The White Mask Society

By A.M. Colwell

ISBN: 979-8-8689-3741-5

www.ayliacolwell.com

For Lemon.

Prologue

His first assignment.

Erik had barely joined the White Mask Society, graduating to the field a year early - the first Guardian ever to do so. He had worked so diligently, trained harder than anyone else, and it had paid off.

He wasn't proud of the nerves he was experiencing as he marched himself to Zak Glover's office to hear the details of what awaited him. His hands were clammy and cold, his heart pounding a violent tattoo against his chest, as he took long deep breaths, counting with each inhale and each exhale.

Calm down, E.

E. He had to practice calling himself by that letter rather than his full name. Part of the mark of being a Guardian.

Outside of Glover's office were two other Guardians he knew only by reputation, chatting quietly with each other, their voices muffled by the carpet. They both looked so calm and powerful. It was intimidating. He hoped he didn't look as nervous as he felt.

"Hi," said the man among them, turning to Erik with a warm smile. "I'm R."

"E," said Erik, shaking his hand.

He didn't need to introduce himself. Erik had done his research. R, or Robin, was one of the most well-liked members of the Society. He was only a year older than Erik. But with his blonde curls, golden skin, and blue eyes, Robin was a stark opposite of Erik who was instead all sharp angles and dark hair. His grin was infectious and Erik found himself smiling back.

"I'm C," said the shape shifter standing next to Robin, extending their hand. Erik shook it. C, or Carter, was one of many shape shifters who worked for the Society. Like many shifters - though not all - Carter did not assign themself any specific gender. After all, they could change so easily between male and female forms. The only part of their appearance that a shifter could not change was their eyes. They could all be identified by the bright shade of amber that was now twinkling at Erik from behind round, rimless glasses. "You're the one who graduated early, right? This must be your first assignment."

Erik nodded. Carter was the oldest of the three of them, though not by much. Guardians in the field tended to be on the younger side, but at the age of 20, Carter's accomplishments were already legend. They had been the Guardian who caught the San Fernando Arson, what turned out to be a fire nymph with a taste for scorched humans, responsible for the deaths of at least 8 civilians not to mention significant destruction of property.

Robin looked about to say something when the door behind the three of them opened. Glover peered around the door, looming at least a foot above them, the light bouncing off his bald, black head.

"Come on in, you three," he said in his deep, slow voice.

Both Robin and Carter looked graceful and composed as they followed Glover into his office. Erik hoped that he was bearing at least some level of calm, but his hands were still sweating.

"Close the door behind you, would you, E?"

He complied and joined the other two Guardians in the wooden chairs in front of Glover's desk. His office was one of the few rooms of the White Mask Society above ground, and the sun was shining a weak, orange light through the curtains as it inched toward the horizon.

"E, I'd like to formally introduce you to your new partners. They'll have a chance to debrief you on the specific parameters of your assignment, but now you've joined the team, I wanted to personally tell you a little bit about your new Ward."

With a slap of paper, Glover dropped a thick folder on the desk in front of them.

"Her name is Yara Rivers. And she is a hydan."

CHAPTER ONE

Headaches

She could feel a headache coming on.

Crowds always made her nervous, and when she was nervous, she got headaches.

She could feel the heat of the people around her pressing in like a crucible, their breaths and the rustle of their clothes and the smell of their perfume. She kept her eyes closed, focusing on her exercises. *Inhale patience and calm.* In her mind, she could see it; a warm, liquid gold. *Exhale the need for control over those around you.* That was a thick, curly red smoke. But it just wasn't working.

Thankfully, at that moment, the bus hissed to a stop, the doors opened with a loud *pssh*, and Yara Rivers pushed her way out, trying as hard as she could not to touch anyone.

The moment she was out in the fresh air, she took several deep breaths. It was cleaner and cooler out here without the thick scent of bodies. Her whole life she had never been comfortable being touched. For years she thought everyone at school was weird for hugging all the time. The fact that other people didn't seem to care if they accidentally rubbed up against some other sweaty body at a school dance boggled her mind. It wasn't until recently that she realised that she was the weird one. But it was in moments like that - when she was surrounded, trapped - that her headaches came most frequently. And it was particularly inconvenient to have them when she was in a public place because they often blinded her with strange daydreams that swallowed reality.

She took public transportation home from school - none of the school buses went near her neighborhood - but it was a short walk from the bus stop to the apartment in which she lived with her aunt. Aunt Catherine (or "Annie", as she had taken to calling her as a child, evolved over time from "auntie") had been Yara's mother's sister, and whom Yara went to live with after her parents died.

Yara walked the whole time with her eyes on the pavement in front of her, tuning out the sounds and smells of central Los Angeles, still trying to inhale the liquid gold and exhale the thick, red smoke.

Which was probably why she didn't notice that she was being watched.

"You still have eyes on the target?"

"Affirmative," said Erik, not bothering to lean in to his ConvOrb, the small communication device pinned onto the high collar of his uniform. It had been almost two years since Erik had received his assignment, and he was still not completely at ease on duty.

"Good," replied Carter, their voice clear through the little device tucked into Erik's ear. "You're on duty until 0100. See you back at HQ."

"Got it." Carter's shift had just concluded, and having confirmed that Erik was able to pick up where they left off, they were no doubt off to get some rest before they were back on duty.

Erik tucked his hands into his pockets and started walking behind Rivers. His eyes flitted back and forth across the street, ahead of her, behind her, trying to assess any possible signs of danger. In the 22 months since he had been her Guardian, Ramsey Kain had made five attempts at apprehending her. Fortunately, he and his partners had managed to prevent it. So far. But whatever Kain was doing to his henchmen, they were getting stronger and harder to stop.

A man holding a briefcase approached Rivers on the sidewalk and Erik tensed for a moment, but the man passed, and she kept moving, completely oblivious. As far as they could tell, she still had no knowledge of the attempts made to kidnap her.

There were times when Erik felt uncomfortable with the arrangement. Watching Rivers without her knowing. But it was his job. The White Mask Society had made that very clear. Rivers was valuable. And she could not be harmed. And now, with two of the hyden taken already, the stakes were higher than ever. So he swallowed his discomfort and followed orders.

Yara's exercises were doing nothing to calm her anxiety. She couldn't hold back the worst of her headache much longer. She was close. Just half a block and she would be home, and Aunt Catherine would be back from work in a couple of hours, if she could just make it—

The stuffy apartment was blissfully warm after being in the chilly October air. It never truly got cold in Los Angeles, but any time it fell below 70° she used the excuse to load on the sweaters and scarves. Now, she stripped them off gratefully, not bothering to put them away and instead letting everything drop to the carpet before she collapsed on the sagging sofa with a loud sigh of relief.

Her head had been pounding since getting on the bus, pressing against the backs of her eyes. Despite whatever breathing exercises and visualizations her doctors suggested, her headaches never truly went away until she could find a nice, quiet place to ride it out. She had never been able to fully explain to Aunt Catherine - or to herself or to any doctor - what exactly was wrong. Only that when she got uneasy, she got the headaches. And they would only dissipate if she let herself give in to the strange daydreams that accompanied them. But those daydreams were often unpleasant and all-encompassing. She did not find herself capable of, for instance, paying attention in class while she was daydreaming, which made for either very painful lessons if she refrained from succumbing as her headache worsened, or else large gaps in her memory if she did.

Now, in the solitude of the living room, she was able to let go. It felt very much like trying to swim to the surface of the water when something was trying to pull you down, and then finally allowing yourself to sink. The pounding in her head ebbed away as a pair of golden eyes behind glasses materialized in her mind, staring at her through a thick, colorless fog. The eyes blinked, and a face took shape around them, emerging from the fog. A plain, soft face. A woman. (Or perhaps a young man? It was hard to tell.) They had short brown hair that fell in subtle waves around their forehead. They gave a wan smile. Yara, always an observer in these dreams, turned to see who the person was looking at. Charging toward them, moving in slow motion as the fog licked at their limbs, were two men whose faces did not betray even a hint of emotion. One of them was bald, the other had pale eyes, though they both remained completely expressionless. Why, Yara wondered, was this strange golden-eyed person smiling if two men wanted to attack them? But suddenly, the roiling fog parted around a man standing beside them. He was handsome, Yara thought idly. Stunning green eyes and dark hair, his straight nose as sharp as his jaw.

Yara watched as the four of them fought. A battle that looked perfectly choreographed, as though lifted straight from an action movie. It soon became uncomfortably violent. Yara had never been a fan of movies like this. She was eager for this dream to end. Shortly after having the thought, the two emotionless attackers were disabled. The green-eyed man said something to the golden-eyed person as fog consumed the two unconscious bodies on the floor. Then, Golden Eyes turned to run toward something Yara couldn't see as Green Eyes knelt by the bodies—

Bzz bzz.

Yara sat up on the couch, her vision clearing as the fog of her daydream dissipated.

In a moment of confusion, before her head cleared, she wasn't sure what had pulled her out of the daydream. She blinked, trying to remember if she had really heard anything in real life, or if it was just a residual effect from her daydream.

A few moments later, however, her phone vibrated again.

She blindly fumbled for it, and saw a message from Aunt Catherine. "Stuck at work. Don't wait for dinner." followed by "See you tomorrow morning. Love you! xoxo"

Another night alone. Yara couldn't fault her aunt. She worked long shifts at the hospital to make ends meet.

Looking around the small apartment, Yara wondered idly if she should clean it up a bit as a surprise for Aunt Catherine when she came home. Tissues on the coffee table, dirty dishes on the counters, various sweaters and blankets draped over every bit of furniture. Then she thought about that calc homework in her backpack that was due on Monday that she should get a head start on. Her stomach gurgled hungrily. Perhaps she should make some dinner.

She fell asleep on the sofa trying to decide what to do first.

CHAPTER TWO

The Tenebrae

Zak Glover took a deep breath, staring at the mahogany door in front of him. The name on the plaque read "BORA BLACK" in big, bold letters, and in a neater, more elegant script underneath, "Head of Los Angeles Branch". He respected Bora Black. She was, after all, his boss, and certainly the most qualified and skilled member of the Society that he had ever met. But she had an intimidating presence, and he always had to brace himself before facing her.

He knocked on the door.

"Enter," came the calm reply.

He turned the brass doorknob and took a step, the light dimming significantly the moment he crossed the threshold.

"Zak," she said by way of greeting. "The Shadow Men made a move for Rivers."

After taking a few moments for his eyes to adjust to the dark room, Zak saw where Black was standing. She was bent forward, writing notes fervently at her desk, wisps of darkness curling around her. As far as Zak knew, there was only one dark nymph, or Tenebrae, currently working at the Los Angeles branch of the Society, and it was Bora Black.

"They were successfully apprehended."

She stopped writing and moved around the desk, wringing her hands. She was not only a force to be reckoned with, but her physical appearance was also intimidating to those who had never seen a Tenebrae before. Her eyes were completely black from edge to edge so it was hard to know if she was looking at you. She had hair as black as

7

her eyes that fell around her in graceful waves, skin so pale it was nearly translucent, and darkness always rippled off of her. Matched with her black turtleneck uniform, broken only by the small, embroidered white half-mask over her heart, she was a vision of night.

"It is the third attack this month," she said. "The girl must be warned. I'm open to suggestions."

"I think we should send in her Guardians."

Black considered Zak for a moment. He could see her mind whirring. When she was thinking hard, the curls of darkness around her thickened.

"And you think they should inform her of the situation?"

Zak nodded. "I think they would have more luck than anyone else."

After a moment, she said, "Very well. Send them in."

Several hours later, the three Guardians left Black's office, the oak door quietly clicking shut behind them.

"That's always fun," said Robin. He looked to his left, where Erik and Carter walked next to him. He was the most talkative of the three. They had worked to protect Yara Rivers together for years, and for a while that protection had been relatively straight forward. But in the last few months, a threat had arisen against the hyden.

And Yara Rivers was one of the last few hyden alive. For decades, they had all but disappeared. Many at the White Mask Society even believed them to be extinct. Perhaps all killed off by religious extremists, or else shunned into hiding where their bloodlines eventually died out. But then about seventy years ago, stories popped up here and there of people with unusual abilities. When the Society looked for them, they found that the hyden had survived after all, however limited their numbers were.

"What's always fun?" said Carter. They threw Robin a sideways look. He caught their eyes and nodded over his shoulder at the door behind them.

"Talking to Black."

The three of them reached the elevator and waited for it to arrive to take them back underground, where most of the Headquarters of the Society was located.

"Fun isn't exactly the word I would use," said Erik with a dry chuckle.

"But we get to make contact. Finally," said Robin. "That's exciting, right?" He gauged Erik's reaction, watching his face closely for any signs, but saw nothing other than a small pursing of his lips before he nodded.

"I think it should be me," said Carter without hesitation.

"That's bold. Any particular reason?"

The elevator arrived and the three of them stepped inside. Robin pressed his hand to a small sensor next to the door. It scanned his palm, and a hidden panel opened up with a selection of floor numbers. He pressed the button to take them seven floors down where their quarters were.

"I think it will be less alarming if she's approached by a woman."

"You a woman now?" said Robin, grinning.

Carter punched his arm. "I can be."

He hated to admit it, but Carter was probably right. As a shape shifter, Carter had the ability to become whatever they wanted, and being approached by a woman would likely seem less menacing. He looked at Erik again. This time, Erik's expression was easier to read: disappointed. So was Robin, though he wasn't about to admit it. He was better at hiding things than Erik, who had a tendency to wear his feelings about Yara right on his sleeve.

"Alright, fine. C, you make contact. Try to get at her when her aunt is home. Since we have to tell both of them, anyway, might as well do it at the same time. Could give us some credibility, too. And I have a feeling we'll need it."

The so-called "senior slump", which Yara had always scoffed at as an underclassman, was - as it turned out - very real. The first semester of her senior year had barely started and already she felt as though she were suffocating in all of her classes. Had her fellow classmates always been this insufferable? (Aunt Catherine had long ago abandoned trying to encourage any friendships between Yara and any other students. They had all been superficial and short-lived relationships, and as it turned out, Yara was just as happy by herself.)

When the bell rang, she could not get out fast enough. But she did not find what she expected when she got home. Whereas Aunt Catherine normally worked late on Fridays, Yara found her sitting at the small wooden table in the kitchen, and she wasn't alone.

"Annie!" said Yara by way of hello. "You're home early."

"Yara, there's someone here who would like to speak to you."

The other woman at the table turned so Yara could see her face. Behind a pair of frameless glasses were the same golden eyes she had seen in her daydream yesterday. She wasn't the same person. Her lips were fuller, her nose smaller, her hair longer. But she had the same brown curls and the same soft face. Confounded by the similarities, Yara blinked and forced herself to stop staring. Most likely the woman worked for the school and Yara had seen her before but not fully registered who she was, then subconsciously applied similar qualities to the person in her daydream.

"Hello," said the woman.

"Hi," nodded Yara, putting down her backpack and feeling suddenly panicked that she was in trouble. Her hands began to sweat, and her head started to throb as anxiety closed in on her.

The woman smiled warmly. "There's no need to be nervous, Yara. You're not in trouble or anything. My name is Carter. I work with the White Mask Society." She held out a silver badge, but it didn't look familiar, nor had Yara ever heard of any white mask anything.

"OK…"

"Sit down, Yara," said Aunt Catherine, pulling a chair toward her.

Her legs feeling like they might collapse under her, Yara went to sit next to her aunt, afraid to make eye contact with the strange golden-eyed woman. "What's going on?" she asked.

"I'm afraid this is going to sound quite strange," said Carter calmly, her words slow and careful, "but you are in grave danger."

Her words were met with a moment of silence, Yara's brain trying to process what had just been said, but instead her thoughts repeatedly rammed up against a giant wall that was preventing any understanding. "Did I do something wrong?" she said.

"No, not at all," said Carter. "But it may be easier to explain all this if you come with me to my office."

"No!" said Aunt Catherine. Yara jumped slightly at the outburst, looking at her aunt with surprise. "No, you can tell us here."

Carter considered Aunt Catherine for a moment before nodding with a tight lipped smile. "There's no easy way to say this, so I'm afraid I'm going to be very blunt. The truth is, Yara, there is a man who is after you. His name is Ramsey Kain. For some time now, he's been developing a new kind of… weapon. And we have reason to believe that he intends to use you to help him build it."

At this, Yara actually snorted. But Carter did not smile. Neither did Aunt Catherine, whose brow was slightly creased. "Is this a joke?"

"Unfortunately—"

"Why would he want *me*? I'm in high school, for crying out loud.

What the hell do I know about building weap—"

"Do you ever have visions? Vivid dreams? Premonitions?"

Yara raised her eyebrow. "What?"

"You're special, Yara. You have a skill, an ability. And Kain desperately wants it."

"I'm not special," said Yara, standing up. She tried to inconspicuously wipe her sweaty palms against her jeans. "And this is getting ridiculous. You must have me confused with someone else."

"Then why did we apprehend two men trying to break into your apartment late last night?"

"What?" said Yara, half laughing, half exasperated. Aunt Catherine's hand was over her mouth, but she still said nothing. "Look, you obviously have me confused with someone else. We're not interested in your help, or your company, or anything else you have to offer."

Yara could feel her face burning from discomfort, but she stood her ground, waiting for this Carter woman to leave. After a few moments, Carter picked up a bag she had brought with her and shuffled inside it. Yara wasn't looking, focusing instead on trying to calm her rising anxiety. She heard Carter set something down on the table before quietly saying, "I'll leave this here. I sincerely hope you change your mind."

As the door shut, Yara let out a shaky breath and looked to Aunt Catherine.

"What the hell was that?" said Yara with an aggravated laugh. But her aunt did not respond in kind. Instead, she kept her eyes on her hands which picked absently at a knot on the table. Anger rose quickly in Yara's chest. Her aunt had let a stranger into their home, a stranger with tall tales of weapons and dangerous men, and instead of coming to Yara's aid, Aunt Catherine sat there in silence.

"Thanks for all your help," said Yara bitterly, before going into her room with no intention of coming out until morning.

CHAPTER THREE

His Laboratory

Miles away from the headquarters of the White Mask Society, Ramsey Kain was sitting in his laboratory. No. It was more than just a laboratory, it was his home. He had never had a home growing up. He never stayed with a foster family longer than a few months. He heard a few of them complain behind his back about his off-putting demeanor, how he made people uncomfortable. Then he bounced from dorm to dorm during the few years he attended college. He had convinced himself throughout his youth that the absence of a place to call his own didn't bother him. That the way people avoided his eye was normal.

But then he had joined the Society.

And he had met *her*.

And suddenly he had everything he had lacked as a child; a home and a family. A fierce obsession had devoured him. The Society had been his home. She had been his family. Their laboratory, which he built - with her - from scratch, was their child. Together, they had explored ideas previously only dreamt about. But the two of them together had nearly made them reality.

This new lab was built from everything he had managed to take with him when he left. She would be proud. He had never given up her work. The lab was more than his new home, it was his life's work. His love letter to her.

It was in the silence before the day started that he would close his eyes and imagine that nothing had changed. Long hours spent in only her company, his heart leaping every time her dark eyes fell on him, his skin tingling whenever she smiled, her teeth pearly white against her coffee-colored skin.

He had painstakingly recreated every part of the lab here in his underground fortress. It had taken him years to build and more money than he had possibly imagined it could cost. (But that was of no consequence. Selling only a fraction of his research to the highest bidder had been enough to cover everything and then some.) And it had been worth it, if only for those quiet moments when he could just sit and remember what it had been like. *Before*.

But it never lasted long.

There was a knock on the door.

At first, Kain didn't move, keeping his eyes closed and trying not to lose the image of her, sitting across from him, frowning as she did whenever she was focused on her work, her long, ebony hair tied in a knot on top of her head with a few loose strands framing her graceful face. When the knock came again, however, Kain could no longer ignore it. With a groan, he pushed himself up, leaning heavily on his cane. His leg was stiff after sitting for so long, and it whined at him as he put weight on it.

At the door were Cesium and Lithium, dressed in the red uniform that all of his Shadow Men wore. These two were a matching pair, and as such were identical, save the brands on their necks which he used to identify them. Matching pairs were hardly put to work together, but the Alkalis seemed to function as a team adequately.

"What?" said Kain impatiently.

"Dysprosium and Rhenium have been apprehended by the Rivers Guardians," said Cesium.

A dangerous, burning heat rose quickly through Kain's chest, his breathing becoming more rapid as he could feel his anger growing. "And Rivers?" he said, trying to keep his voice low.

"The girl is, at the moment, alive."

"Does the Society have her?"

"No," said Cesium calmly.

The most frustrating thing about his Shadow Men was how unflappable they were. Kain enjoyed having control over things, and while they obeyed his every order without question, they never gave him the satisfaction of looking nervous or afraid or ashamed. He rolled his eyes and resisted the urge to slam the door in their faces.

"This is your third failed attempt in a month," he said, keeping his voice at a quivering controlled volume with great difficulty.

"Sir."

"Bring her to me. Tonight. I don't care how many Shadow Men you send. I want the seer."

"Yes, sir."

The pair turned to leave, but Kain stopped them. "And I want operations to begin working on bringing in the next one, too." His men looked back at him. "We have to make up for lost time. Which one is it?"

"Roberto Diaz, sir," said Cesium.

The mind reader, thought Kain. Excellent. Perhaps he would help in future abductions, assuming Kain could crack the formula he was working on. "Good. And after him?"

"Janya Varma, sir," said Cesium.

Kain bristled at the name. He looked hard at Cesium's expressionless face. Cesium didn't flinch. "See that you are careful with her," he said. "I want them by week's end and I want them alive and unharmed." And with that, he closed the door before either of them could say anything.

Janya Varma.

He had intended to save her for last. Perhaps it was his subconscious postponing having to deal with the repercussions of what it would mean to apprehend her.

But he needed her. Every time he looked down at his mangled leg or struggled to walk, he was reminded of how important she was for his plan.

It didn't matter who she was.

All that mattered was what she could do.

CHAPTER FOUR

Officer Knox

Yara lay in bed on Saturday morning, staring up at her ceiling, and replaying for the nth time the events of the night before.

After Carter left Friday afternoon, Aunt Catherine had knocked quietly on her door, but when Yara had refused to answer, she left her alone to her obsessive thoughts. They chased themselves in circles and eventually lulled Yara into a fretful and restless sleep plagued with confusing dreams.

She dreaded getting up and having to face her aunt. While the entire situation had been incredibly stressful, Yara was ashamed of her behavior. She had acted childishly and jumped too quickly to anger, which was more a reflection of her own discomfort than anything Aunt Catherine had done. The thought of dealing with the aftermath was less than enticing. But as her stomach gurgled hungrily (she had not eaten since lunch the day before, after all) she decided that waiting would not make it any better. Nor would her increasing hunger.

Aunt Catherine was sitting at the kitchen table, two mugs of hot tea in front of her.

"Hi," said Yara after a moment.

"Good morning," said Aunt Catherine.

"I'm sorry," they both said at the same time.

Yara chuckled. "Well, I'm glad she's gone, at least."

Aunt Catherine nodded, chewing on her lip.

"Come have some breakfast," said Aunt Catherine, getting up to fix Yara a plate.

"Thank you." She sat down at the table and took a grateful sip of her tea. "Did you call the police?"

"What for?"

"Really? For the crazy lady who threatened me!"

"I'm not sure it was a threat," said her aunt without looking.

Frowning, Yara took another sip of tea. In the corner of her eye, she saw an unfamiliar folder on the table. It was undoubtedly whatever the woman named Carter had left yesterday. "You didn't throw this away?"

Aunt Catherine looked over her shoulder to see what Yara was talking about. "Oh. No, I guess not. I didn't think to."

Yara humphed quietly and tossed it in the trash. Aunt Catherine hesitated for a moment, before putting a forced smile on her face and bringing Yara a quartered orange and some toast with peanut butter. "I was thinking maybe today we could go out to lunch."

"Really?" said Yara, a mouthful of food. Eating out was a rare occurrence in their household. Money was tight, and restaurants were an unnecessary expenditure. "What's the occasion?" though she already knew the answer. Aunt Catherine wanted to make up for last night.

"No occasion. Just to spend some time together. I've been working a lot lately, and haven't seen much of you." Aunt Catherine was a nurse which meant she kept long and sometimes unpredictable hours. It was true that for the last few weeks, they had been like ships passing in the night. Yara felt as though her aunt wasn't being entirely truthful, but she wanted to take advantage of the offer. Getting to spend some time out with her only family sounded nice.

They decided to eat at a little bistro in Silver Lake. After stuffing themselves in an uncharacteristically affluent manner, they walked around a few blocks and chatted over the sounds of traffic. It was nice to look up and see blue skies and palm trees instead of the grey skyscrapers of downtown.

Aunt Catherine asked Yara all about Thomas Mendoza, the boy she had a crush on in her Social Studies class, and Yara lamented about the fact that he seemed to be in an early courtship with one of the girls in the drama department, Stephanie Cantzoukas, and besides the more she spoke to him the more she realized he was a little stupid anyway.

It was the first time in a long time, Yara noticed, that she had gone this long without a single headache.

Around three in the afternoon, they decided to head home. Aunt Catherine had to be at the hospital early the next morning, and Yara supposed she should get a start on her homework. She hated calculus, was bad at it, which often meant that it took forever to get through the assignments.

The city bus was crowded enough that Aunt Catherine had to take a seat near the back, while Yara squeezed into a window seat behind the driver and started focusing on her breathing, trying to make herself as small as possible so as not to touch the man next to her. Two stops later, he got off the bus, but before getting her aunt's attention to come fill the seat, someone else took it.

Inhale liquid gold, she thought, *exhale red smoke.*

But that all became much harder when he grabbed her arm.

A gasp of surprise and fear escaped her lips.

"Don't say anything," said the man in a flat voice. He was not even looking at her. Calmly, he took a gun from his coat pocket and rested it on his knee. Her breath caught in her throat. He did not need to tell her not to speak. She probably couldn't have even if she wanted to. She could barely hear him over the sound of the engine and her own pounding heart. "At the next stop, get off the bus and go left."

She couldn't tell if she was just trembling or if she actually managed to nod, but either way, they continued to sit in silence, his hand painfully gripping her arm, until the bus huffed to a halt and the doors opened. The man let go of her long enough to stand up, tucked the gun back into his pocket, and let her go in front of him. Walking on legs like jelly, forcing herself not to look back at her aunt lest she put her in any danger as well, Yara stepped onto the sidewalk and went left exactly as she had been instructed. It felt less like she was walking, and more like the world was moving past her as she stood still. She didn't even know if Aunt Catherine had noticed what happened, let alone if she had followed her off the bus. Yara was too scared to look.

Yara didn't know where they were. She had never been to this neighborhood, but in every direction, all she saw was gray, save for the few bursts of green from the palm trees high above their heads.

The man no longer spoke, his hand back on her arm. He tugged her to the right leading her down a dirty alley of crumbling brick and cement. Real fear blossomed in her stomach, greater than any she had ever felt in her entire life, and to her dismay, she felt a headache coming on. But she could not afford to give in to any daydreams now. Her life may well depend on it. She didn't know when she started crying, but tears were freely streaming down her face.

"Please don't hurt me. Take my bag, take whatever you want, just…

please just let me go…"

He didn't respond.

In a few moments, the city was muted by the walls on either side of them, the only clear sound Yara's own panicked sobs. Just as she was about to start pleading again, a lot of things happened in very quick succession.

The world was suddenly filled with movement. Several more men appeared at the end of the alley where they had no doubt been waiting. They were indistinguishable from the man holding her in every way. From the tops of their coarse brown hair to the tips of their gnarled fingers. Quadruplets? How many were there? Quintuplets?

Simultaneously, there was a sound not unlike a hoard of bees that accompanied streaks of silver out of the corner of her eyes. She ducked and screamed as the man holding her was pulled backward and forced to let her go.

Keeping low to the ground, her heart beating impossibly fast, Yara tried to run back to the main street.

"Help!" A few people walked across the opening of the alley on the sidewalk ahead, but none of them seemed concerned with what was happening despite her cries for help. She tripped over a loose piece of concrete. She hit the ground hard, and not two seconds later, someone else was grabbing her and pulling her to her feet. She screamed again and struggled violently to get away, but it was useless. Whoever was holding her was too strong.

"It's OK!" said the person holding her. "It's OK, hang on! Hang on!"

"Get off me! *Help!*" she screamed again.

She turned around to see what on earth was happening. At least half a dozen people were in an all out brawl. Most of them looked like the same tall, hulking man who had kidnapped her on the bus. Two other men dressed in black were fighting back all of the twins. Most of them were wearing what looked like a giant metal glove on one of their hands and waving their arms around frantically. One of the men in black did a complicated little flourish and Yara saw the same silver streak whoosh toward one of the identical attackers. What looked like a metal frisbee collided spectacularly with him, knocking him to the ground.

Yara screamed again and continued trying to get away, but the person's grip was too strong.

"Yara! It's OK!" they screamed. It was a woman's voice, and it sounded familiar, but Yara didn't waste any time trying to figure out where she knew it from.

"Get off me! Let go!"

The woman then turned back to the action and shouted something. Yara wasn't listening, however. She had managed to take advantage of the woman's split attention to free herself, and sprinted back toward the street, not bothering to look behind her.

"Yara!"

But still she ran. Her legs were carrying her so quickly that she wasn't able to turn in time and ran straight into the street. A car honked and swerved, narrowly avoiding her, but Yara did not stop to apologize. She didn't know what to do. Where to go.

Phone! Call the police! Call Annie! The thought came to her as though from a stupor beneath her pounding head. She reached for her phone, but realized she had put it in her bag, which had fallen back in the alley. She cursed and kept running, trying to put as much distance between herself and the attackers as possible. Not a single person seemed at all concerned about her distraught state. She weaved through them as fast as she could. She stopped at the nearest intersection, looking desperately to either side, hoping to see something familiar, but she had no idea how to find anything without her phone.

"Yara Rivers!"

She jumped at the sound of her name and spun around to see a police officer in big sunglasses walking quickly toward her from the direction she came.

"Oh, thank god!" she screamed, not bothering to wonder why on earth this police officer would know who she was. A few curious people walking by looked in their direction, but for the most part, they were ignored. "Please, you have to help me," she said breathlessly, walking over to him. She pointed back toward the alley. "There were these men back there and they attacked me and—"

"Ms. Rivers, I know. You have to come with me."

"—they got me on the bus! I didn't know what to do, I just followed him. He had a gun! My aunt doesn't know. They're still back there, please!"

"Ms. Rivers, calm down," said the officer in a very demanding voice. "I need you to listen to me."

Yara swallowed her next words and tried taking a few deep breaths. The officer had a round belly and was short. Barely any taller than Yara, who was already on the smaller side.

"You have to come with me to the station. Can you do that?"

"I need to call my aunt. She's still on the bus. Catherine. Catherine Tanners. She's going to worry if I'm not home. Do you have a phone? I dropped mine. Are you going to call for backup?"

"Ms. Rivers!" The officer's voice was stern, and at last Yara stopped talking. Her heart was still beating too fast. "Everything is being taken care of. Right now I just need you to come with me to the station. We will call your aunt and have her meet us there. Alright?"

After a few moments, Yara nodded, and followed him

The car the officer led Yara to was black and unmarked. Next to it, Yara recognized one of the men who had been involved in the fight she had just escaped from. She had not gotten a good look at him before, but she was sure it was him. He looked to be about her age, maybe a few years older. His black uniform was glistening with blood and filthy from the alley. His blonde curls were pasted to his forehead with sweat and he had a huge gash across his cheek. He smiled at her.

She stopped in her tracks.

"What's going on?"

The officer stopped and, after a moment, took off his sunglasses. Yara tore her gaze off the man by the car and met the police officer's eyes. Her breath caught in her throat. She was looking into eyes that were a brilliant golden color. The same color as that woman Carter's eyes (though the similarities stopped there). The same eyes she had seen in her daydream. How strange that she had never seen eyes like that, and now it was the third time in as many days - even if one of those times had only been imagined.

"Who are you?"

"Yara, I'm Officer Knox," said the police officer, holding both of his hands up placatingly. "I work in law enforcement, as does my partner here." He gestured to the blonde man.

"What do you want from me?" said Yara. "Who are you?"

"We are here to help you. To protect you."

"Protect me from what?" said Yara, taking a step backwards.

"This would be a lot easier to explain if you would just come with us," said Officer Knox.

"Let me see your badges," said Yara, her brain working frantically. She didn't know what the right thing to do was. Knox certainly seemed like a real cop, but this wasn't a police car, and his so-called partner looked much too young to be working in law enforcement.

Officer Knox pulled his badge from a pocket and showed it to Yara.

She frowned. It was the same unfamiliar badge Carter had shown her. In any case, this was not the LAPD.

"Get away from me," said Yara, backing away from them.

"I understand your caution, Yara, and frankly, it's well warranted. But it is very important that you come with us right now. The men who just attacked you are a small number compared to what is coming."

"I need to call my aunt."

The man next to the car reached into the glove compartment. Yara flinched as he came out, his fingers wrapped around... a phone. He handed it to her. "No 900 numbers," he said with a crooked smile and a playful wink.

They waited patiently as Yara turned around, the phone ringing as she waited with bated breath for her aunt to answer.

"Hello?" came Aunt Catherine's breathless voice on the other side of the phone.

"Annie! Oh thank god, Annie, it's Yara."

She could hear her aunt cry with relief on the other end before saying, "Are you alright? Where did you go? What happened?"

"I got attacked."

"What!"

"No, I'm fine now. But..." Yara lowered her voice and cupped her hand around the phone. "Remember that weird woman who came to talk to us yesterday? And the people she said she works for?"

"Yes..."

"Well, they found me. I think they... ugh, this sounds so stupid. I think they saved me. They want me to go with them somewhere."

"Where are you? I'll come meet you."

Yara looked around and told her the intersection.

"Don't move! Don't go with anyone! I'll be there as fast as I can."

Time passed in a painfully awkward silence, the blonde man humming to himself, barely audible over the traffic, and the inane conversations from passersby. Yara's body was tense as she kept her eyes on the two alleged officers, ready to flee if she had to. *Inhale liquid gold, exhale red smoke.* But within twenty minutes they were joined by Aunt Catherine, her graying hair falling out of her top knot, her face shining with sweat.

Now, with the feeling that imminent danger was out of reach, Yara tried to let herself calm down. Her head was pounding like mad, a buzzing in her ears tuning out all conversation.

It was OK. It was all OK. Aunt Catherine was here now and she would take care of everything.

It hadn't been easy, but Carter, under the guise of the male police officer, had successfully managed to convince Yara and her aunt to come in to Headquarters. The three Guardians had agreed not to introduce them to any other Society members of the non-human variety - aside from Carter and Erik, of course. They had been given permission to use one of the offices above ground.

When they arrived, Carter excused themself long enough to shift back into the same form they had taken when first meeting Yara. They rejoined their partners on the top floor in Glover's office.

Both Yara and Catherine were sitting in the elegant chairs facing Glover's desk. Yara's red hair had half fallen out of her braid. Her backpack - retrieved from the fray by Erik - sat untouched in her lap. She looked shell shocked. Carter was sure that if it weren't for her aunt's presence, she would be in much more of a panic. As it was, she kept pressing her knuckles against her temples, her lips pursed. Her aunt, on the other hand, was fidgeting nervously. Carter took a seat behind the desk, Robin leaned casually against the bookcase, and Erik stood behind them. Yara's eyes, they noticed, were glued to Erik's face, and she had a strange expression, as though she recognized him from somewhere. When Erik noticed however, Yara quickly looked away, her cheeks turning red.

"Do you need anything? Water?" said Carter.

"Let's just get this over with," said Catherine shortly.

Carter nodded respectfully. "Did you have a chance to look over any of the information I left with you yesterday?"

It was clear from their expressions that they had not.

"Well, I'll just dive right in, then. You met me already, and this is Robin," they indicated him leaning against the bookshelf.

"Hey," he said, shaking his curls out of his eyes.

"And this is Erik." They indicated Erik standing behind them. It felt strange, saying their full names. Guardians referred to each other only by their initials, a policy enacted by the White Mask Society in an alleged effort to maintain professionalism, though it was common knowledge that the true reason was because being a Guardian was a dangerous job. Using initials instead of names was meant to ensure a level of detachment from their coworkers. It didn't work, but Carter had become so used to thinking of their fellow Guardians as "E" and

"R" that the names "Erik" and "Robin" felt foreign in their mouth. But Yara didn't need to know all that.

"We are your Guardians."

"What the hell is that supposed to mean?"

"Yara, you are what we call a hydan. You're… slightly more than human. Hyden are capable of many different abilities. You are of the seer variety, which means you have the ability to see the future."

As expected, Yara raised an eyebrow in disbelief. "Sure."

"I noticed you recognized me when I came to your home. We'd never met before. How was that possible?"

"I didn't recognize you…" said Yara, but her voice trailed away and she looked down at the floor in an obvious lie.

"And did you also not recognize Erik, here?"

"No…" said Yara, even less convincingly than before.

"Yara, no one here will think you're crazy if you let yourself admit that what I'm saying is true."

At last, Yara met their eyes. Carter could see the wheels turning behind them.

"How could you—"

"Know? Because we knew your father. Theo. In fact, he used to work with us."

At this, Yara turned to look at Catherine, her eyes wide, but Catherine didn't meet them.

"Here at the White Mask Society our jobs… our entire facility is dedicated to keeping a peaceful coexistence between the human and the Devi— the non-human community." Carter had almost said "Deviants", the word for all humanoids who were… just a little extra. Carter themself was one, but they knew that saying the word out of context to someone with no knowledge of this world could sound misleading.

"'Non-human' community?" said Yara. "You expect me to believe all this?"

"I suppose the easiest way to prove that what I'm saying is true is to show you." Carter had a feeling it would come to this. They hated using their ability as a party trick, but it was unfortunately the most effective way of initiating someone into a completely hidden world. They stood up, took a deep breath, and shifted.

CHAPTER FIVE

Reckoning

Yara's mouth actually fell open. She could feel her heart nearly stop in her chest from surprise. A faint "oh!" from Aunt Catherine told her that her aunt was just as shocked by what had happened as she was.

Right before their eyes, Carter's face and body transformed. A soft face expanded; her body lost its feminine curves to be replaced with the straighter form of a man; her hands got thicker and hairier, until suddenly, Yara was staring straight at the same police officer who had apprehended her an hour ago. The only thing that stayed the same was the color of those golden eyes.

"I am a shape shifter," said Carter, her voice completely changed. Or was it his voice? "There are many of my kind, and we are protected by the Society." She held out her hands— his hands?— and turned around in a slow circle. "I may look like a police officer," and just as quickly as she had transformed into the man, she changed back to her previous form, "but I am still me."

Yara could not find any words. Her brain felt like a jumble, a battle raging between the fact that what Carter was saying could not possibly be true and what she had just witnessed.

"I know this is a lot to take in," said Carter, sitting back down. "I just wanted to show you that you're not alone. You're not the only one who is different."

"So…" began Yara, her voice sounding very distant, "none of you are human?"

Carter smiled. "Not exactly. The Society works to maintain a peaceful coexistence with humans, and as such, many of our ranks are just as human as your aunt, here."

The young blonde man with the gash on his cheek named Robin gave a lazy salute, grinning. "Heyo."

"And like Robin," added Carter.

"What do you expect me to do about all this? If what you're saying is even true, how does it concern me?"

"You remember I told you about a man named Kain?" continued Carter. "The one working on a new kind of weapon? He has been targeting all known hyden, and we believe that he is using them to build this weapon."

"Assuming I *can* see the future, what good is that going to be for building a weapon?"

Carter chewed her bottom lip, thinking of how to respond, but Robin spoke first.

"We don't know."

At this, Yara actually laughed. "This is ridiculous. You want me to accept what you're telling me, that some man is out to get me and use some alleged super power that I have but *somehow* don't know about, and you don't even know what he wants from me?"

"You were attacked," said the one named Erik, speaking for the first time. Her eyes flew to his, and she felt locked in like a magnet. Despite what she had said to Carter, she had in fact recognized Erik from the daydream she'd had a few days ago. He had the same stunning green eyes, the same straight nose and sharp jaw, the same dark hair... All coincidences, of course. "We didn't make that up," he continued. "And those men will keep coming."

Yara swallowed. "Well, if that's the case, it's a good thing I have you three on the job. You've prevented them from getting me so far, right? So as far as I'm concerned, I don't need to do anything about any of this." She stood up and walked toward the door, only to realize that Aunt Catherine wasn't following her.

"Annie, let's go."

Her aunt hesitated. She was still looking at Carter. Yara got the distinct feeling that there were unsaid things passing between the two of them, though she had absolutely no idea what they could be.

"I'm going to give you my card," said Carter eventually. "I get the sense that you threw the last one away?"

Carter handed a business card to a pale faced Aunt Catherine before she got up and joined Yara at the door.

* * *

For fourteen years Catherine had kept the truth from her niece. It hadn't been her choice to get wrapped up in all of this. Hadn't been her choice that her sister, Sierra, had fallen in love with a seer. There was no denying that Theo Rivers was a charismatic man. He could charm the reflection off of a mirror, and men like that had always given Catherine pause. Men like that knew they could get anything they wanted from anyone, and it usually meant they were in it for themselves. But as quickly as Sierra had fallen for Theo, he had fallen for her.

Catherine had never had much interest in men. She'd had a few boyfriends in high school. Then a few girlfriends in college. As it turned out, she was much happier on her own.

But that was not to be her fate.

Shortly after they met, Theo and Sierra were married. And several years after that, they had a baby girl. Yara.

Catherine knew that Sierra had wanted a child for a long time, and before Yara was born, when Catherine had asked her sister what they were waiting for, Sierra had some unsettling - and unbelievable - news.

Theo Rivers was not human. Sierra had called him a Deviant. And more specifically, a hydan. A hydan who could see the future. Naturally, Catherine did not believe her sister, immediately jumping to conclusions about drugs, brain washing, cults. But Sierra had proved it. Theo had had a vision that the Berlin Wall would fall.

"Absurd," Catherine had said.

But a few days later, the announcement was made in East Germany that travel regulations were being lifted. Catherine stayed with Sierra, watching the news all day and all night, as West Germans inundated the wall, welcoming the outpouring of East Berliners who came flooding through in droves. People were dancing on top of it, bulldozers were sent to ram through to allow for more gateways, and joyful citizens hacked away at it with sledge hammers, holding up hewn off pieces of graffitied cement to the camera.

But Theo was more than just a seer. He worked for a secret agency known as the White Mask Society as something called a Guardian, and as if that weren't enough, he wanted to recruit Sierra.

"I'm going to do it," Sierra had said. "And starting a family now would be too complicated. Too risky."

"So what now?" Catherine had cried. "You're going to abandon your life to go work for the secret alien police?"

"Theo showed me the whole thing. It's incredible. The people who work there, Catherine, you would love it."

Catherine could remember the look in her sister's eyes when she told her. A brightness, a fervor. Something she had never seen in her sister.

For the next several years, she hardly saw Sierra. Training, initiation, and, eventually, work took up most of her life. Any spare time she had was often spent with Theo.

At a certain point, they evidently decided that it was an appropriate time to have a baby, and Yara was born. Catherine barely ever saw her. Baby Yara spent most of her life at the Society.

Until one day, when she was four years old, a tall, Black man in a neat suit with a white half-mask embroidered on his tie, came to Catherine's door.

He had introduced himself as Z and informed her that her sister and brother-in-law had been killed in action, leaving behind their little girl. Sierra and Theo had put it in their will that Yara would go to Sierra's closest family: Catherine.

A quiet life of solitude had been replaced with school enrollments, clothes that were grown out of in months, legos strewn across the floor of her tidy apartment, an accident prone child who had a hard time socializing with kids and would come home from school every other day complaining about headaches. Catherine knew, of course, what these headaches were. Yara had inherited her father's gift, but without being properly taught how to use her new power, it manifested as migraines. At first Yara remembered some of her life at the Society, but as she grew older, she stopped asking questions about it, until eventually, it seemed she had forgotten completely. Catherine did not see fit to remind her. She wouldn't be able to answer many of Yara's questions anyway, so what was the point?

She had let Yara forget about all the magic that was hidden in her brain. She had hoped that there would never be a reckoning, but Catherine knew that her time had run out.

She had managed nearly fourteen years of a life resembling normalcy, but it was over now.

The only problem was finding the courage to tell Yara what she had kept from her all those years.

CHAPTER SIX

Definitely Not Visions

Robin could not necessarily say he was surprised about how the afternoon had gone. Wards were not frequently contacted by their Guardians, but the situation with Kain had become drastically dire. Two hyden were already in his custody, and they knew there were at least four more - including Yara - that he had his sights set on.

Carter, however, wasn't pleased with the outcome. Neither was Robin, frankly, but it had pretty much gone as he'd imagined.

"What did you expect?" said Robin with a small laugh as Carter raged against a punching bag in the Guardian rec room, having returned to what Robin considered to be their natural state - if shifters even had such a thing. It was a form not unlike the one they had taken when meeting Yara, the same gentle curls were now shorter, their face less soft, their body less curvy.

Erik had not spoken at all after their failed attempt at bringing Yara in for protection, and was now on duty keeping an eye out for any Shadow Men who might be after her, but Robin had been able to tell from the gleam in his eyes that Erik was no more pleased about all this than Carter was.

"I expected that she would at least believe us!" said Carter. "That watching me shift in front of her would do something to convince her! Not to mention," they added, turning from the punching bag, their face shining with sweat, "doesn't her aunt know about all this already? I mean, her sister was a Guardian, for crying out loud!"

"Well, listen. The first thing you need to do is stop shouting. It's annoying, and it's not helping anything." He smiled, but Carter did not find him funny, and turned back to their bag. It was unlike them to get so worked up. Carter usually kept their cool. They were the level head of the three Guardians. "Look, Bobby Diaz's Guardians haven't been able to secure him either--"

"Comparing yourself to someone else's failure is not a measure of success."

"It is in *my* book."

Carter snorted. "Besides, there haven't been nearly as many attempts to capture Bobby. He seems to be a lower priority. Yara's ability could enable Kain to predict the Society's plans, our moves. It could make him unbeatable."

"There's no indication she can control her visions, and we have no reason to believe that he would have access to what she sees."

Carter punched the bag, their lips pressed tightly together.

"Look," continued Robin. "She's safe right now. E is on duty, and you and I both know for a fact that he doesn't take risks when it comes to her safety."

Erik was notorious for calling for backup at the slightest sign of trouble, often when there was no real need for it. Carter and Robin took it for granted that when he was on duty, they would be summoned to his aid. It had become something of a joke, taking bets as to how long it would take, and what the "emergency" would be.

"I predict we'll hear from him in three hours, two minutes."

"No," said Carter. "It's gonna be way sooner. He's already on edge. I say sixty-eight minutes."

"I'll bet you two of my simulator credits."

"Deal."

It had been a few days since Yara had met the trio who called themselves her "Guardians". Several days during which school had been unbearable, homework was impossible to focus on, and there was nothing but tense silence between her and Aunt Catherine.

From the moment they left that place and made their way back home in a fancy car that the Society-whatever-it-was had sent for them, Aunt Catherine had been tight lipped and pale. No matter how much Yara vented about how ridiculous the situation was, or how absurd it was that they thought she could see the future, or when she tried to speculate how the Carter person had given the illusion of transforming into the police officer, Aunt Catherine said no more than the occasional "Hmm." Yara had the distinct impression that Aunt Catherine knew more than she was letting on, and was intentionally hiding something from her.

Not to mention, Aunt Catherine had flat out refused to answer any of Yara's questions about her father. Anytime she asked, Aunt Catherine responded with a short "I didn't know him that well. He said he was a cop."

Yara tried not to let herself get upset with her aunt. Perhaps this was her own way of coping with a strange encounter, though at some point, Yara would need answers. She barely had time to think about that, however. She was having too hard a time keeping up in school that week.

On Monday, she had gone to the nurses office in the middle of third period with a head-splitting migraine. Laying in the dark during the twenty minutes she was allowed before the nurse sent her back to class, Yara gave in to her daydream. The familiar fog filled her vision, curling and licking around new faces speaking to each other though Yara couldn't make out what they were saying. There was a tall, handsome man with dark skin and a neat suit. He was speaking to a woman wearing a black turtleneck, though Yara thought she must still be partly obscured by the fog. Surely she couldn't be seeing her clearly, because no one Yara had ever seen looked like that. Her eyes were like black marbles, her skin pale but somehow darkening the swirling mist around her.

On Tuesday, rather than go back to the nurse's office when her migraine hit, she let herself give in to the daydream in the middle of Social Studies. The fog revealed the same woman with the black eyes, though this time, she was speaking to the three alleged Guardians.

"Miss Rivers!" Mrs. Taylor's voice cut through the fog in Yara's vision like a sharp gust of wind, and she jumped to attention.

"Yes!" she said, trying to clear her head and return to her surroundings.

"Perhaps you'd like to join the class?"

Yara nodded, her cheeks burning. Looking around the class, she saw that almost everyone was looking at her, snickering, including - to her horror - Thomas Mendoza.

On Wednesday, she actually collapsed in the hall between classes. Her head had been pounding all day, but she was too afraid to let herself have a daydream to ease the pressure behind her eyes after what had happened yesterday. But there was only so much she could take. She ended up being sent home early, and was surprised to find

Aunt Catherine waiting for her at home.

"They called me at work," she said. "Said you collapsed?"

Yara, her head still heavy with pain, forced a nod. "I just need to go to bed," she managed, before stumbling into her bedroom and slamming the door shut behind her. At long last, she crumpled onto her bed, finally giving way to the daydream that had been nagging at her all day.

She was in this one. Something that almost never happened. She could see herself emerging from the thick fog. Her long red hair was pulled back in a messy bun, her lips pursed in the way Aunt Catherine said they did when she was uncomfortable. But she was not alone. As the fog cleared around her she could see one of the Guardians standing next to her. The one with the dark hair and green eyes. The one whose gaze made her stomach flutter. He was looking at her here, in this dream world. Not the Yara who was watching the scene, but the nervous Yara. His face was unreadable. He said something to her, his words muffled and impossible to discern, but dream Yara - who was obviously having a hard time looking away from him - clearly heard him. She nodded and he handed her something that she could not see before walking away and disappearing into the fog.

Stupid dream. And stupid, handsome, green-eyed man.

The fog cleared, replaced by the surroundings of her room when Aunt Catherine knocked lightly on the door, startling Yara.

For a moment, she didn't move. Instead, she stared at the walls of her room, every inch of which had been wallpapered with pictures. Aunt Catherine was frequently sent free calendars from various environmental groups, and Yara had saved every page depicting places she wanted to visit. The Na Pali coast in Kauai, Machu Picchu in Peru, Petra in Jordan, the Northern Lights in Iceland. There was so much to see in this world, and Yara wanted to see it all, but she knew that these calendars would be the closest she ever got. A few years ago, she had taken to cutting out pictures of herself and her aunt and superimposing them onto the beautiful images, as though they had actually been there. As though they were memories of wonderful vacations rather than wishful photoshopping. Her favorite was one of some vineyards in Napa Valley. Not because Napa was the place Yara wanted to see most of all, but because of the picture she had glued to it. The original photograph had been taken the summer before Yara started high school. She and Aunt Catherine had driven down to San Diego during a comic convention that happened there every summer.

Tickets were notoriously difficult to come by, but you didn't need tickets to just walk around the Gaslamp District and look at all the people in their costumes, drinking and eating as though sitting next to Batman and a Star Trek officer drinking beers were the most natural thing in the world. Yara and Aunt Catherine had gotten ice cream from a pop-up promoting some new TV show when they had run across a group who were all dressed as different Keanu Reeves characters. Aunt Catherine had always been a huge Keanu Reeves fan and had asked all of them to take a picture with her. They were happy to oblige, and the one dressed as Ted from *Bill and Ted* insisted on taking a picture of Yara and Aunt Catherine together. He had been so completely in character that Aunt Catherine was nearly dying of laughter. The two of them just looked so happy in that picture. The Gaslamp may have been cut out of the image, and there was no sign that a fake Ted Logan had taken the photo, but all the same, it made Yara happy to remember that day.

Aunt Catherine knocked again. "Yara? I need to speak to you about something."

Yara rolled out of bed and opened the door. Aunt Catherine's face could not have been more different from the picture Yara had just been looking at. There were dark circles under her eyes and she looked wan. Had Yara been so preoccupied with herself that she hadn't noticed how miserable her aunt had been these past few days?

"What's wrong?"

"It's time I told you the truth, Yara. It's time you knew about your father."

CHAPTER SEVEN
Bobby Diaz

Bobby Diaz was a simple man who led a simple life. He was born in El Salvador and when he was four years old, his papá got a job in New Mexico. His entire family packed up and moved to the States, where Bobby grew up. He still lived in New Mexico, and visited his now widowed mamá every Tuesday and Friday night to bring her tortilla soup from her favorite restaurant and clean out the cat's litter box. His siblings had scattered across the continent, leaving him to care for her. He had a good job at a waste extraction company where he kept his head down and punched his forty hours a week. Sunday mornings he went to church, and in the afternoons he volunteered at the library.

From looking at Bobby Diaz's life, you would have no idea that there was anything unusual about him.

But Bobby Diaz was very unusual indeed.

Bobby Diaz could read minds.

As a child, he was constantly getting into trouble for asking people questions relating to silent musings they had - and frequently very *personal* questions - which elicited fearful and angry responses. How could he possibly know that Mr. Rodriguez was having an affair with the volleyball coach? And how did he know that little Becky had replaced the creamy stuffing in Sam's Oreos with toothpaste? It had taken a little while for him to grasp that he was the only one who could hear these thoughts, and that people did not want him to hear them at all.

He asked his parents about it when he was in first grade, only to be spanked by his papá, insisting that it was inappropriate to joke about witchcraft and the devil. Later that night, his abuela had snuck into his room and told him a story in a hushed voice.

"When your abuelo and I met, I remember thinking, 'this man is so charming. This man knows exactly what to say!' My mamá, your bisabuela, she had made me this ugly dress from an old table cloth. I did not want to wear it, but she insisted. She wasted nothing, my mamá. I was so self-conscious in this dress on my first date with your abuelo, and the first thing he says to me is, 'you look beautiful in that dress.' For months, he is sweet, and saying the perfect things to me, to my mamá and papá. After we were married, he says to me that God had gifted him with a second sight. The sight of seeing into one's soul. And he could see so clearly into mine I knew he was not lying. God's gift did not get passed on to your papá. Or if it did, he does not see clearly. But you, my Roberto, God has given you the sight."

Bobby had listened with wide eyes, his heart pounding wildly against his chest as he listened to his abuela tell the story. "It wasn't the devil?"

"Do you feel the devil inside you, sweet child?"

Bobby shook his head.

"No, because you are good and pure. The devil cannot get into your soul if it is good. Only God can do that. And He has chosen you. But you must be careful, hijo. People do not always see the difference between a gift from God and a curse from the devil. Keep this gift secret. And do good. Like your abuelo did. He made me so happy, just by saying he liked my dress."

He had kept his word. Bobby never spoke of his gift to anyone. He had never gotten close enough to anyone to feel safe confiding in them. Not like his grandparents. And while his abuela had shown him kindness and understanding, he never forgot that his papá had jumped to violence and anger.

And Bobby had every reason to believe that he would find the same fear from others if they knew what he could do.

But some people did know. Just outside of Albuquerque, the White Mask Society had a small operation monitoring Mr. Diaz. Three Guardians took it in turns to ensure that he got to work in one piece, got back home safely, that his church and his library and his mamá's house were all secure.

Headquarters back in LA had been sending inquiries regarding his safety with more and more frequency, as rumblings were surfacing in the city about an imminent threat to all the hyden, and that included Mr. Diaz.

The Guardians had noticed no strange activity, however. All was quiet in the life of Roberto Diaz. Which was why they were caught so spectacularly off guard when Mr. Diaz's home was invaded in the middle of the night by half a dozen hulking figures in dark red cloaks.

Dusty was on duty. Perched on the roof, as was her custom every time she was on night watch. She had a tumbler full of strong black tea wedged next to her when she caught movement out of the corner of her eye. Squinting, she tried to make out what it was. Definitely not an animal nor a vehicle. It was likely nothing, but just to be safe, she activated the ConvOrb on her collar and called her fellow Guardians.

Monique answered. "What's up?" her voice was groggy. No doubt the call from Dusty had just woken her up.

"I got movement here," said Dusty in a low voice. She pulled her mask over her face, pressing a small button on the side which activated the night vision built into it. She focused on the horizon.

Shit.

She spilled her tea as she leapt from the roof. "I got Shadow Men! Six of them! I need backup, now!"

She didn't take any time to turn off her ConvOrb properly, instead sprinting full speed toward the figures who were fast approaching. Dusty had been briefed on the Shadow Men so she knew what to expect, what to look out for, but she had never seen them in person. They were enormous. Especially compared to Dusty's small frame, something she had always gotten teased about during initiation. (She had taken to training harder than anyone else in her class to prove that size wasn't everything, though in this case, she had to admit that size was, in fact, a lot.)

She launched herself forward and collided with the nearest Shadow Man, wrapping her legs around his neck and slamming him to the floor. Slipping her hand into her gauntlet - a glove used to control the Guardian's weapon of choice, the solenoidal star - she summoned it from where it was tucked safely against her back, and sent it spinning lethally toward another Shadow Man as she kicked the legs out from a third.

But there were six of them, and only one of her. She might be able to disable a few of them, but it was clear that their priority was not fighting her. It was getting to Diaz. The other three were all sprinting toward his house, not bothering to look back or help their fallen comrades. She sent the solenoid flying toward them, but the Shadow Man she had attacked with it before grabbed it out of the air with both hands.

Despite herself, Dusty watched in horror as his hands got ripped to shreds by the impossibly sharp edges of the carbon fiber blade of the solenoid. His face, however, showed no signs of pain or discomfort. It was only a matter of time before the blade tore his hands apart. Her heart was beating quickly, not from the adrenaline of the fight, but from the panic of the realization that the enemy they were fighting had no fear of death or pain.

By the time the solenoid flew free from his shredded hands, the Shadow Man she had downed came back toward her, making it impossible for her to pursue those who had gone for Diaz.

It had all happened so fast. By the time she disabled the Shadow Men, leaving three men dead on the ground, Diaz's house was ransacked and empty. Her fellow Guardians had gotten there in record time, but it was still too little, too late.

For years, there had been nothing. No movement from Kain, no hints of Shadow Men across all of New Mexico. Dusty had even resented being assigned here after having trained in Los Angeles. (Her very first week on the job, a few drunk shape shifters had gotten into a bar fight with human civilians in Highland Park which had ultimately ended with them transforming into mirror images of the civilians. Aside from risking exposure as the whole thing had been caught on camera by some nosey patrons, the brawl had ended with five broken ribs, two broken noses, one concussion, and a handful of death threats. Dusty had been among the few Guardians called to break up violence, and had marveled at the efficacy of the Society. Several other departments were brought in to clean up the mess, leaving no loose ends and ultimately wrapping up the whole snafu with only a couple of bandaged humans who had no memory of the incident, and some hungover shape shifters with several hours of community service ahead of them. Anything like *that* had yet to happen in New Mexico.)

But as much as she missed the constant activity of the city of angels, she kept her mouth shut because she knew the job here was just as important.

And she had failed.

CHAPTER EIGHT

Theo

A stained teapot sat on the table between Yara and her aunt, a faint wisp of steam swirling peacefully from the spout. Yara's fingers lightly touched her piping hot mug, letting her tea cool before she drank any, Aunt Catherine's words hanging heavily in the air between them.

She took a deep, shaky breath. "I'm so sorry I never told you before. I honestly didn't think it was anything you'd ever need to know."

The information moved like molasses through Yara's head. The hope that she had been clinging to all week - that this had all been a sick joke - was quickly evaporating, replaced instead with a tangible fear that gripped her chest, suffocating her.

"All this time… you knew."

"About your father?" said Aunt Catherine. "Yes, I—"

"Not about him. About me."

Aunt Catherine's lip trembled as she met Yara's eyes. "I didn't know, Yara. I wasn't sure."

"You weren't sure?" said Yara, her voice getting louder. "What did you think my headaches were? What did you think my daydreams were! I can't believe it, all this time…"

"Your dad never had headaches. I thought— I'd *hoped*… perhaps it was just that. Migraines and a vivid imagination."

"Doctors appointment after doctors appointment. MRIs, CT scans… I can't believe you put me through all of that when you knew there were people out there who could actually *help* me! Who knew what was happening to me!"

"Yara, please calm down…"

"Calm down?" screamed Yara, indignant. "Don't tell me to calm down! My god! You just told me that my whole life I've been having visions of the future and you were letting me suffer like that... for *years!*"

"I was afraid!" Aunt Catherine retaliated. "Your father took my sister away from me by making her join that... that stupid White Mask Society. He made her a part of his dangerous world, and now she's dead, and my only other family is being hunted by some madman!" After a few moments in which they both tried to regain composure, Aunt Catherine continued. "I didn't want it to be true. I was hoping those doctors would tell me it was something else. And for the longest time, it didn't seem like... like it mattered. You were doing okay. You were safe."

"Okay? You think I was doing okay? I came home from school today because of these stupid headaches! I'm constantly behind on homework because I can't concentrate, or else I have daydreams in class and I miss half of what the teacher is saying! I have no friends because people think I'm weird, I can't participate in after school activities because I always need to come home and lie down... I mean, what about my life makes you think I'm okay?"

Tears were now falling freely down Aunt Catherine's cheeks. Yara knew she was in pain. Knew that her words were making it worse, but for those vindictive moments, she wanted to hurt her. She wanted to punish her aunt for keeping her in the dark and lying to her her whole life.

"I didn't see you," said Aunt Catherine in a small voice. "I didn't want to see it."

"Well, now you see me."

They stared at each other, Aunt Catherine too distraught to speak, and Yara too stubborn to. Until finally, "So, what now?"

Aunt Catherine wiped her nose on her scrubs. "I think now we call your Guardians."

CHAPTER NINE

Changes

Roberto Diaz had been left to wait for him in his laboratory. Though Kain was beyond excited to get to start working on a new hydan, he needed to take his time. He had to give his mind a chance to calm down. Proceeding with Diaz would be unlike the work he had done on the other two hyden. Of course, the wonderful thing about the hyden was that they were all different. But Diaz had a skill that could disarm Kain, and he needed to have his wits about him before exposing himself to the mind reader. Which was why he waited three full hours before limping into the lab, his cane softly thudding against the tile with every other step.

His Shadow Men had left Diaz strapped to the metal exam table in the center of the room. He was dressed in flesh colored underwear, leaving his rotund belly exposed. The man's face was white with fear and his skin prickly with cold.

"Mr. Diaz," said Kain. "A pleasure." He pulled his rolling stool up next to the table and sat heavily, relieved to take the weight off his leg. He leaned forward so he could look more closely at Diaz's face. Could the man tell what Kain was thinking? Right at this moment? How did he interpret people's thoughts? Perhaps words or images or both? Soon he would know. Soon he would be able to know everything that Diaz knew.

His question about whether or not Diaz was currently reading his thoughts were answered when his eyes widened, flitting back and forth between Kain's.

"Shh, shh..." said Kain, brushing the curly hair from Diaz's forehead, gently, as though he were calming a child after a nightmare. "There's no need to be afraid. We're in this together."

"I'm assuming what you're both wondering," said Carter, "is what happens now?"

Aunt Catherine and Yara nodded. The three of them sat around the small kitchen table. It hadn't taken long for Carter to get to their apartment after Aunt Catherine called to accept their offer of protection. Carter looked a little different than Yara remembered her. A little less feminine. Perhaps she had shape shifted? *No*, thought Yara. *That's impossible.*

This was going to take some getting used to.

"We have arranged for you both to stay at Headquarters for a little while. At least until we resolve the issue."

"How long is a little while?" said Aunt Catherine.

"There's no way to know, unfortunately," said Carter. "But you'll both be much safer there. Our Headquarters are virtually impenetrable."

"But I can still go to school and stuff, right?" said Yara. "I'm supposed to start college in the fall, and I'm graduating this summer." She had yet to decide what school she would be attending, nor had she determined how she could pay for it, but the prospect of leaving LA was something she had been looking forward to.

"We can arrange to postpone your admittance into the school you choose to attend. As for finishing out your senior year, that will be slightly more complicated, but we can have myself, Erik, or Robin escort you to and from campus then bring you back at the end of the day. You wouldn't miss anything."

Yara rubbed her face. The severity of the situation had not truly set in. What lengths were these people willing to go to in order to protect her from this alleged threat? "So what, you guys'll just hang around outside the school for seven hours?"

"Yes."

Yara blanked. "OK…" she said, more because she couldn't think of anything else to say.

"And what about my job?" said Aunt Catherine. "I'm assuming you're not going to have anyone escort me to and from work every day and hang out for twelve hour shifts at a time?"

"The Society can negotiate a leave of absence from your work for the time being until we get a better sense of things."

"We can't afford for me to stop working—"

"I'm sorry," interrupted Carter. "I should have been more clear. The Society intends to take care of your finances. At least for the next few months. You both have enough to worry about as it is."

At this, both Aunt Catherine and Yara fell completely silent. This was too good to be true. Here came this magical organization filled with shape shifters and other mystical creatures giving Aunt Catherine a paid vacation while offering free room and board. There had to be a catch.

Imminent danger, thought Yara. *There's your catch.*

"I'm sure you have many more questions," said Carter, "but perhaps I can answer them on the way. If you would like to take a minute to pack a bag, I have a car waiting downstairs."

Erik was wired.

Carter had insisted that they wouldn't need assistance from Robin or Erik to bring in Yara and her aunt, leaving the two Guardians to fret restlessly around Headquarters.

It wasn't necessarily common practice for the White Mask Society to house Wards in their bases, but it wasn't unheard of when situations demanded it. And the situation certainly demanded it. With Kain having recently apprehended a third hydan, the Guardians - particularly those assigned to the remaining hyden - were all on edge. And Erik was no exception.

An entire wing of Headquarters was designated for civilian use. It was the floor above Erik's quarters, who lived alongside the rest of the Guardians.

Everything was already prepared for Yara's arrival. Though Erik desperately wanted something with which to distract himself, there simply was nothing to do. As a result, he and Robin were in the main lobby on the ground floor, ready to greet them when they arrived.

"Did you try the new chocolate pudding they have in the commissary?" said Robin, clearly in an attempt to put Erik at ease.

"No, not yet."

"You should. Especially considering how much you like chocolate."

Erik nodded, but he wasn't really listening. He wanted to let Robin distract him. Wanted desperately to alleviate the heavy knot in his stomach. But he simply didn't work that way.

Seeing it was a losing battle, Robin sauntered over to one of the chairs next to the receptionist with an air of nonchalance Erik had never been able to attain, and started chatting with a nearby fern.

Erik, on the other hand, was pacing by the fountain.

It felt like hours - though Erik was sure it couldn't have possibly been that long - before Carter walked through the glass lobby doors, followed closely by a very pale Catherine Tanners and a thin-lipped Yara Rivers, both of them rolling small suitcases behind them. Erik's heart jumped slightly in his chest, but he tried to hide it. He stopped his pacing and watched them step lightly on the marble floor toward him, Robin rousing from his position to join them as well.

"Welcome!" said Robin jovially, just as Erik opened his mouth to say the same. He shook Catherine's hand - she took it very gingerly - then extended it to Yara, who was gripping herself so tightly that it seemed she might fall apart if she were to let go. "What would you like to do first? Set your bags down? See your rooms? Grab some food?"

Watching Robin interact with people so effortlessly reminded Erik how inept he was at social interactions. He so badly wanted to be the one with a big crooked smile on his face, welcoming them warmly to Headquarters, offering to give them a tour. Robin was the kind of person who knew everyone's name. And what was more, everyone knew *his* name. But Erik had never been like that. He never *would* be like that. One of the many reasons he had grown so fond of Yara Rivers in his time as her Guardian. They both felt more comfortable alone, away from crowds, in the quiet moments of life.

Catherine and Yara exchanged nervous glances. "Can we put our bags away?" said Yara.

"Bags it is! Let me get that for ya," said Robin, taking Yara's suitcase from her and pulling it toward the elevator. "E, wanna grab Ms. Tanner's bag?"

Feeling embarrassed at being told what to do, as though he were merely a bag boy as opposed to a Guardian, Erik did so, bringing up the rear as they all headed through the lobby.

Robin stopped at the front desk and introduced Larry at reception. "This is my main man, Larry. Larry, meet Yara and Catherine. They're going to be staying with us for a few weeks!"

Erik tried not to scoff at the idea that this would all be over in a few weeks, but he didn't say anything. Yara and Catherine already looked uncomfortable enough with the arrangement, he didn't want to make things worse by informing them that it could be months, perhaps even years before Kain was stopped.

"Hello," said Larry, smiling from under a mop of curly red hair. He pushed his thick glasses up the bridge of his nose, taking a moment to look away from his computer and smile at the two civilians.

"Hi," said Catherine.

Yara waved awkwardly.

"Larry will be the one you check in with anytime you come and go," continued Robin. "Onward!"

Erik saw Carter roll their eyes, but a smile tugged at their lips. Everyone packed into the elevator and Erik found himself right next to Yara. Their shoulders were touching, but she quickly shrunk into herself so that there was an inch of space between them.

"Why are we going down?" asked Catherine.

"Most of the building is underground," answered Carter.

The residential floor was the third floor down. The elevator dinged happily, the doors opening to reveal the gray walls and dark carpets of the large atrium that branched off in multiple directions. Robin gestured to the hall off to the left.

"E will show you gals to your rooms and we can give you some time to settle in, get comfortable. What time would you like us to come get ya for dinner?"

"Dinner?" said Catherine.

"Yeah, you know. Food. The last meal of the day. Unless you count midnight snacks, which how could you not, right?" He chuckled. Catherine gave a careful smile, but Yara still looked too tense to react with anything other than nervousness. "How about we come get you around six?"

"Sure," said Catherine. "Sounds good."

"I'm very much looking forward to getting to know you better," said Robin, his blue eyes twinkling as he nodded his head to Catherine and then to Yara. Erik noticed he held the latter's eyes for a moment longer and Yara, who Erik had noticed normally avoided eye contact with strangers, didn't look away. Erik felt a twinge of jealousy. At that, Robin and Carter turned around and headed back into the elevator, leaving him alone with Yara and her aunt.

CHAPTER TEN

Nayla With an N

It was hard for Yara to get a grasp of the scale of the White Mask Society Headquarters. From the outside, the building seemed completely ordinary. It looked like an older building, not even a particularly big one, brown and nearly crumbling, tucked in a quiet corner of downtown she wasn't familiar with. Next door were several warehouses that appeared abandoned with signs advertising filming spaces and scrap metal.

You wouldn't believe it once you walked through the front doors, however. The interior was everything shiny and new; polished marble floors, a sparkling fountain in the center of the lobby, plush armchairs in the waiting area, bright green potted trees.

They headed below ground, however. (Only three floors down, and if the elevator were to be believed, there were at least seven more floors below them, plus the four floors above.) While Yara wasn't very enthusiastic about the idea of living in a basement, when the elevator doors opened to reveal a spacious atrium filled with warm light, her anxiety eased.

She and Aunt Catherine were led to their rooms by Erik. He was stoic and quiet, which made Yara think he didn't want to be there. He stopped in front of two doors facing each other marked with brass numbers.

"Miss Rivers, you'll be here, in room 246. Miss Tanners, room 247."

Yara tried not to stare at his face, but it was hard. He was very handsome, and his eyes were quite simply alarming. She thought back to her first encounter with him last week. Carter had mentioned that there were many humans working for the Society, and that Robin was one of them. She'd said nothing, however, about Erik. Perhaps his eyes were so green - so bright - because they were not, in fact, human eyes. He looked completely normal, otherwise. But so did Carter. *And so do you, Yara,* she thought bitterly to herself. Evidently, no matter how human someone looked, there could always be something different. Something more.

"You won't be able to get any cell reception down here," said Erik, "but if you need to contact anyone, there are secure phones in each of your quarters." He handed them both keys, extracted from a hidden pocket in his elegant black uniform. "I'll see you at dinner."

Aunt Catherine and Yara both watched him walk away, silent for a long while before Aunt Catherine said, "Let's see your room."

Room 246 felt very much like a hotel suite. There was a small kitchenette with not more than a mini fridge, sink, and microwave next to a dining nook smaller than the one they had at home. The kitchenette branched off of a small living space that looked clean and comfortable with a loveseat and armchair. The ceilings were high, the walls bright, there was a television, and - as Erik had promised - a phone. Depositing her suitcase on the floor by the door, they went to check out the bedroom. The en suite bathroom was clean and simple, a double bed was framed by two small nightstands, but the room was otherwise unremarkable. Even without windows, the room felt spacious and warm.

"Not bad," said Aunt Catherine.

"I guess," said Yara.

"What's the matter?"

"This is all just weird. I guess I'm having a hard time believing it's real. I keep expecting to wake up from a dream."

Aunt Catherine said nothing, but touched Yara's cheek lightly.

"Had you ever been to this place before? With my mom?"

"She showed me around a little bit, but it's not much as far as tourist destinations go. I saw her room. She lived here with your dad. I mean in this building, not in this room. Though it was pretty similar to this."

Yara laughed lightly, and realized it was the first time she had laughed in days. Faintly, her head started to pang, but she ignored it.

"I'll let you unpack," said Aunt Catherine, and she left for her own room across the hall.

It was going to be strange to live alone. While she was only across the hall from her aunt, having her own private bathroom and private living space would take some getting used to. Though she couldn't say she was upset about it.

Yara spent about an hour unpacking her clothes, putting away a handful of books, and taping to the walls the few pictures she had taken from her bedroom, including the one of her and Aunt Catherine superimposed on the Napa Valley calendar page.

Erik had not been lying when he said they would get no service. Her phone didn't work.

Already bored, and with nothing else to do, she decided to lay down for a bit and try to shake off the blossoming headache. The most drastic difference between this room at the Society and her room back home was the sound. They lived in an overcrowded part of LA, which meant that silence was never something truly experienced in their apartment. There would be occasional moments of calm, but Yara had grown used to the ambient chaos of a city just outside her window. Cars honking, people shouting, ambulances sirening. But here there were no windows, there was no sound. She was completely cut off from the world, and the oppressive silence was a constant reminder of the life she left behind.

How strange, she mused to herself, that a girl who preferred being alone felt more at home in a crowded city.

Her head gave a painful throb. She pressed her palms into her eyes, groaning. The moment she closed her eyes, her mind filled with the same familiar fog that accompanied her daydreams. No. Her visions. After all, it had been established that these weren't just products of her imagination. The whole reason she was here was because they really truly were visions of the future.

At first, she hesitated before yielding to the vision. The knowledge that what she was about to see was real - or at least, *would* be real - gave her a new sense of trepidation. But the pain was too great, so she let herself succumb.

She could see a man through the fog. He looked frightened. He had dark, curly hair and a round face. Hispanic perhaps, though it was hard to tell. His wide eyes followed someone who was lurking around him, though all Yara could make out was a tall shadow. *It's real,* she thought. *It's all real...* Her heart started to beat faster, and her palms were sweating.

Who was this man looking at?

And why was he so afraid?

* * *

With the luxury of a few hours off to himself, Robin thought he could use the time in the simulator, or perhaps catch up on some reading. Carter had lent him a trilogy and he was nearly finished with the third book. But when he opened the doors to his quarters, it was clear the universe had something else in mind for him.

"N. Fancy seeing you here."

Her name was Nayla Jackson. She, too, was a Guardian, though she and Robin had never worked together. They had been initiates in the same class. Along with a dozen others, Nayla and Robin had trained and studied and fought and drilled. And in the crucible of initiation, they found each other. For several years, they had managed to make a relationship work despite their hectic responsibilities as Guardians. When Nayla had been sent up north to quell a growing movement of anti-nymph extremists, they had stayed together. When Robin had broken his leg after chasing a man who had killed a shape shifter, they stayed together.

But one day, Robin realized he could not offer her what he felt she deserved, and he broke things off.

She was still as beautiful as ever. She had long blonde hair, frequently pulled back into a tight braid, and almond shaped brown eyes. Her nose was sprinkled with freckles, and at this moment, her full lips were parted slightly in a smile. Though Guardian policy dictated that they never refer to each other with their full names, during their courtship Robin had come to know her as Nayla. It therefore took great effort to call her "N" now that they were forced back into a professional relationship. If you could call breaking into his quarters professional.

"I hear you brought in your Ward," she said. "Congratulations."

"Well, you've had yours brought in since the beginning."

Nayla laughed. "Easy, considering she's a member of the Society herself."

Robin took a seat in a chair facing Nayla, who had made herself comfortable on the loveseat. "I must admit, I always thought it weird to assign Emmanuelle with three Guardians herself when she already is one. You'd think you could hit two cans with one stone in that situation."

Nayla raised an elegant eyebrow. "Emmanuelle?"

Robin shrugged. "Sorry. 'E' in my head is Erik. Does she still want you to call her 'E' now she's a Ward in addition to being a Guardian?"

"You know, I never thought to ask. I just kept on calling her 'E' and she never corrected me."

Robin nodded.

"So, how is she?" asked Nayla.

"E? Isn't that your job to know?"

"I mean your hydan. Yara River, is it?"

"Rivers," corrected Robin. "And good. Considering."

Nayla studied his face, but Robin pulled his lips into a crooked smile, revealing nothing.

"Tell me. Has she seen your future?"

"Why don't ya tell me what you're doing here, N."

Nayla closed her mouth, for which Robin was thankful. He had always had a weakness for the natural pout she was able to produce by the simple act of keeping her lips parted.

"I guess I just missed you," she said eventually, her eyes bright.

Robin's smile faltered. "Well, I *am* addictive."

"You never were able to be very serious," said Nayla, smiling, but not quite able to hide her irritation.

"It's part of my charm."

She nodded to the cut on Robin's cheek. It was healing quickly, but had been deep enough to warrant a butterfly stitch. "What happened?"

"Nothing I couldn't handle."

"Well, we'd all love to meet Yara, now she's here," said Nayla, standing up. Her movements were lithe and graceful, like a deer. "I know *Emmanuelle*," she winked as she said the name, "especially is curious to meet another hydan. Maybe we'll see you in the commissary later."

"Cool," said Robin.

She waited for another moment, but when it was clear that he wasn't going to do or say anything else, she left him alone in his quarters.

CHAPTER ELEVEN

The Commissary

For dinner, Yara and Aunt Catherine had been taken to a place the Guardians called the commissary. It was two floors above their quarters, and looked very much like an ordinary food court, large enough for at least two hundred people. The open space was filled with round tables, the walls lined with stands that all offered a different variety of food. The choice was overwhelming, and Yara wasn't very hungry to begin with, so she ended up just following her aunt to a sandwich stand, before meeting her three Guardians at a table near the far end of the hall, all three of whom were eating something different.

"You find something good?" asked Robin, digging in to a giant plate of what looked like Pad Thai.

"Yeah, I guess," said Yara shyly. "They didn't have any cheese."

"Oh yeah," said Robin laughing, his mouth full. "We don't do that here."

"Do what?" asked Yara, confused.

"He means there are no animal products at the Society," said Carter, who was eating much less aggressively than Robin.

"At all?" Did they mean she wouldn't be able to have *any* cheese while she stayed here?

"Many of the Deviants that we work with and protect here are fauna nymphs," Carter explained. "They spend most of their time in their animal forms interacting with other non-human animals. We find it disrespectful to not show the same regard for their lives than we do for humans or other Deviants. It's a show of unity."

Yara nodded, though she wasn't sure she completely understood. At least there would be cheese at school…

"Normally they have some kind of plant based cheeses, though," said Carter. "They must be out."

"I guess." She glanced at Erik who was avoiding looking at her, focusing on his plate. She wondered idly how much he didn't want to be there.

"So. Yara," said Robin, his plate nearly empty already. "I know that Black wants to meet you at some point, we were thinking maybe this weekend? That way you can finish school this week without having anything else thrown at ya."

"Black?"

"Bora Black," explained Carter. "She's the Head of the White Mask Society. At least, Head of the LA branch."

"How many branches are there?"

Carter counted silently before Erik answered without looking up. "Fourteen."

"Well," said Carter, "fourteen Headquarters. We have hundreds more smaller precincts, but they all report to the nearest HQ."

"And *we* all report to the Paris branch," said Robin. "That's the main office."

"Jesus," breathed Yara. "How big exactly is this Society?"

"Big," said Robin and Carter at the same time.

"Bear in mind," added Carter, "we're the only organization that polices any problems that arise involving Deviants, and there are millions of us."

"How is it even possible for something so big to be kept secret?" said Aunt Catherine.

"With great difficulty," said Carter, smiling.

"Anyone sitting here?" came a voice from over Yara's shoulder. She jumped in surprise, her reaction met with a delicate laugh. "Sorry, didn't mean to scare you." Four more people holding trays of food stood behind her, including the speaker, a beautiful woman with bright blonde hair.

"It's fine," said Yara, feeling awkward, her cheeks burning.

"N!" said Carter happily. "Join us, please!"

The four of them took seats around the table, the one called N sitting closest to Yara. She was stunning, making Yara shrink uncomfortably into herself. In comparison to this blonde gazelle, Yara felt like a troll. When, she wondered, was the last time she had brushed her hair or properly taken off her makeup before bed?

"I'm Nayla," she said, extending a hand to Yara, who shook it, avoiding eye contact. "I'm so excited to meet you, finally. Robin has told me so much about you."

Yara's eyes flitted to Robin, but he just waggled his eyebrows and said nothing.

On Nayla's other side was an even taller woman with the darkest skin Yara had ever seen and long black braids that were pulled back.

"Hello, Yara," she said. She had an accent, though Yara, inept at identifying accents and different languages, couldn't place it. "My name is Emmanuelle." Yara shook her hand. "Nayla is one of my Guardians, as are Guy," she gestured to the bearded man on her right, "and Jack," the freckled boy next to Guy who looked entirely too young to be there. They both waved and muttered friendly greetings in turn. "I, too, am hydan."

"You are?" said Yara, strangely excited by these words. "You mean, you can see the future, too?"

"No," said Emmanuelle. "I believe you are the only living hydan with that gift. Mine is a physical one."

"What is it?"

"Jumping."

Yara's heart fell. Her disappointment must have shown on her face because Emmanuelle laughed.

"You were hoping for something more impressive?"

"No! It's just—"

"Wait 'til you see her jump," said Guy. "It's closer to flying, really."

"She's like Spiderman!" said Jack.

"I'm sure this is all very overwhelming," said Emmanuelle smiling, her teeth a dazzling white against her complexion. "Like everything, it will all become more familiar. With time."

Yara nodded, but doubted it very much.

Yara did not say much over the course of dinner, listening instead to all these impressive people chat casually about things like the fauna nymphs who had tried to rob a bank in their animal forms before being captured by Robin and the shape shifter in Research who was caught illegally smuggling an herb from the Casablanca branch, alleging they could use it to cure something called "nymphoma".

Instead, she tried to absorb as much as possible. Robin laughed easily and knew just as well how to make others laugh. Carter always seemed to know the answer, chiming in with corrections and additional tidbits of information while maintaining a sense of calm that felt impossible considering how much noise filled the commissary. The stunning blonde named Nayla reminded Yara of Stephanie Cantzoukas from school. Part of every conversation, interacting with people effortlessly, and throwing flirtatious glances at Robin that no one other than Yara seemed to notice. Emmanuelle was rigid yet warm. She spent most of lunch peppering Aunt Catherine with questions. (Yara got the feeling Emmanuelle wanted to talk to *her*, but Yara was hiding behind her aunt and not making herself readily available for conversation.) Guy never opened his mouth when he laughed. Jack spoke so quickly Yara often missed several words, a problem exacerbated by his unusually large front teeth.

But most of all, she watched Erik. A few times she caught him looking at her, too, his eyes like spotlights. He was completely unreadable. He barely participated in the conversation, smiling politely and responding when someone addressed him, but for the most part he listened, same as Yara.

Their food long gone and the commissary beginning to empty, people started excusing themselves one by one. Yara and Aunt Catherine were among the first to go.

"Thank you so much for…" said Aunt Catherine, gesturing around her as she searched for the right words.

Robin and Carter, who had both stood to say goodnight, waved away her thanks and wished them both a pleasant evening.

"Do you need someone to take you back to your quarters?" said Carter.

"We remember the way," said Aunt Catherine. Yara hoped she was telling the truth because Yara certainly did not remember. She locked eyes one last time with Erik, who gave her a nod and the shadow of a smile (her heart skipped a beat) before she turned with her aunt and headed back toward the elevators.

"Do you actually remember how to get to our rooms?" Yara whispered when they were out of earshot.

"We'll figure it out," said Aunt Catherine. "I just figured you'd had enough socializing for one day."

Yara smiled.

CHAPTER TWELVE
Bora With a B

As exciting as it sounded to be living in a secret underground base filled with magical beings, the next few days were disappointingly mundane. Yara had fewer headaches than usual, and her Guardians took it in turns to escort her to and from school. It was on the first day with Robin that she learned she had been misgendering Carter. Carter did not identify as female, but instead was non-binary.

"Oh my god!" Yara had said, her cheeks flushing. "I feel horrible!"

Robin laughed and patted her on the back. She had tried very hard not to instinctively flinch away from him, still uncomfortable with being touched, but she managed to get through it. His ease and comfort were almost infectious. "Don't feel bad. You didn't know! And now you do."

If she thought she'd had a hard time focusing in school before, it was nothing compared to now. Her mind constantly wandered in class back to the maze that was the Society, questions about what filled all the other floors, how many people lived and worked there, what all their special powers were, and what were the coolest missions they'd been on. Instead of being scolded for dozing off with what she now knew were visions, she was scolded for tapping her pen against her desk as she mulled over questions about the world that had just been revealed to her, and trying to remember if she had ever called Carter a woman to their face.

That Saturday morning, eager to sleep in, Yara's hopes were dashed when someone knocked on her door around nine.

"Who is it?" she called from her bed, bleary eyed.

"Uh, it's a prince. I've come to rescue you." Yara kept her eyes closed, trying to determine if she was still asleep, but then, "Hello?"

"No, thank you. No school today, please."

"Yara, it's Robin. I'm supposed to take you to see Black."

She groaned. "Uh, give me ten minutes, please."

"Ten and that's it. I don't want to get yelled at 'cause *you're* lazy."

She chuckled and pulled on an oversized t-shirt from her dresser and her most comfortable pair of pants, still on the floor where she had left them after undressing last night.

Robin was waiting for her just outside her door, leaning against the wall, fiddling with a small, silver sphere attached to his high collar which he tucked away as soon as she appeared. "Morning, princess."

"Don't call me that," she said, grumpy from having been roused in such a manner.

"Morning or princess?"

"Ha ha. Does my aunt know where I'm going?"

"We left her a message. Didn't want to wake her up."

"How thoughtful."

"I think she's really enjoying this time off from work, if I'm being honest," said Robin, smiling.

"Yeah, well, give it a week."

"I don't think I've ever seen a woman sleep so much. Unless she was under a spell, of course."

"A spell?" said Yara. She hadn't thought of this world containing magic like that.

"Oh no," he laughed. "I was just kidding. Sorry. Hard to remember that since this is all new to you, you might believe anything I tell ya."

Yara lifted an eyebrow. "Great. I'd always hoped that my gullibility would be tested with new laws of nature."

Robin led Yara all the way up to the top floor, the same place where they had initially brought her and Aunt Catherine to tell her of the whole debacle they were about to become intricately involved with.

"We call the people who work up here the 'shoots'," explained Robin.

"Why?"

"'Cause they're above ground. Get it?"

The feel of this floor was very different from those below ground that Yara had been seeing a lot of the last few days. Not only were there windows, but the floor was hardwood and the doors were mahogany. There were, however, the same brass signs that marked each one. Robin led her straight down the hallway, all the way down to the door marked "BORA BLACK".

At the door, Robin stopped.

"What are you doing?"

"This part is just you," he said, again with that crooked smile.

Suddenly afraid, Yara turned back to the door - had it been this big just a moment ago? - reached up, and knocked.

Bora Black opened the door to see Robin Green sitting on the small bench in the hallway behind Yara Rivers, who looked frightened and disheveled.

"Hello," said Bora, beckoning for her to come inside. "I was expecting you a little earlier, but I suppose you were sleeping in?"

Yara didn't respond, her mouth a thin line, though Bora detected a hint of annoyance. Her hazel eyes were looking anywhere but at Bora. Bora was not unfamiliar with this kind of greeting. Newcomers, particularly those who had never interacted with nymphs before, were always wary of her appearance. The Tenebrae were perhaps one of the most intimidating of all nymphs. Bora didn't mind. She often used it to her advantage. It didn't hurt to know you could unnerve someone if you needed to.

"Take a seat," said Bora, moving around her desk and sitting down herself. Yara, shoulders tight, gingerly obeyed. "I knew your father quite well. Though I admit you look more like your mother. But I can see him right here." Bora tapped her own mouth. "He used to purse his lips just like that, too."

Yara tried to relax her mouth at these words and bit her lip instead.

"Well, I can see you don't want to be here, and I'll try not to keep you for long. What I'd like to do, Yara, is work with you on honing your gift."

At this, Yara finally met Bora's eyes. As a Tenebrae, she could see exceptionally well. That included the smallest fluctuations of Yara's irises. From the waves made around her pupil, Bora knew that she was afraid of what she saw, but the tension around the corona indicated that she was also excited. Bora smiled.

"I can imagine how difficult it's been your whole life to be plagued with these visions. The headaches are a result of you trying to suppress them. Your father got them, too, on occasion. But with practice and training, I believe that you will not only stop having headaches, but you will be able to control when and what you see."

At this, Yara spoke. "I can control what I see?"

"Your father was young when we lost him. He had only just started to fine tune his ability. But he was very much coming into his own, and finding new and unique ways of harnessing his gift. Not to mention the many visions he had near the end of his life that helped the Society greatly. I don't want to overwhelm you with anything, I know you've had a lot thrown at you these last few days. So we'll start out slow. This week, when you feel a headache coming on, find a quiet place and try to focus on your vision. Try to remember what you see. And don't try to end it before it ends on its own. Does that make sense?"

Yara nodded.

"I know you've got a Guardian out there waiting to take you to breakfast, and I know you're hungry."

At the questioning look on Yara's face, Bora waved her hand. It was too complicated to explain that the slightest change in the hue of her skin was enough for her to know that Yara was thinking about food.

"I'll see you next Friday after school. Remember what I said."

And with that, Bora ushered Yara out the door and closed it behind her. With her visitor gone, she filled the room once more with comfortable darkness. Too dark for human eyes. But it was how Bora liked it.

She kept her hand pressed against the mahogany door for a few more moments after Yara left, replaying what she had seen in the young woman's eyes. The set of her jaw was so like her father's.

Bora could only hope that her conviction would be stronger.

CHAPTER THIRTEEN
Donuts

It was surprising how much school had become more bearable for Yara since living with the White Mask Society. The senioritis she had been suffering so desperately from before had quieted as a result of her being able to distract herself with the memory of seeing a spider plant crawl out of a pot in the commissary, transform into a human-like figure, then walk out of the room. While it had been awkward for her at first, she was no longer bothered by her Guardians' constant presence.

That Friday, after the final bell rang, Yara practically bolted out of school to find Erik waiting for her across the street, pretending to read a book. She had grown so accustomed to him in his black, fitted Society uniform back at Headquarters, the half-mask emblem of the organization embroidered on the shoulder, that seeing him in civilian clothing out in the real world felt slightly strange. He was wearing jeans and a dark green long sleeved shirt. Perfectly ordinary - if not for his eyes.

"Hi," she said breathlessly. He glanced up, and an electricity she had come to accept that accompanied his look shot through her.

"Hi," he said. "Ready?"

Yara nodded. He tucked his book under his arm and they began to walk down the street to where the Society cars usually waited. A not-so-small part of Yara was excited every time it was Erik's turn to "guard" her (though she privately hated thinking of it in those terms). She knew it was just a stupid crush. He was handsome, and it was literally his job to pay attention to her. It would be hard for any girl to resist. (Right?) But there was another advantage to Erik being on duty. After school, they would make a small detour together to a donut shop down the street.

"Which one do you think you're going to go for today?" he asked.

"Hmm," said Yara, feigning thinking. In truth, her entire seventh period had been spent entirely fantasizing about this donut. Food at the Society was delicious. But the primary focus of the food was generally health, and Yara was craving sugar. "I'm gonna go with the matcha one."

"Ah," said Erik. "Going for the elegant choice."

Yara laughed. "Is it possible for a donut to be elegant?"

"If it's green tea flavored, yeah I think so."

"It's deep fried!"

Erik laughed. He didn't smile often, much less laugh, and Yara felt a sense of pride every time she elicited one. His entire face transformed, and it was then that she got the sense he didn't dislike her. A logical voice in her head kept reminding her that it would be incredibly unlikely for someone who wasn't fond of her to go out of his way to extend their time together with donut dates - *not a date*, she reminded herself - but her logical voice was never quite as loud as the voice that said she wasn't pretty enough. Wasn't smart enough. Wasn't graceful enough. Wasn't *enough*. That voice tended to call the shots. But when Erik smiled, that voice got a little quieter.

"What about you?"

"Probably chocolate."

"That's what you get every time!" said Yara.

Erik shrugged. "Why mess with a classic? If it's good, it's good."

They sat on the wire chairs outside the shop as they ate their donuts, watching the busy downtown life pass them by. Her school was nestled between a few office buildings and an overpriced parking garage, so the area was filled with people in expensive suits pretending they could not see those in rags. (There were entire city blocks downtown lined with tents surrounded by heaping piles of what looked like trash, but in reality were all the belongings of those who lived there.) The sun was almost always blocked by the tall buildings, but cast bright reflections in the windows, causing Yara to squint down at her donut. She wasn't particularly fond of the city with its maze of one-way streets and the contrast of lavish wealth (the businessmen in their BMWs) and extreme poverty (homeless people around every corner sleeping at bus stops). But now with the sun low in the sky and the street cast in shades of vivid oranges and pinks, she thought it was almost beautiful. Downtown Los Angeles looked like it had once been a beautiful place. Older brick buildings with crumbling moldings that had the promise of having once been elegant, but were now in disrepair, abandoned, and splattered with graffiti. The older parts of the city were deteriorating, neglected in favor of the new and the modern. Yara couldn't help but think it was an appropriate analogy for the entire country.

"Are we allowed to be doing this?" she asked, voicing something she thought she knew the answer to, but had been too afraid to ask until now.

"I'm meant to escort you from school to the car. We're heading to the car." He looked at her, the hint of another smile tugging at the corners of his mouth. "Besides, didn't Black tell you you're supposed to be staying calm?"

Yara nodded, her mouth full.

"Do donuts help?"

At this, she snorted causing a piece of donut to fly out of her mouth. Mortified, she clapped her hand over her lips, but Erik was laughing. With great difficulty, she managed to swallow the rest of her donut and punched him playfully in the arm.

He wiped his eyes. "Sorry, sorry."

"You may think it's funny, but I'm still mourning the loss of that bite."

That earned her another chuckle, but Yara wasn't able to enjoy it, because at that moment, her head started to hurt, indicating an oncoming vision. Evidently it was written on her face, because Erik's composure changed instantly.

"Are you having a vision?"

She nodded, trying to take deep breaths through her nose.

Don't fight it. Don't fight it. Don't fight it.

"Do we need to leave?"

She shook her head, squeezing her eyes shut. "Gimme a minute," she said tightly. "And stop looking at me." It was the first time she had had a vision in front of one of her Guardians, and she wasn't keen to think about Erik watching her try to give in to it. What if she looked stupid? This condition had caused her enough embarrassment already as it was.

While she had not gained any control over when she had visions or what she saw, she had been able to surrender to them more easily since she had been practicing trying to have one before bed every night.

Through the fog in her head, she saw... Robin of all people. He was speaking to someone, and with a slow exhale, Yara tried to clear the thick haze to see who it was. It was the same blonde woman she had met at the commissary. They were standing close to one another, and while Yara couldn't hear what they were saying, it was clear there was an intimacy between them. Nayla's arm reached up to touch Robin's shoulder, the fog curling around her movements. He looked down at her hand, but the moment was short lived, and as soon as it was over, the smoke cleared and the world was once again the filthy gray of downtown Los Angeles.

After a few moments, she looked over at Erik, who was cautiously glancing at her out of the corner of his eye. When it was clear she was no longer having a vision, he turned to face her fully.

"What did you see?" he asked, timid.

"Robin."

Erik's lips tensed, but he didn't say anything else. Yara could tell he was refraining from asking more, but she had the nasty sense that she had just witnessed what would come to be a private moment, and she felt more like a voyeur than a seer. She didn't think that moment needed to be shared with anyone.

In the car on the way back to the Society, after having not said a word to each other since her vision, Yara broke the silence and said, "How do Robin and Nayla know each other?"

Erik didn't say anything for a few moments, leading Yara to wonder whether he had heard her. Eventually, however, he said, "They used to date." And he left it at that.

CHAPTER FOURTEEN
Practice

Kain had sent Diaz back to his cell so he could instead spend some time working on one of the other hydan in his custody. Luan Khumalo had been particularly easy to capture as the White Mask Society did not have a strong or well equipped base in South Africa. He had also been Kain's first target, and as such, the Society had been ill prepared. Khumalo had the unique ability to echolocate, and unlike most of the other hyden, his ability manifested itself with external physical differences.

This would complicate things slightly as it meant Kain would have to physically alter himself, and that could prove difficult. Fortunately, he had already planned for that. The Halogen Shadow Men - or women, as it were - had been specifically designed and trained for assisting him with more complicated scientific procedures. He would just need to start training them now to prepare for any upcoming surgeries.

He poured over the data from the various tests and scans that had been taken of Khumalo. The only fortunate thing was that there didn't appear to be any differences in his skeleton, musculature, or nervous system. The external changes to his ears shouldn't altogether be too difficult. Though if he was unsuccessful in growing tissue he may have to graft it to himself using Khumalo's, which wouldn't be ideal considering he would no longer be able to study the subject. It was the changes to his vocal cords that he wasn't sure about. If *she* were still working with him, if they still shared a lab as they once did, this would all be so much easier. But he had to stop thinking like that. Stop pining after what he'd lost. Instead he had to focus on what he had.

After all, she wasn't truly gone.

Having spent her entire school day thinking about her donut date with Erik, Yara had completely forgotten that she was meant to meet with Bora Black that evening to work on her skills as a seer. She had not braced herself for it at all. So when Erik dropped her off outside the heavy mahogany door etched in bronze with Black's name, Yara's pulse started to speed up, causing an uncomfortable tightness in her chest.

She closed her eyes, trying to inhale liquid gold and exhale red smoke.

Inhale the calm, exhale the anxious.

Inhale, exhale.

She knocked.

Black answered the door almost immediately, as though she had been standing just on the other side, waiting. Black was just as intimidating as she had been before, her skin still emanating spiraling darkness and her eyes two obsidian orbs.

"Come in."

Yara looked over her shoulder at Erik who was sitting on the bench, his green eyes unfocused. When he noticed Yara looking, he gave a small nod of encouragement before the door shut behind her.

"How was your week?" asked Black, taking a seat behind her desk, and gesturing for Yara to sit as well.

"Fine, I guess."

"And school?"

"OK."

Black considered her for a moment. "You haven't done any practicing."

It wasn't a question. Yara didn't meet her eyes. "Well, to be honest, I haven't had any headaches since I saw you." It was a lie, of course, but how could Black know that?

"You're lying."

Crap.

Yara finally looked up. Whatever Bora Black was, she wasn't human. And while Yara didn't know what kind of … Deviant … she was, apparently she had the ability to detect lies. "OK, fine. I'm lying. I had three headaches, each one worse than the last."

"Do you remember what you saw?"

Of course she remembered. She remembered every single vision she had ever had, though often only in broad strokes. Faces were easy to confuse. They faded behind the fog. "Yes," she said simply.

Black waited for a moment, as though hoping Yara would speak, but when it became clear that she wasn't going to offer any additional information Black spoke again. "We'll start out simply tonight. I want you to close your eyes."

Yara pursed her lips. She was not keen on the idea of closing her eyes. It often made her anxiety worsen, as she could no longer see what was around her, making it easier for her imagination to run wild.

Black raised an eyebrow, so - begrudgingly - Yara obliged.

"Think about where you were the last time you had a vision. Before your headache began. Where were you. You don't need to tell me, just picture it for yourself."

The commissary.

"Who were you with."

Aunt Catherine and Erik.

"How were you feeling."

Erik had just laughed at a stupid joke she had made. She had been feeling… almost giddy. And nervous.

"Whatever feeling you had, try to recreate the physical effects it had on your body."

Yara frowned, unsure of what this meant.

"I'll give you an example," Black continued. "If you were happy, try smiling. If you were frightened, try breathing more quickly, tensing your muscles. Does that make sense?"

Yara didn't waste any energy nodding, too busy trying to remember how her body had reacted. She pictured Aunt Catherine. And she pictured Erik. And then pictured him smiling. Her heart hitched in her chest. She imagined his green eyes meeting hers as they had for a moment that afternoon. Her stomach clenched and the corners of her lips twitched.

Then all of a sudden, she felt a pressure behind her eyes.

"Excellent, Yara," said Black. "Don't fight it."

Yara didn't question how Black seemed to know that she had triggered a headache. She took several deep breaths and tried to relax her body, the opposite of her instinctive reaction when she felt the familiar pain in her temples.

"Unclench your fists, Yara," said Black's voice from very far away.

Yara hadn't even realized that she was doing it, but instantly released her fingers. The world filled with fog, but before it could clear enough for her to see anything, it all vanished, and was replaced with Black's dark office, and her unearthly presence.

For an hour and a half, Yara sat in Black's office, her toes barely touching the ground in the too high chair, as Black had her repeat that exercise over and over again.

"That was a very good start," she said at last, smiling. "I want you to remember that feeling that you had. Not just a description like 'angry' or 'sad'. I want you to remember the specific things your body did as a response to that feeling. Spend a few hours trying to calm your mind and summon those feelings. See if you can successfully trigger a vision.

"And every time you have a headache remember to give in. Don't fight it. And actually practice this time. I think I've proved that I'll know if you don't."

She winked playfully, but Yara had a feeling that her reaction would not be so playful if she came back to this office a second time without having done any work.

CHAPTER FIFTEEN

Shape Shifters

Life at the Society had started out so strange and surreal, like Yara was living in a science fiction story. But she and Aunt Catherine had quickly fallen into a normal routine. The trouble with normal routines was that they could get boring. Which meant that Yara found herself frequently looking for things to do. Everyone who worked for the Society always seemed to have something important going on, even her Guardians. And it wasn't as though there were a room filled with board games and televisions. Aunt Catherine had been facing a similar dilemma, but had discovered the research division of the Society, where she was being regularly shown around by one of the Medics, Fatima. Evidently they had use for a skilled nurse, and desperate for something to do, Aunt Catherine obliged.

As for Yara, going out seemed to be out of the question. An "unnecessary risk", Erik had called it, though Yara got the sense that those were not his words. (They had the distinct sound of coming from Bora Black.)

So Yara found herself frequently wandering the halls of the Society, trying to get a sense of the magnitude of the organization. There was something very satisfying about the monotone colors of the property. Each floor was color coded, and of course, all who worked there were constantly in uniform. For the most part, it was a form fitting black jumpsuit with the small white mask of the Society emblazoned on the collar, shoulder, or lapel.

She discovered the gym, where Society members trained, and she spent a great deal of time in the commissary. There were also hundreds upon hundreds of domestic quarters and offices. She had even once managed to wander onto a floor that was evidently used for research facilities. Bright, florescent lights and glass walls created a dizzying maze filled with strong smelling mixtures and shiny, expensive looking equipment, though after twenty minutes, someone had seen her and told her she wasn't allowed down there.

However, her favorite place by far was the library. She was on her way there, wrapped in a thick hoodie - as Headquarters was always too cold - dragging her hand along the wall as she went. She was so absorbed in her own thoughts that she jumped in surprise when someone called her name behind her.

"Sorry," said Carter, obviously trying to hide a laugh as they approached her. "Didn't mean to scare you."

"It's OK," said Yara, hand on her heart.

"Where you headed?" they said.

"I was gonna go to the library."

"Mind if I join?"

Yara shook her head. She didn't want to be rude, but in truth she felt slightly awkward around Carter. Perhaps it was the fact that they were so confident. They carried themself with the self-assuredness of a much older person even though they looked to be about the same age as Yara.

"You OK?"

"Hmm?" said Yara. "Oh yeah. I've just always been really jumpy."

Carter chuckled and nudged their glasses back up to the bridge of their nose. "No, not that. I mean in general. How are you feeling here? We haven't really had a chance to talk since you… moved in, for lack of better words."

Yara gave a sardonic chuckle. "To be honest, you guys always seem super busy. I don't want to impose or anything."

"Nonsense," said Carter. "It's what we're here for."

"What, keeping me company?"

"Well, no," they conceded. "Not exactly, I guess. But we want you to be happy here. As well as safe."

Yara didn't say anything, unsure of how to respond. The idea of "happiness" felt strange and unfamiliar. Not anything she had ever tried to pursue. She had always been too anxious to try. Too many other things to deal with.

"So," continued Carter as they both made their way down the hall. "How are your lessons with Black going?"

"Uh, fine, I guess?"

"Is that a question?"

"I dunno…"

They turned the corner together and Carter nodded to someone who walked past them. Yara, who had gotten very good at identifying the different uniforms worn in the Society, recognized from his that he was not a Guardian, but rather in the Eyes division which - from what Yara could tell - were basically the Society spies. And though she only got a quick glance, she saw he had the same amber eyes as Carter.

"Was he a shape shifter, too?" said Yara.

"They were," said Carter.

"Damn," said Yara, realizing that she had misgendered the shape shifter. Again. "I'm sorry."

Carter laughed. "Don't be! Mistakes happen, and it's a new world for you."

"Are all shape shifters non-binary, then?"

"Many of us," said Carter. "Though some identify more with one gender than the other, and they choose to go by the corresponding pronoun. Honestly," they continued, "when you can easily switch between one sex and the other, gender starts to lose all meaning."

"Wow," said Yara. "I never thought of it like that."

Carter laughed. "Why would you?"

They reached the library and lowered their voices as they made their way to an unoccupied reading nook near the back, far from the entrance.

"So, what were you looking for in the library?"

"Nothing, really," said Yara. "I was just bored."

She settled in a worn chair that had no arms so she could cross her legs, while Carter took a seat on a bench across from her and picked up a nearby book.

"Does it hurt?"

Carter looked up. "Does what hurt?"

"Shifting. Changing shape. I'm sorry, if you don't want me to ask questions about it I totally understand."

"I don't mind," said Carter with a chuckle. "I just had no idea what you were talking about."

"Oh, yeah. Sorry," said Yara.

"But no, it doesn't hurt. Some shapes can be more uncomfortable than others."

"Really?" said Yara, fascinated. "Like what?"

"Usually non-humanoid shapes. You know, like dogs or cats. There's a lot more involved in changing into those shapes. Bone restructuring and all that. So it takes a little bit of getting used to. Not pain exactly. More… discomfort."

"Oh my god, so you could literally just turn into a dog right here?"

Carter nodded. "A big one, though. I mean, we can't change our mass. Basic physics. The conservation of mass states that mass can't be created or destroyed, only rearranged."

"I'm not good at physics."

Carter laughed. "That's OK. You don't need to be."

"So that means if you became a dog, you'd be a dog who, like, weighs the same amount that you weigh? Right now? As a person?"

They nodded and held out their hand. Yara watched, eyes agape, as Carter's smooth, bronze skin sprouted hair, the fingers shrinking and curling in on themselves, nails elongating into curved blades, until she was no longer looking at a human hand, but an enormous feline paw.

"That's incredible! Oh my god, could you become like a giant turtle?"

"Ah," said Carter, shaking their hand until it returned to its previous shape. "No. Turtles are reptiles. I'm afraid we can only turn into other mammals. Changing between animal classes requires too much changing of internal organs, and we can't really do that. That's why our eyes are always the same." They tapped their glasses. "I don't know if you've noticed that. They're way too complicated to change. And the best way to identify a shape shifter."

"Man," said Yara, leaning back. "Must be nice."

"What?"

"Being able to look however you want to look." If Yara could change the shape of her nose or the size of her forehead, she would never stay in her natural shape. She had to wonder if Carter naturally looked like this, with their soft features and the natural wave of their brown hair, or if they chose this appearance because they thought it best suited them.

Evidently, Yara's insecurities were written all over her, because the smile slid from Carter's face and was replaced with a look that suspiciously resembled pity. But Yara was grateful that they didn't say anything. She didn't need to hear any preaching about self-love, especially from someone as beautiful as Carter.

Instead, they grabbed a couple of books from a nearby shelf and inspected the covers. "The librarian tells me you've been hanging out here a lot."

Yara shrugged. "I guess. I like libraries."

"Me too," said Carter. "It's quiet. And it smells kind of dusty, but in a good way. What have you been reading?"

"I dunno," said Yara. "You guys don't have a lot of fiction, so I've been looking at a few of the historical books. Some of them are too dense for me, though. Oh! I wanted to ask you about something I came across."

Carter cocked their head inquisitively, sliding their glasses up the bridge of their nose.

"Do you know what the Omega Project is?"

Carter paused for a moment, their face inscrutable, before answering. "Doesn't ring a bell," they said. They cleared their throat and looked down at the book in their hands. "Why? Where did you read about it?"

Yara chewed her lip. "It was mentioned briefly in a book I found about nymphs, but they didn't say any more about it." Nymphs were something Yara had been fascinated to read about. She felt strange asking her Guardians so many questions about all the rules of this new world. Every answer just filled her with more questions, and she had to imagine incessant interrogations would get exhausting after a certain point. But here in the library she had learned about those called "Deviants" on her own. She had bristled at the term initially. After all, as a hydan she was considered a Deviant herself. It was the term they used to classify all non-human humanoids. But when she learned of its origin, it grew on her. For centuries, Deviants had been discriminated against under the guise of witchcraft or Satanism. The humans had called them deviants as an insult. But when the Society was founded in the fourteenth century, the Deviants took the name back, and used it proudly. It was their own little rebellion against the bigotry that they had faced. The hyden, the shape shifters, and nymphs were all included under that title. But Yara found the nymphs the most fascinating, because there were so many different varieties. Not just flora and fauna nymphs, who could become plants or animals at will, but elemental ones. The Nereids and the Naiads who could control water in any state, and often had fish tails in their human forms. (Yara interpreted this to mean that mermaids existed, which was very exciting.) The Vurwari whose skin supposedly crackled like burning embers. It was all so strange and sensational.

"Are there many nymphs who work for the Society?"

Carter nodded. "Many of them have a hard time integrating into the human world."

"Why?"

"Well," said Carter, thoughtfully. "To be perfectly honest, many of them don't look quite as passably human as you or I do."

"But can't they take human form?"

"Many of them can come quite close to it, yes," said Carter. "Though many aspects of their natural selves often remain."

"Oh," said Yara, thinking of the Nereids and their fish tails.

"Take Black for instance," Carter continued. Yara thought of Bora Black and the swirls of darkness that peeled off her translucent skin, and the way her obsidian eyes seemed to peer deep into Yara's mind. "You would look twice if you saw her walking down the street, wouldn't you?"

Indeed she would. Black was not the kind of woman who was easy to overlook.

"If you want to know more about nymphs, you should ask them yourself," said Carter, getting up.

"Yeah, that wouldn't be awkward," said Yara, snorting.

"Well, one of your Guardians is part nymph. I'm sure he wouldn't mind answering a few of your questions." Carter winked an amber eye and added, "I'm going to go get a little bit of exercise in. See you later?"

Yara nodded, no longer truly listening. One of her Guardians, part nymph. She thought back to the first time she had been brought here to the Society with Aunt Catherine. When Carter indicated Robin as being human, but said nothing of Erik. She thought of his glowing green eyes and how they had seemed too vibrant to be human.

And they hadn't been human after all.

CHAPTER SIXTEEN
The Omega Project

"She asked about the Omega Project?"

Carter nodded grimly.

"How did she even hear about that? I thought all mention of it had been removed from Society records," said Erik, his brow furrowed with concern.

"That's what Z wanted to do," said Robin. "But Black wouldn't let it happen."

"Why the hell not?" said Erik.

"Because we can't be expected to learn from our past mistakes if we erase them from memory," said Robin in a sing-songy voice.

Carter watched the two Guardians argue, running their tongue over their teeth. They weren't quite sure what side of the argument they landed on, so instead they chose to stay silent while the other two hashed it out.

"I think it's a little reductive to say that it was just a *mistake*," said Erik. "Not only did people die as a result of the testing, but it was *Kain's* project. He's the one who warped the whole idea. Hell, ultimately it's the reason we're in this damn mess in the first place!"

"There's no need to get so worked up, E," said Robin. Always a bad idea. Erik had a tendency to get more riled when he was told to calm down.

"Don't you tell me not to get worked up," he said in a low voice. "I can't *believe* Black didn't let them erase the Omega Project."

"What if another mad scientist fifty years from now decides to try the same thing? What then?" said Robin. "Do you want us to go through the same painful learning curve to end up right back here, just because you're too scared people will find out about it? It's not like there are instructions anywhere on how to make any of the viruses. Not to mention, if our suspicions about Kain's motives are correct, it's possible that that research could help us fight him."

Erik turned his green eyes to Carter. "Where did she hear about it?"

"Apparently it was mentioned in a book she found in the library. She was reading about nymphs."

Erik rubbed his face vigorously with his hands.

"Look, it's not a big deal," said Robin, slapping a hand on Erik's shoulder. "It's not like she's gonna find any more information about it, right? She'll forget all about it in a few days."

Carter wasn't so sure. Yara had an obsessive streak, and they couldn't imagine her easily letting something go. "I'll mention it to Black, just in case. So she's prepared in case Yara brings it up during one of their sessions."

"Does anyone know how those are going, by the way?" said Robin.

"I haven't asked," said Erik, tight lipped.

"Alright, boys," said Carter. "I got a date with a simulator, so I'll see you both at dinner."

"Go easy on those Saxons," said Robin.

Carter waved a hand in acknowledgement as they walked away, hoping that Yara would truly let the Omega Project question go, and knowing without a doubt that she would not.

"So are you feeling homesick yet?"

Yara shook her head noncommittally, walking next to Erik to the donut shop after school, taking an occasional skip to keep up with him and his long legs. "I dunno. Most of the stuff I would miss I have with me. What about you?" she asked, avoiding looking up at him. While they had been on multiple donut not-dates, she still felt as though she knew nothing about him. He was exceptionally skilled at deflecting whenever she asked him personal questions. She had yet to work up the courage of asking him about his nymph heritage.

"Homesick?" he said. "Oh yeah. Pies on the windowsill, mama's home-cooked lasagna, ghost stories by the fire."

Yara frowned. "I thought you grew up at the Society."

"I did," said Erik. "That was just... my dickish way of saying that no, I don't get homesick. The Society *is* my home."

"I know, I just mean..." She searched for the right words. A new question she hadn't tried yet that could perhaps unlock the mystery that was Erik Carpenter. "Aren't there other things you wish you could be doing?"

He shrugged. "You mean like skydiving? Going to see shows? Vacationing in Hawai'i?"

"Well, yeah."

They reached the donut shop and Erik ordered his usual chocolate while Yara ordered a lemon one with raspberry drizzle. (She was determined to try every flavor on the menu.) When they took their usual seats on the wire chairs outside to watch the city as they ate, Yara kept her eyes wide and locked on him.

"What?" he said at last, without looking at her, a nervous smile tugging at the corner of his mouth.

"You didn't answer."

"I don't have an answer."

"Yeah, but you never answer *any* of my questions."

"Nonsense," he said with mock affront. "Just this morning you asked me how I was and I answered." He glanced at her to see if she laughed, but she stared down at her donut, running her finger through the icing. "Are you really upset?"

She shrugged. "It's just... I dunno. I don't really know you. And I feel like you know so much about me, and it's weird is all."

"Oh," he said. "I didn't realize it bothered you."

Yara felt her cheeks burn. "I don't know if 'bother' is the right word. It's just..." She didn't want to say the words that were on the tip of her tongue, but she found them spilling out before her brain caught up with her mouth. "It just feels like you don't really like me. Or like being around me. Which is fine, I mean you don't have to like me, I just feel like you're being forced to babysit me or something."

There was a moment in which Erik didn't speak and she was too nervous to look up. "Is that really how you feel?" he said at last.

"That's just what it feels like sometimes."

Ugh. Stupid. Shouldn't have said anything. Now it's gonna be awkward as hell, dummy.

She jumped slightly when she felt a hand on her shoulder. Looking up she was startled to find him staring at her, his eyebrows creased with concern. "Yara, I—" He looked at a complete loss for words, his mouth opening and closing soundlessly for a few moments. "I'm sorry you feel that way."

She tried laughing it off. "Well, what would you think?" Despite her attempt at nonchalance, the defensiveness in her words was clear.

He chewed on his bottom lip for a moment, considering her. Then finally, "OK. What do you want to know?"

She raised an eyebrow and laughed nervously. Her stomach was tight, her chest heavy, and her cheeks were still hot. She was sure they were bright red. "Uh…"

"How about this. My favorite food is chocolate chip cookies. My favorite book is *Charlotte's Web*, but anytime someone asks me why, I don't have a good answer for them. My favorite color is yellow. My dad works at the Society as an ambassador, my mom died when I was four, and I've known I wanted to be a Guardian since I was six. And," he added, "I don't not like you. I actually like being around you. A lot."

Yara's face was on fire. She felt a twinge of pain behind her eyes, a shadow of an oncoming headache, but she pushed it away. Wiping her sweaty palms on her pants, too nervous to eat any more of her donut, she swallowed, trying to think of a response. But all she managed was a quiet, "Oh." She couldn't bring herself to look at him. What were these feelings? Shame? Excitement? She couldn't pinpoint anything, her brain a mess of thoughts moving too quickly for her to identify any of them for what they were.

"As for wanting to do anything else," Erik continued, clearly trying to give Yara enough time to collect herself, "I never really thought about it. I mean, eventually I'll be forced to retire out of the field."

"What does that mean?"

"Being a Guardian is hard and dangerous. They don't like us in the field past 27, so—"

"27 years old? Isn't that kind of young?" In her surprise, Yara forgot her embarrassment.

"We start young. Gives us up to ten years in the field."

"So you've only been doing this for a few years?"

Erik nodded.

"Am I your first assignment?"

"No, before you I was just doing basic patrolling. They had me on the security detail for the Armenian ambassador once when they came to negotiate an installation of Society headquarters out there. Got to stop an assassination attempt. That was kinda cool."

Yara gaped. "No big deal."

He laughed.

"So what happens when you get too old?"

"We can either become a Level 2 Guardian, which is mostly training and dispatching and stuff, or else we can move to another branch. Or retire, I suppose."

"Do you know what you'll do?"

She watched as he ran his tongue thoughtfully over his bottom lip, his green eyes glazing over. "No. Not really. My whole life, all I ever wanted was to help people. I worked really hard to get here. I never thought about what comes next." He looked at her and the familiar electric shock she associated with his gaze shot through her. But rather than the painful twinge in her head which accompanied the butterflies he gave her, she actually felt calmer. The promise of the looming headache was dissipating.

He didn't hate her. He liked being around her. And here he was sharing himself with her. She exhaled heavily and realized that her shoulders had been tensed up to her ears. They dropped and she said, "I don't even know how you could be so sure of anything. I've never known what I wanted to do with my life. Except survive."

"A lofty goal."

"Don't make fun of me."

"I'm not," he said, nudging her lightly with his elbow.

"I guess the only thing is… well, I've always wanted to travel. I've never even been outside of California. But you can't really make a living from that."

"Where would you go?"

"Everywhere." She didn't notice that her tension had ebbed away and that her cheeks were no longer burning. "Peru is at the top of my list, I know that. Also New Zealand. And Egypt."

"Tied for first place?"

She chuckled. "It's a big planet. There's a lot to see. And I haven't seen any of it. Just feels like there's too much. Like I'll never be able to do it all."

"Yeah, I know what you mean."

"You do?" she said, an eyebrow raised skeptically.

"Sometimes, yeah."

"You ever feel like," she started, "like there's so much you want to do, and you sort of freeze with indecision, because they all feel equally important, but you don't know where to start? Then all of a sudden the day is over and you haven't done anything?"

"I guess no, I can't say that I have."

She picked off a piece of her donut and ate it.

"But what I have felt is paralyzed by my inability to help everyone."

"So noble. And here I am complaining that I can't travel the world."

"I didn't mean it like that," said Erik. "But one day I just accepted that I can't help everyone. What I can do is help *some*one."

She looked up at him. He was staring at her. "You mean me?"

"You tell me," he said.

CHAPTER SEVENTEEN
The Gym

"I really think you should try to do some exercise while we're here."

Yara rolled her eyes. "Here we go again."

"Now, hear me out," said Aunt Catherine, her mouth full of oatmeal, wielding her spoon like a professor's pointer. "You have all this time on your hands, you have three professionals who can train you…" Yara tried to interject, but Aunt Catherine spoke over her, "Their job is to watch you, so it's not like they have anything better to do."

"I find that hard to believe."

"Listen," said Aunt Catherine, the playfulness gone from her voice. She set down her spoon and wiped her mouth. "We don't know what this Kain person is like. How determined he is to get to you. I think a little self defense wouldn't be the worst idea."

Yara slumped.

"Please, Yara," said Aunt Catherine. "It would give me peace of mind."

Yara groaned, flopping back in her chair. "Don't say that! It's not fair! Manipulative…"

Aunt Catherine grinned. "My evil plan has worked!"

"Why don't *you* have to do it?"

"Because I can't see the future." She picked up her spoon and tapped her head before digging back into her breakfast. Yara gave another dramatic flourish in her seat in protest.

"What's going on over here?"

Yara jumped in surprise and looked up to see Robin approaching them, a breakfast sandwich in one hand and a smoothie in the other. Embarrassed, Yara immediately sat up.

"It's clearly a scene from Macbeth," said Aunt Catherine.

Yara threw her napkin at her aunt as she and Robin chuckled.

"Looks like an Oscar worthy performance to me."

"We were actually discussing Yara taking some self-defense lessons from you three. Is that something that would be doable?"

Robin's eyes widened in surprise as he took an enormous bite of his sandwich. "No kidding!" he said through the food in his mouth. "I can't believe you convinced her to exercise."

"Yeah, well," said Yara. "We'll see."

"Let's start today!" said Robin. "What else you got goin' on, right, kid?"

"I'll have you know," said Yara, "that I was planning on napping today."

"Nah," he said, waving away her words. "Napping puts you in a bad mood."

"You know, it'll never stop being creepy that you know things like that."

"*You* told me that."

Yara pursed her lips. "Oh. Yeah."

"I'll tell E and C to meet us up in the rec room in twenty minutes," he said, reaching for the communication device on his collar, but Yara stopped him.

"Oh! Maybe… let's minimize the embarrassment to just you on the first day. I don't think we need to involve Carter or Erik with this."

He laughed. "You got it."

Robin had found a white workout uniform for Yara to wear so she matched everyone else in the gym, but she was acting dreadfully uncomfortable in it. Her arms were wrapped around her middle and her eyebrows were scrunched.

"Would you unclench?" he said. He pressed his thumb in between her eyebrows and tried to smooth out the crease.

She slapped his hand away and said, "Let's just get this over with."

"That's the spirit." He led her over to a secluded training area that was often used for Guardian initiates. There wasn't a class at the moment with the Society so preoccupied by the Kain emergency. They couldn't spare the manpower to train an incoming group. It wasn't ideal, but on the bright side the training nook was free. "Technically,

I'm not a trainer. Those are the Level 2 Guardians. Guardians who retire from field duty," he explained.

"I know."

"You do?" he said, raising his eyebrows in surprise.

"Oh. Well, yeah. Erik told me."

"Ah. Well all this to say if you sprain something while we train I refuse to accept any responsibility."

"That's comforting."

They started with simple cardio. Jumping jacks and burpees. After only five minutes she collapsed on the floor, her face bright red and shining with sweat. She managed breathlessly, "I hope you know that I hate you for this."

"Don't hate me, yet, kid."

Struggling to push herself up to a sitting position, Yara said, "'Kid'? Aren't we the same age?"

He offered her a hand to pull her up and said, "We're just warming up."

"Well, I'm warm." She swatted his hand away and fell back to the floor.

"Maybe even a little more than just warm. I don't think I've ever seen a face so red."

"I will never forgive you."

"You ever hit anything before?" he asked.

She looked up at him from the floor, splayed out like a starfish. "Like a home run?"

"Oh my god, no. Not like a home run, you dork." He grabbed her hands and pulled her up to her feet. "This is self defense, not baseball." Since they had paused, he took a swig from his water bottle.

"First of all, I think you know the answer to that question," she said. "Second of all, what's the Omega Project?"

Robin actually choked on his water when she spoke. When he found his voice, he raised an eyebrow incredulously at her. "What the hell?"

She crossed her arms, looking particularly smug. "I asked Carter about it last week and they lied and said they didn't know anything about it."

Rubbing the back of his neck and trying to determine what the best course of action was, Robin chewed his lower lip. "You're a stubborn little pain in the ass, you know that, right?"

"The more you try to hide it from me, the more I'm gonna want to know what it is. Carter would have been better off just telling me and I probably would have forgotten. But I could tell they were lying. It's the only thing I'm good at."

"Reading people?"

"I can tell when they're lying."

He laughed uncomfortably. He certainly hoped she was exaggerating about her skills as a lie detector, but he also didn't see a good way out of answering the question. Of course, *answering* the question wasn't a good option either. But perhaps she was right. If he just told her simply, she would forget about it and let it go. What were the odds that she was going to do anything with the information? *How* could she do anything with the information?

"Alright."

Her eyes lit up.

"Under one condition."

"Uh oh."

"You do not tell anyone I told you. Especially E."

"Why especially?"

"I don't want him to be mad at me."

"Carter won't be mad at you?"

"C I can handle."

"You're really not making me want to hear it less," she said.

"I'll come to your quarters tonight. This is not the time or place. Now plant your feet firmly on the ground and throw a couple of punches. Let's see what you got."

Yara groaned. "How did I end up here?"

As active as Yara had been that morning, being pushed by Robin farther than was reasonable, she was ambitiously lazy the rest of the day. She hadn't bothered exploring the Society at all, and while she had tried to focus on her homework, it was pointless, because her body ached and despite everything, all she could think about was the Omega Project.

What was it?

Why was it a secret?

And most important of all, what if she was disappointed upon finding out what it was?

The White Mask Society seemed to take themselves very seriously, and more likely than anything, it was some boring something-or-other that Yara would have no interest in and would immediately forget about. On the other hand, the Society was also a magical world filled with magical beings. It was just as possible that the Omega Project was some exciting and fantastical … well, project. The suspense was killing her.

Her thoughts were interrupted at eight o'clock when Robin knocked on the door.

"Hi," she said, beckoning him inside. "Sorry, it's a mess."

She hastily started grabbing clothes and rubbish that was strewn around the living area of her quarters and tossed them onto her bed, closing the door to the bedroom behind her to try to hide the bulk of the mess.

"Makes me feel right at home," he said.

Feeling suddenly uncomfortable and awkward, aware that she was alone in her room with a boy (something that had never happened before) she crossed her arms tightly. She felt a twinge of pressure behind her eyes, but she stubbornly pushed it away. She was in no mood for a vision.

"You OK?" he said, furrowing his brow with concern. She wasn't used to seeing him so serious. He leaned forward and tentatively reached a hand out to her shoulder.

"Do I really look that bad? I'm just sore," she lied.

"Mmm," he said. Clearly, she hadn't convinced him. As good as she was at detecting lies, she was lousy at telling them.

"So," she said, her head twinging again, "the Omega Project. Go."

"Ha, not much for foreplay, I see."

"What? Foreplay?"

"Sorry… Do we not know each other well enough for me to make innuendo jokes?"

She pursed her lips and chuckled despite herself. "I promise I'm not a prude."

"This feels like a trap," he said, raising his hands in surrender. "I guess I'll just get right to it, then." He laughed. Always quick to a laugh, Robin. Yara envied him. He made everything seem effortless. It was impossible not to like him.

They sat down in the small living area, Yara in the loveseat and Robin in the armchair facing her. She pulled her feet up and hugged them to her chest.

"So. The Omega Project." He ran a hand through his golden curls several times, trying to figure out how to start. "About twenty years ago, Kain worked here. At the Society."

"Yeah, I know. That was in the file Carter gave me." Yara pointed to it on the coffee table between them. She had kept it, occasionally looking over Kain's file, hoping it would suddenly offer her some crucial information that might help protect her from him. "Apparently the Society screening process needs some work."

Robin chuckled. "Well, he was one of our best, frankly. We all thought we were lucky to recruit him. An exceptionally bright young man. Human, so he had no particular ties to the Society. We snagged him out of a civilian school before he could be poached by anyone else. Anyway, he came up with an idea along with another Researcher. What if there was a way to ... synthesize the abilities of Deviants."

"What the hell does that mean?"

"It means he wanted to be able to do things that Deviants could do. Change his appearance like a shape shifter. Control fire or water like a nymph. Or any number of abilities the hyden possess. What he wanted to do was find out how Deviants could do what they do, and give himself that ability."

"And the Society let him pursue that?"

"Well, he talked about being able to share these gifts with the whole world. Not just himself. If humans could have the same talents as Deviants, then maybe we wouldn't have to hide. Maybe both worlds could finally come together. It was a tempting idea. A utopian dream that many people in the Society found appealing."

"Is that why he's looking for me?" said Yara, her head starting to hurt more, an intense pressure building against the back of her eyes.

Robin considered her for a moment. "We're honestly not sure." She could tell he was lying, but she couldn't bring herself to say so, afraid of derailing him.

"I don't understand," she said, trying to distract herself from the pain of the oncoming headache. "Why is that bad?"

"What? You mean, giving humans Deviant abilities?"

Yara nodded.

"Well," said Robin with a heavy sigh, "as it turns out, the laws of nature don't like to be messed with like that. Kain and his team were never able to iron out the kinks."

"Kinks?"

"Grotesque deformities, other less... pleasant and unexpected side effects, irreversible damage, that kind of thing."

Yara frowned, chewing her lip, curious to know more, but afraid to ask.

"In short, most trials ended up being ... unsuccessful."

"As in…?"

"As in fatal."

"People died?"

Robin nodded.

"Oh… Why is it so secret? There was an idea, and it didn't work. I don't get why it's such a hot button issue."

"That's the thing. Kain didn't want to abandon the project after the Society decided it couldn't go anywhere. The risk was too high, the odds of success too low. What we didn't know was that he kept working on it. With the Head Researcher. Without the knowledge or permission of the Society. And… well, he sort of… transformed it."

"What does that mean?"

Robin hesitated. "He discovered a way to weaponize it."

"Jesus."

"Yeah. And we're not really about that, as an organization," said Robin with a sardonic smile. "So you can imagine how well that was received when people found out about it."

"How on earth could something like that be weaponized?"

"Oh, you'd be surprised. Viruses, mostly. Dangerous, cruel, undetectable viruses. He could have caused unthinkable damage if he wanted. We don't know what he was hoping to get out of it, or what his plans were - if he even had any in the first place. He took most of his work with him when he left, so we never found out."

"The Society let him leave with his work?"

"'Course not. He bolted in the middle of the night after he killed the Head Researcher. No one really knows what happened. The lab was found in shambles the next morning, she was dead, and most of his work was already gone. We just got lucky that he left the viruses he had actually managed to synthesize. Otherwise, who knows what he could have done. Or *would* have done."

"How do you know he's not making more?"

"We don't, really."

His blue eyes were locked onto hers. She shrank under his gaze, suddenly very aware of the fact that she had not yet showered since they trained that morning. Her stomach tightened uncomfortably. Just as quickly, a pain shot through her head, severe enough that she couldn't hide it. She pressed her palms against her temple. He rushed over and she could feel his hand on her shoulder.

"Yara," he said. "Hey, are you OK?"

She tried to say "yes" but the word was swallowed by a groan of pain until finally she couldn't hold it back, and the world around her was enveloped in a white fog.

CHAPTER EIGHTEEN

Janya With a J

It took much longer than usual for the fog in Yara's vision to clear for her to be able to see anything at all. The world was just blinding pain until finally a face appeared. It was the face of a young woman. Her complexion was like a rich chocolate, her long, straight hair an absolute black. She was older than Yara, but not by much, and her dark eyes were wide with fear. The pain in her head finally subsiding, Yara exhaled slowly, trying to clear the haze to see what could possibly be making this young woman so afraid.

As the scene materialized, Yara could see that the woman was looking at four other hulking shapes. They were impossible to see through the fog, and no matter how hard she tried, Yara couldn't get the scene to clear any further. All five figures moved as though time had slowed, the four larger ones lunging toward the woman.

Suddenly, as though by a giant gust of wind, the fog whipped around them in a swirl of movement that was impossible to follow. Muted sounds of screams and cries filled Yara's head, and then, just as suddenly, the scene disappeared, replaced by her carpet.

Somehow, she had fallen to her knees. Her breathing was ragged and her skin clammy.

"Yara?"

She looked up to see Robin's worried face. He helped her back onto the loveseat and she gave a shaky laugh.

"So embarrassing," she said.

"You kidding?" he said, rising to get a glass of water from her kitchenette. "I mean, if I hadn't been incredibly worried that you were having a stroke, it would have been super cool. I just got to see the future be predicted."

He handed her the glass and she took a shaky sip.

"Thanks."

He waited a full minute before saying, "I'm dyin' here. Do I get to know what you saw?"

She looked up.

"It's OK, kid," he said, lightly. "Unclench." He reached out again and smoothed the space between her eyebrows, causing her face to loosen.

"I don't really know, to be honest," she said. "What I saw, I mean. I didn't recognize the people."

"Your visions aren't usually that… violent, though, are they?"

"Violent?"

"Well, you were kinda shaking and gasping. I didn't think they were normally like that."

"They're not…" Had it really been that bad?

"Well?"

She shrugged. "It was a woman. I think she was being attacked."

"What did she look like?"

"Pretty. Maybe in her early twenties. Indian, I think. She was scared."

"Indian?" said Robin, suddenly serious. "Are you sure?"

"I think so. Maybe Middle Eastern. Why?"

"Do you remember what the people who attacked her looked like?" he said urgently.

"Why? What's going on? Who is she?"

"What did the attackers look like?"

"I don't know!" Yara fumbled. "I didn't see them! They— they were big, I guess! What the hell is going on?"

Robin chewed on his bottom lip and Yara watched it blossom under his teeth. "One of the other hyden is an Indian woman. About 23 years old."

"How can we be sure that she actually saw Janya Varma, and not some random unfortunate civilian?" Even as he said the words, Erik knew it sounded far fetched.

"But she couldn't tell you any more details about what she saw?" said Carter.

Robin shook his head. "I've never seen her have a reaction like this before, though. It was like she was there, like she was being attacked, too."

"At least she's OK now. I'll get a message to Janya's Guardians." With that, Carter left Erik alone with Robin. It was unusual to see Robin without his trademark crooked smile. Even under dire circumstances he could always find a way to crack a joke or lighten the mood. Erik, on the other hand, was not skilled at social interactions. He lacked Robin's ease and charm, and as such had no idea what to say in order to make Robin feel better.

"We should try to get some sleep," said Erik. It was nearing one in the morning, but he felt wide awake.

"Nah, couldn't sleep," said Robin. "May just kill some time in the sims or something."

"Mind if I come with you?" said Erik.

"Not tired either?"

Erik shook his head as they started heading toward the simulators.

"It'd be really helpful if her visions had a time stamp," said Robin. "You know, then we'd know exactly when it's gonna happen."

"Do you think it's possible to prevent something that she sees from happening?" said Erik, voicing for the first time something he'd been wondering for a while. Yara's father had been a Guardian and also a seer, but to Erik's knowledge, he had never had a vision of something that didn't happen. Which certainly implied there was no escaping fate.

"Gotta hope so," said Robin. "I mean, if not..." He trailed off and ran a hand through his hair.

"If not, Janya is going to be kidnapped and we're down another hydan." With every new hydan that Kain acquired, both Robin and Erik knew that it would be harder to defeat him. If Black's theory was correct, and Erik was sure it was, then Kain was using the hyden to continue his work on the Omega Project. If he was successful, that meant that each hydan would either give him a new power that they would then have to contend with, or else a new weapon.

"I gotta say, I'm surprised he would actually go through with kidnapping her," said Robin.

"Janya?"

"Yeah."

"Why?"

"Well," said Robin. "She's Zenobia's daughter."

"I know," said Erik. Did Robin think he was stupid? Janya's mother had been Head Researcher twenty years ago. She was a legend. And Janya had lived at the Society after Zenobia Varma's sudden death at Kain's hand. Hell, Erik had even grown up with her. She was only a few years older than he was, so they didn't spend a great deal of time together, but there weren't many children at the Society, so some interactions were inevitable.

"You do know about Kain and Varma, right?"

"I mean, I know they worked together," said Erik. "And I know he killed her."

"He was in love with her," said Robin.

Erik's jaw fell. "If he loved her, why the hell would he kill her?"

"No one knows for sure what happened, but she certainly didn't love him. If you ask me," said Robin conspiratorially, "I think he killed her in a jealous rage."

"Janya's not... she couldn't be... his?"

"No," said Robin. "Ugh. Thank god. But still. She's the daughter of the woman he loved. Seems particularly heartless to want to capture her. And who knows what the hell he does to them once he's got 'em."

"Jeez," breathed Erik. He had been so focused on protecting Yara, he hadn't spent any time considering what the other hyden were enduring. Those who had been less lucky. Or what might happen to Yara if he failed.

They reached the simulators, and as Robin started to click through various programs, Erik said, "Hey, R."

"What's up?"

"Where were you? With Yara? When she had her vision. What were you guys doing?"

"We were hanging out in her quarters," said Robin, not meeting Erik's eyes.

"Oh." Erik could feel his face burn. It was unlikely that anything had happened between them. Romantic relationships with Wards were strictly forbidden. Robin knew that. Erik knew that. Knew that he would be risking everything if he pursued anything of the sort with her. The Society was his home. And while he constantly tried to remind himself that nothing was worth losing that, it never mattered as much when he was near her. His feelings for Yara existed, as much as he didn't want them to.

The thought of Robin spending time alone with her in her quarters made jealousy blossom in his gut like a hot storm. And worst of all, he knew that Robin was aware of how he felt. Carter, too, for that matter.

Erik had never been very good at hiding how he felt about her. And while his fellow Guardians never addressed it, he could feel their pity. And worse, he knew they thought him the victim of a foolish and childish crush.

"Listen, E," said Robin.

Erik shrugged and waved him off. "No, what? It's nothing." He fumbled for words as he awkwardly stepped away from Robin. "I think I am gonna try to go to bed, after all."

"Yeah, OK."

"Anyway, I'm on duty tomorrow morning, so…" He trailed off, and with a final wave, turned and left Robin to the simulators on his own.

Ever since her mother died, Janya Varma had been a bad sleeper. She couldn't remember the last time she had made it through more than three hours at a time of uninterrupted sleep. When she lived at the Society as a child, on particularly bad nights, she would wander the halls. The Society never slept. She could always find someone or something to occupy her. Nymphs in particular were light sleepers - some of them even nocturnal - and those who worked in Research welcomed her like family. She would watch them work under the dimmed lights of their laboratories, seamlessly integrating their various abilities into their routine. It was the safest she'd ever felt, watching a Fazuzu, a nymph of wind, summon folders from the other side of the room with a controlled gust, or a Vurwari, a nymph of fire, create a flame in the palm of their hand to heat a sample.

On nights like this one, in which sleep simply would not come, how she longed to go back to the place that had been her home for so long. But, unfortunately, she had no interest in pursuing a career with the Society. She had always been an artist, and Society quarters were not available to be rented by civilians. Instead, she was stuck in a lumpy bed in a cheap apartment in North Hollywood, staring at her ceiling, blue-gray from the street lights that seeped in through her window.

However, over a month ago, Janya had been approached by someone she didn't know. She recognized him immediately as a Guardian from his sleek black uniform, the mask of the Society embroidered on his collar.

Her Guardian, as it turned out. He wasn't clear about what exactly was threatening Janya, but she knew enough that if she had her own private detail of Guardians, it was serious. He told her not to worry if she saw him or her other two Guardians trailing her. That they would do everything they could to protect her. Even now, one of them was likely to be on the street outside her building, or perhaps scouting from a nearby rooftop, ensuring her safety.

She had wanted so badly for him to invite her back to Headquarters. To tell her that she would be safer there. That she could stay as long as she wanted. But he hadn't offered, and she didn't ask.

She wasn't too worried. The Guardians were skilled beyond imagination. Their training started young and was unforgiving. If she felt safe with anyone, it was with them, knowing they had her back.

Just as her eyes started to drift closed, preparing her for hopefully the final stretch of sleep before it was a reasonable enough hour for her to get up, she heard a small noise. A soft click, like that of a window closing. If she had been asleep, she may not have heard it at all. She turned her head to look out the window. She could just see part of the full moon behind the telephone wires and apartment building next door.

Great, she thought, *once again wide awake. Back to square one.*

But then another bump. She sat up. This one undoubtedly came from above her, which was strange, since she lived on the top floor. For the first time since being approached by her Guardian, she began to feel nervous. More likely than not, it was nothing. Her exhaustion was just making her paranoid.

But maybe…

She slowly got out of bed and went to her closet where she kept her mother's old ConvOrb. It was a relic from the Society, the only thing she had left of her mother's, though still functioning. As soon as she held it in her hands, she felt foolish. Her Guardians were on the job. One was always on duty, and if there really were a problem, they would call for backup. Whatever she heard was simply blown out of proportion by her imagination. She put the ConvOrb away and went back to bed. Sleep was out of the question. Perhaps if she read for a little while—

But then her bedroom window exploded, shards of glass flying in every direction. She screamed, instinctively shielding her face. Her arms were slashed by the broken glass, but the wounds were shallow and healed almost instantly.

A few cuts, however, were not her problem. The four enormous figures who crawled through her shattered window and into her bedroom were.

She didn't even have time to draw breath again before a gag was shoved into her mouth, smelling strongly of chemicals. Her natural ability to heal fought against the drug, so that the man holding the cloth to her mouth had to keep it there longer than usual before eventually the world disappeared into darkness.

CHAPTER NINETEEN
Changing Tides

At breakfast Monday morning, Aunt Catherine and Yara noticed something different. As opposed to the usual laughter and chatter that filled the commissary, people were buzzing around, whispering frantically to each other in hushed voices, eyes wide. Almost no one was eating, making Yara very aware of the fact that she was scarfing down her second enormous slice of avocado toast.

She hoped it was all in her imagination, but when Erik came to get her to escort her to school, she could tell from his demeanor that something had indeed happened.

"What's going on?" she asked him.

He considered her for a moment, not quite meeting her eyes. "You know the vision you had this weekend? With R?"

"Yeah?"

"What vision was this?" asked Aunt Catherine.

"I saw a woman get attacked."

"Well," continued Erik. "It happened. Last night."

Yara's heart sank.

"She was a hydan. C told her Guardians, but before we could get the message to the one on duty…" He trailed off. Yara covered her mouth. "He's in the medical ward now."

"Oh my," said Aunt Catherine breathlessly. "Are we sure it's safe for Yara to go to school?"

"Annie," groaned Yara. She expected Erik to immediately dismiss her aunt as being overprotective, but her heart fell when she saw that he didn't seem to find the idea of her staying home as ridiculous as

Yara did. "Oh, come on. I'm not missing school."

"Some things are more important, Yara," said Aunt Catherine in a maddeningly calm voice.

Yara gaped at them, at a loss for words for a moment. "Are you serious? Is this really happening?"

"We haven't received any specific instructions of that nature," said Erik. "And I'm not at liberty to make a decision like that."

Yara felt a knot in her stomach dissipate with relief. It was enough that her senior year of high school was marred with all this additional stress, but if she had to worry about trying to catch up - or even worse, having to retake twelfth grade - she didn't think she'd be able to make it through the year. She grabbed her backpack and slung it over her shoulder, ready to be accompanied to school as usual by her Guardian.

At the look on Aunt Catherine's face, however, she paused.

"Look," said Yara in a low voice, meant only for her aunt. "There's no need to worry. If anything were to happen to me, more likely than not, I'd see it ahead of time, right?" She tried laughing, but it died quickly in her throat. In truth, this thought had occurred to Yara several times since learning of her ability and of Kain's desire to apprehend her. If he wanted to capture her, would she see it? And essentially then have to live through it twice? If she did have a vision of her own capture, would it even be possible to stop it? She had no way of knowing if her visions were warnings of one *possible* future or true premonitions that could not be avoided. Yara had never believed in fate, but when you could literally see people's futures it made fate seem a whole lot more feasible. Brushing away these fears, Yara tapped her head and added, "I've got a built in warning system."

She could tell that Aunt Catherine was not convinced, but there was nothing else Yara could do or say save staying home from school. And she absolutely did not want to do that. As great as the Society was and as stifling as school could be, it was a welcome respite from the lack of phone service and the recycled underground air. Little did she know, however, that her time away from Headquarters would be even more abbreviated than she had anticipated.

At the end of the day, eager to get her illicit donut with Erik (she had decided on strawberry jelly for today), she made her way to where he usually waited for her. She had spent the day remembering fondly their last excursion together. Yara had never told anyone about her desire to see the world. She had no friends with which to share the information, and she was afraid that if she told Aunt Catherine her aunt would feel guilty for not being able to afford for them to travel. But something had changed when she had finally been honest with Erik about her insecurities. His exterior shell had cracked, and she could see the gentle person underneath, in some ways just as uncomfortable in the world as she was. So she was excited about what this afternoon would bring. Instead, she gave a short yelp of surprise when he grabbed her as she exited the building.

"Jesus, you scared me!" she said, hand to her heart, trying to calm down.

"Sorry," said Erik. She could tell he was trying not to laugh. "You scare pretty easy."

"What are you doing here?" she said as they started to head toward the street.

"Picking you up… just like I do every—"

"OK, smart ass, that's not what I meant. I can't believe they even let you on school property."

"Didn't want to run any risks."

Yara raised a skeptical eyebrow. "Me crossing the street by myself is just too much of a risk, now?"

"Why don't you ask Janya Varma."

That shut her up. After a moment of shameful silence, she said, "So, what donut you going with today? Wait, let me guess. Chocolate."

He didn't answer and Yara's heart sank. No donuts, no strawberry jelly, and no quasi-date with Erik.

They didn't speak again and climbed silently into the car that was waiting for them right outside rather than the short walk away as it had always been before.

Yara rested her head against the cool window of the car as it moved silently through the city, inching slowly through traffic, taking her back to the outskirts of downtown where Headquarters was located. As she watched the world slip by, she felt a new sense of hopelessness. When she had agreed to protection from the Society, she could not have imagined what was in store for her. A temporary displacement. A nuisance, perhaps. But now, feeling more like a prisoner than anything else, she had the sinking feeling that her life would never go back to normal.

Lovely. She was lovely.

Just like her mother.

She had the same heart-shaped face, the same dark eyes, and the same coffee colored skin.

"There's no need to be afraid," he cooed as her chest heaved with fear, eyes wide and taking in every detail of the room. He had her strapped to his exam table, which was propped up so she was nearly in a standing position, enabling him to look at her dead on.

"You look so like your mother," he said, taking a strand of her straight black hair and twirling it around his fingers. He closed his eyes and allowed himself for a moment to imagine it was her. That Zenobia was here with him instead of just her daughter. He breathed deeply. They even smelled the same. Of cinnamon.

"You're disgusting," spat Janya, shattering his reminiscence. He opened his eyes and looked at her, anger bubbling inside him like poison. His lips trembled, an urge to hurt her gripping his body. But he clenched his cane, his knuckles whitening, and fought against the impulse.

He would not let her get to him. What was it about these women that got under his skin like no one else? If he hurt them they only had themselves to blame.

He took a slow, calming breath, and forced a smile. He could see her recoil, and his jaw clenched with a new wave of anger, though he didn't let his smile falter. Instead, he stretched it wider, feeling it tug at the scar on his face. A scar that was the result of a Varma woman, as was his useless leg. He ran a long finger down his cheek, tracing the slippery skin that marked where Zenobia had slashed him the night she had died. The night she made him kill her.

Any doubts he may have had about using her daughter for his work evaporated at the reminder of what she had done to him. Janya would fix him if it was the last thing she did.

"You can fight me all you want," he whispered. "It won't make a difference. You're going to help me change the world."

CHAPTER TWENTY

Suppression

Just one self-defense training lesson with Robin had left Yara feeling heavy and weak and hurting all over. While she knew it was ridiculous to think it would be over after that single session, she had hoped that perhaps they would let her alone.

Those hopes evaporated, however, after Janya Varma's capture. Erik had given her no warning about what to expect on the way back to Headquarters after school, but the rest of her Guardians were waiting for them in the front lobby when they arrived. Larry, the receptionist, gave her a small wave from his desk behind them, but she was feeling so sorry for herself she felt incapable of giving him more than a curt nod. Hopelessness was settling over her like a blanket, exacerbated by Erik's joyless detachment. All the progress she felt she had made in getting to know him was gone and that same angry voice whispered again, "See? He doesn't like you." And just as Yara had feared, Robin, Carter, and Erik were all braced to talk her into more self-defense classes.

She had no will to argue. They gave her twenty minutes to put her schoolwork in her quarters before they led her back to the gym. She managed to get close enough to Robin in the elevator on the way down to whisper so the others couldn't hear, "Do all three of you have to be here?"

He looked at her, bemused. "No, I guess not," he whispered back.

She pleaded with him silently to find a way to tell Erik and Carter to leave. Robin, she had already made herself a fool in front of. He knew how graceless she was and she had absolutely no interest in embarrassing herself in front of more people, particularly Erik. When the elevator doors opened up to the gym, Yara stepped out and watched as Robin hung back to speak to the other two Guardians.

She couldn't hear what Robin was saying, but she saw Erik's bright green eyes, like spotlights, looking at her. He was frowning. She pursed her lips and looked away, her cheeks burning. A familiar feeling deep in her stomach, a nervous flutter, accompanied by a growing pressure behind her eyes, and she thought of Bora Black's instructions to recreate this sensation. It had become a feeling she associated with Erik. It had mostly been an exciting, almost nice feeling. This time it was not.

Her head throbbed.

Whatever Robin had said, Carter and Erik both stayed in the elevator and disappeared behind the closing doors. Robin walked over to her, but upon seeing the look on her face, her arms wrapped tightly around her stomach, his easy smile dropped into a look of concern.

"You OK, kid?"

"Just tired."

"You look a little pale."

"I'm always pale."

He gave a small laugh, then led her over to the same training nook they had used before. Her uniform was waiting for her there, cleaned and folded in the corner. Robin pulled a stiff curtain around the nook, allowing her to change privately. He didn't say anything at first, standing silently on the other side of the partition, but eventually she heard his voice.

"You know, E is one of our best fighters. You'd probably be better off training with him. And C has the most seniority. They've seen it all. And they're a good teacher."

Yara didn't answer, fastening the front of her wrap-around top.

"Why didn't you want them to stay?"

She looked at herself in the large mirror along the back wall of the nook, there to allow her to observe her form while she trained. She looked small. She felt small, too. The white uniform did nothing to make her look less pale, and Robin was right. She did look sickly, as though her hopelessness - which had grown exponentially since being picked up from school - was draining her energy. Her head was starting to hurt in earnest.

"I dunno," she lied.

"You know," continued Robin. She didn't tell him that she had finished changing, trying to savor the moment in which she could be stagnant, but unable to as her head started to pound harder, an immense heaviness closing in on her temples. "They wouldn't judge you. We all know you've never done this stuff before. No one would make fun of you."

"I'm changed," she said abruptly. She did not want to talk about it. Not with Robin. Not with anyone.

Fortunately he did not push the subject, but simply opened the partition and began to put her through her paces. They went through the same routine as before, starting with cardio that involved jumping up and down. She tried to push through it. Tried not to let the pain in her head show, but it was becoming unbearable and every jumping jack was like taking a bat to the skull. But she would not give in. She did not want to see what this vision had in store.

One, she counted in her head, jumping her legs and arms open then back closed. *Two, three...*

Her head was being squeezed as though by a vice.

Four, five, six...

White spots were jumping in front of her, blurring the mirror and Robin. She blinked, trying to clear her vision.

Seven, eight, nine...

But it was no use. Try as she might to push through the pain, she collapsed and retched on the floor. She was aware of Robin crouching next to her, speaking to her in a worried voice, though his words were unintelligible as the world faded...

... the same white fog filled her vision. She didn't know why she fought it, but something deep inside her did not want to see whatever it was that was struggling to get to the surface. It was pain like she had never experienced before, crushing her head to the breaking point. A wisp of fog would begin to clear, but she immediately pushed it away. Rather than the deep, slow breaths she normally used to clear visions, she refused to exhale, and the lack of oxygen made the pain worse. Her head was heavy and light all at once and her lungs were desperate for air. But she wouldn't...

She couldn't...

But the pain was too much, and it eventually won out, plunging her into blissful nothingness.

Robin did not know what had happened. They had barely begun when Yara collapsed, vomiting all over the floor and screaming in pain. The others in the gym had looked over in concern, beginning to form a crowd, until Robin had yelled at them to get a Medic.

She eventually passed out, and without her screaming and writhing he had been able to carry her to the medical ward where the Head Researcher, a shape shifter and Medic named Frankie Sweet, was ready for them, already alerted of their arrival.

Frankie was good at her job. She worked quickly, had a knack for diagnosis, always had classical music playing in the background, and a talent for making patients - and those concerned about them - feel reassured.

Yet Robin did not feel reassured. Yara had been sedated to prevent her from waking up and having another episode, and she was currently getting every kind of test imaginable to determine what went wrong.

"You can't stay here, Robin, you know that," Frankie said. As a Medic, and as head of her department, she was not bound by the Society rules of avoiding full names. Robin knew it bothered some of the Guardians, like Erik in particular, but he didn't mind.

"You have to let me stay, Frankie," he had countered. "Just at least 'til you know what's wrong with her."

"Go back to your quarters," said Frankie calmly. "She's safe, she's sleeping, she's comfortable." She flashed him a wide smile, and pushed him out the door. He stood in the hall for a while, unwilling or unable to move. He hated this feeling. He knew he should be telling Erik and Carter what happened, not to mention Yara's aunt. Black no doubt already knew. Someone would have alerted her. But he couldn't bring himself to tell his fellow Guardians. What would he even say? *Hey! So, Yara had a seizure while we were warming up. No idea what happened to her or if she's OK. Talk to ya later!*

Without any concrete information, he did not want to be responsible for communicating to anyone what had happened. Robin was an easy going person. He was arrogant, charming, and sociable. But he felt none of those things now, as though he had left everything back at the gym when Yara collapsed.

After minutes or hours or days, he was back in his quarters, lying in his bed and staring at the ceiling, when someone knocked on the door. He contemplated pretending he wasn't there, but he was sure his light was visible under the door, so he dragged himself up and answered.

It was Nayla, a look of pity on her face. "Hey," she said.

He nodded to her. He didn't want to invite her in, didn't want to speak to her, but he had a feeling that she would not take no for an answer, so he stepped aside.

"I just saw Yara."

"You were in the medical ward?" said Robin, closing the door behind her.

"Just in passing," she said.

Robin did not ask why she had been there. It was near impossible to just "pass" through the medical ward unless it was your destination. There was nothing else on that floor. But he did not linger on the thought.

"Is she OK?"

Robin shrugged and collapsed into one of his plush armchairs. She took a seat opposite him, leaning forward, never taking her eyes off of him.

"Are you?"

"Am I what?"

"OK?"

"Yeah. Great," said Robin shortly.

She hesitated for a moment, her pouty lips parted, before saying, "Did I do something to upset you?"

He forced himself to meet her eyes and tried to give her an incredulous look. "What? Don't be stupid." Of course she had done nothing. Nothing, that is, except being here when he wanted nothing more than to be alone. Or to be with Yara... A dangerous thought.

"Robin, I know you well enough to tell when something is wrong. You're so good at hiding how you feel." She reached out her hand and touched his knee. It was gentle and intimate. "But you can't hide from me."

They had shared so much in their time together. It would all be so much easier if Robin still loved her. In so many ways she was perfect. She understood his job and what it meant to him. He wouldn't have to spend any time trying to justify how much of his life it consumed. They could have built a life here, together, at the Society. But as much as he had tried, he couldn't convince himself that he still cared for her the way he used to. The way she still did.

He wasn't sure what she saw on his face, but whatever it was led her to hold his hands, intertwining her long fingers with his. She pulled him to his feet and moved in closer.

"I don't know what you're thinking now," she said. "But I want to."

And her lips were on his, her hands moving up his back and into his hair. He closed his eyes, enjoying her warmth and the softness of her mouth. Her tongue ran across his bottom lip in a way that used to send chills down his spine. He inhaled her familiar smell, like almonds and sugar, and as quickly as the kiss had come, it was gone.

Nayla looked at him, smiling. But when she pulled him in to kiss her again he gently held her back, his hands wrapped around her shoulders. How badly he wanted to succumb to the comfort of her arms, but when he looked into her eyes he was wishing they were someone else's. It wasn't fair to Nayla. He brushed back a strand of her blonde hair.

Her smile turned into a frown of confusion. She couldn't quite mask the hurt that she was feeling. "What?" Her eyes searched his and he could see the moment in which she understood. "Her?" she said in a quiet voice.

He looked away and it was enough for her to know that she was right.

She took a few steps back, trying to act as though this information didn't sting. She tucked a loose lock of hair behind her ear and laughed. "Oh," she said simply.

"Nayla..." Robin began, feeling helpless.

She shook her head. "No," she said. She chewed on her bottom lip, her mouth pulled into a smile that did not reach her eyes. "I feel so stupid."

"Don't," he said, taking a step toward her, reaching out to take her hand, but she pulled away, still shaking her head, still forcing a smile.

"So I guess... I guess that's why." It wasn't a question.

How he had tried to prevent her from knowing. Why did she have to come to his room? And tonight of all nights?

She gave a nervous laugh. "I'm gonna go."

He didn't try to stop her. She moved quickly to the door, her head held high. She did not look back.

CHAPTER TWENTY-ONE
Occultatum

When Yara woke up, it took a while for her to remember what had happened. She was in a room she was unfamiliar with. It was sterile and white and quiet. There was soft, orchestral music playing, a steady beeping, and what sounded like someone singing faintly. The beeping sped up, and she realised it was coming from a machine monitoring her heart rate.

The singing stopped and someone said, "You're awake!"

Yara turned to see a shape shifter - she recognized the amber eyes - dressed in white. "Where am I?" she said.

"You're in the medical ward. How are you feeling?"

It was hard to tell. Her head didn't hurt at all. In fact, it didn't feel like anything. She felt like she was full of cotton. Stiff. Numb. "Fine."

"My name is Frankie," said the shape shifter. She (or perhaps they?) had a wide smile with very white teeth and twinkling amber eyes. She was short, shorter than Yara - which was saying something - and had a mess of untamed hair pinned back in a knot that looked like it hadn't been undone in weeks. "You gave us quite a scare."

Slowly, Yara's memory started to resurface. She had been training - or at least starting to - with Robin when she had felt a vision coming on that she had repressed, making her sick. "What time is it?"

"You've been asleep for several hours. It's the middle of the night."

"Am I OK?"

"You are now, but Robin said it was pretty bad before he managed to bring you here. We ran a few tests," Frankie continued, taking a tablet from a nearby table and scrolling through something Yara couldn't see. "Fortunately because of your father we have some information on seers so we know what to look for." She held out the tablet to show Yara who sat up on her elevated medical bed. It was a picture of a brain.

"Is this… this isn't… mine?"

"Indeed it is!" Frankie pinched the screen and rotated it to show Yara the bottom of her brain. Unlike the rest of it, which looked like a never ending worm wrapping around itself, the part of the brain at the base looked more like a wrinkled mushroom. "We were able to take some scans while you were unconscious and you see this area?" She tapped the screen and the wrinkled mushroom magnified. "This is your cerebellum. It generally controls voluntary actions like motor functions. But for seers specifically, the cerebellum also contains the gland that produces your videtonin, which is what makes you hydan. It's what enables you to see the future." Frankie pinched the screen again, zooming even further into Yara's cerebellum. How on earth had they been able to get such imagery of her brain?

"Here it is. We call it the occultatum. This scan was from about an hour ago, several hours after your episode. This is what it's supposed to look like." The gland Frankie was showing her, the occultatum, was very small, buried among the rest of her brain, like a flesh colored pea. Frankie swiped the screen, bringing up a new image. "This is what it looked like when Robin brought you in." The new image was startling. Yara couldn't believe it was the same brain that she had just been looking at. Instead of the little pea sized gland, there was one the size of a peach pit, angry and red, pressing against the rest of her brain.

"I imagine this gave you quite a headache."

"You could say that," said Yara, rubbing the back of her neck, horrified.

"Yara," said Frankie, leaning against Yara's bed, "I'm sorry that Ms. Black didn't explain to you how it worked earlier. I've been telling her for years that in order for the hyden to hone their skills, or *anyone* for that matter, they must know what makes it biologically possible, but she never had an affinity for science." It was clearly a sore subject. "In any case, this gland, the occultatum, it swells an enormous amount when it produces videtonin. And when you allow your vision to happen, that hormone is then carried to the rest of your brain to be interpreted, and the swelling goes back down, because the gland no longer has to hold onto it. But when you suppress visions, like you did this evening, that hormone has nowhere to go. That's when the swelling looks like this." She tapped the screen, bringing Yara's attention back to the alarming, red pit in her brain. "You were lucky this time. It didn't seem to do any permanent damage, but you can't let this happen again. Or what you go through next time may be much worse."

"Yara!" Another voice shouted her name in the hall, and Yara recognized it immediately as Aunt Catherine. She jumped off the bed, yanking off the few sensors still attached to her, and went to the door.

"Annie, I'm in here!" she called after her aunt, who was frantically looking in all the windows along the corridor outside.

"Oh, thank god!" said Aunt Catherine, running toward Yara, arms outstretched. She wrapped her in a bone crushing hug.

"Annie, I'm fine," Yara gasped.

"What happened?" She finally let Yara go and inspected her face for any signs of injury.

"Hello, Catherine!" said Frankie, welcoming them both back into the room. "My name is Frankie. Take a seat and I'd be more than happy to fill you in on everything. I'll start by saying that Yara is completely fine."

Yara let their conversation wash over her, not taking in any of the words. Her whole life she had dealt with these headaches, assuming they were nothing more than chronic migraines. If what Frankie said was true - and Yara had no reason to doubt that it was - every time she suppressed a vision, she had been risking brain damage.

Why on earth had she resisted so much last night? It was unlike anything she had ever experienced. As though she knew on some subconscious level that whatever was in that vision was something she didn't want to see. But if suppressing her premonitions was not an option, she would undoubtedly have to face it at some point.

But what was it?

"Yara?"

Her name snapped her out of her thoughts. "Hmm?"

"I think it would be a good idea for you to see Ms. Black tomorrow night instead of waiting for your session on Friday. What do you think?"

As much as Yara did not want to, she nodded, still feeling vaguely of cotton.

"Is it safe for her to go to school tomorrow?" said Aunt Catherine, and while she didn't say so, Yara knew she was fishing for a reason to keep Yara from going.

"Oh, I don't see why it would be a problem," said Frankie, flashing her white teeth. "Just as long as she doesn't try to ignore any more visions." She winked at Yara as though it were all a joke. "She might be a little tired, though. Getting pretty late."

As Yara left with Aunt Catherine into the corridor and back toward their quarters, she turned back and said to Frankie, "Oh, Frankie? Can I ask you one more thing?"

Frankie nodded.

"What pronouns do you use?"

Frankie's smile grew. "I don't have a strong preference, but I suppose she and her. How kind of you to ask."

Yara nodded at her then followed her aunt back down the hall, wishing that she could view the whole situation with the same light heartedness as Frankie.

CHAPTER TWENTY-TWO
Prisoner

In the end, Yara did not go to school the next day. That morning, she woke up feeling impossible heavy, anxiety pressing down on her like a lead weight, making it difficult to breathe. When Aunt Catherine found that Yara wasn't waiting to go to breakfast with her, she knocked on Yara's door to find her still in her pajamas, immobilized. There were no words to describe how grateful Yara was for her aunt explaining to her Guardians that she wasn't feeling up to school, sparing Yara the chore of having to face anyone. She just wanted to lie in bed, completely still, in the dark, trying to turn her brain off.

Would Aunt Catherine be able to get her out of her lesson with Bora Black tonight, too? And were they still expecting her to train in self-defense? These thoughts bore down on her, so she tried to push them away and replace them with a comforting white noise. She thought of her breathing technique, used to alleviate her anxiety. It often only came in useful when she was in crowded spaces, but right now, the cramped feeling came more from within than without. She pictured the same slow moving liquid gold, inhaling it through her nose, imagining that she could feel its warmth spread through her whole body, pushing out the nervous feelings, and filling all the empty space. As she exhaled, there was the same thick, red smoke that she assigned to those negative feelings. She pushed it out and watched it drift away from her before repeating the whole process.

Aunt Catherine had been kind enough to bring her breakfast and lunch, asking as few questions as she could. Just enough to reassure herself that Yara was OK. Relatively speaking.

But Aunt Catherine did not have authority over the Society's plans. That evening Yara could hear her aunt outside her door, arguing with Robin. She couldn't make out any of the words they said, but the gist of the conversation was evident from their tones. And it was clear who won the argument when there was a knock on her door and Robin called, "Yara?"

She didn't get up, unwilling - or unable - to move. She was terrified that if she got out of bed, her head would begin to hurt, and she would have to succumb to whatever vision she had been so afraid of having.

"Don't do that!" came Aunt Catherine's voice, simultaneously with her door being opened.

"Yara?" called Robin again, ignoring Aunt Catherine.

She heard him look around her living room before sticking his head into her bedroom and seeing her, lifeless, on the bed.

"She's not feeling well," continued Aunt Catherine. "How dare you barge into her room? You have absolutely no right to take her anywhere—"

"It's OK," said Yara, barely lifting her head to look up. As predicted, a pressure increased against her temples.

Her aunt pursed her lips, but didn't press the issue.

"How're ya feeling, kid?" said Robin, leaning against the doorframe. His air was all calm and casual, same as always, but Yara - ever the lie detector - could tell that he was masking concern. His pillowy lips were slightly tighter, and he was carrying tension in his neck which normally wasn't there.

"Great. I could run a marathon."

"Well, that's great news!" said Robin. "Because Black is insisting on seeing you."

"I'm not doing that."

Robin gave an exasperated chuckle, looking down at the floor. She didn't want to make things harder for him. It certainly was not her intention to. But over the course of the last 48 hours Yara had felt more and more like a prisoner. And she did not want to give in to them so easily. Of course she knew it wasn't Robin's choice. He was likely just following orders. As much as Yara would like to think that he, Erik, and Carter were not literally required by their job descriptions to care about her, she knew better.

This was nothing more than a job to them.

She was nothing more than a job to them.

"If Black wants to see me, why is she making you do her dirty work?" said Yara. It would be so much easier to say no to her than to Robin, who had always been so kind.

"I guess that's the advantage of being the boss," he said. "Delegation."

"What happens if I say no?"

Robin sighed. "C'mon, kid. Don't make me the bad guy. We're just trying to help you."

Despite every particle in her being wanting to plant her feet firmly into the floor and melt down into it and never have to move again, she followed Robin down the same elegant hallway and through the same elegant mahogany door to Black's office, where she was promptly placed by her treacherous body in the seat facing the desk.

"You've had quite the eventful weekend."

Yara barely registered Black's voice. It felt distant and hollow, as though coming from a great distance. But then a powerful force took over Yara, like a magnetic pull between her mind and where Black stood. She looked up to see the woman towering over her desk, her pale skin emanating those dark wisps of shadows which always roiled around her. They were moving faster as though caught in a heavy wind and reaching out toward Yara, stretched fingers clawing at her mind. But as soon as Yara met Black's obsidian eyes, the coils retreated and calmed so quickly, returning to their usual state, making Yara wonder if she had imagined the whole thing.

"I understand it's been a difficult few days, Yara, but I need your attention." She held her gaze for a few moments, and as uncomfortable as Yara was in the silence, she could think of nothing to say. "Do you want to control this ability?"

What a question. It had never actually occurred to Yara. Did she want to control it? Did she want to be able to peer into the future, just as she might peer through a window? She had never believed in fate, she had never believed in magic. But what other explanation for her ability could there be? Sure, Frankie could give her all the scientific and medical reasons for it, but it felt beyond science. And if a future could be seen, it meant it was going to happen. And that certainly implied that fate was unavoidable. Unchangeable.

No. If she was being truly honest with herself, she did not want control over this ability. If anything, she wanted it gone. She wanted whatever it was in her brain that made it all possible removed, so she would no longer have to worry about thinking about these things. Her headaches would be gone, the question of fate would not need to be answered, and she could go back to her old life. It hadn't been a glamorous or a particularly easy life. But it had been hers. She had been free. She no longer felt like this life belonged to her in any way.

Evidently, Black could see the answer in her face because she heaved a weighted sigh and sat down at her desk.

"Let me try to explain the situation to you, Yara, and then you can reconsider your answer."

"I understand the situation just fine," said Yara. "If nothing else, I've been told of the situation. In fact, I may understand it better than any of you."

Black raised an elegant eyebrow, a gleam in those endless eyes. "Is that so?"

"Have any of you witnessed the capture of any of the other hyden? Because I have. I've seen faces I don't know, but faces that are also somehow my own, be whisked away by the same men who attacked me. Every night, I dream of those faces, and imagine what it will be like when it actually *is* mine. I understand that my only value is a tiny gland in my brain that makes me into something I don't want to be. And that people are being paid to watch me. And that I'm not free to do what I'd like, go where I want, or eat what I choose."

"You are looking at the situation through the eyes of an individual."

"I *am* an individual!"

"Yara." Though Black did not raise her voice, it vibrated within Yara's bones like an earthquake. "You are looking at this situation as one that only affects you. You may be an individual. But whether you like it or not, Yara Rivers, your actions do *not* only affect you. Your ability, in the wrong hands, would be catastrophic. You no longer have the luxury of only thinking of yourself. Everything is at risk."

Yara seethed. The injustice of it prickled at her skin.

"You can use the anger you're feeling toward me into focusing on honing your ability. Channel it into your training with your Guardians tomorrow."

Yara pressed her lips together, swallowing all the insults she wanted to throw at Black, and tore her eyes away to stare determinedly at the corner of the desk.

"Now, let's get started."

CHAPTER TWENTY-THREE

Foreseen

Three hours.

Three painful hours.

When Yara finally left Black's office, the light in the hallway felt blinding compared to the dark room she had just emerged from. Despite the late hour, Robin was still dutifully waiting for her on the bench in the hall. He was reading a book, a paperback with corners soft from use, the binding lose and apparently on the verge of collapse. He tucked it away when he saw her.

"How are you feeling?"

The truth was not an attractive answer. She was feeling horrible, as though her brain had been opened and left that way, exposed and vulnerable. It was hard to form thoughts, much less words, and instead of trying, she gave him a noncommittal shrug and clutched herself, trying to keep from falling apart.

She was grateful that Robin didn't push it and instead just followed her back to the elevator, down to their quarters, and left her at her room with a soft "see ya tomorrow".

During her lesson with Black, Yara had had vision after vision, all of them vague and ill-defined, none of them sticking with her long enough for her to be able to identify anything with any sort of clarity. Now her mind was filled with images that disappeared as soon as she tried to hold onto them, like a dream she thought she remembered, but as soon as she tried, it disappeared. Water in cupped hands. Had she really seen Erik, or was that just her imagination?

She desperately wanted to sleep, but it felt impossible. As tired as

110

she was, every time she closed her eyes, she was plagued with faces she couldn't recognize and places she couldn't make out. Her head had been pounding mildly throughout her entire session with Black, so when the pain started to increase she didn't notice it right away.

What she did notice, however, was the same dread she had felt last night when she had passed out. She didn't know - couldn't know - where the dread came from. But she knew that this headache, this oncoming vision, was one she desperately didn't want to see. If only Black had taught her a way to block visions without risking damage to her brain, but she had seemed much more focused on giving Yara the tools to summon them. Apparently it was an uncommon desire to want to stop from using one's ability.

And so, with a pit of apprehension and fear in her stomach, Yara let herself fall back into her mind the way Black had just spent the last three hours encouraging her to do. The same fog filled her mind as the pain in her head instantly dissipated, replaced with the sensation of being underwater. She inhaled deeply and watched the fog turn into liquid gold as it went into her mouth, (Black had suggested using the same visualizations Yara used for her anxiety to help control the visions) then exhaled a thick red smoke which faded back to white around her as the scene cleared, and Yara found herself looking at none other than...

... herself.

She was almost never in her own visions. Perhaps this was what the dread had been about. Yara didn't want to know about her own future. But it was too late.

While the Yara in her vision didn't look any older than she was now she somehow seemed smaller. Her eyes were red and swollen, tears streaming down her cheeks, and she was shaking. What on earth would happen to make her so afraid?

Inhale.

Exhale.

The world cleared a little more, giving the Yara in the present a greater view of the scene.

Future Yara, frightened Yara, trembling Yara, was surrounded. Her back was up against a wall, and an army of figures stood in front of her. She couldn't recognize where exactly she was, but it had the same pale walls of Society Headquarters, barely discernible through the fog.

It was true that just a minute ago, Yara would have given anything not to see what this vision held, but now she found herself gripped with curiosity, desperate to widen the lens and see whatever it was that future Yara was looking at. No sooner had she had the thought, the world spun, like a camera swiveling on a hinge, to reveal more of the scene. The army of people standing in front of her were just shadows in the mist, but she was still able to make out a handful of faces, her Guardians among them.

A shaky inhale.

A shake exhale.

The hazy peephole widened, and Yara saw the face of another man, standing much closer to future Yara. A face she had only ever seen in past visions or photos, but that she instantly recognized.

Kain.

How? How had he gotten into the Society? Unless she was wrong, and they weren't at Headquarters? And why weren't her Guardians attacking him?

But as the shadowy shapes of Carter, Robin, and Erik came into clearer focus behind Kain she at least had an answer to one of her questions. All three of them were hunched and battered. Robin's arms were pinned behind him by an enormous crimson-clad person, his face splattered with blood. Erik was pressed up against a wall, his face bloodied and bruised. Carter was on their knees - one lens of their glasses shattered, blotting out their amber eye - held down by several pairs of thick hands. Their chin was held high, but they were as equally beaten as Erik and Robin. Bringing her attention back to Kain she saw that he was leaning heavily on a cane. His right leg was straight as a board and it seemed he couldn't put any weight on it at all.

Then suddenly, in the same way that her visions had slipped away during her lesson with Black, the scene in front of her started to disappear.

"No!"

She had to see more, had to know more. It couldn't have possibly been what she thought.

Could it?

But no matter how hard she tried, implementing every tool Black had thrown at her, trying to relax her mind and fall into the vision, inhaling, exhaling, the liquid gold, the red smoke, the nervousness in the pit of her stomach... it was no use.

It was gone.

And Yara was left alone on her bed staring up at the ceiling and knowing without a shadow of a doubt that the walls of the Society would no longer keep her safe.

Kain was coming for her.

CHAPTER TWENTY-FOUR

Jealousy

Erik had always looked up to Robin. As an initiate, he had found Robin to be everything he wanted to be. Confident, talented, charming. And while Erik was very good at his job (he was, after all, the youngest Guardian to ever be advanced to the field, and the only one to have graduated from initiation early) he lacked the easy going qualities that made it so easy for Robin to talk to people. He had been thrilled to be assigned to a Ward alongside Robin, hoping that he would be taken under his wing and taught - not so much about being a Guardian, but rather about being, well, a person.

Growing up in the Society had plenty of advantages. He already knew the ins and outs of the organization when he started initiation, knew the names of every single person who worked there, knew the equipment and the armor and the weapons that were used by Guardians. But alongside those advantages came plenty of disadvantages as well. There hadn't been many children to play with. A child raised at Headquarters was more often than not a product of parents who worked there. And while there were plenty of couples within the organization, almost none of them had children.

Erik's parents hadn't both been members of the White Mask Society. Just his father, who had been a Nymph Ambassador. But when Erik's mother, a human, died when he was just four years old, his father had little choice but to raise him at the Society. This meant that Erik grew up around grown ups, trying to be serious like they were and quiet so as not to bother them. He had never truly learned to play or to interact with people, always too busy absorbing all the information he could and trying to stay out of the way while he did so.

But Robin was the whole package. He had the skills that Erik had, and all the charm that Erik lacked. And he was kind enough, on top of everything, to train with Erik every week in the simulators while Carter was on duty.

It wasn't anything fancy. Carter preferred to gear up to fight in fictional wars. (The entire Society knew that Carter had the best scores in the Camelot simulation.) But Erik and Robin would activate a simple room and alternate between hand-to-hand combat and using simulated solenoids and gauntlets - the Guardian weapons of choice - to fight.

Robin never seemed to mind Erik's awkwardness or his silence. But tonight, it was Erik who was bothered by Robin's. They had been at it for almost two hours - both of them slippery with sweat, hair plastered to their foreheads, and their uniforms soaked through with perspiration - before Erik decided to say anything. Robin was grabbing a drink of water in the corner, giving them a brief respite.

"You seem preoccupied," said Erik.

Robin didn't look at him right away, but set down his water bottle and wiped his face with a towel. "Nah," he said.

But Erik knew enough to recognize that Robin's stoic behavior was uncharacteristic. After Yara's collapse from suppressing a vision, Erik had a feeling he already knew what Robin's mood was about.

"Ready?" said Robin, getting back into position in front of Erik. He had his gauntlet on his left hand, a heavy metal glove that controlled the deadly solenoidal star. The solenoid was simulated, of course, made of harmless nano technology, and the only real danger Erik faced would be at Robin's bare hands, but it was still hard not to view it as the very real threat that it was outside of the simulators.

Erik nodded, bringing his own gauntleted hand around.

Robin charged at him, bringing his gauntlet around, summoning his solenoid to attack Erik on the right while Robin reached for Erik's left side. Erik was able to dodge Robin's hook while simultaneously bringing his own solenoid around to defend himself. He didn't wait for Robin to recover before swinging his leg around and swiping Robin's out from under him. Robin landed on the floor with a heavy grunt and Erik brought his solenoid to his throat, kneeling on Robin's gauntlet so he couldn't summon his own.

"You're getting tired."

"You're getting cocky."

Erik barely had time to absorb Robin's words when he felt Robin's hand slip out from the gauntlet, freeing him as he rolled away, only to pounce back at Erik with a roundhouse kick to the chest.

The breath was knocked out of his chest as he fell back a few steps, but managed to remain standing. He was disoriented long enough for Robin to shove his gauntlet back on and bring his solenoid back to an attack position.

Had it been any other day, any other spar, Robin would have made a comment about Erik's one and only weakness (his tendency to rely on weapons) alongside a crooked smile and maybe even a playful wink. Tonight, his eyes were blazing with heat and focus. He watched Erik, unblinking, like a predator.

But that gave Erik an advantage. He could see Robin's thoughts in those wide eyes. If he had been grinning or flirtatious in the way only Robin could be, it would have hidden his intention. Instead, it was written cleanly on his face. So when he charged at Erik, faking right and coming back to attack him on the left, Erik dodged the blows and found himself behind Robin. He wrapped his right arm around Robin's neck, pulling him back onto the floor, where Erik was able to use his feet to pull the gauntlet off Robin's hand and kick it across the room.

Robin struggled to break free from Erik's grip, but Erik was strong and he had the advantage. Eventually, Robin tapped the floor and Erik released him, springing back up. Robin slowly pushed himself to standing, rubbing his neck.

"Maybe we should stop for the night," said Erik.

Robin gave a quiet grunt which could have been assent.

Erik went over to the corner where he had his towel and water, and pressed a few buttons on his gauntlet causing his solenoid to disappear back into the ether of simulated equipment, before dropping the enormous metal glove on the floor. He started unwrapping the bindings around his hand and turned to look at Robin.

"You've been really quiet," said Erik, unable to stand the tension any longer, reading too much into Robin's every movement and sigh.

Robin shrugged. "It's been a long week."

"It's only Wednesday."

"You know what I mean."

"She's OK now," said Erik.

Robin frowned. "Who?"

Erik was sure that Robin knew he was talking about Yara, so he didn't answer.

Robin ran a hand through his golden curls. "It's fine. No lasting damage or anything, and Black has it under control now." He leaned against the wall, taking another long drink of water. Erik watched him thoughtfully. Even now, evidently in distress, Robin was able to exude an effortless grace that Erik could never hope to attain.

But Robin was avoiding Erik's eyes. There was something he wasn't saying. Something he was hiding. A thought blossomed in Erik's head. An ugly thought he didn't like at all, and one he hoped against all hope was wrong. The way Robin was preoccupied after Yara's collapse, the way he wouldn't meet his eye, the refusal to acknowledge that anything was wrong...

Robin was in love with Yara.

Hot bile rose in Erik's throat, jealousy burning his face. Erik was not good at hiding his feelings when it came to Yara, so he turned to face the wall, pretending to be focused on wrapping his bindings and putting them away. In truth, he was trying to compose himself before having to face the man he so looked up to, feeling betrayed.

It was not a secret how Erik felt. Carter knew, Robin knew, and Erik knew that they both knew. The trouble was that his feelings were forbidden. There was no loophole that would allow for a Guardian and a Ward to have any kind of romantic relationship. And while it had never been addressed by any of the team, they all knew, and Erik was grateful that neither of his fellow Guardians had reported him. While he had not yet acted on his feelings, he knew that he would be instantly reassigned if any of his superiors were to learn about them.

"Erik."

He jumped at the sound of his name on Robin's lips. Turning around, he could see that Robin had read his every thought, even with his back turned.

Erik shook his head and shrugged. "No, it's fine."

Robin frowned at him, his blue eyes flitting back and forth between Erik's.

"This doesn't change anything."

"What would it change?" said Erik with a laugh. He tried to make it sound natural, but it came out forced and hollow.

"You know it doesn't matter," Robin continued. "For either of us."

Erik tried. He tried so hard to maintain the nonchalance which he knew he wasn't pulling off. But looking at Robin, even now, sweaty and red-faced from exercise, every quality he had once admired and hoped to emulate was all of a sudden a threat. Something to defeat in Robin. How could Yara possibly choose Erik, a stick in the mud, when she had the choice of a handsome and charming person like Robin?

It makes no difference, said a quiet voice in his mind, *because neither of* you *can choose* her.

But that voice didn't matter. It was drowned out by jealousy.

"I looked up to you," said Erik, unable to stop himself. "I was so happy to be able to work with you, and I trusted you."

"E, none of that has changed," said Robin, reaching out a hand to put on Erik's shoulder, but Erik swiped it away angrily. "Hey," said Robin. "Come on, now."

"It's like you couldn't stand the idea of letting me have something."

"Have what?" said Robin, his voice rising in anger as well. "Yara? You *can't* have her. Neither of us can. And besides, who's to say she would even want you in the first place?"

Erik's fist moved with unprecedented speed, colliding with Robin's jaw and - caught off guard - it sent him falling back to the floor. Erik's knuckles burned from the impact, his fingers aching, but he didn't care.

"What the hell!"

"When you were with her the other night," said Erik, "when she had the vision of Janya Varma being captured, what were you doing? Why were you alone with her in her quarters?"

"You need to take a moment," said Robin, standing up, anger carved into every feature of his face, "and remind yourself what you're doing and what you're saying."

"I don't think I'm the one who needs to do that," spat Erik. He opened his mouth to shoot another accusation, but Robin was on him too quickly, and before he knew it, they were on the ground, Robin pinning him face down as Erik tried to get out from under him.

"All we can do," said Robin, pushing Erik's face into the ground, "is try to protect her from Kain. Nothing else matters right now."

"I'm not the one who put her in a position to have a goddamn seizure!" Erik managed to squeeze out between his teeth.

Robin hit him so hard that his vision filled with bright spots and it took several moments before he could regain his bearings.

"If you ever imply again," said Robin, his lips close to Erik's ear and his voice low, "that I am responsible for any harm that befalls her, I'll report you to Black myself."

And with that Robin released Erik and was out of the simulator before Erik could even get back to his feet.

Erik had always thought of the sims as a calming place, when the holos were off and all he could hear was the faint hum of the computers in the walls. But lying there on the ground, staring up at the black ceiling and the thin silver grid that covered every inch of the room, he felt none of the calm.

All he felt was shame.

CHAPTER TWENTY-FIVE

Turning Point

Yara hadn't revealed to anyone what she'd seen the other night. Though the vision had haunted her every moment, waking or otherwise, she couldn't bring herself to tell Aunt Catherine, much less her Guardians.

Thursday morning, Erik had been the one to take her to school. He was still just as distant as he had been, a new behavior from him that she didn't like at all, but ended up suiting her quite well at the moment as she was also melancholy and uninterested in socializing. Once again, they didn't get their traditional post-school donut, and while Yara didn't push it, she thought it might have put both of them in a better mood. Instead, they went straight back to the Society where Erik promptly left her to Carter's care and disappeared.

"Something's come over everyone, it seems, of late," said Carter at the commissary over dinner.

Yara shrugged, but didn't speak. She could feel Carter's eyes on her, but refused to look up from her soup, afraid that if they could see her face they would see what she was hiding.

She could hear both sides of the argument in her head. One voice screaming at her to tell Carter, "They're coming for me! Help me! Save me!" The other said, "No use in worrying anyone. They'll take away what little freedom you have left and the future is unavoidable anyway."

She didn't know which voice she believed. She wanted to listen to them both. Or rather she wanted to believe that somehow telling her Guardians would prevent what she'd seen, but deep down in her gut she knew that no matter what, it wouldn't change the future.

Carter was speaking, but Yara couldn't hear the words. She nodded mutely and it seemed to satisfy them, because they kept going, evidently trying to mimic some semblance of normalcy despite the fact that neither of them felt normal at all.

She could see Carter's face the way they had appeared in her vision. Bloodied, beaten, bedraggled, glasses shattered like a starburst. Forced to their knees by a dark figure dressed in crimson. Erik and Robin on either side, also restrained, equally afraid. Every time she closed her eyes, the scene swam before her. She wanted both to see more and to see less, but instead she kept seeing the same details over and over again.

"I want to train," she said abruptly, interrupting Carter who was in the midst of speaking about juice. Or someone named Joyce.

"Beg your pardon?"

"I think we should go up and train after dinner. You kept talking about wanting to teach me self-defense, right?"

"Yes, I suppose."

"Well, I want to do it."

"Yara, I'm not so sure that's a good idea."

Yara gaped. "Are you kidding me?"

"No," said Carter carefully. "No, I'm not kidding."

Yara dropped her spoon which clattered against her bowl, spilling minestrone on the table. Her heart was beating quickly with frustration. She focused on her breath, trying not to get worked up as that often led to anxiety attacks which often led to visions. "Why the hell not?"

"Last time you did that you collapsed. You had a seizure. And it could have been much worse than it was."

"That had nothing to do with it."

"We don't know that."

"Yes we do!" said Yara, unable to keep her voice down. "We do know that. We know exactly what caused it."

"We know that an increase in your videtonin caused the seizure, but we don't know what triggered that increase--"

Yara stood up, cutting Carter off mid-sentence. "You need to stop treating me like I'm a child who doesn't understand anything."

Carter considered her for a moment, their amber eyes narrowed and steady. "You're right."

"I- what?"

"You're right. You're not a child. If you want to train, we'll train."

"Oh. Good." Yara sat back down, suddenly feeling foolish and ashamed of her outburst. "Thank you."

After a few quiet moments in which Carter resumed their dinner and Yara ran her finger through the spilled soup on the table, Carter said, "What triggered this change of heart?"

Yara wasn't sure how to answer.

Fear.

Fear was the real answer. Fear of what awaited her in Kain's hands. Fear of whether or not she would ever see Aunt Catherine again. Fear of whether she would make it out alive.

She wouldn't be able to avoid Kain. That much she knew. And she wanted to make her peace with that. But so far she had seen nothing of what awaited her after she was captured. Perhaps if she was taken in by Kain as prepared as possible, armed with all the tools and resources she could attain from her Guardians, then maybe she would be able to survive.

Maybe she'd be able to get free.

Carter wasn't sure what had inspired Yara to change her attitude regarding self-defense. But they didn't want to question it lest she decide she didn't want to after all. Yes, she'd had a seizure last time, but they had to trust that Yara knew what was best for herself. It was their shift until tomorrow morning when Robin would take over and accompany Yara to school, but they would wait to tell their fellow Guardians about this new development when they sent their debriefing report before bed.

It didn't escape Carter that it was a little strange that they were still all "on duty" even when Yara was safe at Headquarters, but that was the job so they did it obediently.

They had a feeling that - no matter what she outwardly expressed - Yara enjoyed the company of her Guardians. She had never been a social butterfly, but life at the Society could be particularly isolating, especially for a civilian. Perhaps having an activity, like self-defense, to work on would be a great distraction, and might even help in more ways than one.

Yara hadn't learned much from her first training session. She was clumsy, uncoordinated, and held herself with all the confidence of a sixth grade nerd. Carter spent most of the lesson pressing their fist between her shoulder blades to get her to stand up straighter. Without a strong core, (which often translated to good posture) she wouldn't have any of the strength she needed to protect herself. They expected her to fight back or complain, as she often did when it came to things the Society wanted her to do, but she barely spoke at all except giving Carter an occasional verbal acknowledgement or asking if she was doing it right.

After an hour and a half, Carter called it. They could tell that Yara was disappointed, but she thankfully didn't press the issue. While it was clear that she wanted to continue working, she had gotten tired and it was making her sloppy. Sloppier even than she already was.

"Quite a change of heart," said Carter putting their glasses back on and handing Yara a towel. She took it and wiped her face which was as red as a tomato.

"This is hard," she said.

Carter laughed. "Not much of an athlete?"

"I don't like exercise. It hurts too much."

"But you're doing this."

Yara took a long drink of water, sweat dripping from her forehead all the way down her neck, disappearing into the collar of her white workout uniform. "Guess so."

"And you're not gonna tell me why, are you?"

"What do you mean?" said Yara, avoiding their eyes.

"Alright," said Carter with a small smile. "Keep your cards close to your chest."

"We can do this again tomorrow, right?" said Yara.

"You'll have to ask E. He'll be the one on duty."

At these words, Yara's face turned a deeper red.

"You know, it's his job," they said.

"What?"

"You don't have to be embarrassed."

"I'm not," said Yara shortly. "I get it. It's just his job. Just your job. I'm just a job, I get it."

"That's not what I meant, and you know it," said Carter gently.

"I know it's not what you meant, but it's the truth."

"Hey, Red." They took Yara's hand. She didn't look at them, but while they knew she wasn't keen on being touched, she didn't pull her hand away. "Do you really think you're just a job?"

Yara snorted. "Is this the part where you try to convince me otherwise?"

"I can already see that if you don't want me to convince you, you won't be convinced. All I can tell you is the truth."

"Which is?"

"Which is that Erik, Robin, and I-" it took a concerted effort to say their full names, but it felt appropriate in the moment, "-all care about you. The Society could reassign us tomorrow and it wouldn't matter. We would all still want you to be safe and happy."

"You're right," said Yara. Carter smiled. "There's nothing you can say that will convince me." Their heart fell. Was that really how she felt? "Look. The fact of the matter is that none of you would care about me at all unless Bora Black ordered you to."

"Black can order us to do a lot of things, but she can't order us how to feel. She's the reason we met you, the reason we know you, but not the reason we care about you."

Yara pursed her lips in silence. Carter could see cogs whirring behind her eyes, but she didn't speak.

"What?" asked Carter.

She shrugged. "I don't like compliments. I never know how to respond."

"Well, you could say that you care about us, too. You could say that you're sorry for doubting our intentions."

"Sorry. Thank you."

Carter waited a moment before nudging her gently and adding, "And you care about us, too."

Yara gave a weak chuckle. "Yeah, I do. Of course I do."

They knew that what they wanted to say next could backfire spectacularly, but Carter had a feeling that not saying it could make things worse in the long run. So they took a deep breath and added, "I know that tomorrow you'll be training with E. I just want you to know that..." *Oh boy, here we go,* "...he's not allowed to pursue anything with you."

Yara's face, finally starting to return back to its regular pale complexion, burned again with a fervor. Still not looking at Carter, Yara shook her head as if to say, "why would I care?" Instead, she said, "Uh... OK. I didn't--"

"I don't want to make things awkward or uncomfortable for you. But I just want you to know that the Society takes that rule very seriously. Guardians are not allowed to have any kind of romantic relationship with their Wards."

Her discomfort was obvious and growing. She pulled her hand away from Carter and started to unwrap the bindings on her hands, throwing them unceremoniously into the bag she had been assigned with her gear. "I don't know why you're telling me this. It makes no difference."

"If you want to tell me that it makes no difference to you, that's fine. But it makes a difference to him."

Yara froze, still facing the wall.

"I know he'd be upset that I'm telling you this, so please keep it between us," said Carter. Yara turned to look at them. They pushed their glasses up their nose. "He feels very strongly for you. And he could lose his position altogether if anything were to happen. He could be expelled from the Society. And I don't know that he alone is strong enough to stop himself from pursuing you. You don't have to say anything," Carter added in response to Yara's stunned silence. "I just wanted to make sure you knew what was at stake."

Yara said nothing else before leaving Carter alone in the training cubicle to clean up.

CHAPTER TWENTY-SIX

Gauntlets and Solenoids

Knowing something horrible was coming and not knowing when it would happen was agonizing. Every morning, Yara woke up wondering if this was the day that Kain and his men (her Guardians called them Shadow Men and she couldn't help but wonder why they didn't give them a less ominous name) would come for her. All she knew was that it would happen within the walls of the Society, so the only time she didn't feel on edge was on her way to, at, and coming home from school.

At night she would lie awake and the scene would come back to her, sometimes as a memory of what she had seen and sometimes as a bonafide vision, but it was always the same.

She had tried so many times to induce another vision, desperate to see what happened next. Black said that it would be possible if she honed her skills enough. She had to learn to control when and what she saw, but Yara was no good at it. Since her initial lesson with Black in which she had managed to summon hazy shadows that faded as quickly as they came, she had not improved at all. Occasionally during lessons if she let go enough, if she tried to sink into her mind, she would feel a twinge of pain, and the fog would surround her in earnest. But whenever that happened, she tensed with excitement - or perhaps apprehension - and the fog instantly dissipated.

But in the absolute silence of her quarters - the silence she had been so uncomfortable with upon her initial arrival, the silence so unlike her true home downtown - she could sink into her mind, like falling slowly through water. She tried so hard to see what awaited her after her capture. She had come at it from different angles as well, trying something new every time she failed. She tried summoning the original scene - easily done; it was always waiting at the edge of her mind - and fast forwarding past it like a tape to get to whatever came next, but when she got to the end everything always vanished. She tried jumping directly into the future. She tried focusing on something different in the scene - whether it was Kain or her Guardians or the Shadow Men. Of course, she couldn't know if she was doing any of it right. Black could string any words together and make it sound good, but she had never actually experienced seeing the future so how could she possibly know what Yara had to do? Perhaps it was different for her than it had been for her father. Maybe it was different for every seer and they just had to figure it out on their own. It was like flexing a muscle she had never known she had, one she couldn't always find, and when she did it was so weak she felt like it wasn't even there.

It was all pointless. Nothing she did ever brought any images of what awaited her beyond Kain taking her away. And that stubborn emptiness did more to scare her than anything else. It was as though life did not exist beyond that day.

And of course, for Yara, perhaps it did not.

Erik had refused to take what had been their traditional detour to get donuts ever since Janya Varma's capture, despite Yara's renewed efforts to convince him to do so, knowing she was safer there than at Headquarters. But without telling him directly what she knew she was unsuccessful.

After several weeks of being in a constant state of fear, of training with her Guardians to the point where she no longer felt weak after each session, and of mulling over Carter's words of warning about pursuing anything romantic with Erik, she began to feel accustomed to this permanent anxiety that now filled her life. Nearly every breath was strained with the effort of keeping her head above water.

She was also continuing her lessons with Black and was becoming better at letting visions come to her without suffering the headaches, but she was still unable to truly summon them at will. The most unusual thing had been the repeated vision of her own capture. She was now seeing no other vision but that one, and it was happening several times a day, every day. (She was often having to excuse herself from class for frequent "bathroom breaks" in order to find a quiet place to succumb to her premonitions.) Never had she seen anything more than once, but now she was plagued by the sight of her Guardians hunched and beaten in the hands of Shadow Men and Kain approaching her, but every time she tried to make out any additional details, it all disappeared once again.

Her breathing exercises had done little to ease the tension she was now living with. Instead she found that her evening training sessions were the only things that helped - something she found very strange considering how much she had always hated exercising. But this felt different than regular exercise. She liked having a goal to accomplish, an endgame. Running or weightlifting or cycling or any of the other exercises most people engaged in didn't have any sense of achievement and often left her feeling bored and aimless.

But now she knew what she was working toward.

Thanksgiving break was quickly approaching and the thought of a five day weekend gave Yara a renewed sense of panic. On her way home from school that Monday she found herself feeling numb, as though her body no longer had the energy to feel afraid. It was Robin's day to bring her home from school and she let him chat happily on the way back to Headquarters, thinking only that she hoped today wasn't the day.

After dinner with Aunt Catherine and all three of her Guardians, Robin left her with Erik who took her to train. But instead of leading her down the familiar path to the rec room where they usually went, he took her one floor further down to a place she had never been.

"Where are we going?" she said.

"We were talking about it last week," said Erik, "and we decided that you've made enough improvements to move to the next stage of your training."

"What does that mean?"

"You'll see."

Yara looked at him out of the corner of her eye and saw to her surprise that he was smirking. Erik hardly ever smiled. Before things had taken a turn she had occasionally been able to eke one out of him. These last few months however he had been more stoic than ever. (She had to admit it made following Carter's warning about pursuing anything with him much easier when she felt like he was miserable around her.) So seeing that little tweak in the corner of his mouth made Yara cautiously excited about what awaited her.

The floor he led her to had 12 doors. But unlike most of the mahogany doors that lined the walls in the rest of the complex, these resembled elevator doors. Each one had a big screen above it, numbered from 1 to 12, and space underneath for a message to flash either "occupied" or "vacant" or "reserved".

Erik led her to the panel next to the door labeled "11" and pressed a button, illuminating the screen. Yara couldn't exactly make out what was written on it - he scrolled through everything too quickly - but it looked like some sort of menu.

"What is this?" she asked.

"You'll see," he repeated.

After selecting something from the panel, the doors whooshed open.

Yara stepped inside feeling, despite herself, somewhat disappointed by what she saw. After all of Erik's tantalizing teases, she had been expecting some sort of incredible room filled with robotic training dummies at the very least. (From everything she had seen at the Society they certainly had the technology for something like that.)

Instead she found herself in a room that was a perfect cube, about fifteen feet across. What she had originally perceived as black walls - broken up by a large silver grid that covered not just the walls but the floor and ceiling as well - upon closer inspection proved to be glass covering what had to be thousands if not millions of little bulbs that looked like they belonged on a Light Bright. Only a few of the bulbs were on, giving them just enough light to see each other and the dimensions of the room.

"This is it?" she asked.

Erik shook his head and his smirk grew, transforming his face and giving Yara's gut a twinge she hadn't felt in a while. Remembering that these were often the feelings that had triggered visions in the past, she looked away.

"Generate a solenoid," he said in a clear voice.

In the middle of the room, appearing out of nowhere, a strange kind of plate materialized.

"Wha—" stuttered Yara. "How did you do that?"

He handed her an enormous metal glove, pulled from a hidden cabinet in the wall, as he answered. "We're in the simulators. Basically giant VR rooms where we can run different scenarios. Great for training."

"By 'VR' you mean… virtual reality?"

"Virtual reality," said Erik simultaneously, nodding.

"But we're not wearing a headset or anything. I don't understand how this is possible."

"Well," said Erik, raising one of his thick eyebrows, his green eyes twinkling at her, "I could try to explain to you how the sensors in the walls read our movements and nano tech rearranges itself into whatever matter is programmed into the computer in order to create a seamless virtual experience, but it's a little complicated. So why don't you just take my word for it that it works."

Yara stared, dumbstruck.

"These are our weapons. This," he slipped the metal glove onto his hand, "is called a gauntlet. And it's used to control," he lifted his hand and the strange plate hovering in front of them started to whir with the sound of nails on a chalkboard, becoming nothing more than a silver blur, "the solenoidal star. Or solenoid." Yara reached out to touch the floating silver frisbee, but Erik stopped her, moving his gauntleted hand back, sending the solenoid away from her. "Don't!"

She jumped slightly.

"Sorry," he said with a soft chuckle. "It's very sharp. The edges are a carbon fiber filament. Pretty much unstoppable with enough strength behind it."

"Wouldn't it just be easier," started Yara, feeling awkward, "to use… I dunno, guns?" She had never liked guns, but they certainly seemed simpler to use than these contraptions.

"Nope," said Erik simply. "Guns may seem easier when you're unfamiliar with how to use a solenoid, but this is a projectile, too. Only it's much more powerful. Unlike a bullet, it'll cut through just about anything."

"Oh my god," said Yara, mildly horrified.

"Our armor is one of the only things that'll stop it. Made of the hardest substance on earth. But we'll get to that later. Today, we're just gonna start with the solenoids."

"What?" said Yara. "You want me to… use that thing?"

Erik lowered the solenoid to the floor and slipped off his gauntlet, handing it to her. She shrank away from it, clutching herself.

"I don't think so," she said.

"Oh, come on. The solenoid isn't even real. I put the safeties on and everything. It's very unlikely you'd be able to do any real damage."

Yara raised a skeptical eyebrow. "How reassuring." Nevertheless, she held out her hand to let Erik affix her with the gauntlet. It took several minutes to get everything adjusted to her hand. The glove was heavy and infinitely more complicated than Yara had initially imagined. He spent several more minutes explaining to her the basics of using it to control the solenoid, most of which she instantly forgot.

(She also took it as a very bad sign that her arm was already aching from the weight of the gauntlet.) Then suddenly…

"Begin level one, difficulty 'basic'," he said to the room at large.

Yara jumped a foot into the air as a body appeared next to her out of thin air. "Oh my god!" She clutched at her chest with the gauntlet, staring at the figure, trying to calm her heart. "What the hell!"

It was the body of a person - perhaps not even a person. It barely had a face, just faint divots where eyes should be and a small protrusion for a nose, like a sexless doll waiting to be painted and wigged. Its body was otherwise relatively detailed, and looked as human and solid as Erik. It was even wearing the same white uniform as them.

"Meet your new sparring partner," said Erik, trying and failing to hide his amusement at Yara's shock.

It was hard to believe that this would work, but she tentatively took a defensive stance, holding the gauntlet out like Erik had shown her, the solenoid wavering unsteadily above it. She half-heartedly tapped the dummy with her foot. Or at least she tried to. It dodged her blow and parried immediately with a cross punch to her ribcage.

"Ow!" She fell back a few steps, staring angrily at the dummy as though it had betrayed her, clutching her side. "What the hell! I thought VR wasn't supposed to hurt?"

"Traditional VR doesn't use matter. This is … how should I put this? Completely immersive. How can you learn to fight properly if you think you're impervious?"

"I thought you said I couldn't do any damage!"

"Any *real* damage," said Erik, biting his lip to hold back a laugh.

"A warning might have been nice," she said, but she, too, was smiling. For the first time in a long time, it felt like Erik had loosened up.

Remember Carter, said a small voice in the back of her head. But she brushed it aside and instead faced the dummy.

"OK," she said. "Let's give this a try."

CHAPTER TWENTY-SEVEN

Room 11

After the initial frustration of having to learn to fight a partner unlike any she had combated before, not to mention using an unfamiliar and complicated weapon, Yara started to genuinely enjoy this new sort of training. Any time she had actually sparred with her Guardians, no matter how much they reassured her that she couldn't hurt them, she always held back a little. Just in case. But with this faceless simulation, she didn't worry about it. Instead, she found herself genuinely trying to hit it as hard as possible and slash it in half with the solenoid while Erik stood back and occasionally corrected her stance, or shouted adjustments to her technique.

She wanted to destroy the dummy. It was strangely therapeutic.

She didn't even notice when her muscles started to ache beyond reason until she slowed considerably and could no longer lift her gauntleted hand, a huge disadvantage to the never-tiring simulated dummy.

Erik shut the program down, the dummy and solenoid vanishing into thin air. Yara pulled her gauntlet off and slumped against the glass wall of the simulator, guzzling her water (with her left hand, her aching right hand hanging useless in her lap), taking a moment to enjoy feeling better than she had in a while. In the last hour and a half, since Erik had brought her here, she had not once thought about Kain.

"Well done," said Erik, smiling in earnest. His face was transformed. The hard and sharp lines of his jaw became softer, his eyes brighter. She didn't look at him long. It was too disarming. Remembering something Carter had mentioned over a month ago, she spoke before her mind had a chance to catch up with her mouth.

"Are you human?"

He slid down against the wall next to her, the smile not completely gone, but faded. "Not entirely," he said.

"I'm sorry, should I not have asked that? I don't really have … Deviant etiquette or whatever."

He gave a short laugh and ran his long spindly fingers through his black hair. "I don't mind, but maybe don't run around Headquarters asking everyone you find if they're human." He looked at her and while his smile had faded his expression was still soft.

"Noted. Good thing you told me not to do that. Otherwise, you know." Yara trailed off, picking at the wraps around her wrists. He chuckled. She hesitated, but she couldn't contain her curiosity. "If you're not entirely human…"

"My father is a nymph. Flora."

"He's a plant then?" said Yara. "Sorry. I'm— ugh. I feel stupid. I just don't know how any of this works. I haven't actually… *met* any flora nymphs yet."

But Erik was laughing. "He can take the form of a plant, yes. The moringa tree. But he can also take the form of a man."

"Can you become a tree, too?"

"Not entirely," said Erik.

"And your mother?"

"She was human."

Yara noted the past tense. "I'm sorry."

"It was a long time ago. I barely remember her, actually."

Yara didn't respond to that. She knew what it was like to lose a parent. To have a gaping hole in your heart and your mind where you knew you were meant to love them, but there was nothing left to hold on to.

"You were five, right?" said Erik.

She gave a sardonic chuckle. "I keep forgetting that you guys already know everything about me." She leaned her head against the glass wall and closed her eyes.

"Not everything," said Erik.

No, thought Yara, remembering the vision of her capture. *Not everything.*

She heard a soft rustling and opened her eyes to see Erik holding out his arm in front of her, palm facing the ceiling, and she watched as his smooth, pale skin turned rougher and darker until it looked to be made of unfinished wood. A few branches had even started to sprout.

"Wha—" Yara turned to look at his face to see that, while he was still Erik, he now looked to be carved directly from a tree. He shook his head, and returned to normal before she could fully appreciate the transformation. From between his fingers, leaves were still growing and curling around his hand. They were bright green, the same color as his eyes. Yara stared in amazement. "Oh my god!"

He gave his hand a small shudder and the movement stopped. He plucked a branch from his hand and gave it to Yara. She took it, her mouth still agape.

"That's incredible!"

"You're easily impressed," he said, smiling. "You should see what my father can do."

"Well, don't tell your dad, but I prefer you." She meant it as a joke, but she had never been very good at communicating intent and it came out sounding much more flirtatious than she had intended. She felt her cheeks burn, but Erik looked away, giving her a moment to regain her composure.

A comfortable silence followed, and she was overcome with a strong urge to tell Erik about her vision. Tell him that she was in danger. That Kain was coming for her. That she was afraid and wanted to leave the Society. And most of all that she thought there was no escaping it. But as soon as the words rose in her throat they were choked back down with fear.

"Erik—" she said at the same time that he said, "Yara." Instead they both cut themselves off and looked at each other.

There they were again, those beguiling eyes, green like the moringa tree he had come from, locking her gaze like a tractor beam.

She heard Carter's words in her mind. *He feels very strongly for you. He could lose his position if anything were to happen. He alone isn't strong enough to stop himself.*

Carter had told her that Erik had been harboring the same feelings she had for him. Since she first saw him she had wondered at his behavior. Wondered if he liked her back, wondered if he couldn't stand her.

But he did. He wanted to be with her, and she wanted to be with him. She wanted to fall into his arms. Did he want that, too?

His face was much closer to hers now, moving as if in slow motion. She felt pulled to him like a magnet. And Carter's words became a distant memory as she felt his lips brush lightly against hers. Shy.

Unsure.

She could hear his breath trembling, though she was sure hers was, too. He pulled away and waited.

Waited for her to say no.

To say stop.

To say it couldn't happen.

But no part of her wanted to say anything other than yes, yes, yes.

She leaned forward, closing the gap between them and kissed him again. It was slow and soft and warm. His hands were on either side of her face, holding her gently as he kissed her, pulling her closer to him. They were suddenly on their knees. She ran her hands up his back, ignoring the burn of her aching muscles and still gripping the moringa branch in her clenched fist, unable to let go.

What had started as tentative and tender was becoming stronger. Heated. Unyielding. He kissed her cheek. Under her ear. The crook of her neck.

She inhaled him, sweaty and warm and yet still somehow smelling like summer and something else she couldn't quite place…

Then his lips were back on hers and nothing else mattered.

Kain didn't matter and Carter didn't matter and the Society didn't matter.

All that mattered was this.

CHAPTER TWENTY-EIGHT

Secrets

Erik couldn't sleep.

His mind had found a new way of tormenting him: remembering being with Yara. Remembering kissing her, finally feeding the hunger he had lived with for so long. His chest swelled with the memory. Then, as though intent on keeping him from enjoying it, he would remember everything he risked by giving in to his temptation.

He had worked his whole life to be where he was. Having grown up at the White Mask Society, he had always known he wanted to be a Guardian. And Guardians got to spend so little time in the field in the scheme of things. At the age of 27 they were forced into a quasi-retirement, moving into what was called "Level 2". Instead of being in the field like a Level 1 Guardian, Level 2 oversaw assignments, training, dispatching, all the boring stuff. He had worked so hard to graduate from initiation as early as he could to spend as much time in the field as possible. He just wanted to *help* people. He'd worked so hard that he had set a Society record in being the youngest Guardian in all of Society history.

And last night he had risked throwing it all away.

For her.

Then the pit of anxiety in his stomach dissipated as he remembered kissing her again…

And on and on it went, a cruel cycle of joy then trepidation, all working together to prevent him from getting a single wink.

Worse than not being able to sleep, he knew that as soon as he saw either of his fellow Guardians they would read everything on his face.

He had never been good at hiding how he felt about Yara. For years as a youth he had learned the hard way that anything he was thinking was apparently broadcast to the world. As a result, he had adapted a technique of trying to shut down any potential signals, which ended up making him come across as standoffish, but those techniques did not hold up against those who knew him well. Especially when it came to Yara. Carter and Robin would know. They would likely be able to determine everything that had happened as though watching a movie projected onto his face.

He could trust them, though.

Couldn't he?

At least Carter would not report him. Though they would do everything in their power to prevent anything more from happening. They would try to rearrange the shift schedule so that Erik would only ever escort Yara to and from school but not have any free time to spend with her.

Robin, however…

Erik still hadn't spoken to him since they fought in the simulator. A few polite exchanges here and there when they debriefed each other at the end of each shift. But with Yara staying at the Society, there wasn't much to report, so those conversations - if they could even be called that - amounted to no more than a few words. It changed nothing, though. The events of that night were no less real. And Robin still loved Yara.

Erik smiled despite himself. He wasn't proud of it, but there was a vicious voice in his head that kept saying *I won*. Yes, he had won. Yara wanted him, not Robin.

But had he really won if it meant he lost his position at the Society?

Would he even be allowed to ever see her again?

Perhaps he had won the battle, but it remained to be seen if he won the war.

For the first time since having the vision of her capture, Yara's mind was not filled with the image of Kain's twisted face, but instead of Erik's. His green eyes and parted lips. Instead of feeling the fear that accompanied every recollection of that premonition, she felt his hands on the back of her neck and his trembling breath on her skin.

During the last few weeks every night had dragged on, sleep a thing long forgotten as every little sound would startle her with the thought, "This is it. He's here. He's come." But now that she wanted the night to last, to be able to sit with the memory of the evening and the satisfying ache of her exhausted muscles, time slipped away from her and before she knew it, Carter was at the door to take her to breakfast and then school, the last day before they were out for Thanksgiving break.

It had become a nuisance, going to school. It felt like such a waste of time. It certainly didn't help that during her English quiz she could barely use her right hand which was unbelievably sore from her first foray into fighting with a gauntlet.

When every passing minute meant a minute closer to the fate that awaited her, she found herself filled with a restless need to escape these static classrooms filled with people who were so ignorant to her plight. (She wondered how many of them would actually notice if she disappeared…) But she was also aware that school was the only place she felt safe. Whether or not she actually *was* safer was irrelevant. All she knew was that Kain wasn't coming for her there. He would attack Headquarters, and she was now facing five days there.

The hours dragged by painfully slowly before the bell released her, but had she known what was waiting for her that evening, perhaps she would have simply refused to go back.

She slid into the black car waiting to take her to the Society, Carter sitting patiently in the back seat. Yara kept her mouth shut. She did not want to accidentally blurt anything out that might give away what had happened between her and Erik last night. If Carter noticed anything strange, they did her the kindness of not asking any questions.

If they *had* asked, what would Yara say? Would she confess about Erik and put his position as her Guardian at risk? Or would she tell them instead that she was waiting with baited breath for Kain and his Shadow Men? Instead, to fill the silence, she said, "Is the location of Headquarters secret?" As soon as the words were out of her mouth, she was sure that Carter would be able to deduce what Yara was really asking. Which was, *Am I safe?*

"Secret from whom?"

"You know… everyone. Like non-Deviants and bad guys and stuff."

Carter scrutinized Yara with their bright, golden eyes, and pushed their glasses up their nose. "No, it's not a secret. At least not for people who know about Deviants. Which excludes most civilians." They looked back out the window. "We are a service to the Deviant community. We're there to help them if they ever need it. Wouldn't be very helpful if they didn't know where to find us."

"Hmm." A moment. "So how do you defend it against attacks?"

"It doesn't happen a lot," admitted Carter. "The Society doesn't have many people who want to attack it. This situation with Kain is relatively anomalous. But there are Guardians who are always on duty, and we have various defense systems set up by our other departments."

"Oh. OK."

Carter looked at Yara, and she tried hard to ignore the feeling of being x-rayed by those amber eyes, fixating her own on the world zooming by outside her window.

"It's really not something you need to worry about, Red," said Carter quietly. "It'd be like someone trying to raid the FBI or Langley."

Yara forced a smile on her face and looked at Carter. "I'm not worried."

As good as she was at being able to tell when others were lying, Yara had never been good at it herself, and she hoped that Carter would not be able to see through her.

CHAPTER TWENTY-NINE
The Alarm

The tightness in her chest that evening had become unbearable. Her aunt seemed relatively oblivious to Yara's mental state, having found ways to assist in the medical ward, bored after months off of work. But Yara was starting to panic in earnest, as though a hand had been gripping her for the last few weeks slowly tightening its hold. And now she could no longer breathe. She was heading down to the cafeteria for dinner with Robin, trying to focus on her relaxation exercises - *breathe in the liquid gold; exhale the red smoke* - but it was no use, and the next thing she knew her legs had collapsed from under her in the middle of the hall. Her hand was clenched around Robin's arm, her knuckles turning white, pulling him down with her as she fell.

"Oh no, not again," she heard him say under his breath and then his wide eyes were in front of hers, kneeling opposite her on the floor. "Yara? Can you hear me?"

She couldn't breathe. She tried to nod, her eyes locked with his, trying to communicate without words, hoping that he would understand.

"It's OK," he said. He placed her other hand on his chest and she felt the rise and fall of his steady breathing. "Breathe with me, kid, you're gonna be OK."

Without blinking he started to inhale deeply through his nose and exhale steadily through his mouth.

"Just breathe with me."

Shaking, she tried to match him, focusing on her hand pressed against his chest, trying to match his rhythm. After a few horrible, earth-spinning moments, she had calmed down enough to speak.

"I don't want to go," she managed, her words stilted, still trying to control her desperate gasps for air. The knowledge she had been keeping secret for what felt like a lifetime was draining and, though she didn't want to admit it, she was too cowardly to keep the information from her Guardians any longer. It had taken everything she had to not say anything up until now. But she didn't have the strength, the courage, to go it alone.

"Go? Go where?"

"He's coming—" she gasped. "I'm so— so scared, Robin."

"Hey," he said calmly. "Don't worry, kid, no one is going to take you." He tightened his hold on her hand, pressing it more firmly into his chest, still breathing slowly.

"No. I saw him." The panic tightened its hold on her chest again and she had to take a few moments to try to match Robin's breathing. She couldn't bring herself to look in his face. No matter what she saw, it wouldn't be what she wanted to see. Either the skepticism of someone who didn't believe her or the worry of someone who did.

"Tell me exactly what you saw," he said in a low voice. If he was panicking or if he was doubtful he wasn't showing it.

"It was Kain. And his men. They were in red. They were here, and they had all of us—"

At that moment, it became clear why Yara's anxiety had come to a crest. Somehow, her mind had known on a subconscious level what she had been too scared to deduce.

A loud, blaring alarm starting ringing in the hallway.

"What's happening?" she asked, her chest tightening again. Why she asked she couldn't say. She knew what was happening. Perhaps she simply hoped that Robin would say impossible words to the effect of, "Don't worry, it's a false alarm."

Robin, however, neither spoke nor hesitated. He grabbed Yara and started to move quickly toward the elevators. The hallway, a few moments ago nearly empty, was suddenly a flurry of activity. People were moving with speed and purpose, but everything aside from the alarm was oddly quiet. No one spoke, no one made eye contact. Clearly, this was something they were prepared for, had trained for, and knew exactly how to react to.

Had Yara made a horrible mistake in keeping this a secret? She had been convinced she could not have stopped her own capture, but perhaps other lives would have been saved had the Society had a warning.

Instead of going into the elevator, Robin opened a door Yara had never noticed next to it that led to what looked like an infinite staircase. Robin did not give her any time to marvel, however, and instead started to lead her down the stairs. He wasn't running, but he moved quickly, almost as though he was sliding down the stairs, a stark contrast to Yara's graceless stumbling behind him. He was talking into a device on his collar, his voice too low for her to hear. Her other Guardians were both waiting for them on the next landing.

At least, Yara thought it was them. They were both dressed in black from head to toe - not unusual in and of itself - but rather than their normal form fitting attire, like what Robin was wearing, they were draped in cloaks, barely concealing what looked like chain mail armor underneath. Their left hands were equipped with the same enormous gauntlets that Erik had just had her train with in the simulator, but the most shocking aspect of their appearances were the white masks covering the top of their faces, contouring their jaws like yawning mouths, their bright eyes shining like searchlights from behind them.

Yara had never wondered why it was called the White Mask Society, but now it became very clear.

Wordlessly, Carter handed Robin his own battle attire.

Erik approached her, identifiable by his blazing green eyes. He, too, was carrying a pile of black fabric. He started draping her with the same chain mail that they were wearing. She staggered under the weight. As he leaned forward to wrap the cloak around her, he whispered, "Are you OK?"

She didn't know how to answer, too overwhelmed, too frightened, too not OK.

He seemed to understand.

He placed a mask over Yara's face and pulled her hood up. She barely had time to appreciate that at a first glance they all looked identical - a clever added security measure - before she was being led back down the stairs, one of her Guardians (she couldn't tell who it was) in front of her, the other two flanking her from behind.

Yara wanted to shout at them that this was all pointless. That she had already seen them fail, and that it would be easier if they didn't fight. But she also wanted to shout at them *to* fight. To try to change fate. To not let her get taken by the monster that was Kain. Wherever Robin was among her cloaked Guardians she wondered what he was thinking. Everything had happened so quickly, and he had been so unreadable.

Hoping against hope that tonight would not be the last time she would see him, or Erik, or Carter, she whispered a small prayer that he was not mad at her, and that she wouldn't die before being able to explain why she had kept it all from them.

She had not even been able to say goodbye to Aunt Catherine.

Oh, god.

Robin had not had time to think after Yara told him that Kain was going to attack Headquarters. The alarms only meant one thing.

Infiltration.

Someone had breached the Society's defenses - no small task.

Like a switch being flipped he went into autopilot, following the protocol that had been drilled so efficiently into him during his training as an initiate then again during drills when he was assigned to Yara's case. But after joining up with Carter and Erik, heading down to the bunker where they would stay until Headquarters was secured, his mind was able to catch up to his body.

Yara had known. Her strange behavior the last month... How could she have sat on this information for so long and not told them? They could have prepared! They could have taken shelter at the underwater base. It was far, it was hard to get to, but it was impossible to reach without the help of its assigned Guardian team - all aquatic nymphs.

But no. Stupid Yara had taken it upon herself to keep the knowledge of Kain's oncoming attack to herself. Evidently, they had not earned her trust enough to be informed of something so crucial. His face was burning underneath his mask. Robin was not quick to anger. He hated the feeling. It muddled his decision making. And if Robin prided himself on any one thing, it was his sense of reason, his coolness under pressure. But this...

The alarm continued like a metronome. He tuned it out. The stairs felt endless as they went down to the lowest level of the building. The bunker and holding cells were not open to all White Masks. It wasn't even accessible by elevator. He didn't know exactly how far underground it was, only that this was where they kept haunts and other dangerous Deviants. That was enough for him to not want to spend much time down there. Unfortunately it was also the most secure part of Headquarters, and therefore ideal for protecting Yara. Without being able to check on what was happening outside the stairwell, he had no way of knowing what the status of the attack was. Were they winning? Was Kain himself already here? How many Shadow Men had he brought with him?

At last they reached the bottom. Robin palmed the lock on the door, impatiently waiting for the scanner to grant him access. After only a few seconds that felt like an eternity, the door hissed open to reveal a dark, long hallway. He ushered Yara and his partners inside, and palmed the inner scanner to close the heavy door behind them.

When he turned around to follow the three of them down the hall, however, he found them standing perfectly still.

"Wh—" he started, but stopped as soon as he saw why.

Erik had trained his whole life to be a Guardian, prepared for this exact scenario.

But nothing could have prepared him for this.

He had been sure that if they could get Yara to the bunker that they would be safe until the building was secured. A small part of his brain had registered how unusual it was for them not to encounter anything in the stairway. Not even other Society members scrambling for safety or to their posts. But he had brushed the thought aside, deciding there was not enough time to deal with it, not enough space in his mind to think about it.

He understood now.

The Shadow Men had been inside longer than anyone knew. Somehow, they had found a way to infiltrate the building without setting off any alarms, giving them ample time to set up an ambush. True, Kain had worked at the Society. He had not been a Guardian, however, and therefore could not know their exact protocols. But he was smart. And he was curious. Erik would not have been surprised if he had somehow gotten his hands on information he was not meant to have during his time at the Society. Evidently he had done just that, because Kain knew exactly where to wait for them. He would not have to hunt Yara down. Her Guardians had delivered her straight to him.

After Robin ushered everyone through the heavy iron door that led to the bunker, Erik was the first to see the army of Shadow Men blocking their way. He had no idea where Kain had found men like this. Hulking figures with brick faces, all with the same dead expression in their eyes. There were at least a dozen of them, all dressed in crimson. Despite everything, Erik couldn't help but think that Kain certainly had a flare for the dramatic. (Though he wasn't exactly one to talk given the Society armor.)

He pushed Yara behind him without thinking and felt her body trembling with fear against his arm.

For an instant, everyone was frozen.

And then the moment was over and the dark hallway exploded with movement.

Robin moved Yara back against the door while the three of them simultaneously used their gauntlets to summon their respective solenoids from the sheaths on their backs.

Three silver discs whizzed forward toward the Shadow Men who had pulled their own weapons free.

With a dozen Shadow Men, they would each be tasked with taking down four, no small feat. The three of them split forward, careful not to leave too much room between them and Yara. To his right, he could feel Carter shifting their form. Erik didn't take the time to look though, headed instead for the Shadow Man dead ahead, a bald man who looked to be almost seven feet tall. This close, Erik could make out something on his neck, something like a tattoo or a brand, but in the low light he couldn't tell what it was and he didn't want to take the time to find out.

Despicable that Kain would brand his soldiers.

Unlike the Guardians, the Shadow Men were relatively unprotected from damage. The Guardians were all wearing chain mail made of the strongest material on earth - wurtzite boron nitride - and the only substance which could stop an oncoming solenoid from slicing through them. They had their masks to protect their faces. They had their gauntlets enabling them to both control a weapon and engage in hand to hand combat.

The Shadow Men, on the other hand, wore nothing but their crimson uniforms which looked as penetrable as muslin. Their weapons were, however, formidable. Most were devices of Kain's own invention. A few of them were equipped with solenoids and gauntlets, technology that Kain had no doubt taken from the Society when he left. The Shadow Man in front of Erik had a sort of sword, glowing with a strange pinkish light. He swung it down and Erik had just enough time to send his solenoid directly into the oncoming strike, blocking the blow, though it came so close to his shoulder that he could feel a heat coming from it, as though whatever made it glow also made it burn.

Erik twisted his solenoid, locking its thin, jagged teeth around the sword, making it harder for the Shadow Man to pull it free, giving Erik the time he needed to cut him across the jaw with his gauntleted hand, then a quick punch to the gut, doubling him over.

But Erik had fought Shadow Men before, and knew that they were not ordinary fighters. Pain seemed to have little to no affect on them. If you wanted to slow one down, you had to incapacitate it. There was no room for mercy.

Yara watched her Guardians fight, barely able to make anything out through the commotion.

She knew three things:

The hallway was dark.

Her Guardians were outnumbered at least four to one.

And this was it.

No matter how hard they fought, she knew how this ended. She had already seen it. So many times. The image was seared into her memory. All she could be do was be grateful in the moment that neither Erik nor Carter nor Robin would die.

Would they, though? She didn't know the end of their story. Only the end of hers. Kain would take her from here, but what would happen to them when she was gone?

Fear was gripping her chest with its unforgiving talons, squeezing hard. She couldn't breathe, her line of sight was closing in like an aperture ring tightening around the edges of her world. She clutched at the iron door behind her, trying to stay present, to stay grounded, to keep from collapsing. Her head was twinging painfully, but she could not permit herself to have a vision. She couldn't take her eyes away from what was happening in front of her.

The three Guardians fought so fluidly, moved so quickly, it was hard to believe that she was not watching a sped up video. Carter had transformed themself into a hybrid of sorts, their un-gauntleted hand lengthened into vicious talons, their face transfigured, just visible enough beneath their mask for Yara to make out a wide mouth with elongated canines, which they gnashed at a Shadow Man, taking a large chunk out of his arm. All three Guardians swung their solenoids around so quickly they were blurred. The first time one of the stars sliced clean through a Shadow Man, Yara screamed and closed her eyes. His blood had splattered against whichever Guardian was fighting him, staining their mask like a Jackson Pollock painting.

With her eyes closed, it became harder to push away the vision that was tugging at her mind. Fog started to fill the world and she saw the shape of a face. *Really?* she thought bitterly to herself. *Now?* After how hard she had tried to summon a vision for the last four weeks, it could not have come at a worse time. So she forced her eyes open again before anything could take shape.

By then, two more Shadow Men lay dead on the floor. One of her Guardians - not Carter, who was using their new taloned hand to rip open a Shadow Man's chest - had been pinned against the wall, his gauntlet ripped from his hand, and a glowing weapon pushed against the back of his neck.

She wanted to help. Hadn't that been the purpose of those self defense classes? But everything she had learned was gone. Wiped from her memory as effectively as if from a white board. She was completely paralyzed with fear. And she hated herself for it.

Coward.

She didn't need to know which Guardian was which to know they were losing the fight. One more Shadow Man had fallen, but now Carter was on their knees, clutching their arm, their face and hand returned to their humanoid shape. Two Shadow Men swarmed them and pulled the gauntlet off as well. They were completely disarmed.

The last one standing she recognized to be Robin. Seeing that his partners were incapacitated, he moved slowly backward toward Yara, focusing less on hand to hand combat and instead on swinging his solenoid toward the Shadow Men, trying to keep them at a distance. But they seemed to have no fear of death. Yara's opposite, they were stoic, calm, and unaffected by any non-lethal blows that Robin landed.

Who were these men? How could they be so fearless and so impervious to pain?

The fight was over. Yara could tell. This was the end. They had fought so hard for her. Risked injury and death for her.

Could I have stopped it?

But it was over now. The remaining Shadow Men, unafraid of the damage the solenoid was causing to them, had managed to wrestle Robin's away from him, leaving him defenseless.

The remaining crimson clad army parted, making a path for someone emerging from the dark corridor. A light thud accompanied every other step as the figure walked haltingly forward.

Before his face came into the low light, Yara knew who it was.

Ramsey Kain.

The man she had been running from for so many months. The man responsible for her life being upended. The man who had haunted her dreams ever since her first vision of him.

He was tall, nearly as tall as his Shadow Men. But where they were thick and built like walls, he was skeletal. It looked as though a strong enough wind would be able to knock him over were he not holding himself up with his cane. His skin was ashy, stretched over bone like vellum, save for a scar on the left side of his face, reaching from his eye all the way down to his jaw, ending just below the ear. As Yara looked into his green eyes, so unlike Erik's, she couldn't help but wonder if he had become evil simply because he looked the part.

"A valiant effort, dear Guardians."

Robin backed up, the only one still standing, his body a shield between Yara and Kain.

"Step aside, boy," he said, not taking his eyes off of Yara.

"Never."

Kain barely twitched in the direction of one of his Shadow Men, but it was enough. The message was clear. *Move him.*

One of them slashed at Robin's leg with a glowing weapon, eliciting a hideous scream of pain and bringing him to his knees. Another few swift movements and a Shadow Man had locked Robin's arms behind him. In the commotion, his mask had gotten knocked off. The bottom half of his face was covered with blood - though Yara couldn't tell if it was his - and his eyes were fierce. She had never seen him look so angry. She hated it, so she quickly looked away and found herself looking directly at Kain who now stood not two feet from her.

He positively loomed over her. She felt herself shrinking away. He reached toward her suddenly with one of his long, spindly fingers. She flinched, but all he did was pluck the mask from her face and toss it to the floor where the clatter echoed in the now silent hallway.

He spoke so low, as though to a lover, she almost didn't hear him over the pounding of her heart. "I have waited a long time for you, Miss Rivers."

CHAPTER THIRTY

Shadow Men

"Don't touch her!" It was Erik's voice. He was pressed against the wall where two Shadow Men were holding him down.

Unconcerned, Kain slowly turned to see who had spoken. "Let me see his face," he said to his men. Their expressions still blank, they pulled Erik roughly forward so he was facing Kain and Yara. His mask had fallen off, his cloak was torn, his lip cut, his eye bruised… She was sure there were many more hidden injuries as well. Despite all that, his eyes burned into Kain, hatred etched into every line of his face.

Kain cocked his head, as casually as if examining a piece of art in a museum.

"Erik Carpenter, correct? Youngest Guardian in Society history, stop me if I'm wrong. From looking at those eyes it seems to me you are a nymph, yes?"

Tears were falling down Yara's cheeks, hot and sticky, her body trembling. How could Kain be so casual? He was enjoying it, the bastard.

"But not entirely. Hmm. Shame." His head turned to her other two Guardians, both in as bad or worse shape as Erik. "A shifter, too. I watched you fight. Impressive. Partial transformations are no small feat. And… aw. Just a human." Kain shook his head, and ran one of his long fingers up and down the scar on his face. He continued to address Robin. "Me too, I'm afraid. We were dealt an unlucky lot, you and I, Mr. Green. These three wouldn't understand." He gestured at Yara, Erik, and Carter with his cane. "They were given an enormous privilege and what do they do? Do they share it with the world? No.

They keep it to themselves. But we must spread the wealth. Wouldn't you rather have the skills of your partner here?" He nodded at Carter whose glare was visible even through their broken glasses. "Being able to transform into whatever or whomever you wanted. Perhaps you'd be able to make yourself more… appealing to those you'd like to appeal to."

Yara was not listening to anything Kain was saying. Her fingers and toes were becoming numb. She just wanted it to be over. But at the same time, she dreaded the unknown beyond. The blackness she could never see past when she tried.

Kain slammed his walking stick on the ground causing Yara to jump. "Well! What a thrill this has been, my dears." He signaled to two of his Shadow Men who moved wordlessly to Yara. She backed away instinctively, pointlessly, until her back was against the wall. There was no mercy in their faces as they grabbed her. She didn't even have the strength to struggle. Her body felt impossibly weak. "But I'm afraid my time is short and I have places to be. It's really been quite a pleasure."

As much as she had wanted this to be over just a few seconds ago, now she longed to reach for Erik, to hold him and be held by him one more time before possibly never seeing him again. Why had they wasted so much of their time together? It was Yara's fault. He hadn't known there was an expiration date. But she had.

Just as she tried to move toward him, his name a garbled mess as it wrenched free from her throat, one of the Shadow Men hit her hard in the side of the head. The shock was stronger than the pain at first. She could hear Erik screaming her name. But soon the world faded out of focus, until she fell into oblivion.

It had gone perfectly. His Shadow Men may be bland company, but they knew how to execute orders. And that was all he really needed from them.

He had been planning his incursion of the White Mask Society Headquarters for months. After all, he would only have one shot. Any failed attempt would alert the Society that he was not above breaking into arguably one of the most secure locations in the state, if not the country, and they would have doubled their security measures, possibly even taken the hyden to the underwater base where they would be all but unreachable.

And this mission would give him not just one hydan, but two.

The last two he needed.

And the Society still did not know about his upper hand. Not the fact that he used to work at the Society, no. That alone would have offered him little to no advantage. But that he had help from within. That gave him access to everything he needed, plus ample time to prepare before the alarms went off.

He was buzzing with excitement when they arrived back at the lab, despite the ache in his leg after standing for so long. The hyden's cells were ready, but Kain was eager to get started, so he had his Shadow Men bring the jumper immediately to him. She would likely be in better shape than the other one anyway. A better specimen.

At this point, after having done the painstaking research of mapping a hydan brain with his first four subjects, he had nearly perfected his process. The difficult part for hyden who did not have reflexive or involuntary abilities was getting them to employ their powers under the correct circumstances.

But that was also part of the fun.

Cesium and Lithium were the two Shadow Men who brought him his prize. As they both came from the same batch, they were identical, the same coarse brown hair and gnarled fingers, distinguishable only due to the brands identifying them on their necks. "Cs" for Cesium and "Li" for Lithium.

Between them was the limp form of Emmanuelle Moreau.

Her skin looked particularly dark under the white lights of his laboratory, her long braided hair hanging over her face as her head lolled unconsciously against her chest.

Cesium and Lithium knew the drill. Cesium put her on the examination table and began to strap down her extremities while Lithium prepared the injections.

The excited buzzing in Kain's head was growing into a frantic energy.

A new hydan. A new challenge. And a new skill that he would be able to harness.

"Wake her," he said with a smile, fingering his scar, and he watched as Lithium gave her the first shot.

CHAPTER THIRTY-ONE

Aftermath

The first thing Yara noticed was the cold.

The second thing was the pain.

She was no stranger to headaches, but this one was different. It was localized above her right ear. She reached up to touch it and gasped in pain. There was indeed a sizable lump.

Oh, right… A Shadow Man had hit her there. She remembered now.

She was on the other side. The other side of time, beyond where her vision had shown her, the place she could not see. Her stomach dropped like a rock as she opened her eyes for the first time to see what was indeed beyond the black.

She was in a cell. No more than a small cement box. On one side, a stone slab protruded from the wall that had a thin mattress, stained pillow, and threadbare blanket. On the other, a metal toilet, if it could even be called that. It was minuscule and looked like not more than a modest seat over a hole in the ground.

There were no windows.

She expected fear to accompany this new environment, but all that was left was a hollow numbness. Her body had been wrung dry of fear back at Headquarters.

Headquarters…

Where she had left her Aunt Catherine, Robin and Carter and Erik…

Were they OK? Were they alive? She squeezed her eyes closed, hoping that a vision would magically appear with all four of them smiling and happy and safe, but all she saw were dizzying spots against the darkness of the inside of her eyelids.

She tried to push herself up and noticed why she was so cold. Her Society armor had been taken - of course - but they had stripped her of her clothes as well. She shuddered to think of her body being handled, unconscious, by either Kain or any of his Shadow Men. Otherwise she seemed relatively unharmed - aside from the lump on her head. They had instead dressed her in tan underwear and a band of the same fabric wrapped around her chest.

Pulling herself toward the makeshift bed jutting out of the wall, she wrapped herself in the blanket. It was scratchy against her bare skin which was already rough with goosebumps, and it smelled musty. But it was all she had.

Leaning against the wall, feeling impossibly tired and heavy, tears started to fall, stinging her skin. She didn't want to cry. She didn't want to be afraid. She made a half-hearted attempt to sink into her mind, probing for a vision that might indicate what the future would hold, but nothing came. After all, it would be near impossible under such circumstances to achieve the relaxed state necessary for such a thing. Even Black would have to admit that.

"HOW DID THIS HAPPEN?"

Bora Black was not quick to anger. In fact, most people described her as stoney. Unflappable. A brick wall, she had even heard. It was a mark of her kind, the Tenebrae. Dark nymphs were by nature relatively unfeeling. That was not to say that they were incapable of emotion. They just often didn't access it.

Now, all she felt was rage. It had blinded her completely. She could feel everyone in the room shrink away from her and the churning coils of blackness that emanated from her skin, but she didn't care. The thought of her Headquarters being infiltrated, of Shadow Men having had enough time to ambush her Guardians before the alarms went off, made her angrier than she thought possible. Two hyden were snatched out from right under their noses. And one of them a Guardian herself.

"*HOW?*" she bellowed when no one answered her.

"We have reason to believe—" started her second, Zak Glover, but she didn't let him finish.

"Not you," she said sharply, silencing him with a look from her obsidian eyes. She stared back at the six Guardians standing in front of her, bedraggled and beaten, cloaks torn, chain mail bloodied, heads hanging in shame. "I want to hear from you all *how* you let this happen!"

They hesitated long enough for Black to think that they wouldn't answer her at all, but finally Nayla Jackson, one of Emmanuelle's Guardians, spoke up.

"Kain must have had knowledge of our operations, sir," she said in a voice that did not match her submissive posture. "He did used to work here—"

"Irrelevant," said Black. Jackson flinched as though physically hurt by the word. "Kain was in Research. He was never given any information about Guardian protocols. *Especially* during a siege."

They said nothing in response.

"Are you suggesting," said Black, taking a step toward them; she could see them fighting to hold their ground, "that someone within the Society has given him information on our procedures?"

Again, silence.

She closed her eyes, fighting to regain composure. She needed to find her calm, to reign in the fierce darkness that wafted off her, threatening to engulf those around her. Her rage hindered her perception, made her blind to any signals she might have normally picked up on with her heightened Tenebrae senses.

"Go see Dylan." Dylan Meyer was the Head of the Eyes division. He oversaw both the Seekers and the Trackers. "Take what other Guardians aren't already out looking. Coordinate with him. *Find the hyden.*"

The six of them filed out of her office, heads bowed, silent.

Once the door clicked shut, Black turned to Glover.

"As if there wasn't already enough work to do."

"It may not be as bad as it seems," he said, his deep voice reassuring. He was as tall as she was, and seemed to be unaffected by her presence, unlike most humans. While they never did it consciously, they all seemed to shrink away from her, whether or not she was angry. The Tenebrae, it was true, were not the most unassuming in the nymph family.

"Explain."

"We've already had eight Guardians out looking for the first four hyden to be taken. Four more working with our Eyes trying to find out any additional intel on where Kain could possibly be hiding them. They've been working for months. Now we've added six more to that pool and they're not starting from scratch."

Black ran her tongue over her teeth, thinking about his words. She was still angry. Angry at her Guardians for letting this happen. Angry at Kain for causing it. But most of all, she was angry with herself. She could yell at Guardians and at Glover and at anyone else until she was out of breath, but as the Head of the White Mask Society, she was the one responsible. And she would always be remembered for having failed to protect the hyden from a psychopath that *she* had hired in the first place.

"What makes you think they'll find them now, after all this time?"

"Determination," said Glover.

She raised an eyebrow. "Are these Guardians more determined? Is there something I don't know?" She meant it mostly in jest - though she had never had much of a sense of humor - but the look on Glover's face told her she had inadvertently stumbled onto something. "I see."

Glover was as ever inscrutable, but the fact that he did not elaborate was enough to give him away.

"Who?" Which one of her Guardians had broken a cardinal rule? Which one had somehow developed a personal relationship and with which hydan?

He pursed his lips. He would not answer. Whom was he protecting?

But she didn't have the time for this nonsense gossip. She would deal with it when the time came. She had several other cases to attend to.

For now, perhaps it would behoove them to have a lovestruck Guardian.

Seeing a Tenebrae be as angry as they had just seen Black was hopefully something Robin would only experience once in his life. He had never seen anything like it and hoped he never would again. Based on everyone else's expressions, he was not alone.

"That was fun," he said with a small laugh as they filed into the elevator to head down to the Eyes eleven floors below them. No one else laughed. Nayla's shoulder was pressed against his, but she was determinedly looking forward.

"What makes her think that we'll be able to find where Kain has taken the hyden?" said Guy, Emmanuelle's bearded Guardian. He wasn't looking at anyone either. He might have been talking to himself if not for the fact that he was crammed in an elevator with five other people. "He's had four of them for months and no one has been able to get even a glimmer of information."

"Did we get anything from the Shadow Men? The ones who got left behind?" asked Carter.

"They're dead," said Jack, Emmanuelle's other Guardian, the fauna nymph.

Robin had barely had time to recover after the attack. He had been knocked out by the Shadow Men holding him when Yara was taken and woke up in the medical ward. As soon as he had been cleared, he was summoned to Black's office with the rest of them. "How many were killed?" he asked, not sure if he wanted to hear the answer. He knew he was responsible for at least two.

Two more to add to his short list.

Two more faces he would never forget.

"Twelve of theirs. Four of ours." It was Erik who spoke. Robin looked at him out of the corner of his eye. He looked worse than any of them. There was a huge bandage along the side of his face and a dark bruise around his neck. But more than that, he looked drained of life. His shoulders were slumped forward, his eyes unfocused and heavy. Robin wanted to help. Wanted to reach out and tell him it would be OK. But he couldn't bring himself to.

Nayla shifted next to him and he tore his eyes away from Erik, looking back at the elevator doors in front of him.

They opened onto a floor Robin rarely visited. It looked more like a traditional office building than any other floor at Headquarters. A hall filled with cubicles and glassed-in conference rooms which were currently abuzz with activity. The Eyes consisted of both Trackers and Seekers. Robin didn't know much about their operation. He didn't even fully understand how their jobs were different from one another, but it wasn't his responsibility to know. The Society may have been about cooperation among all Deviants and humans, but there was surprisingly little overlap between its own divisions. None of them truly knew where to go from there, but fortunately someone was ready for them.

Robin recognized her. Rice was her name. Something Rice. It started with a J... James. That was it. She was the Head Seeker, dressed in an elegant black pantsuit with a white mask on the lapel.

She nodded in greeting. "Mr. Meyer is coordinating our next moves and will see you all in a few moments if you want to wait over here." She gestured to a small area that looked like a kind of breakroom. Two tables with a few chairs, a small kitchenette, a couple of plants for color, and someone in a Tracker uniform eating oatmeal with one hand while working frantically on a tablet with the other.

Robin moved to sit with the other Guardians, but Nayla held him back.

"Can I talk to you for a second?"

He nodded and followed her a few paces away from the others.

"What's up?"

"I just want to make sure you're OK."

He wanted to laugh. To brush off her words. "Are you OK?" was not a question he often took seriously. But he kept seeing Yara's face, not only when she'd had a panic attack in the hall, but also the fear in her eyes when she saw Kain in person. He felt sick. "Why? Are you?"

"You know why I'm asking," she said. "*I'm* not in love with Emmanuelle."

"You could do worse."

"Stop that."

"What do you want me to say, N?" He ran a hand through his hair, trying to find words that would get him out of this conversation. "I want to find her. And I'm sure you want to find Emmanuelle. We all want this over."

Nayla didn't look away from him. He tried not to avoid making eye contact with her too much, knowing it was a sign of weakness.

How stupid to be worrying about showing weakness to a woman he had once loved. Nayla knew more about him than anyone else did and now he wanted to hide everything from her.

"OK," she said simply, and walked toward the others, leaving him with a strange feeling of guilt he couldn't understand.

Yara didn't know how long she sat there. She had never been a good judge of that, and without a window of any kind, the only thing she had to indicate the passage of time was her own hunger. She'd never ended up having dinner before Kain captured her, and it wasn't long before the numbness gave way to the gnawing pain in her stomach. While she and Aunt Catherine may have lived paycheck to paycheck, they had been lucky enough to never go hungry. For all she knew, at this point it was likely already Thanksgiving.

The thought of sleep was laughable. A lumpy cot, a stained pillow, one ratty blanket, and no food. She tried to focus on anything other than her empty stomach. Eventually she thought she might have drifted off, but woke up abruptly, her neck cramping from having been resting at a strange angle, her lips cracked from thirst.

Hours passed - it could have been days, and Yara would not have known - before the oppressive silence of her cell was broken.

Bolts on the outside of the massive door locking her in clanked loudly and the door slid heavily open, revealing Kain, dressed exactly like his Shadow Men.

He looked different than she remembered. For one, he wasn't limping and he didn't have his cane. Had it all been an act? Like an opossum playing dead? Not only that, but the scar on his face was gone. Rather than the curve from his eye to his jaw, there was a very neat letter "P" on his neck. It almost looked like a brand, not the slippery texture of a scar, but rather an indent in his skin, still red and brown. His eyes were different as well. When Kain had looked at her before, there was a madness and a hunger. Now, she detected nothing inside. Perhaps it was the light, or maybe she was imagining it…

He didn't speak as he approached her. She didn't have the energy to try to fight back, so she let him grab her arm and yank her to her feet. She clutched desperately at the blanket, but he tore it from her and tossed it on the ground before pulling her out of the cell.

She tried to cover herself up, humiliated by her near nakedness, but Kain showed absolutely no interest in looking at or touching her, other than the painful grip he held on her arm.

They began to walk down the hallway outside of her cell. It looked similar to where she had just been in that it was bare, cement, and windowless. Perhaps this place was underground as well, just like Headquarters.

It was a winding maze of identical corridors. They passed a few doors, but didn't stop at any of them. She wanted to ask him where they were going. Where they *were*. What he was going to do to her. She wanted to ask if her Guardians were still alive. But she was afraid of the answers to any of those questions, and her mouth was so dry she doubted she could have spoken even if she wanted to.

The door he took her to was not quite as threatening.

In fact, it was not unlike the doors she had seen at the Society in the medical wards. Without hesitation, Kain took her inside.

"Sir," he said.

Yara frowned up at him. If Kain wasn't in charge, whom would he be addressing in this way? Was there someone else? Someone more dangerous?

But the person he spoke to turned around and—

Kain. The real one. The Kain with the wild eyes and the slippery scar and the mangled leg.

She looked back at the man holding her, her eyes wide searching for any other differences... he had to be a brother. Or a twin! There couldn't be two of them...

"You can go," said the real Kain to the other.

He turned and left. Without him there holding her up, Yara staggered under her own weight. She grabbed the wall behind her for purchase, not wanting to fall in front of Kain, thinking it would somehow make her more vulnerable than she already was. She swallowed hard, wanting to speak, to say something - *anything* - to make her seem like more than a defenseless teenager in her underwear. But she could not.

Kain grinned, his skin tugging at his scar.

"We're going to have some fun, aren't we, Miss Rivers?"

CHAPTER THIRTY-TWO
Captured

Kain had decided to only call on one Shadow Man to bring the seer to his laboratory. She was not only the smallest hydan in his possession, but after having spent 18 hours alone in her cell she would not pose much of a physical challenge.

Phosphorous, his favourite Shadow Man (obviously) had brought her and she looked even more pathetic than he'd expected.

"Yara Rivers," he said to her, beginning to undo the restraints on his exam table, his cane leaning up against it as he kept all his weight on his left leg. "Born to human mother, Sierra, and hydan father, Theodore. 17 years old. Skilled - as was Theo - in the gift of divination. I use the word 'skilled'," he added, turning to her, "for lack of a better term."

A crease appeared between her eyes. It was hard to tell if it was from fear or contempt.

He gestured to the table. "Go ahead and lie down."

She didn't move.

"Either you come lie down on the table," he said jocularly, "or I put you there."

He gave her a moment, and she finally began to step forward. He could see her trembling. What a pointless response to fear, trembling. The hyden were evidently not so much more evolved than he was.

She gasped slightly at the cold metal when she pulled herself onto the table. Another pointless reaction. His Shadow Men perhaps weren't great conversationalists, but at least he was never irritated by any of their stupid reflexes. They didn't have any.

"All the way down," he said when she hesitated. She flinched as she followed his instructions, her skin prickly from the cold. "Good girl. Now, where was I."

He began to fold the metal restraints, securing her to the table as he spoke. His left leg was starting to shake from the weight of holding him up. "I took what information I could get about your father from the Society," two restraints over the wrists, "evidently he had quite a hard time learning to use his ability," two over the ankles, "but it seems that his hard work before you made it easier for you to learn to control yours. At least, that's what Ms. Black seems to think—" one more over both thighs, "Now, now, Yara Rivers. Don't cry. It's pointless and you'll only dehydrate faster," and the largest one over her sternum. He left the head restraint undone for the moment.

"Every single one of you have all been so scared, but you don't seem to understand," said Kain. He leaned over so that his head was directly above the seer's, finally clutching his cane. "I need you. All of you. So why would I hurt you?

"Together, we will remake the world."

"The whole point of this," said Catherine, "the whole point of coming here, of putting our lives on hold, was to avoid this."

Carter had gone to her quarters in order to try to fill her in on the situation. Now she sat on the edge of one of the armchairs in the sitting area, Carter on the coffee table in front of her. She would not look at them. Her skin was pale with heavy, dark bags under her eyes. She wasn't crying. Hadn't cried, as far as Carter knew. Catherine resembled more a shell of a person than an actual person. Her voice was so quiet they had to lean in to make sure they heard what she said.

But finding a response was the true challenge.

Yes, all this felt pointless to them, too. Putting Yara and her aunt through this had ended up being fruitless. Kain had won in the end.

No. Kain had won a *battle*. This battle. But the war was not over.

"We're doing everything we can," they said. They reached out and held Catherine's hand gently. She did not resist, but her hand stayed limp in theirs. "Kain had resources we couldn't— didn't anticipate."

"How."

Carter didn't know how to answer that. As involved as Catherine may have been with Yara's case in particular, it did not give her clearance to know everything. Including the new alarming suspicion that there was a mole within their ranks.

"We don't know."

Catherine said nothing. Her eyes were unfocused, her body still. Carter almost wished she were crying or screaming. Anything other than this would have been easier to handle. They just didn't know how to help someone who looked so lost.

Carter let them both sit in the silence for a while. But they couldn't stay forever. Carter had work to do. They had left Robin and Erik with the Eyes for the time being, knowing that they were the best person for the job to break the news to Catherine.

"I want to know what's happening," she said eventually.

Carter looked up. She was still staring aimlessly at the spot where the wall met the floor behind them. Her face was so still that Carter would have believed that she hadn't even spoken and they had just imagined hearing the words.

"We'll try to keep you as informed as possible—"

"No," she said. She brought her eyes up to meet Carter's. "I don't want to be given the PG version. I want to know what's happening."

Carter licked their lower lip, considering her words. "There are… regulations against informing civilians—"

"I don't care." She didn't raised her voice. She didn't need to. "You tell me what's happening."

Carter took a deep breath, rubbing the back of their neck. They had been fighting a tension headache since being chewed out by Black and this was not helping. "The truth is, Catherine, that we don't know very much. And telling you anything would just put you in danger." It was a cookie cutter response, and it was clear that she could tell.

"If I were in any danger, I'd already be dead. This Kain person has what he wants already. My daughter."

Carter had never heard Catherine refer to Yara as her daughter before. She wielded the word like a weapon, knowing the weight it would carry. But she had a point. Catherine was not on Kain's radar. And it was unclear how keeping her apprised would jeopardize anything any more than it already was, including hers and Yara's lives.

"We're trying to find where Kain is keeping the hyden," said Carter, unable to keep looking at her. "We already know they're somewhere in the city. Our Guardians, including Emmanuelle - who was also captured - are all equipped with tracking devices so we were able to follow hers for a little while, but he's disabled it and we lost the trail. So we're still trying to find the exact location."

"How did he get in." Her voice was still flat, though she seemed to be zeroed in on their words.

"That we don't know. And that's the truth," they added.

"What is he doing with her. Why is he doing this."

"We can only guess."

"Then guess."

Carter sighed. At this point, they were speculating about Kain's true motivation. The Society had theories - one in particular - but nothing had been confirmed. They weighed the options. Telling her could make things worse. She might panic. But it would be less likely to make things any better, so they opted for the lie.

"I'm sorry, Catherine. I really don't know."

Despite having felt like she had exhausted her body's supply of fear, it turned out there was still a secret reserve deep inside her. There seemed to be nothing off limits with this man. No part of her felt safe. Anything could happen and she had no idea what to expect.

The lab she had been brought to was not unlike the medical ward at Headquarters where she had been treated. But instead of the elegant white and glass walls of the Society, this room had walls of cement, just like everywhere else she had seen in this place. But little of the walls were visible through all the equipment that had been placed throughout the room. There were shelves filled with labeled jars of all shapes and sizes, some of them containing what looked like blood. There were several touch screens hanging on the walls showing things she might have seen in her chem class at school though much more complex. And surrounding the entire perimeter of the room were metal cabinets with all sorts of paraphernalia scattered along the surfaces. Kain was busying himself with taking things from inside the cabinets and pulling some of the labeled jars from the higher shelves. She couldn't see most of what he was doing since he kept going behind her.

There was no hope of trying to induce a vision under the circumstances either. What remaining body heat she had left had leeched into the exam table she lay on, her skin shrinking away from the cold restraints he'd closed over her. She tried to take steadying breaths through her nose, remembering how Robin had led her through her panic attack before the alarms went off, but now it did little to calm her.

Kain had not stopped speaking since she had been brought here by his inexplicable doppelgänger, though she had stopped listening, his voice intercut with the soft sound of his cane as he moved around the room. At first she tried to follow along with what he said, hoping to glean any idea of what she was in for. But he spoke quickly, used words she didn't know, mumbled, and was often not facing her as he prepared whatever horrors awaited her.

He brought a metal tray on wheels closer to her and she felt another wave of terror wash over her when she saw the surface had five needles neatly arranged on a clean towel.

"—so that's what the paralytic is for," she heard him say, his voice coming back into focus. He picked up the first needle and tapped the syringe lightly, squeezing a few drops out of the tip. Then he picked up a small alcohol wipe and rubbed the nape of her neck. For the first time, she began to struggle. It was an uncontrollable reflex. She knew it would amount to nothing, but her body and her mind were not in sync. The metal restraints, however, had no give, and all she succeeded in doing was hurting herself.

Kain's hand came down on her head, pressing it into the table, keeping her still long enough to inject her with whatever was in the needle.

Paralytic indeed.

At first, it burned. She let out a garbled scream of pain and fear through clenched teeth, but the burning dissipated quickly. It took only seconds before she felt her body completely deaden. It was the same sensation as having her mouth numbed at the dentist, only it spread everywhere. As though she were no longer there. A brain floating in space. The cold vanished, but the fear remained.

"Good girl," Kain said for the second time, and she felt a well of hatred pooling inside of her.

How Kain had the energy to keep at it as long as he did, Yara didn't know. She might have fallen asleep from exhaustion if her palpable terror hadn't kept her awake.

After the paralytic injection, he had unstrapped her, which somehow had made her feel worse. The knowledge that she wasn't physically restrained made her hate herself, wanting so badly to just get up and walk away. Swipe his cane out from under him, beat him senseless with it, and make a run for it. It was pointless to think that way, though. After all, she *was* physically restrained. It was just a prison inside her body rather than outside.

He spent hours happily alternating between humming and speaking - it was impossible to tell if he was speaking to himself or to her. At one point he had attached sensors to her temples. She couldn't see what the wires were connected to, unable to turn her head or even move her eyes. The only movement she could do was blink, and while it was hard to tell with her body deadened of all sensation, her vision was blurred with what she assumed were tears.

When he gave her a second injection, also in her neck, she couldn't feel it at all. Shortly after, he placed a machine over her head blocking out any view she'd had. It was loud, but she could still hear him, humming and speaking, the soft thuds of his cane as he walked, and the blips and beeps of his equipment.

Hours later and he gave her the last of five injections. Her sensation began to come back, prickly and bordering on painful. Her body was stiff, the cold came back with a vengeance, and bruises were forming where she had struggled against the restraints which were once again fastened over her. She didn't notice Kain had left til she heard the door close behind him, followed by the absence of his voice and his gait. She tried to lift her head to see, but she was still heavy from the drugs he had used. Whatever he had injected into her, she did not know. There had been five needles with five syringes, and they all lay empty on the tray beside her.

She had a sudden urge to be sick. Barely able to turn her head, she managed to throw up to the side, though much of it still got all over her shoulder. Fortunately, without having had food in what had to be over a day, it was mostly bile.

A wave of self pity and disgust overcame her.

How long would she be left here, alone? Would Kain come back? Or would she be taken back to her cell? Would they feed her? Or would they let her starve?

She tried flexing her fingers and gasped with pain at a sharp stab in her left arm. She tried to see what it was and noticed an IV port had been inserted below her elbow. Nothing was feeding into it. It had a cap, and was otherwise taped down. She had never felt him insert it. Did he mean to leave it there?

Eventually, two people came to get her. One man and one woman. The man looked dumb. Yara could think of no other word to describe him. He had a low brow that hung heavily over his dead eyes and a thick-lipped mouth that hung slightly open. He had the same kind of brand on his neck as the Kain doppelgänger, only his read "Pb". The woman was solidly built. Her head was shaved, but Yara could see a shadow of growth which suggested she had black hair. She had sharply angled and hooded eyes as well as a brand on her neck. Hers read "Th". And just like every other Shadow Man she had seen, they both had that same empty gaze. Nothing was behind their eyes. Was Kain drugging them? She couldn't think of another explanation. But Yara didn't have the strength to wonder what any of it meant.

They wiped the bile from her shoulder using a strong smelling alcohol wipe - apparently unbothered by any of it - unstrapped her, and hoisted her up by the armpits. The two of them had to half-carry-half-drag Yara back to her cell. She wanted to walk, to be able to hold herself upright. But whether it was the paralytic still wearing off or just having been weakened from her experience she was unable to carry any of her weight. After a point, she stopped trying and let her feet drag on the floor. She knew her skin was getting scraped and torn by the rough cement, but it wasn't yet as painful as she knew it would be (the feeling was still only just creeping back into her body). She couldn't bring herself to care.

They dumped her in her cell which was just as barren and sad as it had been before. She collapsed on the floor and listened to the door lock behind the Shadow Men.

Silence.

She was trembling.

She thought of Aunt Catherine. How worried she must be. If Yara died here, Aunt Catherine would have lost her entire family. And Yara never even said goodbye. Erik. His beautiful green eyes and the way he looked at her like she was the only person in the world. The feel of his lips. His hands in her hair. Would she ever feel such joys again? Or would this cell and that laboratory be her entire life now? Carter. Comforting. Calming. Wise beyond their years. She had barely gotten to know Carter and now she might never see them again. And Robin. Was he angry with her for having kept this all a secret? Or was he too busy trying to find a way to get her back? Assuming, of course, that any of them were still alive. That Kain hadn't completely eviscerated the entire White Mask Society in his quest to apprehend her.

Oh god.

What had she done?

CHAPTER THIRTY-THREE

Pointless

Pointless.

On Thanksgiving Day, Erik obediently sat at the long tables in the Eyes division, surrounded by a flurry of quiet activity and hushed voices. Trackers, Seekers, and Guardians were all murmuring to each other various ideas and plans for retrieving the hyden.

Useless.

He said nothing. He had nothing to contribute. He watched as Robin and Carter, both looking very serious, tapped a screen held by a Tracker named George. But there was no point in any of it.

Incompetent.

These people, this entire division, had been searching for months already and to no avail. If they hadn't found where Kain was hiding yet then they never would.

How could they be expected to succeed at all if Kain had as many resources as they believed, not to mention an army of Shadow Men? An army he was keeping in the middle of a crowded urban city that they were still - somehow - unable to find. Sure, Los Angeles was big, but there were only so many places they could be. And if Kain really did have someone working for him from within the Society…

Pointless. Useless. Incompetent.

Erik had always had faith in the White Mask Society. He had seen them do countless things that helped the Deviant community. Aid extended to injured nymphs, centers built to help unhoused shape shifters, humans imprisoned for hate crimes against them. But after Yara had been taken, that faith was wavering drastically. Did they deserve his faith? If the Society couldn't keep one girl safe, what *could* they do? If Erik were only allowed to go on his own perhaps he would be able to get *something* done, rather than waiting here as useless as the rest of them, sitting at a desk like he was a schoolboy.

"What do you think?"

"Hmm?"

He looked up to find Carter, Robin, and George looking at him expectantly.

"I said, 'what do you think'?" repeated Carter.

Erik tried to look as though he were considering their words rather than floundering in confusion, having not heard a single word they had said in the last hour.

Evidently, Carter could tell that he was struggling and offered, "About George's plan to inform the civilian law enforcement?"

"If we can get them to put out an APB on Kain, maybe we can get information from civilians," said George, who had also cottoned on to Erik not having been paying attention.

"APB?"

"It's an emergency broadcasting system used by the human police to alert the public of wanted suspects."

"Why the hell haven't we already done that?"

"It's not exactly easy," said George, sounding defensive. "It requires getting the PR team to contact the police, then we have to disclose a certain amount of information in order to convince them that it's a significant enough threat to the civilian population, not just Deviants."

Bureaucratic nonsense.

"But Kain hasn't made any indications that he's threatening civilians," said Robin.

"No, not yet."

Not yet. Not yet. Not yet.

Not knowing what Kain was up to, why he wanted Yara, what he was doing to her, was torturous. Erik imagined the worst, often having to snap out of horrific scenes in his mind of her body being mutilated, trying to convince himself instead that she was still alive.

Still alive. Still alive. Still alive.

Please let her be still alive.

The three of them continued to speak, offering their idea to a few others around them. Erik didn't need to listen to their words in order to understand there was a general consensus that they would propose the plan to Black for her approval before moving forward with it. Of course, then it would need to be taken to the Society's Head of Human Public Relations. So much bureaucratic red tape. This was one aspect of the Society he could do without.

There was a buzzing under Erik's skin. An impatient energy desperate to hit the streets himself, to try to find her. These people were slow, they played by the rules, and they accomplished nothing. God only knew what Kain had already done by now. What more he would do before they found him.

Erik could not wait.

Together, we will remake the world.

The words Kain had said to Yara rang in her mind. She wasn't sure why, but they stuck there like a song she didn't know all the lyrics to, spinning around her brain.

She didn't know what time it was. Time had no meaning. It was simultaneously stagnant and never ending. It might have been noon, or just as likely it was the middle of the night. None of it mattered, because when she wasn't in the lab, she was in her cell, huddled in her worn blanket on the wafer thin mattress which she had dragged underneath the protruding slab that was meant to be her bed.

Together, we will remake the world.

Those were the exact words Kain had said. He wanted to remake the world.

And suddenly she remembered, a lifetime ago, sitting in her quarters at the Society with Robin, when he had promised to tell her about the secret Omega Project. What had Robin said?

She heard his voice, warm and calm, like a dream. *If humans could have the same talents as Deviants, then maybe we wouldn't have to hide.* He had said the worlds could come together, human and Deviant. He had called it "a utopian dream".

When Yara had asked him if that's why Kain was after her, Robin had lied. He said he didn't know. But he had known.

And now Yara knew.

Together, we will remake the world.

Periodically, Yara would open her eyes, expecting to see something different as though she had dreamt this whole ordeal, convinced that it wasn't real. How could it possibly be? Things like this didn't happen in real life, and certainly not to people as ordinary as her.

But, she supposed, despite how she felt, she was not ordinary. And that was the problem.

Things like this *didn't* happen to ordinary people.

And every time she opened her eyes, she found herself still in the same oppressive environment.

If she thought the Society was quiet, it was nothing compared to here. Somehow the walls absorbed even the sound of her own breath, giving her the feeling of being buried alive, a sense she never had at Headquarters despite being underground.

But every day or so she would be fetched by the Kain doppelgänger, strapped down to the metal table in Kain's laboratory, injected with the paralytic, tested on for several hours, given the antidote to the paralytic, then brought back by the shaved-headed woman and the dumb looking man. The only person who ever spoke was Kain. His Shadow Men were always silent, always stoic, and always unsympathetic to her plight.

She wondered during the long hours in her cell where the other hyden were. She had seen no one else here. But she knew it was likely that when Kain had broken into Headquarters, he had also gotten his hands on Emmanuelle Moreau.

Lucky Kain. Two hyden with one blow.

But who were the others? Yara realized she didn't even know their names. Aside from Janya Varma. Janya whose capture she had seen before she fully appreciated the danger she was facing. Janya whom she had never actually met, but whose face she could not forget. Was she here? Was Emmanuelle? Were the others? And what were their abilities? If Yara's theory that Kain was trying to use his research from the Omega Project to take their abilities was correct, they would make him stronger than ever. Would he even be able to be defeated if he managed to do what he had set out to do? If he had the abilities of six hyden, he would become superhuman…

But her thoughts most frequently strayed back to the four people she had been torn from at Headquarters.

Poor Aunt Catherine. Now with Yara gone, would they send her back home, back to work? Or would she still be at the Society until this whole thing was over? Surely she was no longer in danger. Yara didn't have many memories of Aunt Catherine after the deaths of Yara's parents. She had been too young to remember much. But there was one image she had never let go of. It was hazy. Yara couldn't even say with any certainty that it was real and not just a warped amalgam of different memories.

Five-year-old-Yara had built a fort out of cardboard boxes. In her memory they were blue, though where they could have gotten blue boxes she didn't know. She was talking to herself, making quiet noises. Aunt Catherine was sitting on the sofa watching TV and crying silently. Yara remembered that, in her curiosity, she had stopped talking to herself in order to observe this strange behavior. These silent tears. Yara didn't cry silently. It was not in a child's nature to suffer in silence. If she was crying it meant something was wrong, and if something was wrong, it was the job of a grown up to fix it. But Aunt Catherine had her eyes glued to the television, her cheeks glossy as a constant stream of tears fell from her eyes. When she had noticed that Yara was no longer making any noise, she glanced over, but Yara turned away quickly and continued to play.

If any of the memory was genuine it was hard to know which part. But Yara thought of it frequently over the years. She never thought of the death of her mother being a loss that affected Aunt Catherine like it had affected Yara. But her aunt had lost her sister, a pain Yara could not imagine.

And now Aunt Catherine had lost her last connection to Sierra Tanner.

"We're going to try something a little different today," said Kain.

Yara could not move. She had learned to fight the claustrophobia that accompanied the drug Kain routinely injected her with. It took all of her concentration, so having to focus on Kain's words made her panic a little.

He moved the machine that usually surrounded her head, blocking her vision, and replaced the view with his own face. Unable to turn her head or move her eyes she could not look away.

"You're going to have a vision for me."

Oh am I, she thought bitterly to herself. Her body was vibrating with hatred. His condescending nature, his demands, his joy at her pain. Every single part of him filled her with revulsion. For the first time since being in his custody, she wanted to say something. To spit at him and tell him that even if she knew how she would not cooperate. At least, she wanted that to be true. But if it came down to it, she didn't know if she'd have the courage to resist. She was afraid. Afraid of pain, afraid of death, afraid of anything he might do to her.

"Don't give me that look," he said, tapping her nose lightly. (What look he was referring to she didn't know since the drugs made it impossible for her to so much as raise an eyebrow.) "I know that Bora Black was teaching you to control your visions. I know," he whispered gleefully, "what you're capable of, Yara Rivers."

She closed her eyes, the only respite she was allowed from his presence.

Thud, thud, thud. "It'll be fun!" His voice was farther away, so she chanced opening her eyes and sure enough he was back to puttering around with his equipment. "Would you like the bad news or the good news first? I'll give you the bad news. The bad news is that I can't sedate you." He turned back toward her. "The good news is that this is going to be a lot of fun. For me," he added, then laughed.

Despite herself, despite the numbness that had been settling in over her confinement, she felt herself cry. She could recognize it when it happened now, even with her body devoid of all sensation. She hated herself for it. She didn't want to be weak. Didn't want to show Kain how afraid she was. But her body betrayed her cowardice.

She tried to distract herself, as she often did during the long hours in the lab. The usual images of Aunt Catherine and her Guardians came into her head, but then a sudden shock sent those images scurrying back out.

A strangled cry of pain came from her throat.

"Felt that? Good."

Whatever had happened, she couldn't understand how it had hurt her. She had never felt any pain - felt anything at all - under the effects of the paralytic agent. It often took hours after he gave her the antidote before her full sensation returned.

She tried moving, but no, she was still under the drug's effects. So he couldn't have reversed it. Then what had he done?

"Now, let's see about getting a vision out of you."

She wanted to scream at him, "I can't control them!" but she couldn't move her tongue, her jaw, her lips. The feeling of claustrophobia was returning in her frustration and terror. She thought of Robin, her hand on his chest, the rise and fall of his breath. *Inhale liquid gold, exhale red smoke.* But it was no use. She couldn't drown out the sound of Kain's voice.

"The rules are simple. Have a vision, no shock. *But*, no vision..." He didn't need to finish his sentence. She felt the same electrifying spasm. It was short, but it left a shadow of pain.

"So, let's give it a try."

CHAPTER THIRTY-FOUR

Coward

Yara had no strength left in her. When the two Shadow Men came to fetch her to return her to her cell, they carried her entire weight between them, dragging her feet. Her face was swollen from tears, her head pounding distantly, her muscles limp and exhausted.

She had never felt so defeated.

Time had been impossible to track while Kain tried to induce a vision. And what was worse, it had worked. She'd had no control over it, however. It was almost as if her brain went into some self-defense mode and was able to produce a few images she could not even distinguish. It had felt and looked unlike any other vision she'd ever had. Instead of the white fog that usually obstructed the faces and surroundings of the subjects of her premonitions, it was dark and turbulent, roiling as though in the heart of a storm. She could barely make out any of the details. But it ended up not mattering.

Kain had whooped loudly as soon as it had happened and everything faded just as quickly back into the recesses of her mind. Evidently, it had been enough of a victory for him, because that's when he ended their session. But she knew that next time they came for her it would be more of the same.

And she didn't know what outcome she wanted. Should she fight? Try to stop from having visions? Did he want to see the future, log it, and use her as a kind of forecast? Or was he trying to do something else by inducing them? Was it dangerous for her to give in? Because she wanted so badly to give in. If she was being honest with herself, all she wanted to do was practice controlling her visions all night so that the next time he tried she could call upon one immediately and avoid the pain she had endured all day. (Morning? Afternoon? Evening? Was it still even November?)

"Coward," she said out loud. Her voice was raspy from the strangled screams of pain. It was the first time she had spoken a word since being taken away from Headquarters.

Coward.

Coward.

"Coward," she said again. *Let the word change me*, she thought. *Let me be so ashamed by the truth of it that I find the courage to fight back.*

Fight back.

"Fight back."

Carter sat in Black's darkened office. The last time they had been alone with Black, they were being evaluated after their graduation out of initiation. It was not an experience they particularly relished, but after the break-in and the rising suspicions that there was an informant among the ranks of the White Mask Society, everyone now had to be assessed by her. As a Tenebrae, she could function as a virtual lie detector. There was an added measure: Carter was also strapped to a device recording their reactions to each question for further evaluation.

"Have you had any interactions with Ramsey Kain?" said Black, her obsidian eyes locked onto Carter.

"Not beyond the altercation last month. That was my first and only encounter with him."

"Have you had any interactions with his Shadow Men, or any others who associate with Kain?"

"No."

Black scrutinized Carter, her face unreadable. But Carter had nothing to hide.

"Did you have any prior knowledge of Kain's planned siege?"

"I did not."

"Are you aware of any White Mask consorting with Kain or his Shadow Men?"

"I am not."

Black made a note without taking her eyes off Carter, then nodded. "You may go."

"Can I join you?"

Carter stood next to Erik who was, as was often the case these days, reading something on a tablet while absently putting food in his mouth. He glanced up long enough to see who had spoken and nodded.

"Sure."

Carter sat down and took a long drink, keeping their tired amber eyes on Erik. They had just come from their assessment with Black after working for the last 14 hours with the Trackers. They wanted nothing more than to go to bed, but they had one more thing to do. Why did this responsibility always come to them? They had no interest in being the parent to their fellow Guardians, but Erik was so young and Robin could not be trusted to have difficult conversations. And so it fell to Carter.

"I know what you've been doing," they said.

Erik stopped eating and looked up. Carter focused instead on their own food, trying to keep things casual.

"R and I both know."

"What am I doing?"

"The Eyes are trained for this, E. They know what they're doing. We have to trust their process."

Erik put down his fork and tablet and stared at the table. Carter could see a war going on inside his mind: whether to admit he was planning something or continue to play dumb. He eventually opted for the former.

"And look where that's gotten us."

"I know it can be frustrating—"

"Frustrating?" Erik laughed dryly. "Frustrating is your shoe lace becoming untied. This is *incompetence*. Kain has all six of the hyden, C. The hyden *we* were trying to protect. The Society has *failed*. Playing by their rules has *failed*."

"I would watch what you say," said Carter quietly. They did not mean it to sound like a threat. But words like that often found their way to Black and she was not fond of that rhetoric. "The hyden are not our only responsibility. Yes, Kain has bested us. For *now*. Only for *now*. But you grew up here. You should know better than most what the Society does every day for Deviants living among civilians. In the time Kain took the hyden, how many Deviants has the Society helped?"

Erik bit his lip and looked away. Carter sighed heavily and laid a hand on Erik's arm.

"We all want Yara back. We're all worried. But if every White Mask went on a spree, following their own judgement whenever they disagreed with protocol, we'd never get anything done. Our system would collapse. The Society works because of our command structure."

Carter could tell that Erik was not about to say another word. People had a tendency to find it hard to admit when they were wrong. While Erik had a lot of strengths, that was not one of them.

"I'll see you tomorrow morning."

They squeezed Erik's arm one last time and left him alone, hoping that their words had sunk in.

CHAPTER THIRTY-FIVE
New Skills

She didn't know when she had fallen asleep, but Yara woke up with a terrible headache. She hadn't had one so bad since the night she collapsed with Robin after trying to suppress a vision. But in the same way that the visions induced by Kain's cruel methods of persuasion were different from her usual ones, so too was this headache. Rather than the pressure she was accustomed to, this was an echo of pain. Like the soreness that came after exercising.

Later that day in Kain's laboratory, he tried something different. Rather than the painful shocks when she didn't cooperate, he injected her with something else. She was barely able to see him insert the needle into the IV port below her elbow. Another tube was already feeding into the line as well. (She had determined several days ago that it was a nutritional supplement, since they hadn't been feeding her much in terms of solid foods.)

As his finger squeezed the syringe, a strange feeling overcame her. A sort of weightlessness. She felt her muscles - which had been so tense from fear and cold and paralysis - loosen, and while she still couldn't move, it didn't seem to matter quite so much. She would have smiled, had she been able to.

Kain's face appeared above hers. He pulled one of her eyelids up and shined a light into her eye.

It was lovely. Blinding and white, brighter than anything she had seen in days. A star.

But it was gone too quickly and she heard Kain say, as though from a dream, "Excellent."

He continued to talk as he always did, but his words didn't matter.
She could stay here forever.

Let her stay here, like this, forever.

Robin tried not to fidget as he sat in front of Black. (Was fidgeting a sign of guilt? Of course it didn't matter. He had nothing to feel guilty about.) The device recording his reactions was tight and cumbersome. He wanted nothing more than to scratch his nose, but the camera attached to his head and pointing at his face made it impossible.

"Have you had any interactions with Ramsey Kain?"

"Yes. When he infiltrated Headquarters. The night the last hyden were apprehended."

"Have you had any interactions with Ramsey Kain prior to the invasion of HQ?"

"No."

Black made a note, her glossy eyes not moving from his face.

He swallowed.

"Have you had any interactions with his Shadow Men, or any others who associate with Kain?"

"Negative."

"Did you have any prior knowledge of Kain's planned siege?"

Robin hesitated. "…Yes," he said cautiously. "About a five second warning."

"Explain," said Black, her brow furrowing.

"Yara Rivers had a vision. She told me moments before the alarms went off. She was mostly incoherent. She was experiencing a panic attack at the time." He tried not to picture her face as it happened and focused instead on Black and the whirls of darkness surrounding her.

"And are you aware of any White Mask consorting with Kain or his Shadow Men?"

"No, sir."

After a moment, Black said, "You're dismissed."

Another day, another drug.

As it turned out, what Kain was doing was mapping her brain.

The drugs he injected into her IV port enabled him to trace how she responded to different stimuli.

Pain. Fear. Euphoria. Sadness. Anger.

He had a drug for everything, and unfortunately most of them left her feeling sick afterward.

How many days, how many tests he had done, she couldn't know. Time no longer had any meaning. She measured time by the growth of hair under her arms and the weight she lost. Her body no longer looked like her own. Occasionally when she got too filthy, they would leave a sponge and bucket in her cell for her to clean herself with, along with a fresh chest wrap and underwear. But with nothing but dry protein bars and whatever nutrients were administered to her via the IV, she was deteriorating. Her skin, already pale, had become papery and covered with large bruises where the straps held her down to Kain's table, giving her the look of wearing a striped prison uniform.

She sometimes wondered if she hadn't died, and this was all some horrible dream in the moment before oblivion. She had read somewhere that in the moment right before death, a gland in your brain released a hormone which caused a sense of eternal euphoria. Similar things had been described by those who had had near death experiences. But if that were the case, why was her brain making her live here in hell? So she had to still be alive. Unless, of course, she really *was* in hell.

It had been longer than usual before she was fetched by Kain's doppelgänger, but when he finally brought her back to his lab, Kain looked happier than she had ever seen him.

"We're going to see the future today, Yara Rivers!" he said, limping toward the examination table as she was strapped to the frigid surface by his Shadow Man.

She watched miserably as the paralytic traveled into her arm and the familiar heaviness settled in on her.

Deep breaths. Inhale gold. Exhale red.

"I have found your trigger! Isn't that exciting?"

It didn't sound particularly exciting to Yara.

"See this?" Kain held up a syringe filled with a viscous liquid, opaque and white. She didn't need to know what was in it to know she didn't want him injecting it into her bloodstream. "This is what's going to activate that special part of your brain that lets you see the future! But I haven't even told you the most exciting part." He walked out of her line of sight (*thud, thud, thud*), but didn't stop talking. "I have been developing an enhancement of my own. That's the advantage of having other hyden at my disposal.

"This hydan," said Kain, flicking the syringe, "is named Roberto, but his friends call him Bobby. Lovely man. Wouldn't hurt a butterfly.

And boy, does he have a useful skill. More useful than yours? I couldn't say."

When Kain returned, he was carrying another syringe. He lay the opaque white one on the rolling tray next to her, and held up the other for her to inspect. It was clear, though perhaps with a slightly yellowed tinge, not unlike the stains on the pillow back in her cell.

"Oh, don't worry. This one's for me." He leaned his cane against the table, his weight on his left leg, and rolled up the sleeve of his button down shirt. He tapped the needle before inserting it into the crook of his arm. She closed her eyes. She had never liked needles. For that matter she had never liked Kain, and given the choice, she'd rather not look at either.

When she opened them back up she saw him, needle still in arm, face toward the ceiling, the veins on his neck distended and strained. It didn't look as though he was breathing at all, his chest completely still.

Please let him die, she thought to herself. *Please let something have gone wrong...*

But then he took a great shuddering breath and looked at her, his murky eyes wide and crazed, so unlike his Shadow Men.

"Nope. Not dead," he said. And grinned.

CHAPTER THIRTY-SIX

Something to Fear

Enough people had gone through Black's assessments by now that Erik had a relatively good idea what to expect. That did not make him feel any more comfortable as he sat in front of her, a camera in his face and a heart monitor strapped around his chest. While he knew nothing of a mole, Erik did have something to hide from Black. He could only hope that he would be able to avert her talents at detecting lies.

"Have you had any interactions with Ramsey Kain?" Her voice was flat. No doubt she had asked the question a million and a half times by now.

"Just during the invasion."

"Have you had any interactions with his Shadow Men, or any others who associate with Kain?"

Erik shook his head.

"Please respond verbally."

"No, I have not."

"Did you have any prior knowledge of Kain's planned siege?"

"Absolutely not."

"Are you aware of any White Mask consorting with Kain or his Shadow Men?"

"No."

Black stared at him. It was evident from the intensity of her gaze that she knew Erik was hiding *something*, but he had not lied. If she didn't ask the right questions, he didn't *need* to lie. He tried not to think about his plans to search for Yara, to bring her back, afraid that his thoughts might be read on his face. Instead he focused on Black.

Those black orbs that were her eyes, the dark smoke that wafted off of her in delicate coils, the way she sat so impossibly still. They stayed in silence for several minutes. Erik was careful not to be the one to break it.

It felt like an eternity, but at last, Black said, "Very well. You're dismissed."

That horrible smile stretched Kain's face, contorting it, his scar pulling his mouth into a frightening grimace.

"Be careful what you think, Yara Rivers," he said, tapping his temple with one of his skeletal fingers. "You can thank Roberto Diaz for that. What's that?" He tilted his head, as though straining to hear something, though the only sounds in the room were the usual beeps and hums of his machines. "Yes! Yes, you're right. I can hear your thoughts. No, you're not imagining it. See, Roberto has the very impressive skill of reading people's minds. He was a tough nut to crack, that much is certain. But I discovered how he uses his ability and now... Well now, dear Yara. Now it's distilled. Bottled. And ready for use. Impressive, no? Ah, yes. Yes, that is why I've been searching for you, hydan. You've figured it out at last."

Yara squeezed her eyes shut, the feeling of claustrophobia returning in full force. She was trapped in her body, and now even her mind wasn't safe.

"To think, for so long you Deviants have hoarded your abilities from us humans, looking down on us. But now, at last, your power is mine!"

Inhale liquid gold! Exhale red smoke!

She could hear Kain laughing.

"What an unusual technique you have," he said.

She began to cry of frustration and anger. How unfair. The only solace she'd had here under Kain's control were her thoughts. And now she had nothing. He had taken every single part of her.

"Well, aren't you feeling sorry for yourself," he said. "How incredibly privileged." His tone turned angry, the amusement suddenly gone as quickly as turning off a light. "You have no idea what you've been given. You have no idea what the world is like for a mere *human*." He slammed his cane on the ground as he said the word. "No idea the mediocrity we have to endure while watching you Deviants with your god given gifts, unaware of the power you hold! But no more.

"However," he said, his voice back to normal, "we have other things to press on to."

She opened her eyes long enough to watch him empty the contents of the second syringe into her IV line. What horrors awaited her with this drug? Kain said it would trigger a vision, but how long would it take? What horrible side effects would it give her?

At least one of her questions was answered right away. No sooner had he emptied the syringe than she felt a painful throb in her mind. It was strangely welcome in its familiarity. Instinctively, she tried to fight it. If Kain could read her mind, he would see whatever she could. But then she remembered how dangerous it was to suppress a vision, and knew that suppressing a drug induced one might be even that much more dangerous. So she let herself fall into it, very aware that Kain was there in her brain, right alongside her.

The white fog settled in, almost comforting by comparison to the storm that had obstructed the visions Kain had been inducing. She thought about letting the fog stay, of making no effort to clear it to get a better view of the future. Let Kain see nothing, let him dismiss her ability and leave her alone. Perhaps he would. She tried to push the thoughts from her mind, remembering that he was no doubt aware of everything that went through it.

But then something caught her attention from behind the fog. Something that made her desperate to know what was beyond it.

A flash of green eyes, too green to be human.

Erik.

She exhaled, clearing the fog, though in her excitement she was doing a lousy job of it. It didn't take long, however, for her to know that something was wrong. More than anything she saw, it was a feeling in her gut. But as the mist cleared around him, she saw that Erik was ragged, worn, exhausted, beaten. His face was bloodied, his clothes torn, his hair matted. His fitted Guardian uniform was barely recognizable in the state it was in.

Exhale. Exhale. *Exhale.*

She tried to get a clearer image.

Let me see more! she thought frantically, forgetting momentarily that Kain was watching it all unfold in his own mind.

She could feel the pressure in her head releasing as the videtonin stopped being produced, the swelling going back down, and knew that this meant she was about to lose the vision. She tried to cling to it desperately, at least long enough to see where he was.

In the moment before it all disappeared into nothingness, she saw that Erik, bedraggled on the ground, was approached by two hulking figures dressed in crimson.

Shadow Men.

She gasped, her eyes flying open, as the dregs of the vision faded into the void.

Her eyes met Kain, and while she felt nothing but fear, he was smiling victoriously, because they both knew what they had seen.

Kain and his Shadow Men were going to capture Erik.

CHAPTER THIRTY-SEVEN

[In]evitable

Yara screamed in anger the whole time she was dragged back to her cell. She begged over her shoulder, hoping that wherever Kain was he could hear her pleas.

But it was useless. She screamed herself hoarse and was thrown back into her cell just the same as always. But instead of falling to the ground, she managed to stay upright and launched herself at her cell door just as it slammed shut in her face.

"No!" she screamed, banging on the hard surface. "Please! Please don't hurt him!"

She heard the loud clicks of her door being locked, and then silence except for her own ragged sobs.

She continued to pound on the cell door until her hands bruised and she lost her voice so completely that all that came out was a crackly whisper.

Erik.

Erik in a cell just like this one.

Erik beaten by Shadow Men.

Why? What did they want with him? How did they get him? She tried to find the vision again, tried to sink into her mind and see what would happen to lead to his capture or what happened to him after, but it was no use. She was too worked up and it was impossible to find any semblance of the calm that was needed.

Perhaps Kain went back to Headquarters to get him. But why Erik? He wasn't hydan. And even if Kain were interested in nymphs to further his research on harvesting their abilities, Erik was only half nymph. What would be the use of that when he could have his pick of pure nymphs, of which there were many at the Society? And who knew how many out in the real world? Unless it was a self fulfilling prophecy, and seeing the vision of Erik in his possession was what made Kain want to bring him in in the first place.

None of it made any sense. The only thing that could possibly lead to the scene that Yara saw was if Erik were stupid enough to try to break her out on his own. And somehow he got caught.

She pressed the heels of her palms into her eyes until she saw stars.

This was all her fault.

If she had just said something about her capture in the first place…

If she had listened to Carter and not kissed Erik…

If she had fought harder against Kain…

If, if, if.

But even if what caused Erik to be so foolish was the evening he and Yara spent together in the simulators, Yara couldn't regret it. She had clung to that memory so desperately these last few… weeks? Months? (She guessed it had been around two weeks based on the growth of hair in her armpits. Sometimes she thought it was more based on how much weight she had lost.)

She had done nothing after the vision of her own capture. What would have been the point, she convinced herself, of trying to avoid the inevitable? It had been easier to accept her visions as representing the unpreventable when she was the only one at stake. Easier still when they had been visions of people she did not know.

But now it was Erik's face she saw swimming in her mind.

Erik's green eyes. Erik's straight nose and soft lips and curved mouth. Erik's long fingers in her hair. Erik's palm stretched toward the ceiling as bright green leaves curled around his hand. He was so gentle. So kind. She could not let this happen to him.

She closed her eyes and tried to sink into her mind.

Let me see something - anything - *that I can do to stop this,* she thought desperately.

Nothing came.

But it didn't matter. Now she had a goal. Something to fight for. She knew what she had to do. And she would work all night if she had to.

In her effort to calm her mind, Yara had accidentally dozed off a few times, woken by the hunger pains in her stomach and the ever present cold. Her body was aching, but it didn't matter. Every time she woke, she would immediately return to her efforts to find that place in her mind where she could summon a vision.

A couple of times, she managed to feel the familiar pressure in her head that meant it was working. Her vision fogged, but in her excitement it all dissipated too quickly.

She was about to give up, try to get whatever rest she could muster, and resume her efforts later. Presumably after her next session with Kain, whenever that would happen.

But then, she took a deep breath, trying one last time, and imagined herself falling backwards into black water. The ground beneath her disappeared. The cold was gone, if only for a moment. Pain in her head swelled and faded just as quickly, but the fog in her mind stayed. Her heart pounding, she stayed perfectly still, afraid that the slightest movement would make it disappear as it usually did, but the fog was thick. She exhaled slowly, her breath shaky in her anticipation, watching it part before her.

It was Erik again. The same vision Kain had managed to induce with his newfound drug. She stared for a few more moments, hoping to see something else, but the vision never changed. It never moved past those initial images.

She opened her eyes, letting the whole thing collapse around her. She felt excited that it had worked, but just as disappointed that she hadn't seen anything new.

Try again, Rivers.

And so she did. And it happened again. The fog stayed long enough for her to clear it.

Erik, beaten and broken.

Again and again she tried, and every time she saw the same thing. Yara had now seen it so many times she could have drawn it perfectly from memory. As much as she wanted to try again, her head was pounding, the pain no longer receding with every vision. The bottom of the slab under which she slept was blurred, her eyes unable to focus. She needed to take a break.

In fact, she was surprised she hadn't been fetched yet. Though she could never be sure, it felt like a strangely long respite from Kain. Shouldn't his doppelgänger have fetched her by now? Perhaps it was only her imagination.

Or perhaps Kain had gotten what he wanted from her and no longer needed her.

There was a strange feeling in her gut at the thought. Both hopeful and terrified. If he truly didn't plan on using her again, then she would never have to endure another session with him. But then what was he planning on doing with her? Would she spend the rest of her life in this cell, starving and cold and alone, with nothing but her own thoughts for company? Or would he kill her? Perhaps preserve her brain in case he ever needed it?

No, he couldn't possibly be done with her. He had learned how to trigger her visions, but he had not yet - as far as she knew - managed to harvest her ability for himself. Whatever awaited her, it was unlikely it would end in her death. He still needed her.

Though by that time tomorrow she would wish that he didn't.

CHAPTER THIRTY-EIGHT

Hole

It had not been Yara's imagination. She had indeed waited longer than ever for the Kain lookalike to come fetch her. But it was not he who came. It was someone she had never seen before. A woman. She was slender with white blonde hair braided down her back. With her thick framed glasses, she would have looked completely ordinary save for the same deadened eyes that marked the Shadow Men and the brand on her. The letters "At". She was wearing a lab coat that was the same crimson as the rest of the Shadow Men's uniforms.

As she stepped into Yara's cell, she saw that this woman was not alone. Behind her were the same Shadow Men who usually brought Yara back after Kain's experiments were done.

The blonde woman did not need to speak. She simply stepped aside and let the two others do their work, pulling Yara out from under the bed, stripping her of the blanket she had wrapped protectively around herself, and lifting her under her arms.

They led her out of her cell, down the hall, the same path they always took, the blonde woman walking quietly behind them. But when they reached Kain's lab, it looked different than usual. Much of the equipment had been clustered off to the side and a clear plastic curtain had been erected around the metal table. The table itself, however, was also different. Rather than the one she was normally strapped to, this one was clear and curvy, as though it would contour the shape of her body.

Fear crept down Yara's spine like icy water.

Kain was behind the clear curtain. He looked up as the foursome entered his lab. A woman was next to him, slipping latex gloves onto his hands. Despite the terror that muddled her brain, Yara couldn't help but look twice. She was identical to the blonde behind her. She tried to look over her shoulder, made difficult from the way she was being held, but watched as the woman with "At" on her neck stepped casually forward and started to wash her hands.

There was no mistaking it. They were identical in every way.

"Aha!" said Kain happily. "She joins us at last. Prep her, please."

"No, no," said Yara, unable to stop herself. She had barely pleaded, barely begged during her entire incarceration - admittedly much of the time it was a result of being paralyzed - but she had been proud of that fact. Now, the words spilled from her mouth freely, and there was no stopping them. "Please don't do this!"

She continued to cry and beg and struggle as she was dragged past the plastic curtain. She did not make it easy for them, though she stood no chance against the two enormous people holding her. She flailed as much as she could, but their arms were like vices around hers, and eventually they got her onto the table.

As she had predicted, the table felt molded to her, so that when they strapped her down she was completely immobilized. None of it mattered because the same paralytic was soon injected into her via the IV port that had stayed in her arm since she had been first captured, making the straps redundant. She screamed and cried until her jaw was forced shut by the drug.

The two Shadow Men then closed a lid attached to the table over her head, covering her forehead and chin, leaving her face exposed.

She felt dread the likes of which she had never experienced. There were so many of them in the room... Everything was different today, and she had a very bad feeling about it.

The Shadow Men left and Kain continued to give orders to the two identical blonde women left in the room. But she couldn't focus on his words, the world spinning and blurring in her terror.

There was a loud click, followed by a buzzing. One of the blonde women moved into her line of sight and Yara saw she was carrying an electric razor which, without hesitation, she lowered to Yara's head and started buzzing off big clumps of hair.

Tears were streaming down Yara's paralyzed face as she watched the woman work, her eyes dead behind her glasses. She paused briefly, gripped the table, and spun it so that Yara was facing the ground. It was clear now why they had to use the restraints in addition to the paralytic. The drug was meant to immobilize her. The straps were meant to keep her attached to the table. Her whole body shifted, straining against the harnesses, her head now pressed into the strange lid that had been closed over her face.

Yara stared at the ground, watching tears drip down her nose and land with a small splash on the floor amidst a growing pile of red locks of hair.

Yara felt none of it.

She couldn't even bring herself to close her eyes, as much as she wanted to drown everything out. She was too afraid to look away, too scared of what would come while she couldn't see.

The buzzing stopped.

Feet were moving back and forth on either side of her; the two pairs of identical shoes of the blonde women, and Kain's much larger feet. Yara tried to calm her mind enough to listen to what they were saying.

Kain's voice was uncharacteristically hushed. He sounded more focused than she had ever heard him before.

A strong smell reached her, like rubbing alcohol, and then she saw something else drip to the floor beneath her head.

Blood.

A long, steady stream of it. It was coming from her. Dripping down the back of her now bare head, and pooling on the floor.

What was happening?

What are they doing?

A spasm of fear shot through her when she considered that she was lucky she didn't know what they were doing because she was mercifully numbed.

The pool of her blood on the floor was now large enough to show her reflection - something she hadn't seen since she'd been taken from Headquarters. She forgot herself, for a moment, staring into the sunken eyes that looked back at her. She did not recognize herself. Whoever this girl was, it was not Yara Rivers. Her cheeks were hollow, devoid of the roundness she had once loathed and now missed.

She was so mesmerized by her own transformation that she didn't immediately notice the sound of a drill until her head was pressed further into the restraint, and reality snapped back like a rubber band, bringing the terror along with it.

The drill was getting louder.

Kain's feet were right below her. He was standing so close.

Despite the anesthetizing qualities of the paralytic, she could feel pressure against the back of her head, a cold and sharp feeling, distant through the drugs, but undeniably there.

With her jaw forced shut, the scream that escaped her throat was not loud enough to drown out the sound of a hole being drilled into her skull.

CHAPTER THIRTY-NINE
Broken

Broken.

Beaten.

That was how Kain and his two surgical assistants left Yara.

Her eyes stared at the ground, the pool of her blood still reflecting her face, the image fractured by locks of red hair that were still scattered on the floor.

Broken.

Beaten.

After what might have been hours alone in the lab, she heard the door open and people shuffling over to her. She could see feet out of the corner of her eyes, but she did not try to watch what they did or determine what was going to happen next.

None of it mattered. Nothing mattered anymore.

Broken.

Beaten.

Instead of trying to lift her off the table, however, the Shadow Men who came to fetch her wheeled it out of the room, leaving her strapped to it and face down. She watched the ground pass by underneath her in a blur. It was hypnotizing and she let herself be lulled by it.

Once they reached her cell, the two Shadow Men went about the long and arduous process of detaching her from the operating table. They managed to lay her facing down on her meager bed, though she had never used it that way, and set up an IV drip - which was feeding into her arm - right next to her.

Then they took the operating table with them and were gone,

leaving an echo of the door closing behind them.

The drugs were starting to wear off and the cold was starting to set back in as Yara became aware of a dull, throbbing ache in the back of her head. She tested her fingers to see if she could move yet, and found that her mobility was starting to return, though she was still stiff. Kain had not administered whatever antidote to the paralytic that he usually used. She would have to wait for it to dissipate on its own.

Though she wasn't entirely sure she wanted that to happen.

As claustrophobic as it was not to be able to move one's own body, Yara knew that once the paralysis was gone, the numbness would be gone with it. And then she would have to face the reality of what had just been done to her. But lying facedown on this makeshift bed forever was not an option. She thought of Erik, thought of his battered face and imagined him here, living through this same hell. She couldn't let that happen. She had something to fight for.

And that gave her strength.

As soon as she had enough mobility to move her arm, she tentatively reached up to feel the back of her head.

At first what she noticed was the absence of hair. Her skin was tender and even the gentle touch of her fingers felt coarse. She felt foolish for being sad that her hair was gone. It was, after all, such a trivial loss all things considered. But now she was completely naked without it. She felt alien.

What she noticed next, however, was much worse. There was a thick gauze taped to her head. She tugged at it tentatively, wincing as the tape pulled at her sensitive skin, freeing it enough to reach a couple of fingers underneath. A plastic tube, not unlike the permanent IV port in her arm, protruded from the base of her skull, stitched into place. She gasped as soon as her fingers found it, though she couldn't immediately tell if it was from pain or simply shock.

She felt clammy and panicky, her skin hot and cold at the same time. The world was closing in on her and she took several forced breaths, desperate not to give in to the panic attack that was threatening to engulf her.

Inhale liquid gold. Exhale red smoke.

So this was how he did it, she thought, shaking and filled with revulsion. This was how he took the abilities of the hyden. Whatever tests he had done had given him the information he needed to find her *occultatum*, the gland deep inside her brain that released the hormone which allowed her to see the future.

No doubt this tube that had been drilled into her skull was his access to that gland, to that hormone.

No doubt he would be back for more.

No doubt Ramsey Kain - if he couldn't already - would soon be able to see the future.

Too much time had passed.

Erik's skin was crawling, and with each passing day, the feeling of restlessness increased. He was barely sleeping, his nights plagued with twisted images of Yara as he imagined what horrors she was enduring with Kain. She had to still be alive. He couldn't even let himself entertain the idea that she was dead. If his theory was right - the same theory the Society was operating on - and Kain was in fact continuing his work on the Omega Project, more than likely he needed Yara to continue. She was an asset. And as evil as Kain might be, he wasn't stupid. Far from it.

So instead of sleep, Erik planned. He poured over all of the notes accumulated by the Eyes on where Kain might be hiding his lab. He scoured Kain's research from when he had been part of the Society. (There wasn't much left, Kain had taken most of it with him, but a few bits and pieces here and there remained. Erik now knew them all by heart.) He trained in the sims, using what they knew about Shadow Men to program realistic opponents so he could prepare for what it would be like to fight against them.

And a handful of times he had been able to sneak out of Headquarters after hours to follow a few leads. Strictly speaking, recon like this was meant to be performed by the Eyes. But they were too slow. Despite reaching out to the civilian police force, no progress had been made. It had gone exactly as Erik had anticipated.

But he'd had a breakthrough. That night he had spent hours downtown following what turned out to be an empty lead, but on his way back to Headquarters, he caught a flash of crimson.

Stalking was certainly not his strength. As a Guardian, his duty was to fight and protect. Trackers were the ones trained to follow undetected. But it was late - or early, depending on how one looked at it - and this figure seemed unconcerned about the threat of being tailed. It was a rare opportunity. There was no time to second guess himself. Erik stuck to the shadows, barely breathing, stepping as lightly as possible. He followed the figure, and though they were barely lit from the occasional street light, Erik saw enough to make out a bald man, nearly seven feet tall.

No…

It couldn't be possible.

It was the same man, the exact same man that Erik had fought the night Yara was taken. But Erik hadn't simply fought the Shadow Man. He had killed him.

And yet, here he was. Very much alive.

There wasn't time to linger on the man's miraculous resurrection. Erik looked up and saw where they were: 6th Street. He knew his way around downtown pretty well, but he couldn't imagine what this man was doing here. It was a crowded area, the skyscrapers looming and plentiful. Even now, in the dead of night, it wasn't empty. People were lingering on corners or walking quickly with their heads down or sleeping at bus stops. In short, it was not exactly a spot conducive to hiding a lab filled with an enormous army of Shadow Men.

But the man surprised Erik by turning down Hope Street. He moved away from the bustle of the city, heading instead down a dead end that led directly to the central branch of the Los Angeles Public Library.

A Shadow Man going to the library?

It made no sense.

It was harder to remain unseen here with less cover from the street lamps, so it forced Erik to stay farther back. As he neared the dead end, the Shadow Man made no moves to turn back, no signs of slowing down. He was clearly heading exactly where he wanted to be going. When he reached the locked gates of the library, he turned and vanished out of sight.

His heart pounding violently in his chest, Erik sprinted down Hope Street, desperate not to lose sight of the man.

But as soon as he rounded the corner, the wind was knocked out of him with a fist to the gut. Caught off guard, Erik stumbled backward. He reacted without thinking, ducking from another attack and swinging his legs around. He caught the Shadow Man, but his height and weight made him nearly impossible to topple. He lost his balance just long enough for Erik to stagger back to his feet and try to collect his bearings. He hadn't worn his armor. He hadn't expected a physical altercation, (not to mention it tended to draw attention which he had desperately wanted to avoid) though he had fortunately thought to bring a gauntlet and solenoid. He reached for the gauntlet, strapped to his leg, but the Shadow Man was faster. He whipped out his weapon, the same hot, glowing sword Erik had fought against back at

Headquarters.

Under the soft light from the sword, the man's face was illuminated enough to see that he was indeed the man Erik had killed.

His moment of fixation was enough for the Shadow Man to swing his weapon. Erik managed to twist out of the way just in time, preventing the burning sword from slashing through him, but it did yank the gauntlet off of his hand, leaving him with a now useless solenoid he could not control strapped to his back and a gauntlet out of reach behind the Shadow Man.

Erik had a split second to decide what to do. Stay and fight, likely leading to injury, or try to run and report all this to the Society. There he would face retributions for his actions, and the Shadow Man would also be able to report back to Kain that he had been followed. While Erik still didn't know where Kain's secret base was, he had a feeling he was close. Closer than anyone had ever been to finding it.

He had to run. He had to tell the Society. He would do Yara no good if he died here without being able to share this new intel. (He had even deactivated his tracker so as not to be followed during his illicit excursions away from Headquarters, so there would truly be no way for them to ever determine what happened to him.) He kept his eyes on the expressionless Shadow Man who was lumbering forward.

Erik leapt toward the high wall to his left, pushing off of it and landing a high kick to the man's face, hoping it would disorient him long enough that Erik could get a head start that might enable him to get away. Without stopping to check, he turned and started to run, but a searing pain in his leg knocked him to the ground. He screamed as he fell. The Shadow Man had thrown his sword which had pierced Erik's calf, protruding straight through to the other side of his leg. Erik tried to grab the hilt to pull it out, but it burned his hand.

The Shadow Man was approaching, not bothering to hurry. He knew he had won. After all the preparation Erik had done, it all came down to this. A burning sword through the leg crippling him, dying inexplicably at the hands of a Shadow Man he had already killed.

An enormous hand wrapped around Erik's throat, pulling him up enough so that the Shadow Man could yank his sword out of Erik's leg. Another scream of pain was caught in Erik's throat. Erik pulled a blade from a hidden pocket in his sleeve and sank it into the hand gripping his neck, but the Shadow Man did not let go. His hold did not even loosen. Erik twisted the blade further, tearing through muscle.

Let me go! he thought desperately. He could feel his work start to break the Shadow Man's grasp, until he was at last dropped to the floor. Pain shot through his injured leg as he landed on it. It took every bit of strength he had to stay upright. Taking no time to catch his breath, still coughing and spluttering, he dove for the Shadow Man and stabbed him in the side. He didn't wait before wrenching the blade out and sinking it back in. Again and again he shanked the Shadow Man, but the man was still able to slam his unbroken hand against Erik's side. His leg unable to stand against the blow crumpled under him, he fell backward, slamming his head against the curb. The world faded out of focus.

"No…"

But it was useless. He could not fight this. His body was failing him. The Shadow Man kneeled on his chest, his dead eyes locked on Erik's, and he watched as Erik's eyes rolled back into his head.

CHAPTER FORTY
Action

Yara's heart was racing. If Kain could see the future, he would become unstoppable. He would be able to anticipate every move before the Society made it. And that wasn't even accounting for the abilities he would poach from the other hyden. She didn't know them all, didn't know what their abilities were. But she knew already about Roberto Diaz who could read minds and Emmanuelle Moreau who could jump. One of Emmanuelle's Guardians had said it was as close to flight as a human could get.

Kain was on his way to becoming a superhuman force. A god.

There had to be a way to stop him. If he left a tube in the back of her head, it meant that he needed to be able to access her videtonin again. Possibly many times. It would seem that whatever he was taking from her didn't give him a permanent ability.

He had to keep her alive.

And if Kain wanted to harness the abilities of the other hyden, he needed them alive, too.

They were all alive. They had to be.

The thought gave her strength.

But what about Erik? He was not hydan. Not even a full nymph. Kain had no reason to keep Erik alive. And Yara could not stomach the thought of him dying.

She tried to push herself up. Her whole body screamed in protest, her arms shaking from the weight. She felt sick, and even heaved off the side of the cot, though nothing came up after having had no solid food in days. Her limbs were trembling, weak from disuse and lack of food. Now that she thought about it, she realized she hadn't stood on her own two feet since having been brought here. She tested it now, using the IV drip to steady her.

Everything hurt. Her head was screaming in protest, her muscles straining, but she was determined. It was strange how different the world looked from up here. She was still trapped, still in her small cement box, but she felt bigger.

Despite being weaker and more insubstantial than she had ever been in her whole life, she had a renewed sense of purpose. For the first time, her desire to fight was stronger than her fear. Kain may have taken from her everyone she loved. He may have robbed her of her body and mutilated her mind.

But as it turned out, she still had something left.

Erik was late and he was not answering.

Robin had gone to Glover, the second in charge of the White Mask Society, for permission to trace Erik, hoping that he wouldn't find what he feared. Erik's tracker had been self-deactivated. A bad sign. Then they traced his ConvOrb to his quarters. Robin's suspicions were reaffirmed.

"What is the meaning of this?" said Glover in his impossibly deep voice when Robin relayed what he had found.

What was the right move here? Robin had spent so much effort trying to protect Erik from himself, but this was the end of the line. "C and I think..." began Robin, speaking slowly as he clung to the hope that Erik would burst into Glover's office and save him from having to do this, "... we think that E is trying to find Kain on his own."

Glover raised an eyebrow. "Kain? Or Yara Rivers?"

Robin ran a hand through his golden curls. "I admit, sir, we don't know what the protocol is in this situation."

Glover sighed heavily. "Yes, we do have an unusual situation on our hands. We've never had a rogue Guardian before." He stared down at his mahogany desk for several moments before saying, "I am not going to tell Black. Yet."

A weight lifted from Robin's shoulders, one he hadn't even realized was there. "Thank you."

"Don't thank me yet. You have—" Glover checked his watch, "—six hours to try to get a hold of this situation at your own discretion before I have to report him."

Robin nodded and headed toward the door. He had to get Carter, hoping they would join him in trying to find Erik. He had no idea how they would go about it, or where they would even start, when Glover stopped him.

"It is very likely that E will not remain with the Society after this. If he's found."

Robin hesitated, his hand on the doorknob. "I understand," he said eventually, and left.

CHAPTER FORTY-ONE

Paradox

Weaker than she had ever been, the idea of escape was laughable. Yara knew that if she tried to fight, she would lose. And it wouldn't take long. (So much for all her self-defense training…)

But she did have one strength, and a mutilated skull to prove it. Whether or not Kain had her power by now, she couldn't be sure, but it would be wise to assume that he did. Though he showed no inclination of giving hydan abilities to his Shadow Men, so that at least gave her an advantage over them.

The problem now would be figuring out how to use that advantage to get out in time to save Erik. The only way she could think of doing that was trying to summon a vision. She had managed it before, but things were different now. Would she even be able to do it with this tube in her head? Perhaps Kain had taken all of her videtonin, leaving her with a deficit that would take time to replenish. Maybe the tube even blocked its production… She didn't know how any of it worked, of course, but it was easy to imagine that the surgery would certainly not make things any easier.

The other problem was that she had not yet been able to control *when* she was seeing. All visions she had managed to summon up until now had been things she had already seen. That wouldn't cut it now, though. She needed new information.

She sat up against the wall, one hand wrapped around her IV stand, and closed her eyes.

"OK, Rivers," she breathed in a hoarse voice. "Let's do this."

As expected, the catheter in the back of her head was not helping.

Whereas before she'd simply had to sink into her mind, she now had heavy obstacles to push through.

She slowed her breathing. *Inhale liquid gold, exhale red smoke.*

It was working. Slowly, but surely. She was sinking further down, her body getting heavier, the ever present cold and ache in her muscles becoming less noticeable as the world around her was exchanged for a sea of fog. It was like leaving her body behind as she recoiled into her mind.

It would have been so easy to stay here, and be rolled away by the thick clouds in her mind. Let them take her where they wanted. But no. She needed to be in control. She needed to see something helpful.

The fog started to swirl as if caught in a low wind. She still could not see anything past it, but it was all accompanied by a different feeling. She was no longer in the recesses of her mind. She had surfaced, yet somehow remained here in this strange place where the future lived. It was like a lucid dream, when you leap off of a cliff because you realize you can fly if you want to.

She was in control.

And then a wild thought occurred to her. The idea was ludicrous. Impossible, even.

What she wanted to do - what she *really* wanted to do - was escape. If she was successful, then it was part of her future. And if it was part of her future, then she would be able to see how she did it... Or how she *would* do it...

It was a paradox. It couldn't possibly work. Right?

She had to try.

With a deep exhale, she grabbed the reins and did something she had never done before. She gave a command.

Show me how I escape.

At first, nothing happened. Yara wasn't surprised. She hadn't necessarily expected it to work, but then the fog started to move in a strange way. It took several moments for Yara to realize it was moving backwards, tracing over the same patterns it had just followed but in reverse.

She could feel her heart start to beat faster. With so little meat on her bones, it resonated through her entire body, causing her skin to tremble. Her grip on her mind started to slip in her excitement and she redoubled her efforts to stay present.

Everything continued to rewind around her, disorienting to the point that if she hadn't been sitting she might have fallen over. At last it slowed. As it began to part she saw…

… *herself.*

Her head was shaved, her face sunken and pale, her body bruised and insubstantial. She looked so small. A strangled cry escaped her lips at the sight. But she couldn't linger on it.

Vision Yara was standing against the wall next to the door to her cell, both of her hands gripping the IV stand.

Real Yara watched the whole scene unfold, her heart pounding in her chest the entire time.

Her eyes opened, bringing her abruptly back to her cell, and with it the cold and the pain. She was breathing heavily, blood pumping so loudly through her ears she could barely hear herself think.

If she hadn't just watched it all happen, she wouldn't have believed any of it to be possible. But it had to be. She had just seen it.

Her bones were vibrating. She knew what she had to do now. So she used the IV stand to pull herself up to her feet. Everything hurt, but she ignored it all. Pain was temporary. At least, it would be if she managed to pull this off. She moved slowly, every step sending shooting pains up her legs. Her arms cramped and her head throbbed faintly. (She wondered idly if there were some sort of painkillers in her IV drip because this was not nearly the amount of pain she expected after having her skull drilled open.)

At the door to her cell, she assumed the position she had seen in her vision, took a deep breath, and waited.

CHAPTER FORTY-TWO

Discovery

What in reality must have only been a few minutes felt like an eternity to Yara as she stood by the door to her cell. Her mind replayed her self-defense lessons, and she could feel the ghost of Carter's fist pushing between her shoulder blades, lecturing her about a strong core being key to a strong defense. Her back straightened. Meanwhile, her knuckles were turning white from gripping the IV stand so hard. She was trying to stop from trembling. She strained to hear outside her cell, but the walls were thick enough to mute the sounds outside. Her heart was beating so loudly, blood thrumming through her head, that she doubted she could have heard anything anyway.

Then, at last, came the familiar clicks of the door being unlocked. She was shaking from fear and from cold and she was sweating, but she was determined.

She closed her eyes, trying to remember every detail of her vision. It had to work, because it already *had* worked... She had *seen* it.

The world shifted into slow motion as the door opened. In came the Kain doppelgänger and Yara didn't hesitate before whipping him in the head with her IV stand, wielding it like a Bo staff. It tugged at the port in her arm, but she ignored it. The Shadow Man was completely caught off guard, having not expected anything other than a weak and unresisting prisoner, as he had found every day until now. He stumbled back a few steps, but Yara didn't wait to let him regain his bearings. She grabbed him by the front of his crimson uniform and yanked him into the cell, exactly as she had seen herself do in her vision. He was so much taller than Yara, it was like trying to topple a very skinny tree. He stumbled forward, showing no signs of surprise on his face, and she slammed her makeshift weapon into his back. Already off balance, it was all it took to get him to fall to the floor.

She didn't stop hitting him. She couldn't control herself. She could feel herself crying, though she didn't understand why. She kept slamming the stand down. His back, his legs, his neck, his head. She didn't stop until he fell to the floor and lay completely still.

Gasping for breath, shaking - now from adrenaline - she dropped the IV stand and backed away from his body. The stand followed her, dragging against the cement floor with a loud screech, pulling painfully at the port in her arm. It took several moments for her to realize that her gasping had turned into a laugh.

She had done it. It had all gone perfectly. Exactly as she had seen in her vision. But it wasn't over yet. She picked up the IV stand. She couldn't leave it. It was the only thing she had that resembled a weapon, not to mention the drugs it was feeding her were possibly the only thing keeping her standing. She didn't want to risk disconnecting it.

She crouched next to the doppelgänger's unconscious body and searched his pockets. His keys were under him. Grabbing them, Yara walked quickly out to the hallway, closed the door, and locked it behind her with some difficulty, her hands still shaking violently.

Thankfully, the hallway was empty. She was operating blind now. She had played through everything she saw in her vision.

It was just as cold out here as it was in her cell. Her skin prickled uncomfortably, colder still because of the sheen of sweat that coated her body.

"What now?" she whispered. She looked both ways down the hall. They looked identical. She had no idea what to do, except…

Feeling panicked and exposed, Yara darted into a small alcove not far from her cell, breathing heavily.

"C'mon, c'mon, c'mon…" she muttered impatiently to herself. She felt lightheaded and simultaneously impossibly heavy. Her head was throbbing, though not as the result of a vision but rather of the wound at the base of her neck.

She needed to calm down. She needed to find that same place in her mind. She needed another paradox.

Yara leaned against the cold cement wall and closed her eyes. When she accidentally nudged the catheter in her head against the wall, she gasped in pain, forcing her to start from scratch.

Don't think about how you might get caught any second...

It wasn't easy, but it wasn't as hard as it had been the first time, either. After only a few minutes, she had found what she was looking for.

She saw herself in her mind, reeling that this was actually working. How it could be possible, she couldn't afford to spend any time dwelling on.

The Yara in her vision walked out of the alcove and turned right around a corner. Despite having been led down these halls countless times, she had no idea where anything was situated. It was all starting to feel impossible. She was injured, alone, frail, unarmed - aside from medical equipment - and she was completely lost. Vision Yara had only been walking for a few moments when, as though pulled from thin air, two Shadow Men appeared in front of her. Yara watched with horror as they wrestled her to the floor.

She gasped, her eyes flying open. Yara came back to her body so fast it was like a rubber band had snapped, bringing with it her frantically beating heart, the pain, the cold.

No...

No!

This couldn't be how it ended. Had it really all been for nothing? What would be her punishment for an attempted escape? Would Kain even bother keeping her alive? Or would she have proven herself to be more trouble than she was worth?

In her desperation, a wild idea occurred to her. What she had seen... what if...

She took a deep breath, sank back into her mind (harder now with her heart beating in her throat) and went backwards through the vision, watching everything unfold in reverse until she was back where she started. This time, Yara thought frantically, *Don't turn right!*

She watched, her breath hitched in her throat, as Vision Yara went not right, but *left*. Yara couldn't believe it. Had she just changed her fate? Was it even possible for her to make a decision that was different than the one she had already seen herself make? All she had done was make the conscious choice to go a different way, and the future had changed. Did that mean she not only had the ability to see the future, but the ability to see how her choices would affect things?

She was so intoxicated by this discovery, that she lost all concentration. The vision faded and the world came crashing back. Her pain seemed to have increased, the cold now more intense, but none of it mattered. She might actually have a chance! Yara pressed her trembling hands into her eyes. She didn't have time for confusing thoughts about paradoxes. There was only one way to know for sure.

Taking a deep breath, she plunged back into the recesses of her mind. It came more easily to her this time as though the vision was still there, waiting for her to return after her last attempt. At the end of the hallway, she watched herself turn left instead of right. She could feel the presence of the Shadow Men behind her, although they had not actually rounded the corner yet. Yara watched herself speed up down the hall, turn into an alcove and hide until they had passed. Then, she turned around and went back the way she had gone, stopping at an unguarded door.

She committed everything to memory, focusing hard on not missing anything. It was over quickly, only showing her, as before, a small step at a time.

Yara opened her eyes, smiling. It was so simple that she couldn't help but laugh.

"I did it…"

After all that time, after everything she had been through, the lessons with Bora Black and the torture with Kain, to think that she had managed to achieve it under these conditions and all by herself…

All in all, less than five minutes had passed since she had locked the doppelgänger in her cell. She scrambled up and started to run down the hall, turning left at the fork, her feet somehow knowing intuitively where to carry her. Her fear was almost non-existent. She felt practically giddy. She knew exactly where and when to hide when she heard voices coming. Could anticipate their movements as though she were in a video game that she had played a hundred times before, though the colors were brighter, the sounds clearer, everything more defined. Her visions had always been viewed through that thick fog in her mind, and now the fog was gone.

Almost effortlessly, she reached the door from her vision. It looked like the one to her own cell. Could this really be the exit? The door was marked with a small number "1". Yara looked through the keys she had taken off the unconscious man's body, finding one that was engraved with a matching "1", and stuck it in the lock.

One hand still wrapped around the IV stand, she unlocked the door. Pushing it open took some effort, however. It was solid iron and impossibly heavy.

Definitely not an exit. Instead, she could tell through the small opening between the door and the wall that it was a cell identical to hers, right down to the stained pillow.

"Help… me…" she managed through gritted teeth to the occupant.

The door had opened perhaps a foot, but she could push it no further. The view was blocked by an unfamiliar face.

He was a handsome man, his skin the color of rich chocolate. Older, perhaps in his sixties. He wore the same tan underwear as Yara. The most striking aspect of his appearance, however, were his pearly white eyes. He was blind.

He lifted his chin slightly, his milky eyes pointed directly at her, then said, "Who are you?" His voice was weak, with an accent she couldn't place. (Australian perhaps, or English? Yara wasn't good with accents.)

Yara frowned. Why had she been brought here? Who was he?

"Uh… I'm Yara. Who are you?"

The man frowned right back at her. "Are you hydan?"

Yara's heart skipped a beat. She was able to squeeze through the narrow opening because of her frail frame, not wanting to stay exposed in the hall. It was only a matter of time before Kain noticed she was missing and sent people to look for her.

"Yes. Are you?"

He nodded. "Luan," he said finally, extending his hand. "Luan Khumalo." She shook it. Looking at him more closely she saw that he, too, bore the scars of his time with Kain. Massive wounds, barely healed, ran down his throat and both sides of his face all the way to his collar. The stitches circled his ears - which were also strange, though Yara looked away too quickly to get a good look, not wanting to stare. (Not that he would have necessarily noticed…) His dark skin looked as though it had grown duller during his incarceration. Gray was starting to grow in his short, tightly curled black hair, his face gaunt and prematurely lined. "What's going on?" he asked.

"Do you know where you are?" asked Yara, starting to speak quickly, aware of every second as it passed.

He shook his head. "America. Is this a government building?"

Yara looked at him in disbelief. Luan Khumalo must have been one of the first hyden to have been captured. He might never have even heard of Kain or the White Mask Society. No doubt, he didn't even know who his Guardians were, let alone that he even had any.

Understanding washed over her. Her vision had purposefully led her not to any kind of exit, but to the cell of another imprisoned hydan because she was meant to help all of them escape.

A war raged in her head. She wanted to leave this place. She wanted to save Erik. To run back to her Guardians, to her aunt, to her life. And the more of them there were, the harder it would be. They would all be injured and weak. Then again, they would all have strengths. They were hydan, after all. But maybe, like Yara had been not long ago, they didn't know how to control their abilities.

If she left him and the other hyden here, would she be able to live with herself?

No. But she wouldn't be able to live with herself if she failed, either. *Coward.*

"Come with me. We have to hurry. I'm going to get you out of here."

CHAPTER FORTY-THREE

The Hyden

Unable to tear her gaze away from Luan Khumalo's eyes, Yara said, "I need you to come with me. We're going to try to get out of here after we find the other prisoners."

Yara could feel her fleeting hope start to dissipate. Trying to escape while helping a blind man would slow her down. But she had no choice.

"Just put your hand on my shoulder and I'll lead you. Try—"

But Luan cut her off. "I don't need to be led."

"How—"

He pointed to his ears. "Echolocation."

"Holy shit," said Yara with a laugh, despite herself. "That's cool. OK," she said, collecting herself. "OK, just give me a minute. I need to figure out where we need to go next."

She used the IV stand she was still gripping to lower herself to the floor, preparing to swim through the fog and find their next steps, when Luan reached for her shoulder. She flinched slightly. Already uncomfortable being touched by strangers, Yara had spent so long being abused by Kain and his Shadow Men that she instinctively reacted with fear, though his touch was gentle.

"You're bleeding." Somehow, despite his sightless eyes, Luan had noticed what Yara had not. From beneath her bandage, a thick trail of blood was gushing down her neck and spine.

"Shit," she said, feeling with her fingers and pulling them away red and shiny. "I'm fine." She had no time to worry about that. In truth, she was in incredible pain. But she couldn't stop now.

"Wait," said Luan. He grabbed the blanket off of his bed and tore a strip from it. When he turned away from her, Yara could see a tube protruding from the back of his head amidst a healed scar. She resisted the urge to vomit, wondering if her head looked as bad. "Here," he said, tying it with unexpected gentleness around Yara's head. She flinched as he tightened it enough to stem the bleeding.

She gave him a weak smile of thanks and closed her eyes.

It was harder this time, to sink into her mind. She was very aware of Luan's presence.

At last she was able to fall into the fog. She had to test out several different paths before she found one in which they didn't get caught. Each time she watched the two of them encounter Shadow Men, her pulse quickened with fear, but she simply rewound everything like an old video tape, then made another choice to go a different direction or double back to avoid detection. But there was a safe path, and she found it.

She opened her eyes to see Luan patiently standing in front of her, looking trepidatious, but determined.

"We're gonna move fast," she said, struggling to stand. He helped pull her to her feet. "Thank you."

He nodded, then pointed his head toward the open door, opened his mouth, his chin lifted as it had been before, and said, "No one's coming."

"Man, that's cool," said Yara under her breath.

Luan smiled.

They slipped out the narrow opening together, closing the cell door behind them, and started to run down the hall. Yara was filled again with the euphoric feeling of knowing exactly where she was supposed to go, and moving with Luan was effortless. He didn't need to be told when to stop. Every time Yara paused to hide from a Shadow Man or two, he knew just as quickly. He too could tell when someone was coming and they moved in unison, working perfectly together.

Luan and Yara found themselves at a door marked with a "3". Using the matching key, they opened the door to find another identical cell. This one housed a short man huddled at the foot of the makeshift bed. He looked like he had been larger than either Yara or Luan to begin with, so he wasn't as wraithlike, but he was still clearly unhealthy, underfed, and abused. Another hydan bearing the mutilation in the back of his skull. Yara could just see his catheter protruding from beneath his short, curly, black hair.

He stared at them both with wide, fearful eyes.

Luan moved slowly over to him, but before he could say a word, the man cocked his head and said, "You're trying to escape?"

The mind reader, then. What was his name? Kain had mentioned it. Roberto Diaz.

"Yes," said Yara.

The man shook his head. He embodied the fear that Yara had felt during her entire incarceration. The fear she wanted so badly to succumb to. But then she thought of her vision of Erik, and managed to push it back down.

"Please come with us," said Luan calmly.

Roberto Diaz cocked his head again as though trying to hear something very far away. His eyes were locked on Luan. He was reading his mind. Whatever he found there seemed to be enough to convince him, because he nodded nervously and got up from his cot, keeping the ragged blanket wrapped tightly around him.

"I'm Luan. This is Yara."

"Bobby," said the man.

Luan turned to Yara and indicated it was time for her to do whatever she had to do.

It was becoming a familiar routine, now. Like taking the same path to work in what had once been a strange place. It came to her more easily, despite both Bobby and Luan watching her.

After barely thirty seconds, Yara had already found their next route and the three of them were out in the hall, heading to the next cell. The next hydan. It was more difficult to move now, however. Bobby was also able to detect when people were nearby - no doubt able to hear their thoughts - but he moved slower than either Luan or Yara, and the Shadow Men were moving faster. There were more of them now.

They had finally registered that something was wrong.

"Shit," Yara whispered, watching them run down the halls. They had armed themselves which might prove to be a serious complication - some with glowing swords or double-ended spears, others with gauntlets, their corresponding solenoids following them like a hoard of angry birds.

By the time they reached the next door, marked "2", Bobby was panting heavily and Yara felt lightheaded. The makeshift bandage that Luan had wrapped around her head was soaked through with her blood.

"Hurry!" whispered Luan frantically. "People are coming!"

Yara's cold, stiff fingers fumbled with the keys until she found the one.

"Hurry!"

"I am!" she hissed back, and jammed the key into the door. The three of them pushed it open and darted inside, trying to close the door as quickly and quietly as possible without letting it latch shut, unsure of whether or not they would be able to open it from the inside, even with a key.

Luan stayed by the door, his mouth open, sending signals out that bounced back to him that the others had no hope of detecting.

Footsteps rushed past outside the cell and rounded a corner. A few moments of baited breath and Luan finally said, "OK. They've gone."

Yara realized she was trembling again. Her body collapsed with relief. She tried to calm herself down (*inhale liquid gold, exhale red smoke*) as she looked for the occupent of the cell.

A woman was sitting in the far corner of the room. Of the four of them, she looked the worse for wear. Her face was gaunt, like a death mask, her dark hair graying, her skin sickly white. But the most noticeable difference was that she was wearing a collar around her throat. One that glowed like the weapons of the Shadow Men. Yara had no idea what it could possibly be, but had an ugly moment of selfish relief that she had not been affixed with one herself.

Bobby was already moving toward her, looking deep into her eyes, the same tilt of his head.

"She doesn't speak English," said Bobby, not looking away from the woman.

"*Nima bulyapti?*" said the woman in a small voice.

"We don't have time to try to explain anything to her..." said Yara. "They're looking for us. We need to move fast."

"Can she walk?" asked Luan.

Bobby offered his hand to the woman and Luan smiled encouragingly at her. Yara remained stoic, too busy trying to sink back into her mind while they tried to convince her to join them. Her heart was pounding, her head was throbbing, and her neck was slick with blood. Yet everything relied on her getting them to their next step. She remembered that Kain had been after six hyden. That meant there were two more, and - if her vision had already come true - Erik. How they would manage to successfully evade anyone, she didn't know. Perhaps the best plan would be for them to leave this woman, escape, and come back for her later with reinforcements.

Coward.

Fine. They would do it together. Unbelievably, Yara was able to find a safe path to the next cell. When she opened her eyes, Luan and Bobby were supporting the woman between the two of them as she was too weak to stand on her own. They all looked as scared as she felt.

"Her name is Anna," said Bobby.

"We need to hurry," said Luan. "There are more people. They're moving quickly."

"Luan," said Yara. She didn't need to finish her sentence. Looking into his sightless eyes, she could tell that he knew what she needed from him. She would lead the group, but he had to ensure that their six-legged procession stayed out of sight. Luan was capable of knowing where the Shadow Men were better than even Yara.

She led them out the door, nervous despite knowing that if she followed what she had seen in her vision to a T they would be safe. But she was getting so lightheaded, how long before she couldn't remember her next step?

How long before she bled out?

CHAPTER FORTY-FOUR

Escalation

There was no time to be angry, though Kain could feel it bubbling under his skin like poison. It was the same toxic rancor he felt that night in his laboratory back at the White Mask Society. The night she had died. He hadn't been able to control it then. He had to now. Because he could not lose what he had worked so hard for.

Those hyden were *his*. They belonged to no one else.

His Shadow Men, infuriating in their calm demeanors, were obeying his orders, spreading throughout the entire base to stop the hyden from being able to reach the exit - if they could even find it. How they had even gotten this far, he couldn't know for sure. But he still had time.

He just had to work quickly.

He pressed a button on his collar, and the crackly voice of Phosphorous said, "Sir?"

"Block the exits, but call off the search."

"Sir," replied his Shadow Man.

Kain grinned.

The serums were lined neatly before him. He had yet to perfect them all, and a few of the Shadow Men on which he had tested the newest solutions had displayed unpleasant side effects, a few of which had even led to fatalities. They certainly weren't ready for him, yet. But that didn't mean he couldn't use some... The ones he knew were foolproof.

He injected himself once.

His bones tingled. It was bordering on painful, though he knew that

216

each prickle was his body becoming *more* powerful. *More* than human.

A second shot.

This one sent an electric current through his head. He seized for a few moments, his jaw clenched shut, but it was over as soon as it had started, leaving his brain feeling strangely inflated, like a balloon. He shook it off.

One more.

The most useful of them all. A pain shot through Kain's leg and he felt itchy all over, but he clenched his fist, resisting the powerful urge to scratch himself until it faded.

Let's see them fight me, now, he thought, smiling, testing how much weight his leg could now hold. Incredible. His leg wasn't even weak. He dropped the cane with a clatter and took several steps, reveling in the sound and feel of his even gait.

If he knew Yara Rivers, which of course he did, all thanks to Bobby Diaz, he knew where she would go before she made a run for it.

And Kain would be there waiting for her.

The woman named Anna had really slowed them down. Bobby and Luan would have been able to carry her easily under normal circumstances, but they were far from operating at a hundred percent. The halls were crawling with crimson Shadow Men, and with people running down every hallway, they had to double back so many times that Yara forgot where they were supposed to go. Trying to stay as concealed as possible, they had to stop in a corner to allow her to retrace the path.

Miraculously, they made it to the next cell. The halls seemed to have thinned of activity, and Yara was starting to feel more nervous about their successes. There was no way they had managed to evade detection this long with an army of Shadow Men searching for them. Perhaps it was all a trap laid by Kain. For what purpose, she couldn't begin to guess.

"The key?" said Luan, snapping Yara out of her morbid thought spiral.

The four of them hobbled clumsily inside, but instead of finding a figure cowering in a corner, they saw a tall, dark woman standing defiantly in the middle of the room. Even with her head shaved, her long dreadlocks gone, Yara recognized her immediately.

"Yara?"

Emmanuelle Moreau had gone through the same transformation as the rest of hyden. Her normally rich, dark skin was gray and ashen, her face hollowed, and her body just as weakened as theirs. But in addition to the catheter in the back of her skull and the IV line in her arm (also connected to a drip just like Yara's), Emmanuelle showed signs of even more damage.

Along the outside of her thighs were enormous bandages that trailed the length of her legs. Yara didn't want to imagine what kind of scars were healing beneath such large swaths of gauze.

"How—" said Emmanuelle, her eyes flitting between Yara and the other three hyden. She stopped herself, however, clearly able to see there was no time.

"We're..." said Yara, unable to finish the sentence. *We're getting out of here. We're escaping. We're going home.* The words got caught in her throat, afraid that they would sound foolish or jinx the entire operation. Yara had never been superstitious, but now was certainly not the time to test anything.

"What do you need?" said Emmanuelle, evidently understanding the situation without Yara needing to explain anything.

Grateful beyond words that they now had a member of the White Mask Society, no matter how injured, Yara could have cried. "Are you able to walk?" she said, gesturing to Emmanuelle's legs.

Emmanuelle tightened her jaw, her gaze steely. She was clearly bracing herself, but she nodded. She had the determination of a Guardian, and no matter how mutilated her legs were, Yara knew she would keep up.

"How have you been navigating the passages? It's a maze. I can't make heads or tails of it. How have you been avoiding the Shadow Men?"

"Luan's echolocation has made it possible to avoid detection so far, and I've been using my visions to see what path we need to take."

Emmanuelle gave her an impressed nod.

Yara sat down and prepared to sink back into her mind, but was interrupted by Emmanuelle's accented voice.

"I need something sharp."

Yara shook her head, confused. They were all as naked and unarmed as Emmanuelle was, equipped with nothing other than their meager coverings, two IV stands, and the keys Yara had taken from the Kain doppelgänger.

"Those will do," said Emmanuelle gesturing for the keys.

Bewildered, Yara handed them over. They weren't particularly sharp. Was Emmanuelle hoping to use them as a weapon? Her own IV stand would work better. Yara opened her mouth to say as much but Emmanuelle had already jammed one of the keys into her right arm.

"Jesus!" said Yara, at the same time as Bobby gasped and Luan said, "Oh my!"

"What are you doing!"

Emmanuelle did not respond. Her eyes were closed, her jaw clenched, as she dug the keys around in the gaping wound in her arm. Yara didn't want to watch. It was horrifying and she didn't understand why it was happening at all, but she couldn't bring herself to look away.

With a loud grunt of pain, she yanked out a small, flat piece of silicon.

"What the hell…" said Yara.

Emmanuelle threw the keys back at Yara who nearly dropped them, not eager to hold anything still hot and dripping with blood. Without speaking, the Guardian pressed a few buttons on the thing she had just pulled from her arm. She tucked it into the band of her underwear then nodded at Yara as if to say, "Where to next?" as though what she had done was perfectly ordinary.

"What the hell was that?"

"My tracker. Every member of the Society has one. Kain disabled it, but he didn't know that it could still be activated manually."

"There wasn't… an easier way to do that?"

"I thought we were in a hurry."

Yara slammed her eyes shut, trying to erase the image of Emmanuelle digging in her arm. But what she saw next certainly wasn't what she *wanted* to see.

"We have a problem," said Yara, opening her eyes. "The next cell is being guarded."

"Lead the way," said Emmanuelle shortly.

CHAPTER FORTY-FIVE

Guarded

Emmanuelle would not have believed it had someone told her that she would be attempting escape from Kain's secret laboratory, crawling with Shadow Men, led by a high school girl who was perhaps one of the most awkward people she had ever met.

But now she found herself in a pack of five hyden, closer to escape than she thought possible. She had never met another hydan before Yara, aside from her parents. Emmanuelle was born in France. She had inherited her mother's hydan ability. Her father, also a hydan, was a strongman, able to move impossibly heavy objects with little effort. Upon learning of the White Mask Society's existence in Paris, she was determined to join, much to the chagrin of her otherwise passive family.

Then, a few years ago, Kain had become a serious threat against the hyden. There were rumors of what he wanted with them, and what lengths he would go to to achieve his goals. As a result, Emmanuelle was temporarily transferred to Los Angeles where she had been living for much longer than she had ever hoped.

Her experiences with Kain had been traumatizing to say the least. So when Yara told them of another hydan they had to rescue, Emmanuelle couldn't even entertain the idea of leaving them behind to endure more of what she had faced in this wretched place.

Taking stock of who all were with them, Emmanuelle figured they were now heading toward Janya Varma, the healer.

Emmanuelle knew of the rest of the hyden. Luan Khumalo and his echolocation, Roberto Diaz and his telepathy, Yara Rivers of course, and Anna Karimov. Emmanuelle knew that Anna had an unusually powerful and dangerous gift. She could control people. Their bones, their muscles. She could move them with nothing but her mind. The Society called her "the puppeteer". How Kain had managed to keep her from controlling him or his Shadow Men, Emmanuelle did not know, but she imagined it had something to do with the glowing collar locked around Anna's neck.

Kain was twisted. What he did to them was unforgivable and inhumane. Staring at that collar and Anna's half-conscious body, Emmanuelle's own legs aching in pain as she pushed them to keep her upright despite her recent ordeal in Kain's laboratory, she vowed to destroy him.

And she would show no mercy.

They moved like clockwork. Yara led the way, Luan and Bobby carried Anna, finally finding a rhythm and moving seamlessly using their abilities in concert, and Emmanuelle brought up the rear. Yara felt foolish, still carrying the IV stand with her like a hospital patient trying to run away from her nurses. Only she and Emmanuelle had one despite them all having the permanent rubber ports left in their arms. Evidently, everyone else had recovered enough from whatever surgeries Kain performed on them that they didn't need a constant intake of drugs. But Yara did not want to let go of it. She was still hoping that the drugs being pumped into her were helping keep away the pain and it was the closest thing she had to a weapon. As much as she wanted it not to be true, they would likely need it.

Kain's base was so much bigger than she had imagined. The halls were emptier now, and Yara felt a growing sense of unease.

"It's around the corner," Yara whispered.

Emmanuelle slowly moved past the other three hyden and whispered to Yara, "I'll get the guards. You get the last prisoner out of there as fast as possible, then head for the exit."

Yara bit her tongue. Emmanuelle didn't know about Erik. Nor did she know that if he really was here Yara would not leave without him. She bit her tongue. Now was not the time to mention it. How Emmanuelle was envisioning being able to take out four Shadow Men on her own, especially with such severe injuries, Yara didn't ask. Instead, she turned to Luan, Bobby, and Anna.

"You wait here. It'll be faster if I go alone."

Yara barely had time to prepare herself when Emmanuelle took a huge leap toward the opposite wall, clutching her IV stand like a Bo staff, and rebounded out of sight around the corner. Yara followed her at a sprint and saw Emmanuelle already immersed in a fight with the Shadow Men. The air was filled with Emmanuelle's yells, and the sounds of bodies colliding. Yara didn't slow down to look, fumbling with the keys to find the last one, labeled "4".

It didn't work.

"Dammit." She looked around and saw Emmanuelle trying to get out of a bald Shadow Man's chokehold. Blood had begun to seep through her bandages and she had lost her IV stand, leaving her weaponless and her arm bloodied. Yara instinctively started to move toward her to help, but Emmanuelle gave her a sharp look that clearly told Yara "no!" before flipping the Shadow Man onto his back.

Not expecting any of the other keys to work, Yara tried them all. Sure enough, none of them fit.

So close.

They were so close.

This couldn't be how it ended... Yara had not seen past opening this door. She didn't think there would have been any point. Up until now, every door had opened, they'd saved a hydan, and moved on. There was no purpose in wasting any time with a longer vision, but now she kicked herself, wishing she had done it. Looking up, she saw no markings on the door whatsoever, whereas the rest of them had all been numbered, matching their corresponding key.

Perhaps this cell was empty... Or perhaps they couldn't get it open and this was how it all ended...

"None of the keys fit!" Yara screamed, her hands starting to shake violently.

"Here!" Emmanuelle yelled. Yara turned just in time to catch a set of keys that Emmanuelle had thrown to her from the belt of one of the guards.

Unbelievably, Yara guessed the right key on her first try and the door clicked open.

Yara gasped.

"You..."

CHAPTER FORTY-SIX

Surrounded

There was no hydan in the cell.

It was Erik.

Unlike her cell door, there was a narrow window near the top through which he had been trying to see what the commotion was. When she opened the door, he collapsed into Yara's arms.

"I thought I'd lost you," he said, his voice choked with tears.

Yara wanted to speak. There were so many things she wanted to say. She wanted to tell him that she was OK, that it would all be OK. But, of course, she was not OK. Not in the slightest. Not that any of it mattered, because the words wouldn't leave her throat, and instead she sobbed in disbelief into his shoulder.

"What have they done to you?" he said, pulling his hands away, drenched in her blood. Otherwise he looked exactly as she had seen him in her vision. Relatively intact, fresh wounds, still dressed in his Guardian uniform though it was torn and filthy.

"Yara!" said Emmanuelle's strangled voice from behind her. It was enough to jolt Yara into action.

"Come on. There's no time."

She grabbed Erik's hand and went to find the rest of the group. Emmanuelle had - somehow - managed to incapacitate the guards, though she had suffered for it. She wasn't putting any weight on one of her legs, both bandages were soaked through with blood, and she was clutching a massive wound across her side. Her face remained determined.

Before Yara could reach the other hyden, however, Luan came from around the corner, his white eyes wide with panic.

"We're surrounded."

Yara looked to Erik and Emmanuelle, hoping that one of them would know what to do. But this was Yara's operation. She was the one who had gotten them this far, she had to get them out. Emmanuelle had taken a gauntlet off of one of the Shadow Men and handed a fallen glowing sword to Erik.

"Where are we supposed to go now?" said Emmanuelle, affixing the gauntlet to her hand.

"They're here," said Luan. Anna and Bobby came limping over to them. They were cornered animals; vulnerable and terrified.

Footsteps were getting louder from all sides. With nowhere else to go, the six of them ran into Erik's cell and slammed the door shut.

"We're trapped…" said Bobby.

"What are we gonna do?" said Yara, looking at Erik who looked just as lost as she felt.

"Yara," said Emmanuelle's strong voice. "Close your eyes. Focus."

"Oh. Right."

Despite her uncontrolled shaking, still clutching Erik's hand, Yara had never been able to sink into her mind so quickly. Whether from the imminent fear of recapture or the relief she felt at having found Erik, it took her no time at all to find their next steps.

The real problem would be getting past the Shadow Men.

The other four hyden waited as Yara returned to her mind.

Minutes passed in silence.

Finally, her eyes snapped open, bright despite her otherwise gaunt appearance.

"I know what to do."

"The last hydan is with Kain," said Yara. "In his lab."

Erik started to ask how she knew this, but stopped at the sound of the lock clicking open.

Yara took a deep breath, bracing herself.

The Shadow Men flooding the halls had unlocked the door and before Yara could fully comprehend what was happening, they came spilling into the small cell. The space was suddenly filled with echoing screams and yells. Emmanuelle had summoned a solenoid from the belt of an unconscious guard in the hall and it zoomed clean through three Shadow Men. Their limp, crimson robed bodies crumpled in a pile, a pool of blood growing beneath them. Erik, meanwhile, had slashed violently with the sword he had been given, though it was clear it wasn't his weapon of choice. He was locked in combat with one of the Shadow Men while Emmanuelle continued to use the solenoid to keep the rest at bay. She felled another, and then another. Erik landed a blow to the Shadow Man's gut and fumbled for the gauntlet on one of the arms of someone Emmanuelle had killed. Once he managed to slip it on, the two Guardians made quick work of the rest of the men who charged at them. It was lucky the Shadow Men were clearly under orders not to kill the hyden, or Yara had no doubt they would all be dead. Erik now had a fresh gash across his left arm which hung limply at his side, and Emmanuelle looked on the verge of collapse, but somehow remained standing.

In the wake of the slaughter, the cell was stunned into silence.

"We are following you, Yara," said Emmanuelle, her voice weak but calm.

Yara tried hard not to look at the floor as she finally dropped her IV stand, disconnecting it at last from the port in her arm, and instead took Erik's abandoned sword. She wasn't a fighter, but it would be better than medical equipment. The other hyden all followed suit, picking weapons from the fallen Shadow Men. She reached for Erik's hand and led them out of the cell, carefully trying not to tred on any bodies. How the six of them had managed to get out alive was a miracle Yara could not explain. Though in her logical mind she knew she should be grateful, she couldn't shake the feeling that there was something she didn't know.

It's just because Kain wants us alive, she thought to herself, trying to shrug away the sense of foreboding.

They moved in silence, the only sound their gasps, sobs of pain, and the slapping of their feet on the cold ground. They encountered no more Shadow Men, and the feeling of unease in Yara's gut grew. There was no way Kain would make it this easy. And where was he, anyway? He had to know what was happening. Was he really content to entrust the situation to his goons?

"Here," said Yara. They had reached it. The door to Kain's lab. Yara recognized it, and she felt her body seizing with renewed fear at the sight. It was the absolute last place she wanted to be. None of their stolen keys would be able to unlock it, however. Yara, during her many times being brought here, had seen Kain palm the screen next to it, and his hand seemed to be the only way to get in or out.

"Uh, Yara?" said Luan. She turned around, and - even though she knew what she would see - her heart stopped.

The six of them were surrounded, an army of Shadow Men blocking any means of escape. Behind her, the door opened. She jumped and turned to find Kain, towering over her, smiling dangerously.

CHAPTER FORTY-SEVEN

Trapped

"You made it," said Kain. "I've been waiting."

Yara gaped at him. Kain, who usually leaned heavily on a crutch, his right leg mangled and incapable of supporting his weight, was instead standing perfectly upright. He had no crutch and his leg was straight as an arrow. Yara felt her jaw drop. Despite knowing that she would find him here, the sight of him still made Yara's blood run cold. She did not remember seeing in her vision that he was no longer disabled. Perhaps it was another doppelgänger, like the one she had locked in her cell. But he had no brand on his neck, and his eyes were as crazed as Yara remembered. This was undeniably Kain.

So what had happened to fix his leg?

His Shadow Men stayed perfectly still, their faces masked in shadow, but showing no signs of surprise at Kain's transformation.

"You've even found your pet," he said, looking to Erik. Though his voice was low, it was laced with danger. Beneath his calm demeanor, there was a rage Yara could feel emanating off of him. "You know, it had never been my plan to fetch this boy. But he was kind enough to deliver himself directly to me and as is it turns out, he bought me that much extra time to get situated."

Yara backed into Erik, trying to draw strength from him. His ungauntleted hand squeezed her shoulder.

"Ah," said Kain, his eyes flashing. He looked at Emmanuelle and cocked his head. The movement triggered a memory. It was the same way he had looked when he read her mind. The same way Bobby did when he'd met Luan and Anna and Yara. Kain was reading

Emmanuelle's mind. "A tracking device," he continued. "I suppose you were able to reactivate it, then? An upgrade since my time."

The tracker! Emmanuelle's tracker! Yara had forgotten it in all the commotion. Then there was still hope that they would be able to get out of this alive. The Society knew where they were, and with any luck they were already well on their way.

Kain shoved Yara and Erik to the side carelessly as he moved soundlessly toward Emmanuelle. It was strange without the usual *thud* accompanying his every step. He grabbed Emmanuelle's injured arm, mutilated in her attempt to retrieve the tracking device. Behind Emmanuelle, Yara could see that Anna had passed out. Luan and Bobby were doing their best to keep her upright, but it looked like a losing battle. They were all so weak. Too weak. Yara could feel her hope rise and falter with each passing moment, as fragile as a butterfly wing.

Emmanuelle tried to wrench her arm away from Kain, but she had lost so much strength. Out of all of them, she was in the worst condition. Her battle injuries, her mutilated arm, her fresh and bleeding surgical scars down the sides of her legs and on the back of her head. It was a miracle she was still standing, let alone alive. And yet somehow, she still had strength to fight. Kain did not try to keep his hold on her, however. As soon as she was free, she didn't hesitate, not in the slightest deterred by the hoard of Shadow Men around them. She summoned her solenoid and was about to bring it down on Kain when something incredible happened.

Kain held out his hands and Emmanuelle's body, and subsequently her solenoid, froze.

"I'm sure you know what's happening to you right now," said Kain, his mad eyes locked on Emmanuelle. "After all, you know all about Anna Karimov and her... unique ability."

Yara looked to Anna, unconscious in Luan's arms, and the strange collar around her neck that none of the others had. She did not know what Anna could do, and therefore what Kain could now do. Yara's vision had not gone this far. She was in unfamiliar territory now. And the fact remained they were still one hydan short.

Kain turned to look at Yara, still apparently keeping Emmanuelle frozen in place. "Don't worry, she's right inside the lab," he said in response to her thoughts.

Yara glanced past him through the open door into his laboratory and saw a woman strapped to the table. Yara recognized her from a vision she'd had what felt like a lifetime ago. Janya Varma, whom Yara had been too slow to help.

Janya's eyes were wide as she stared at the commotion happening just outside the door. Other than being physically restrained to the table, she looked utterly unharmed.

Just then, there was a distant sound, so low Yara thought perhaps she had imagined it.

It happened again.

Erik tightened his hold on her and Kain looked distractedly in the direction of the sound. Not imagined, then. It was a far off rumbling, and it sounded like it was coming from above their heads.

"Sir," said one of the Shadow Men to Kain.

"Do nothing," said Kain. "They don't know where we are."

It was the Society. It had to be!

The White Mask Society had found them. It was over now. It had to be over.

CHAPTER FORTY-EIGHT
Heart Stopping

Yara could have cried with relief. Her body started to collapse from the damage it had taken. They were saved. She no longer needed to lead the charge.

Emmanuelle seized the opportunity of Kain being distracted and managed to break free of whatever hold he'd had on her. The solenoid had been taken by one of the Shadow Men, but she didn't seem to need it. She leapt spectacularly into the air and landed on top of him, catapulting him at a wall before landing catlike on the floor. It all happened in one smooth motion, but Yara could see color draining from Emmanuelle's face. Every movement was costing her greatly.

Kain's body was limp, his arms bent at a strange angle.

The distant sounds now forgotten, movement erupted from all sides. The Shadow Men lunged at the hyden and Erik. Yara wasted no time, screaming, "Run!" as she sprinted into the lab. Erik was keeping the door clear, using his own solenoid - which he had somehow kept control of - to fight back any Shadow Men long enough for them all to scramble into the lab. Emmanuelle was dragging Kain's unconscious and twisted body in with her.

"Leave him!" Yara shouted, afraid that Emmanuelle wouldn't be able to make it in time. And as far as Yara was concerned the more doors there were between them and Kain the better.

But Emmanuelle did not listen. "They can use him to unlock the door!" she yelled back. Luan left Anna with Bobby and ran to help Emmanuelle drag the man inside. And not a moment too soon. Yara was just able to slam the door shut in the faces of the Shadow Men and locked it.

Emmanuelle dropped Kain's unconscious body and collapsed on the floor, her eyes closed, breathing heavily. Luan and Bobby lay Anna down and rushed to help Janya. The metal straps binding her to the table were magnetically locked, and no matter what they did or how hard they pulled, they didn't budge.

"What the hell is going on?" said Janya.

"I can't get these things off!" said Yara, starting to lose any semblance of control over the situation. She wanted so badly to drop next to Emmanuelle on the floor and fall asleep... It was only the thought of waking up back in her cell that kept her standing.

The door to the lab was being pummeled by the Shadow Men outside. Their dead eyes could be seen through the small window as they hurled themselves at the door with no regard to their own safety. The hyden's only hope now was that the door would hold. Without Kain, the Shadow Men wouldn't be able to unlock it.

"Stand back," said Erik. He brought the solenoid so close to the table that Yara was sure the spinning disc would cut straight through Janya, but he wielded it expertly. His eyes were wide with focus, unblinking, as he cut through one, then another, and another restraint.

As Yara watched him work, she could feel herself falling apart. She was getting shakier, though she didn't think it was as much from fear as it was from blood loss. She could still feel it continuing to run down her back. Her skin felt both hot and cold. Her head had not stopped hurting, and the door was close to its breaking point.

"No!" It was Bobby who yelled, and Yara looked around just in time to see Kain rising from his crumpled form on the floor, unfurling like a beanstalk, his face lit with rage. His arm which had just moments ago looked horrifically broken was now completely normal. He pulled Emmanuelle's gauntlet off of her, and while she initially resisted, he simply held up his hand and once again she went still.

Kain had his head cocked and she knew he was reading their minds.

She wanted so badly to hide her fear from him, unwilling to give him another weapon against her, but she barely had time to have the thought before Erik went spinning past her toward Kain, yelling as he hurled his solenoid. Kain threw up his hand, the same way he had managed to stop Emmanuelle, and Erik slowed down, but he didn't stop. The solenoid still soared toward Kain, who threw up the gauntlet he'd taken from Emmanuelle to try to gain control of it.

Tearing her gaze away, Yara returned to Janya who was tugging at the IV drip plugged into her arm. There were tears in her eyes, but they didn't seem to be of pain or fear, but rather anger. Finally free, she clambered off the metal table.

"He can't win," she yelled over the commotion, nodding to Erik who was wrestling with Kain.

Yara felt completely lost. The Shadow Men were going to be able to break into the room at any second and they would lose the fight. And to think the Society was *here*. Somewhere so close she could hear them. How was it possible that they couldn't find the actual location of Kain's operation? The hyden would have to find *them*. But they were cornered, the only exit blocked by more than fifty people.

Erik was still fighting. Emmanuelle had managed to get back to her feet, though she looked unsteady and her face shone with sweat. She grabbed the glowing sword Yara had dropped on the floor and crept up behind Kain while he was locked in combat. She moved quickly, only one of her arms usable, the other clutching her wounded side, and sank the blade deep into Kain's back.

His scream was deafening, half rage and half pain. His distraction was enough for Erik to grab Kain's head and slam it against the corner of a counter.

A loud crack.

The hyden froze, panting.

Kain's body toppled.

And fell.

It was over.

Kain was dead.

Panting, Erik hurried to Emmanuelle to help her stand and she looked calmly to Yara and said, "Where to?"

Yara couldn't tear her eyes from the wide pool of red under Kain. His head was turned too far to the side, his temple was gushing, and a bright white spot was just visible through the blood. His skull.

Hating herself, Yara felt no pity. She didn't want to be the kind of person who relished in death, but staring at Kain's skull she felt... satisfied.

"Oh..." came a faint voice from next to her, and she saw Bobby with his hand over his mouth and his eyes squeezed shut.

"Yara!" Erik said sharply, pulling Yara's focus back to the present.

"Right," she gasped, closing her eyes, trying to sink into her mind. But all she could think of was the sound of the Shadow Men outside the door as they continued to try to break it down. "I can't," she cried. Her body was now shaking so uncontrollably that she had to lean against the table for support. She was too tired. She couldn't do it again.

"Yes you can," said Emmanuelle.

"I can't..." Yara was fading.

"Yara?" Erik left Emmanuelle to stand on her own as he rushed over to Yara, limping heavily from his injured leg. Each step burned, but it didn't matter. Grabbing Yara's shoulders he tried to look into her eyes, but they rolled into the back of her head. She was drenched in blood, her back soaked in it. She had lost so much. Too much.

"Is she OK?" Janya asked, but Erik barely heard her.

"We're losing her. Quick, find me something. Anything. Amphetamines. Whatever you find."

Janya gaped at him.

"Do it!" he yelled.

Janya and Bobby rushed to the cabinets lining the room and started searching frantically.

"Here!" said Janya, thrusting a massive syringe into Erik's hands. "Epinephrine."

Looking at the size of the needle, Erik cringed. "I'm sorry," he said to Yara's nearly unconscious body. He tried not to focus on how close to death she looked. "This is gonna hurt." She didn't seem to hear him. Janya's face was screwed up with apprehension as she watched Erik place the needle next to her arm. He hesitated for a fraction of a second before jamming it into her skin, sinking it into muscle, and emptying the contents of the syringe into her failing body.

She didn't move for two heart stopping seconds.

CHAPTER FORTY-NINE

Hurt

Yara could feel her heart start beating frantically. Her muscles buzzed with energy. She was aware of pain in her arm and in her head, but it didn't seem to matter. She sat up, panting heavily, panicked by the sudden surge of energy.

"What the hell…"

"You OK?" Erik's green eyes came swimming into focus.

He looked brighter, more vivid than he had before.

"Yara, we need you to see what our next step is," said Emmanuelle. "Can you do that?"

Her blood was pumping so loudly it drowned out the creaking of the metal door that the Shadow Men had nearly succeeded in knocking down. She could feel it pulse through every part of her, right down to her fingertips. She nodded and squeezed her eyes shut. But it felt impossible. Even had she not been at death's door, her bones were practically vibrating.

"Yara!" said Emmanuelle.

She felt hands on her face and opened her eyes to see Erik in front of her. He was holding her close, pressing his forehead to hers. "You can do this," he said. Yara inhaled the smell of him, like summer and roasted nuts. The world melted around them. Here was Erik, the first man she had ever loved, on the verge of being killed, and she was the only thing standing between them and freedom. She could do this. She had to.

Everything disappeared.

And she sank into the fog.

"They're breaking through!" said Luan. He had grabbed Anna who had started to regain some consciousness and was backing up from the door. He nudged Yara and it knocked her back into the present, but she had already seen what she needed.

"What do we do?" asked Bobby.

Yara looked around the room frantically, and spotted what she was looking for. An air vent in the ceiling. "There!" she yelled, pointing.

Without hesitation, Emmanuelle leapt into the air and grabbed onto a light fixture, hanging upside down from it like a spider. Yara, remembering how she had once scoffed at Emmanuelle's gift, felt ashamed of how skeptical she'd been of that talent.

Emmanuelle managed to single-handedly detach the cover of the air vent before jumping back down to the ground to help the rest of them reach it. She grabbed Anna first. Despite not being able to understand what they were saying, Anna knew enough to hold onto Emmanuelle. The Guardian looked up at the ceiling, her hard eyes focused intently on her destination, and took a great leaping jump. Anna managed to clamber into the vent, leaving Emmanuelle hanging from the ceiling, her face contorted with pain. She would not be able to do it again.

But it didn't matter. "Help me!" said Yara, grabbing the wheeled tray Kain used to carry his syringes. She swiped them to the floor and brought the tray directly underneath the open vent.

"Bobby!"

He rushed over and they helped him onto the small table, holding it steady. Anna and Emmanuelle managed to pull him up.

"Start moving!" Yara shouted up at them. The three of them didn't know what direction they needed to go but at this point it didn't matter. They needed to get out of this room. The door was dented, the hinges faltering, and Yara doubted it would last more than a few more seconds.

"Woah!"

Bobby's shout of surprise tore Yara away from watching him to see what had made him yell.

Kain who, moments before, had been bleeding and motionless on the ground, was beginning to stir. The gaping gash on his temple, once open enough to expose his gleaming skull, was closing up. New skin was forming rapidly, and hair was growing over it. He unfolded himself from the heap on the floor, like a majestic being that was waking from a deep sleep. With a sickening crack he snapped his broken neck back into place. Just as before he was now apparently completely devoid of injury. Even his leg was still miraculously healed. "How…"

"That hurt," he said.

Erik launched himself at Kain, scooping the bloodied sword from the ground as he went. "Go!" he shouted over his shoulder.

Luan rushed over to help Janya climb into the vent next. Behind Yara, Erik was thrown backwards by Kain and crashed into a pile of equipment. Trying hard to ignore his cries of pain, Yara gestured for Luan to go next.

One of the Shadow Men had gotten their weapon through the door and was slashing at the lock.

"You next, Yara," said Luan from the ceiling. She looked at Erik. She couldn't leave without him. She wouldn't. After all, he had been the one who had given her the strength to fight.

"Erik!"

He glanced at her, made a final effort, sinking his sword deep into Kain's gut, and extricated himself. Sprinting toward her, limping from his own injuries, he yelled, "Go!"

Trusting that he would follow, Yara leapt for Luan's outstretched hand, her body still buzzing with energy.

Below them, the Shadow Men had at last broken into the lab. "Hurry, you fools!" screamed Kain.

"That way!" she yelled at the hyden, pointing down the vent. They started to clamber in the direction she pointed as she turned back to the open vent to see Erik climb onto the small table.

"Jump!"

She didn't need to tell him. He had already leapt for her, the table rolling out from under his feet as he did so. Yara managed to catch his hand and pull him up enough for him to grab onto the vent. Shadow Men appeared beneath him. One grabbed his leg, the other sliced at him with their weapon. Erik yelled, but did not let go. Using every ounce of strength she had, Yara was able to keep hold of him and won the tug-of-war with the Shadow Man below, pulling him fully into the vent. He looked about ready to collapse, but there was no time to rest.

"Come on," she said, army crawling through a trail of blood after the others in the cramped space. She could hear Erik behind her, grunting in pain as he moved.

It was harder to keep the map of where they needed to go in her head in the near complete darkness. More than once, someone gasped in pain as they got caught on a screw or snag they couldn't see. Every time Erik accidentally bumped into her, she jumped in surprise.

Yara had to shout ahead to Bobby who was leading the pack when and where to turn anytime a fork presented itself. They were loud as they moved, clanging against the cold metal. If she hadn't seen it already in a vision, she would have expected them to fall through the vents at any moment, but they held. She couldn't imagine where they were in respect to the lab or Kain's base below them, but the sounds of the Shadow Men faded as they moved, though she was sure they would catch up in another room. Yara could only hope that her vision was accurate and that they wouldn't send any solenoids or glowing swords through the vent, sure that it would slice straight through the metal. They would be completely defenseless. But no doubt Kain wanted them back alive, and a solenoid could accidentally kill someone. More than likely, the Shadow Men had gone to prepare to intercept them wherever the vent would spit them out.

No one was speaking. Their breathing was labored over the muffled sounds of chaos below them.

"I see a light!" said Bobby at last.

"That's it!" said Yara, her heart racing. "Go towards it!" She couldn't see it with everyone in front of her, but as they got nearer, the faint light bounced off the metal walls, casting a modicum of illumination through the darkness, growing as they got nearer.

Their scrambling sped up until Bobby shouted back, "Now what?"

It was impossible to see what he was looking at, with nothing in front of her but the bottom of Luan's feet, so she had to rely on the images in her mind. It had been a soft, diffused light, like looking through an opaque window. It had a different quality than the lights where they had come from. In Kain's lab, in their cells, in the halls, the lights had all been cold and blue. But this one was warm and yellow.

"Push it! Break it down!" called Yara.

She heard Bobby grunt as he pushed against the window, but nothing happened.

"Kick it," suggested Emmanuelle.

There was a moment of awkward clambering during which Bobby reoriented himself feet first and kicked at the window.

Once, twice, and on the third try, the window pane went flying away with a crash, letting light flood the vent. Yara squinted from the brightness.

It was really going to happen. They were going to make it.

"Go! Go!" she yelled.

How long before Kain's men caught up to them? Surely they knew where these vents led.

One by one, they crawled clumsily through the opening Bobby had made, each turning back to help the next. When Yara reached the window she saw Bobby supporting Emmanuelle who looked on the brink of death and Luan holding up Anna. Janya, who looked, as before, entirely unharmed, reached out to help Yara. She climbed over a sink, of all things, just below the window and into what looked like the handicap stall of a public bathroom. Turning back to help Erik, she saw they had emerged from what had once been a mirror, which now lay shattered on the tile floor.

"We should hurry," said Erik. He wasn't putting any weight at all on his left leg, but when Yara tried to say something, he waved it off impatiently.

They all moved as quickly as they could, stepping carefully around the broken glass. The bathroom tiles were alarmingly colorful in comparison to the cement prison from which they had just escaped. They scampered toward the exit, allowing Yara to catch a glimpse of herself in another mirror as they passed. Her eyes were sunken and wide, giving her a crazed look, which was not helped by the bloody rag tied around her head nor her lack of clothing. She knew that the only reason she was still able to function at all was the shot of adrenaline Erik had given her. How the rest of them were still standing, Yara didn't know.

Keeping a firm hold of Yara's hand, Erik took the lead, limping heavily, and signaled for everyone to stop. He cautiously pushed the bathroom door open, listening for any sign of trouble. Finding none, they slipped out one by one.

"Do you know where we are?" whispered Janya.

"Is this…" said Yara.

"The Los Angeles Library," said Janya.

Directly in front of them were long, grey, metal shelves filled with volumes of books, stretching the length of the entire room illuminated by fluorescent lamps. The ceiling was low and the shelves were high, making the room feel small, an impression not aided by the loud carpet which they were now staining with blood as they moved forward. Tables with tall silver lamps and desks with privacy partitions were scattered around the room, equipped with ornate wooden chairs.

It was beyond strange. The world was still there, unaware of their ordeal, looking completely normal, even though beneath their feet was a maze of horrors.

"Let's go," Erik whispered. They moved as quickly as they could down the length of the bookshelves. (Yara was painfully aware that they were all - except for Erik - essentially naked. It felt much stranger now that they were back in the real world.) He moved with intention, apparently knowing where to go, and turned sharply at the end of the shelf. They passed an Information desk further down - mercifully empty - and Yara wondered idly what time it was. The library was clearly closed. Past a flickering light, which gave the already low ceiling the impression of caving in, they reached a door that led out into the atrium of the library. The warm carpet was replaced by red and green stone tiles, and the ceiling was suddenly eight stories tall, made entirely of glass, enormous pieces of abstract art hanging like giant birds. It was dizzying after so long being trapped underground. Along the walls were towering green pillars that stretched all the way to the top, giving her the sensation that she was falling up toward an empty gray sky.

To their right were escalators to the next floor, and beyond that another escalator, and then another, until it reached what had to be the ground floor. Like Headquarters, Yara knew that the majority of the library was subterranean, leaving a paltry four stories above ground in comparison to the high rises of downtown.

"Wow..." said Bobby, also looking up.

Yara had only been to this branch of the LA Library once on a field trip when she was in middle school, and it had been just as impressive then, too.

"Where is everyone?" Erik muttered, and she knew he didn't mean patrons, but rather the Society. It was true, Yara had expected to find people waiting for her when they emerged, whether they were Shadow Men or Guardians. But the library was empty. Except for—

"Excuse me!" A plump woman with white, curled hair, thick glasses, and a pinched voice came ambling over to them from the room they had just left. "Excuse me," she repeated as she got closer, sounding appalled. "We don't open for another—" She stopped mid sentence when she took them in. "Goodness!"

Erik spared her a split second's worth of attention before limping toward the stationary escalators. They had only made it halfway up the motionless staircase when a great crash and loud yells sounded from behind them. No less than fifty Shadow Men clad in crimson were storming out from amidst the bookshelves as though they were jumping out of the library walls themselves. Yara didn't spare any time wondering where they had come from.

Where was the Society?

The few Shadow Men who had gauntlets were hurling solenoids in their direction, the others charging with weapons in hand. Yara screamed, though none of the solenoids were apparently aimed at them. They zoomed around, propelling into books, slicing lamps in half, shattering glass. They weren't trying to injure the hyden. They were trying to herd them.

The librarian was swiftly cut in half.

It was hard to register anything about what was happening, other than Erik's grip on her hand and the metal from the escalator cutting into her bare feet. She didn't know where the other hyden were, if they were still following them or even alive.

Hope was draining from her body as quickly as her energy. They had been so close that she could see the orange light from the rising sun in the high windows above them.

But then a streak of black. Several dozen Guardians were flooding in from the top level, pouring down the escalators and leaping to the aid of the hyden and Erik. Yara had never seen anything so magnificent as the sight of the black shadows filtering into the room, their white half-masks glowing angelically, their solenoids zooming toward the exposed Shadow Men. Almost half of the Shadow Men had fallen before they realized what had happened. The air was filled with the clang of metal on metal.

"Run!" screamed Erik.

It took everything Yara had to urge her legs to move. Her muscles screamed and ached, her body was weak, her skin slick with sweat. She was cold and hungry and completely drained. But she managed to pull herself forward with Erik's help, her feet as heavy as the steps beneath her.

But there was too far to go. They had barely made it up two flights and she could no longer muster the strength to continue. She had hit a wall. Her legs were collapsing, her vision sliding out of focus.

Hands were tugging at her. She could not even tell if it was a Guardian or a Shadow Man.

Chaos ensued all around them, echoing grandly in the massive atrium. Screams. Yells. Cries. The occasional sound of a solenoid slicing clean through something. Or Someone. Whoever had a hold of her picked her up and carried her up the remaining escalators. She was too heavy to help them, assuming it was a good guy, and too heavy to fight if it wasn't. Her head was lolling on their shoulder. Behind them she could just make out Luan being pulled along by an anonymous Guardian, though he seemed to be in better shape than she was. He, at least, was supporting his own weight.

"Hang on for me, Yara," said the person carrying her. She swung her head to look at them, but all she could register was that they were wearing a white mask. A good guy then. She didn't recognize their voice. The world was spinning.

So much screaming…

"This way!"

"I've got her!"

"They're on our tail, we've got to hurry!"

"The cars are waiting on Hope Street!"

The next thing Yara knew, the warm library lights were gone, replaced by the bright morning sun. And the cold which had permeated her for so long was evaporating at last.

CHAPTER FIFTY

One Week Later

Yara was afraid to open her eyes. Had it all been a dream? Would she find herself still in her cell? But even before opening her eyes, she knew it had been real. The air was warm, she was no longer in pain, and the surface on which she slept was soft.

She was back at Headquarters.

But upon looking around, she was not immediately sure where in Headquarters. This room was unfamiliar, though she could safely deduce it was indeed part of the medical ward. She was in what resembled a hospital bed and wearing a white gown. She reached up to scratch her cheek only to find - much to her dismay - that the IV port was still in her arm, attached to a drip. Though perhaps it was responsible for the feeling of being filled with cotton.

The room was quiet, but not silent. She could hear a few voices murmuring quietly, as though trying not to wake anyone, and soft beeps. Yara tried to sit up, but found that her body was too stiff to move.

"Yara!"

She would recognize that voice anywhere. "Annie?"

Aunt Catherine, who had been sitting in a nearby chair, came to sit on Yara's bed. She looked tired, gray hairs flying in all directions, pale skin, red eyes. Worse than Yara had ever seen her.

Mad relief swept through Yara, tears pouring out of her eyes.

They embraced awkwardly, Aunt Catherine leaning forward as Yara could barely move, but they clung tightly to each other and didn't let go. Yara hadn't realized how alone she had felt in the time she had been with Kain. To have the soft touch of someone who loved her compared to what she had endured…

"I thought I'd lost you," cried Aunt Catherine into Yara's shoulder.

Yara couldn't answer. Her chest was heaving with sobs. She couldn't catch her breath enough to say a word. But she didn't need to.

"I thought I'd lost you," said Aunt Catherine again. "I thought I'd lost you. I thought I'd lost you."

Aunt Catherine had let Yara cry herself to exhaustion before letting go, though still keeping a tight hold of Yara's hand. She wanted to squeeze her aunt's hand back, but her body was impossibly weak and all she could manage was a small twitch. Aunt Catherine seemed to understand.

"I was supposed to go get Frankie when you woke up," she said.

"Where is everyone?" said Yara.

"The other hyden are in their quarters, except for Emmanuelle. She's still recovering." Aunt Catherine gestured toward a bed on the far side of the room which Yara now recognized to be a sort of recovery ward with half a dozen beds. Only hers and Emmanuelle's were occupied. Emmanuelle was unconscious and a Medic was hunched over the desk next to her.

"Where's Erik?"

"He's fine. He and the others have been trying to chase down Kain for the last week before—"

"*Week*?" said Yara. "How long have I been asleep?"

"Well, about a week, honey," said Aunt Catherine, her brows furrowed.

Yara gaped. One week. Seven whole days. How injured must she have been to warrant that?

"They almost lost Emmanuelle. You both lost so much blood. The Medics told me you'd just had a surgery hours before you went through all that. Is that true?"

Yara gave a noncommittal shrug, not really listening to her aunt.

"How horrible. When I think of what you went through with that man—" Her eyes were gleaming and her voice caught in her throat.

"I'm OK," said Yara, trying to catch her before she started to cry. "We're OK."

"I just can't believe you got out."

"It wasn't easy," said Yara.

"The others couldn't say, everyone is dying to know how you did it.

They just said you were the one who got them out. Even Erik couldn't tell us how it all happened. Bora Black wants to 'debrief' you, but I don't think it's appropriate, if I'm being honest. Frankly, you are not a part of this organization. It's not your responsibility."

"But Annie, if I can help them, shouldn't I?"

"You've been through so much! How could she possibly ask you to relive all that?"

"So they don't have Kain?"

Aunt Catherine shook her head. "I'm afraid not. He wasn't in the library when they found you, and by the time they went back to look for him his whole place was emptied. They couldn't even find a way in except through that mirror in the bathroom. And it's so small they could only send a few people to investigate. They said the whole place was abandoned. Nothing left. Not a trace of him."

Yara's heart sank. "After all that, and he's still out there."

"I keep asking them to move us," said Aunt Catherine. "It doesn't feel safe here. After all, Kain broke in once. Of course they keep saying they've upgraded the system, changed it all, but..."

"But what?"

Aunt Catherine hesitated. "Maybe I shouldn't be telling you all this."

"Are you serious?" said Yara. "You don't think I've earned a little inside info?"

Aunt Catherine chuckled and squeezed Yara's hand. "You make a fair point." She sighed and lowered her voice. "There are whispers that the way he broke in before was because he has someone. You know. On the *inside*."

Yara frowned. "You mean like a mole?"

Aunt Catherine nodded.

"That's not possible," said Yara, shaking her head, though she stopped quickly when it made the world spin. "Who in the Society would ever do that?"

Aunt Catherine shrugged. "It's hard to swallow to be sure. But I've heard several people talking about it as a very real possibility. It's one of the reasons I think they should move us out of Headquarters. If there really is a spy, what's stopping them from telling Kain all the new security measures they've set up?"

Yara felt a familiar grip of fear in her stomach, made worse when she jumped in surprise at the sound of the door opening.

"I see someone neglected their responsibilities." It was Frankie, the shape shifter who had treated Yara after her collapse from the suppressed vision. Though her words sounded reproachful, she was smiling her wide smile, showing every single one of her white teeth.

"Was just hoping for a little one-on-one time," said Aunt Catherine, standing up to make space for Frankie.

"How are you feeling today, Yara?"

"Thick."

"Is that some new slang I'm not familiar with from the kids these days?"

"No," said Yara. "I just feel thick. You know, like... heavy and stuff."

"I see." Frankie checked a gauge on the IV drip and some measurements on a nearby monitor. "You seem to be moving in the right direction. They did quite a number on you."

"Do I still..." Yara started. She didn't know how to ask the question, too afraid to reach up and feel the back of her head for herself. "Is there still the..."

She didn't need to find the words because Frankie knew what she meant. Yara's heart fell at the expression on Frankie's face. "Unfortunately, we weren't able to remove the funnel. Any of them."

Yara could feel the world closing in on her. There was a crawling under her skin. Something she desperately needed to claw out. She felt violated.

"I'm sorry, Yara. We would have risked too much brain damage if we'd tried to remove it. We don't know how Kain managed to avoid any while putting them there in the first place. What I can say is that the damage to your skull was minor, so we trimmed the funnel and plugged it up. And now your skull is healing normally thanks to a hydrogel I myself developed," (she looked quite proud of herself as she said this,) "that can stimulate bone regrowth. You should take it easy for a few weeks at least, but I imagine you'll make a full recovery. You likely won't even notice anything is there at all."

Yara knew that Frankie's words should have made her happy, but all she felt was unsettled. Yes, they had made it out. Yes, she was recovering, she would survive, she would be back to her normal self. But after all that, Kain was still out there. And she would always know that he had left a part of himself inside her mind. The war was not over. She was still in danger. Still needed Guardians.

Life wouldn't really go back to the way it was.

"Don't celebrate too much," said Frankie.

"Sorry," said Yara. "It's just... a lot."

"Of course. Well, I'll go inform Bora that you're up. I'm sure she'll want to talk to you—"

"Do you really have to do that right away?" said Aunt Catherine. "She only just woke up."

"Sorry, Catherine. She's the boss. I do what she says."

Aunt Catherine shook her head, her lips pursed as Frankie left. "Honestly."

"Is she gonna be OK?" said Yara looking at Emmanuelle.

Aunt Catherine followed her gaze. "She's stable, at the very least." She lowered her voice. "I was surprised they managed to save her, if I'm being honest. But apparently hyden are more resilient than humans. I suppose I should be grateful. You all took quite a beating." She trailed off and when Yara looked at her, she saw her head bowed and tears running down her cheeks.

"I'm OK," said Yara.

"I would never have been able to forgive myself," she said, "if I'd lost you. Your mother—"

"You didn't lose me," said Yara. They hugged again and did not let go.

CHAPTER FIFTY-ONE

Fault

It wasn't long before Frankie came back, this time with Bora Black at her heels. Yara had forgotten how intimidating Black was, with tendrils of darkness curling off her skin, like black ink moving through water. Her obsidian eyes were trained on Yara. (Even though it was hard to know exactly where she was looking without any discernible pupils, her gaze always provoked a sense of apprehension.)

"Yara," she said matter-of-factly. "It's wonderful to see you awake. Dr. Sweet here tells me you're well on your way to a full recovery. I'm glad."

Unsure of how to respond, feeling very far away from a "full recovery", Yara didn't speak. Instead she felt her lips tighten with unease.

Black pulled a chair to Yara's bed and sat down, looking at Aunt Catherine pointedly, but Aunt Catherine ignored her.

"Perhaps it's best we give them a minute," said Frankie politely.

Evidently, Aunt Catherine was not up to resisting a second time, and Yara knew that she respected Frankie quite a bit more than she respected Black. So, reluctantly, she let herself be guided out of the ward by Frankie. The Medic who had been tending to Emmanuelle followed them as well, leaving Yara alone with Black and the unconscious form of Emmanuelle Moreau.

The door clicked shut. They sat in silence for a few moments, the only sound the faint beeping of the machines monitoring both her and Emmanuelle.

"Yara, I can't pretend to know what you've been through this last month."

Had she really been with Kain a whole month? What had happened in that time? Thanksgiving. And Christmas. And her eighteenth birthday…

She realized she didn't even know what dayr it was.

"And I don't relish the task of asking you questions, but unfortunately, you're the only one who may be able to shed some light on the situation."

Not having been asked a direct question, Yara remained silent.

"Mr. Khumalo, Mr. Diaz, and Ms. Varma were able to tell us what their experiences were, but it seems they didn't—"

"What about Anna?"

Black licked her lips before answering. Perhaps it was just Yara's imagination, but she thought the curls of darkness started to move more quickly in the wake of her question. "I'm afraid Anna Karimov did not survive."

Yara's stomach dropped. She knew next to nothing about the hydan named Anna. Only that she did not speak English, and that whatever her ability was, it was the most powerful of all of them, evidenced not only by the collar Kain had put around her neck, but his confidence when he had wielded her skill against Emmanuelle and Erik. Anna had been in the worst shape of all of them. What had Kain done to her, Yara wondered, to leave her in such horrible condition? How much more frightening must that whole experience have been when she couldn't even speak the language?

"What happened?"

"I'm not sure that's relevant—"

"What happened to her?"

Black hesitated again. "She was injured by a Shadow Man during your escape, and her injuries were too severe."

It was a lie.

Yara didn't pride herself on much, but she knew one thing. And that was when someone was telling a lie. What on earth could have happened to Anna Karimov to make Black want to lie about it?

"But from what the other hyden tell us, it seems you were instrumental in the escape. I'd like to know more about that."

So Yara told her. She recounted everything that had happened. Everything Kain had done, from the drugs and his attempts to stimulate her ability to the procedure in which he had drilled into her skull. She explained about the first time she was able to control her ability, not just *having* a vision, but *when* and *what* she saw. That if she made different decisions she could change the outcomes of what she saw, and how she was able to use that to see how to survive.

She did, however, omit a few details. The vision she'd had of Erik that had triggered her desire to escape. (She did not want to compromise his position at the Society by hinting at anything between the two of them.) In as much detail as Yara could remember, she told her all about retrieving the other hyden, fighting off Kain, his added abilities - how he seemed to be impervious to injury, how his leg had healed, how he had stopped Emmanuelle in her tracks, and how he could read their minds. She told Black how they had crawled through the vents to find themselves in the bottom floor of the library, before finally being rescued by the Society thanks to Emmanuelle's tracker.

Black listened without interruption, her obsidian eyes unblinking and narrow as Yara spoke, taking everything in.

"I must say," she said at last, "you've come a long way. Your father worked on honing his ability much longer than you, and he was never able to wield such specific control over it. I'm impressed."

"Thank you," said Yara in a small voice, if only because she didn't know what else to say. In truth, she wanted Black to leave. She wanted to ask for her aunt to come back, and to see her Guardians. To see Robin and Carter, and most of all to see Erik. To know he was OK. The last time she saw him, he had been almost as battered as her. Now she was desperate to see him alive and well, to hold him and be held by him. But there was no way to convey all this to Black, so instead she said nothing, hoping that Black would just leave.

Before she had the chance to, the door to the ward opened again. Not only did her aunt return, but she was followed by Frankie and Robin, who looked more tired than she had ever seen him, though still cheerful, a big crooked grin plastered across his face.

"Welcome back to the land of the livin', kid!" he said.

Yara smiled back at him, though it felt strange. She realized then how long it had been since she last smiled.

"It's good to see you," he added more quietly, the words meant just for her.

"I assume you have information for me, R," said Black.

Robin turned to her, his demeanor changing. "Yes, sir."

"I'll take it in my office." Black turned to Yara and gave her a small nod. "Thank you, Yara. You've been very helpful. Five minutes," she added to Robin. "Oh, one more thing." She looked at Yara. "We'd like to equip you with a subcutaneous tracker. In case." She did not need to finish the sentence. "In case" meant "in case Kain captures you again".

Yara nodded.

"Good. I'll see to it, then," said Black before heading out the door. Frankie went to Emmanuelle's bed to occupy herself, giving Yara a moment with Robin before he had to report to Black. Aunt Catherine stayed close by and put on an air of not paying attention to them.

"How ya doin'?" said Robin in a quiet voice. His eyes still twinkled, his smile lopsided, but she could tell something in him had changed.

"Been better. You?"

"Been worse."

"Where is everyone? Where are Carter and Erik?"

"Everyone's been working overtime since you got back," said Robin. "Trying to find the main entrance to Kain's base. So far, we can't find anything. The only way we've been able to get in is through that vent you used. I still can't believe you managed to do that."

"Desperate times," said Yara dryly.

"I guess so."

"Did anyone else— get hurt?" She had been about to ask if anyone else had died, if she had to carry the weight of another life on her conscience, but she couldn't bring herself to say the words.

"A couple of Guardians had some relatively minor injuries. Three casualties. One of them civilian. Not counting Anna Karimov. Or Kain's men."

Yara could feel a tightness in her chest, a vice around her heart and lungs.

Inhale liquid gold…

"Don't do that, don't put that on yourself," said Robin sternly. He grabbed her hand and squeezed it. "Listen to me, kid. You did the unthinkable. You managed to save five people from Kain and his Shadow Men. You're a hero. You risked your life to save them, and that will never change. The Guardians who died knew that was part of the job. We all know it's a possibility. And we know there are things worth dying for."

"But—"

"No. No 'but's. You are not responsible for those we lost. OK?"

Yara looked down.

"I wanna hear you say it."

Hot tears burned her eyes. She couldn't find any words. She knew that it had all happened a week ago. Robin may have had time to make his peace with it, but to Yara it was fresh, those wounds still open and bleeding. She remembered everything so vividly and felt bile rise in her throat. Panic settled over her like a heavy blanket so quickly she didn't have time to remember to do her exercises. But then she felt Robin's fingers between her eyebrows, smoothing out the crease that often lived there. "Unclench. And tell me you know it wasn't your fault."

She looked up at him, weak and tired. She didn't want to be crying. She bit her lip to stop it trembling and nodded, if only to make Robin look away.

"Let me hear it, kid."

"It wasn't my fault."

He gave her a small smile, the corners of his lips tugging upward. "I gotta go. I'll tell C and E to come by when they're done with their shifts."

Yara watched him go, feeling lighter.

CHAPTER FIFTY-TWO

Readjusting

Yara had been allowed to leave the medical ward a few days later, on New Year's Eve. In that time, Emmanuelle had still not recovered. Yara stared at her lifeless body as she was escorted from the ward by Frankie and followed her aunt back to her quarters.

It felt strange to be back in this familiar place. Or at least, what had once been familiar. It had been over a month since she was here last, but Yara was no longer the same person she had been then and the room now felt like it belonged to someone else. Her clothes didn't fit. Everything hung loosely on her now. All in all, she had lost nearly twenty pounds in Kain's custody. The Society was feeding her a diet meant to help her put the weight back on, but it still left her shy of being able to fit in her old clothes. Staring at herself in the mirror, she did not recognize the woman looking back at her. Her hair had started to grow back but was barely more than an inch or so, giving her the sickly appearance of a cancer patient. Any youthful roundness of her face had been hollowed out and replaced with sharp edges. And while she couldn't see the back of her head, she could feel a tender scar where Kain had drilled into her brain.

Aunt Catherine spent as much time with her as possible, but Yara had a hard time filling the silences. She was always tired yet she didn't want to sleep. Nights were plagued with memories of being with Kain. Even waking, her mind replayed the worst experiences of her incarceration. Not wanting to burden Aunt Catherine with the details, she ended up not speaking much.

Carter had visited her when she had still been in recovery, looking just as tired and worn as Robin had been, but still happy to see her. They told her as many details as they could. They were scouring the library, and had evidently gotten permission from the civilian city government to close it off to the public allowing them to run a more extensive search of the area. It still turned out nothing. As to where Kain had moved everything, from his equipment and research to his Shadow Man army, no one had any ideas where to start looking.

But still Yara had not seen Erik.

She didn't know who to ask or even how to ask. He was her Guardian, which meant in theory it would be completely natural for her to be curious as to his whereabouts. But she was too afraid to ask. She didn't want to risk revealing anything that could cost him his position with the Society.

That night when Robin came by her quarters with two packed dinners for them so she wouldn't have to go to the commissary - for which she was very grateful, still not ready to face large groups - she couldn't help but blurt it out.

"Why hasn't Erik come to see me?"

Robin, who had just taken an unreasonably large bite of his sandwich, chewed exaggeratedly before being able to answer her. "So, you noticed, huh?"

"Of course I— Oh. You're teasing."

"Well, the truth is he's been asked not to see you."

"What?" Yara exclaimed. "What— why?"

Robin rubbed his hands together staring at his own fingers. It was clear that her question was not one he wanted to be answering. "Z found out. About you two. About E specifically."

"Oh."

"We don't know how, exactly. But when you got captured, E got... well, he didn't handle it very well. He went looking for ya. Against regulations. Against direct orders. And that's what got him captured. Z said he wouldn't tell B, so he hasn't lost his job or anything. But it's been made clear that if he... well, that if you two keep..." He paused, evidently searching for the right words. "He's been advised under serious penalty to try to limit his interactions with you."

Yara's face burned with embarrassment. "I'm sorry," she said. And she was. She was sorry to have put Erik in that situation, to have been the cause of his capture, to make Robin uncomfortable in talking about it. The whole thing had gotten so far out of control, but then it had never really been in control in the first place. It wasn't Yara's fault that the Society had that stupid rule, and that she was unlucky enough for Erik to be *her* Guardian. It wasn't her fault that she loved him and that he loved her. "This is all so stupid."

"What do you mean?" said Robin, resuming his dinner.

Yara stared forlornly at the soup he'd brought her. "I never asked for any of this, you know? I didn't ask to be special, or to have my very own Guardians, or to fall in love with one of them."

"You love him?" said Robin through a mouthful of food.

"I dunno. Sorry. I shouldn't be talking to you about this. It's weird."

"No, I don't mind."

Yara shrugged. She wrapped her arms around herself and leaned back in her chair, her unfocused gaze on the table. "I dunno, I guess. He was... I didn't tell Black this, but he was what got me out of there."

"What do you mean?"

"I had a vision," she started, feeling awkward, but at the same time as though a weight was lifting off her shoulders. "Of Erik. Kain spent a lot of time trying to make me have a vision, and when I finally did I saw him. He had been captured by Kain. And it scared me. I dunno, just thinking of him trapped there, thinking of what Kain would do to him..."

"It scared you more than *you* being trapped there?"

Yara scoffed. "I know, it sounds stupid. But that's what kinda gave me the kick I needed. You know?"

Robin nodded, running a hand through his golden hair. "It doesn't sound stupid. Well, maybe a little."

Yara chuckled.

"No, I just mean love can make us stupid." He smiled, and Yara was reminded just how young he was - barely a year older than her. How young they all were to have faced so much already. "But the thing that concerns me more is that you cared more about E than about yourself."

"Why is that concerning? Isn't that what you do?"

"Care about E more than myself?"

"You know what I mean. You put your life on the line for me, for the Society. That means you value the Society more than your own life."

"It means I know what purpose I want to *give* my life."

Yara bit her lip.

"What purpose do you want to give yours?" asked Robin.

It was a question she had never asked herself. She had always believed that life had no meaning other than what you decided for yourself. But she had never bothered to ask what meaning she wanted to give her life. Now that Robin said the words, the answer seemed obvious.

"I want to make sure Kain can never do what he did to me again. Not to anyone."

CHAPTER FIFTY-THREE

A New Year

Robin had asked Yara if she wanted company to usher in the new year. She lied and said she just wanted to go to bed. Instead, she sat in the chair of the small living area of her quarters, exactly where he left her, staring at the wall, her mind spinning.

It had been three days since she had woken up at Headquarters. She thought of Kain, as she often did these days. The longer they went without stopping him, the greater the potential for him to become stronger. Even become unstoppable. If Yara's suspicions were correct and he had successfully harnessed the abilities of all six hyden, then fighting him would be near impossible. She knew he had already taken Janya's ability - it was undoubtedly how his leg had miraculously healed. And also having the ability to see the future, read people's minds, control people (which Yara had learned had been Anna's dangerous skill), all combined with Emmanuelle's and Luan's physical enhancements, it would be like fighting a god. (Not to mention if he bestowed those gifts to his Shadow Men as well.) How many abilities had he been using when they fought him before? Despite what Yara had at the time believed to be death blows dealt to Kain, he had recovered within moments, good as new. Better, even. And now with the entire force of the White Mask Society, they were no closer to finding him. Either the Society was not as powerful as Yara had been led to believe, or Kain was masterful at hiding. Yara was inclined to believe the latter.

As the minutes ticked away, inching toward a new year, she let her mind wander. She thought of Erik - painful as it was that she hadn't seen him. Her aunt. Carter and Robin. She thought of the other hyden. Her old, ordinary life which she now suspected she would never get back. And how all of it was in danger because of Kain. Kain, who wanted to be like the hyden. Wanted to steal the powers of Deviants and use them for himself. And to think, the Society had given him the tools to do it. Kain had, after all, been a Researcher *here* when he started working on the Omega Project, and—

Yara sat up.

An idea was on the edge of her brain, not yet fully formed. She could feel it forming, but was afraid to reach for it in case it disappeared before manifesting completely.

Robin had told her about the Omega Project, and no one had wanted her to know about it. They had insisted that Kain wanted to use her as part of a weapon, but Kain *was* the weapon. Yara pressed the heels of her palms into her eyes, desperate to remember the details. Her memory had never been very strong. The Omega Project had been all about harnessing abilities of Deviants, and the Society had stopped research on it because they hadn't been able to get it to work. People died in trials, Robin had said.

The idea was getting clearer, but she would need to talk to one of her Guardians first.

Outside, the world celebrated as they ushered in the new year.

Carter wiped their glasses meticulously, taking all the time in the world, before looking back up at the scene in front of them. It was early. Too early for this.

As the Society decided what their next steps were, the Guardians and the Eyes working on the Kain-hyden case had been summoned to discuss their best options. And - as these meetings often were - it was a mess of differing opinions and contentious debates.

Carter sat between Robin and Erik who were both, like them, keeping their heads down and their thoughts to themselves.

"The seer has confirmed that Kain is wanting to use the hyden abilities on himself," the Head Guardian Xaili Williams (known to the Guardians as X) was saying. "Who's to say how long before he imbues these abilities on his Shadow Men as well?"

"He would never!" interjected Milo Porter, the Head Tracker. He had studied Kain more than anyone else at the Society. "Kain *wants* to feel special, he would never—"

"The entire purpose of the Omega Project was to eliminate anyone being 'special' or more powerful than anyone else," another Guardian cut in.

"In it's origin, perhaps," retorted Porter, "but that's not what Kain is working toward anymore."

"How can you be sure?"

Carter shot a glance over their glasses at Robin who was chewing his nails, his eyes out of focus, clearly not paying attention. Carter chortled, catching Robin's attention, who smiled back and shrugged.

Why was Black not taking charge of the meeting? She had not spoken in over an hour, letting everyone scream themselves hoarse, and as a result they were nowhere nearer a conclusion. How long would she let this go on?

In the end it was not Black who silenced the room, but her second in command. Glover stood, an impressive figure, and the room eventually fell quiet as attention turned to him. He didn't speak, but instead yielded the now silent floor to Black.

"Several things are clear," she said, the light in the room dimming as she spoke. "The longer we wait, the harder it will be to fight Kain. From the accounts of the hyden we now know he has the abilities of five of them."

Carter bowed their head, thinking of poor Anna Karimov. Anna's three Guardians sat, ashen faced, on the opposite side of the room. Rose, a flora nymph, looked the worse of the three of them.

"For now," continued Black, "the fact remains that we are no closer to finding Kain, his Shadow Men, or his new base of operations. This means our priority is to ensure he does not succeed in taking back the hyden."

Carter rubbed their eyes under their glasses. They knew what was coming next, and they didn't want to hear it. The Society's last resort had always been the same. Move the hyden and their Guardians to Atlantis, the underwater base which could not be found without the help of the Nereids, the nymphs who guarded it.

And stay there. Until Kain was stopped.

"So," said Black. "Start preparing for a move. You have two days."

CHAPTER FIFTY-FOUR

A Plan

Kain had raged for days.

So close. He had been *so close* to having what he wanted. What he *needed*. And just like that it was gone. He had underestimated the hyden. Underestimated the seer.

Yara Rivers.

He had anticipated she'd be more as her father had been. Pliable, weak-willed, undisciplined. Instead, the bitch had ruined everything he had worked for. His base, on which he had worked so long and hard. All of the equipment he had designed and built. Years and years of research. Most of his stockpiles. They had had enough time to clear most of it away, moving it to his new temporary location. With an army of Shadow Men at his disposal, they had made quick work of evacuating the base. And, most importantly, *she* had made it out.

He was going through his stores of the hyden serum faster than anticipated. He had found that his doses lasted about 12 hours, except the healing serum from Janya Varma. Evidently, as a result of his leg, that one went through his system much faster. He meant to ration it, but as soon as he started to lose mobility he became too frustrated. He could not go back to what he was before. And he would run out in a few days.

Whatever he did, he would have to do it fast.

"I need to know more about the Omega Project," Yara told Carter the next morning. It was late enough after breakfast that the commissary was relatively empty, giving the two of them a modicum of privacy.

Carter choked on their oatmeal.

"Excuse me?" they said, an eyebrow raised as they dabbed their mouth with a napkin and straightened their glasses.

"The viruses that Kain made. What are they? What do they do? How do they work?"

Carter searched for words before speaking. "Uh, listen, Red. I'm not sure—"

"Carter, please."

"It really isn't your place to know any of this stuff."

"I think I've earned some information," said Yara, surprising herself with the sternness in her voice. "After everything." Carter looked at her, and Yara could see a pity in their amber eyes that made her uncomfortable. She wrapped her arms around herself, but did not let up. "Look, I have an idea. But I can't… I just need to know more."

"You're gonna get us all fired by the end of this, aren't you?"

Yara's stomach dropped. "What? Did Erik get fired?"

"Oh, no," said Carter gently. "No, I was just trying to lighten the mood. I guess I should leave the comedy to R."

"Oh, thank goodness."

"Look, Red, I can't just tell you about that. It's secret for a reason. The Omega Project is incredibly dangerous."

"I *know*," said Yara through clenched teeth, fighting for patience. Why did everyone treat her like she was a child? Had she truly not earned any respect after everything she had done? Everything she had been through? "Please, Carter. Trust me. Do you trust me?"

Carter's eyes flicked back and forth between hers, thoughts clearly running rampant behind them. "I trust you," they said at last.

"Thank you."

They heaved a sigh, put their napkin on the table, and said in a low voice, "So what do you want to know, exactly?"

"The viruses. What are they?"

"Well, there were a lot of different kinds. Anything made from hyden or shape shifter DNA was relatively harmless. It was the nymph viruses that were the most dangerous."

"And what did they do?"

"It depends," said Carter.

"On?"

"On what kind of nymph it's derived from. Each one had a different effect. But since the original purpose of the work on the project was to help transform humans into Deviants, the viruses were all developed from that research. So these viruses sort of… transformed people."

Carter paused, but Yara just stared until they continued.

"For instance, if you infect a human with, say, a Tenebrae virus—"

"Those are dark nymphs, right? Like Bora Black?"

Carter nodded. "Then the subject would be sort of… consumed by darkness."

Yara's eyes widened. *Consumed by darkness.* What did that entail? What would it look like? How would it feel? The prospect was frightening. "I heard the viruses were undetectable," said Yara, remembering words Robin had told her when she had first asked about the Omega Project. "What does that mean?"

"Well, that's the thing. There is no test that can reliably identify someone who's infected. And as far as we know, no cure."

"How is it transmitted?"

"I'm not sure I should be telling you all this—"

"*Please.*"

Carter sighed. "Through direct contact."

"So, that means… he would have to be directly infected with it?"

"Who would? Red, what are you talking about?" Carter was starting to look genuinely worried.

"I mean, it's not airborne, or anything. Or like, you couldn't infect a water supply?"

"OK, why don't you tell me what you're thinking."

"You're not gonna like it."

"No," said Carter. "No, I'm not. But either you tell me, or I report all this to Black."

"But that would get you in trouble, too."

Carter shrugged. "You asked me to trust you. Now I'm asking you to trust me."

"You're right," said Yara. Her idea was still ruminating, and she felt foolish now she was suddenly on the spot, but she had considered every option the whole night. Woke with a splitting headache this morning after having spent hours upon hours running through a million different scenarios in her mind, testing the boundaries of the future, the outcomes of her decisions. She could never change the actions of anyone else in her visions. But she could change what she did. And after all that, she had found one possible path to success. Just one. And she knew Carter would hate it as much as she did.

"Absolutely not," said Carter when she told them her idea. "Out of the question."

"I knew you would say that."

"Then you know why I would say it, too. Too much could go wrong."

"You think I haven't tested this?" she said, tapping her forehead. "I spent all night seeing different scenarios, and—"

"I'm serious, Yara."

"So am I."

"It's suicide."

"I'm willing to do this, Carter. I'm scared, but not nearly as scared as the thought of Kain still out there. I know what he's capable of. *You* know what he's capable of."

Carter buried their face in their hands. "There has to be a better way."

"If there were, you all would have found it already. You'd have *done* it already. Kain has been out there for years, and you're no closer to stopping him now than you were when this all started."

Carter looked up at Yara, and she could see tears gleaming in the corners of their amber eyes.

Then, at last, they nodded.

"But that's insane," said Erik.

A few moments ago, Carter had called Robin and Erik to meet them in their quarters - an unusual occurrence which hinted at something serious and potentially mutinous. And sure enough, as Carter spoke, Robin listening in silence, his suspicions were confirmed.

"Her mind is made up," said Carter solemnly. "I very much get the sense that she's going to do this with or without us."

"This is—" Erik struggled to find words. "This is beyond absurd! R, say something!"

Robin ran a hand through his hair, trying to buy time before he spoke. He had no idea what to say. He felt the same as Erik did. Angry, helpless, confused. "There has to be a better way," he said at last.

Carter shook their head, their amber eyes dark as they looked at both of their fellow Guardians.

Erik stood up, evidently too full of angry energy to stay seated.

"E," said the shape shifter, reaching for him. But Erik slapped their hand away. "We've seen what Kain is capable of," Carter continued calmly. "And now we know that our suspicions are confirmed. From what the hyden reported, he *has* found a way to take their powers. And if he can truly use the abilities of all of those hyden..." Carter trailed off.

"He would become unstoppable," finished Robin.

Erik stared from one to the other, his eyes wide with disbelief.

"The alternative could be worse," said Carter.

"This is bullshit!" Erik raged. He kicked the table in between them, breaking the leg and sending it crashing to the floor. Neither Robin nor Carter moved or tried to stop him as he stormed out of Carter's quarters. The door slammed shut behind him, and still the two Guardians did not speak. Robin stared down at his folded hands, his elbows resting on his knees. There was nothing to say. He wanted to think, to find another way, but his mind was not working. It was frozen on exactly one thing, and that was Yara.

Everything they had done to keep her safe would all be for nothing. In the end, she had been broken by Kain, and now she was running headfirst into a one-way trip.

CHAPTER FIFTY-FIVE

Stay

Yara had decided not to tell Aunt Catherine her plan, and Carter had promised to tell no one but Robin and Erik, leaving the rest of the Society in the dark. Indeed she had induced a vision in which they asked for help from the Society and things rapidly escalated out of Yara's control. And as undesirable as her plan was, it was simply the best option they had. The only option.

It wasn't easy, the idea of facing her own death. And more than that, going toward it willingly. But Yara knew that if she wanted to protect those who mattered most, she had to go through with it.

In preparation, she spent even more hours submerged in her own mind. She saw every various version of her future. What changes could she make, would it actually make any difference, was there any path that led to her survival? But every vision ended the same.

The most difficult part of preparing, however, was when she sat down in her quarters to write a letter to Aunt Catherine. She stared at the blank paper for nearly an hour before finally being able to set the pen to it. She was uncharacteristically calm, as though numbed by Kain's paralytic agent. She felt neither sadness nor fear as she wrote, only difficulty in finding the right words.

She had just finished the letter when there was a knock on the door. She thought for a moment about ignoring it, but then they knocked again, so she said, "Come in."

It was Erik.

"Hi…" she said uncertainly. It was the first time she had seen him since they'd been at Kain's base. She had almost forgotten how beautiful he was. Seeing him, she felt a sudden urge to tear up the letter she wrote to Aunt Catherine, to tell Carter she had changed her mind about the whole thing. They'd had so little time together.

He didn't speak right away. His face was unreadable. He simply stood in the doorway, his green eyes locked on her face, as she waited for him to make the next move.

Then, without saying a single word, he crossed the distance between them in three long strides and they crashed together like waves. His lips were on hers, his hands pulling her close. She could feel his heart beat through her own chest. Tears began spilling from her eyes as she inhaled him, the smell of summer and wind and of roasted nuts. They embraced hungrily, knowing it would be the last time.

"Please don't go," he whispered at last into her shoulder.

"Don't," she said.

He pulled away to look into her eyes, brushing tears from her cheeks with his thumb. "Yara, I'm begging you. There has to be something I can say to stop you."

She shook her head. "Don't make this harder."

"I'll make it as hard as it takes for you to change your mind."

"You know as well as I do there's not another way to stop him. And the longer we wait the more powerful he'll become."

Erik looked down, his black hair falling in front of his face. They sank onto the couch, Erik still clutching her arms, his shirt crumpled in Yara's fists. She did not want to let go of him.

"I missed you," she said at last when her tears had started to dry.

"They told me I couldn't see you," said Erik. When he looked up at her, his eyes were glossy. "I wanted to, but—"

"I know," she said. He brought her hand to his lips and kissed it gently before pressing it to his cheek. He lightly brushed her forehead as if to push aside a lock of hair - though she no longer had any.

"When I think about what he did to you..." He trailed off, his chest rising and falling faster, his nostrils flaring with anger.

"I'm OK," said Yara untruthfully. She leaned into his chest and stayed until his breathing slowed, her eyes closed, listening to the beat of his heart. She wanted to stay there forever. She wanted the night to never end, knowing what she had to do in the morning.

Afraid he might leave as soon as she fell asleep, she whispered, "Will you stay with me?"

He wrapped his arms around her. "Always."

* * *

Yara was back in Kain's lab. It was darker than it had ever been, colder than it had ever been, and their was noise all around her, a buzzing like thousands of angry bees. Kain was there, and his doppelgänger, and another doppelgänger… She was surrounded by Kains. Only they all had the same crazed look in their eyes, the same scar on their faces. They loomed over her, coming from every direction, each one holding something sharp and shiny. Scalpels here, needles there.

She tried to cry out, to beg them to leave her alone, but her words were stuck in her mouth, which was suddenly full of what felt like pebbles. She tried to spit them out and found to her horror that they were her own teeth, and she was choking on them. No matter how many she spit out, her mouth filled with more.

The Kains laughed and ignored her strangled pleas for mercy, and just as the closest one pressed a needle to her neck—

Yara woke with a start on the small sofa in her quarters, still wrapped in Erik's arms. It was not yet four in the morning. She had set an alarm for herself the night before, but as it turned out she hadn't needed it.

She could tell Erik was still dozing by the even rise and fall of his chest. She watched him for several minutes, trying to calm down from her nightmare. His brow was slightly furrowed even in his sleep. She longed to reach out and trace the sharp edges of his jaw, his cheeks, his nose. But she didn't want to risk waking him, so instead she memorized every detail. She never wanted to forget the way his black hair fell lightly over his forehead, the pulse in his neck, the curve of his lips. The longer she stared, the harder it was to look away. But she had to.

She carefully tried extricating herself from him, but found that in his sleep he had somehow grown branches - just as he had that night in the simulator - sprouting from beneath his sleeves and coiling themselves around her. Bright green leaves, small and round, wound around her middle. She smiled as she peeled them carefully off.

Erik did not wake, but Yara hesitated before leaving. Then, on a whim, she carefully plucked the end of one of the branches and tucked it into her pocket.

"Will you stay with me?"

"Always."

CHAPTER FIFTY-SIX
Breaking

Yara dressed in the dark as quietly as possible so as not to wake Erik. She grabbed the armor the Society had equipped her with, though there was really no need for it. This was, after all, a one-way trip. But it was familiar, and it felt safe. Last time she had been with Kain she had been nearly naked. She didn't want to experience anything close to what had happened before. And with any luck, it would help her survive long enough to carry out her plan. The chainmail was heavy, but easy to move in. She transferred the leaves she had taken from Erik into one of her many pockets and covered it all with a hoodie with the White Mask Society logo on the front. If anyone looked at her, they shouldn't give her a second thought. The hoodie was baggy enough to hide the fact that she was wearing armor. She reached up to tuck her hair behind her ear and felt foolish when she felt nothing there.

She slipped silently into the hall. Erik still had not stirred for which she was thankful. She might not have the strength to do what she needed to do if he were awake.

The elevator took her up one floor to the medical and research labs. Yara had by now spent enough time in the recovery wards, but she was unfamiliar with the research area. The floor was still dark which would be her only cover. Otherwise, every wall was made of glass, giving anyone a clear view of the entire area.

Her heart was beating so loudly in her chest that she was afraid someone might hear it. She had walked the halls of the Society countless times, but never after hours, and never had she tried breaking in anywhere. But her Guardians had made it clear that they could not be caught helping her. Carter had tried giving her directions, and she had scouted the path herself in her visions, just as she had done when escaping from Kain. So at least she knew where she was going.

She walked as silently as possible down the narrow halls between glass cubicles, reading the small plaques next to each door, looking for the one Carter had told her to find.

Right on cue she heard movement down the hall. She ducked. She just had to wait it out. Despite knowing how it would play out, her heart was still pounding, her chest constricting with anxiety. Daring to peek above the desks she hid behind, she saw two people in white coats speaking quietly. They were far from her, distorted through multiple glass walls. They did not look up and shortly after disappeared from the ward.

"Right," she whispered to herself. "Focus."

At last she found it. A room at the far end of a corridor, tucked away as far from the elevator as it was possible to be. This door, unlike any of the others, was not made of glass so she could not see what was inside. But she didn't need to. The plaque read "Cold Storage" and that told her all she needed to know.

From one of her many pockets, she pulled out something she had taken from Erik while he slept. Not the leaves, which her fingers brushed as she reached into her pocket, but a key card. She had seen her Guardians, as well as every member of the Society, use them. While many of the doors used some sort of hand scanner, every White Mask carried these as well. Yara swiped the card through the lock.

The red light blinked green and beeped along with a loud click. She tried the door and it opened without resistance.

"You do not wonder, Yara Rivers…"

Yara spun around, the key card flying out of her hand, but before she could shriek in surprise, something crept over her mouth, stifling any sound.

"…why a level 1 Guardian might have access to a locked room in Research?"

Yara was staring at the strangest person she had ever seen. Their hair was long and matted, dreadlocks so rough they resembled bark, actual leaves interwoven with each tress. Their skin was dark and as coarse as their hair. The nymph - at least, Yara was almost certain they were a nymph - had the basic shape of a person, but looked more like a burnt tree.

They tilted their head, their wide dark eyes taking in Yara. When it was clear that she was not going to scream, the leafy vines which had gagged her crept back into the nymph's fingers.

"I am a Kunochi. A wood sprite," they said as though they could read Yara's mind, their voice gravelly. "Though some humans call that nymph."

"Sorry. I didn't…" Yara trailed off, unsure.

"My name is Thuja." They extended the vowels in their name so they were long and airy.

"I—" Yara started, trying to think of an excuse as to why she was there, trying to break into cold storage.

"Do not explain, Yara Rivers," said Thuja, raising one of their wooden hands. "I know why you are here."

"Oh…"

"I know what you are looking for."

They pushed past Yara into the cold storage room, rustling as they moved. How they had managed to sneak up on Yara, Yara didn't know, but she followed the Kunochi inside. The room was enormous, filled with rows of glass refrigerators, not unlike those at a grocery store. Only instead of food, they were filled with neatly lined vials, each one clearly labeled and topped with a different colored lid. Despite the individual cooling units, the room was so cold that Yara's breath rose in plumes before her.

"How do you know what I'm looking for?"

"It is not important," said Thuja. "I am here to help you."

"You want to help me?"

Thuja continued to move through the room to the far end where there was another door. This one had a large sign with big block letters.

"DO NOT OPEN. ACCESS GRANTED BY FRANKIE SWEET ONLY."

Carter had not mentioned anything about this. Yara had not bothered to keep seeing in her visions what lay past the door once she saw herself unlocking it, did not know how they were expected to get in if only the Head of Research was allowed access. But Thuja was not concerned. "The humans hold that every individual life is sacred," they said, placing one of their hands against the lock. Yara did not see exactly what they were doing, but after a few moments, the lock clicked and Thuja pushed the door open. "That in losing one of you, something irreplaceable is gone and can never be found again." They led Yara into the smaller room, this one colder than the first, and lit only with a blue glow. "But my people understand that we all come from and return to the same place. Our energy is borrowed. And if you choose to sacrifice your existence to save us all, I honor that choice. And that is why I help you. As will my kin."

Yara was torn between wanting to grab what she needed as fast as possible, and knowing what Thuja meant.

"If you think life is borrowed, why bother saving people?"

"You misunderstand," said Thuja in their rough voice, speaking slowly. "Saving one life at the cost of many upends the balance. Life must be protected more than the individual. You decide to fight with yours so that others may live."

Erik woke up, his arms empty. It took him a moment to remember where he was and why he was there. Looking down, he saw that he had inadvertently grown branches in his sleep - an unusual occurence. He pinched them off and blearily got up from the sofa. Perhaps Yara was in the bathroom, or had moved to her bed. But they were both empty.

"Yara?" he called in a low voice. When it was clear that there was no one to wake up he tried again, his voice shaking from the fear that was rising in his chest. "Yara?"

The room responded with silence. Looking at his watch he saw that it was just barely after five in the morning. The commissary wasn't serving breakfast this early—

He stopped mid-thought when he saw a piece of paper on the low coffee table. He glanced at it quickly. It was a letter in Yara's handwriting.

"*Dear Annie,*" it started. Panic gripped his chest. Erik did not need to finish it. He knew what it was.

"Damnit," he cursed under his breath and rushed out of the room.

Dear Annie,

My greatest hope is that you won't be mad at me. I can't imagine that there's any hope of that, but I want you to know my intention was not to hurt you, but to help save you. Ugh, that makes me sound like a martyr-wannabe, doesn't it?

The truth is that the thought of anyone having to face that man again makes me sick. I don't want to live in a world in which I could have acted, and did nothing.

I'm sorry that I didn't say good-bye in person, but I knew that if I had, I would have lost the conviction to go through with it. ~~Now you can go back home~~

And please don't be mad at Carter, or any of them. They tried to talk me out of it, but when was the last time that ever worked?

Love love love always,
Y x

Carter woke to a loud, incessant pounding on their door early in the morning. Too early. Nevertheless, they got up, rubbing the sleep from their eyes, not even bothering with their glasses, and answered the door.

"Yara's gone." It was Erik, his green eyes wide.

"What?" said Carter, their sleep addled brain still trying to catch up to the fact that they were now awake. "Gone?"

"She's going after Kain."

"Oh…"

"We need to stop her."

Carter gaped for a few moments, trying to decide how best to react to what Erik was saying. Telling Erik that Carter had helped Yara - as hands-off as the help may have been - would amount to nothing good. But they weren't keen on the idea of lying to Erik, either. "OK. What's your plan?" they said, stalling.

"We go after her. With R. And we don't tell Black."

Carter hesitated. Breaking protocol was not their forte. Of the three Guardians assigned to Yara Rivers, Carter was the voice of reason, the level head, and the one who always reminded the others of the mandate. But that had all gone out the window when they had agreed to Yara's plan, which could be ruined if the three of them went after her.

But it had all become suddenly very real. Yara was going headfirst into a suicide mission… and what if something *did* go wrong? What if she failed?

Why had Carter ever agreed to this? It all now seemed incredibly foolish, reckless, dangerous.

"OK. Get R. I'll get dressed."

CHAPTER FIFTY-SEVEN

Going Back

Yara reached the lobby of the White Mask Society Headquarters and found it empty. Larry's seat, always occupied either by him or one of the other night or weekend receptionists, looked strange empty.

"You must hurry."

Yara jumped, a small yelp of shock escaping her, and looked around for the source of the voice. It was a fern by the door who stepped out of their pot and took on a form much like Thuja's, though considerably smaller. And greener. And leafier.

"We have ensured you a clear path up until here," said the fern. "But you must hurry. Your Guardian has woken. We cannot stop him."

"Right," said Yara, trying not to imagine what Erik must have thought when he woke to find her gone. "Thank you."

"Go."

Yara pushed the doors open and stepped outside. Behind her, through the glass doors, she saw the fern fold themself back into their pot, losing all semblance of having once vaguely resembled a person.

The cool early morning air was particularly frigid against her nearly bald head. She pulled the hoodie tighter around her face and chanced one last look back at the building which had become her home the last few months. It looked so ordinary. Brick trim around modern windows, and a pale facade, giving no hint at what lay inside. Or underneath.

What she had done so far was the easy part. She had managed to say goodbye without saying goodbye. She had gotten what she needed from Research. Now it was time to find Kain. If she knew him at all, he was likely keeping an eye on Society Headquarters. He would want to get the hyden back. He needed them. Whatever he had extracted from them, he only had a finite supply. Otherwise there would have been no point in leaving access ports to the insides of their brains. And he would want more. But Yara did not even need to know that much. She had mapped it all out with her visions - as much as she had been able to - and knew where to go in order to be apprehended the fastest.

Two glass vials clinked in one of her pockets, one of them very warm against her thigh, the other smelling faintly of roasted nuts. But she had to wait until the right time to use them. Otherwise, everything could be lost.

The streets of downtown Los Angeles were not Yara's favorite haunts, particularly when it was dark. Street lights were still on in the cold, blue glow that hinted at a sun just below the horizon, speeding toward daylight. There wasn't much activity yet. A car here, a sleeping unhoused person there, a few pedestrians who paid her no heed.

As soon as she rounded the corner, so that Headquarters was no longer in view, she stopped. A few steps up, closer to the intersection, she would be captured by Shadow Men. After that, she did not know what would happen. No matter how hard she tried, no matter how many different choices she made, every vision ended immediately after she did what she knew she had to do now. She had to believe that it did not mean her death, that something else prevented her from being able to see the future, but there was still a shadow of doubt in the back of her mind.

"The viruses are lethal," said Yara. "And there's no cure. Right?"

"That's correct," said Carter. Yara could tell they were waiting to hold judgement with great difficulty until she was done explaining her plan.

"And the hyden aren't immune?"

"Red—"

Yara cut them off. "If we somehow managed to infect Kain with one of the viruses from the Omega Project, he would die. Even with Janya's healing powers. Right?"

"Well, yes. In theory. Although… I suppose it depends on how quickly the virus would work, and how quickly he can heal."

She smiled at them, waiting for their words of approval, and was instead met with a blank stare.

"What are you getting at?"

"Well," said Yara, "we wouldn't even need to fight. And with Kain dead

his entire operation would collapse. His Shadow Men are drones. With no leader, they won't be a threat at all. It's simple, effective, and it minimizes casualties."

"But Yara, there's no way we could come close enough to Kain to infect him. The viruses aren't airborne. He would need to be physically *infected. And he's always surrounded by his Shadow Men, not to mention we don't know where he is."*

"I've thought of that."

Her heart was beating frantically as she pulled a vial from her pocket. Not the one that burned, but the one that smelled like Erik. The liquid inside was bright green. It did not move like liquid at all, but rather rustled like leaves catching sunlight. She smiled lightly to herself and pulled out one of the syringes she had stored in another pocket.

"Inject yourself in the ankle."

Yara looked at Thuja as she spoke, trying to mask her fear.

"Far from your heart. And only a little. You won't need much. The virus moves quickly, and you must give yourself as much time as possible."

Careful to extract only a small amount of the green liquid, Yara braced herself before slipping the needle beneath her skin on her right ankle. She gasped with surprise. It was more painful than she had expected.

She squeezed the syringe and emptied its contents.

"Kain needs my videtonin. He wants us all back. The hyden, I mean."

"Yes," said Carter.

"And when he gets us back—"

"If."

"What?"

"If he gets you back."

"Oh," said Yara. "Right. If he gets us back, he won't hesitate to take what he needs."

"What are you getting at?"

"Well, theoretically, if one of us were infected with one of the Omega viruses and he extracted our… magic brain juices, then when he used it on himself, he would get infected."

Carter frowned, their amber eyes locked on Yara's face. "What are you suggesting?" they said in a low voice.

"Exactly what you think I'm suggesting."

* * *

At first she felt nothing at all. But when she lifted her foot to move forward she found it had gotten very heavy. "Woah..." she said. The world spun around her as she started to feel lightheaded. It was like moving through molasses. She was not all that had slowed. The world around her moved at half speed as well. She heard a clinking and looked down in time to see the rest of the green liquid spilling sluggishly from its open vial onto the concrete, still winking like leaves caught in sunlight.

Hurry, Rivers, she thought frantically, begging her body to move forward.

Only in the visions in which she was not infected did she see herself get captured by Shadow Men. It happened just ahead, around the corner. Kain must have had people stationed nearby all the time. Just in case. In case something like this happened. In case a hydan was stupid enough to wander alone outside.

But in every vision in which she injected herself, no matter what, she saw nothing after. As soon as she was infected, the world went black, as though everything ceased to exist.

Though of course, it didn't. The world was still there.

She was almost surprised, albeit relieved. And while she had never seen them capture her in this timeline, she had to believe they would still be there, waiting.

Her heart was beating faster now and she could feel the weight in her foot spread up her leg as it crept through her body. It was moving fast.

As the streetlight up ahead became clearer through the low morning fog, so did the knowledge that this was her last hour on Earth.

What had she done?

She made it four steps, all but dragging her right foot behind her, when she could make out two enormous crimson figures lumbering toward her.

CHAPTER FIFTY-EIGHT

An Hour

"Back so soon!"

Yara blinked in the sudden bright light as the bag was ripped off of her head.

As prepared as she was to face Kain again, it was more unpleasant than she could have imagined to see him looking down at her. The Shadow Men had bagged her head and transported her in some sort of van. It did not take long for them to arrive at Kain's new base.

Looking around she saw they were in a much smaller and more temporary-looking version of his lab. He had somehow managed to shove all of his equipment into the room, leaving very little floor space for him to maneuver. He was still moving without his cane. Moving quickly, as though he knew he didn't have much time.

"Scan her for a tracker!" he barked at the nearby Shadow Men, the same identical white blondes who had helped him with her surgery. They calmly approached Yara with a metal wand and ran it over her arms. One of them beeped over her left forearm, exactly where the Society had implanted a subcutaneous tracking device just a few days ago.

Kain ripped her arm out of the restraint with a frustrated sigh. Yara was tied to a chair rather than strapped to an exam table as she had been before. Little did Kain know the restraints were pointless. The virus was working its way quickly through her, making it harder for her to move. She probably couldn't have gotten up even if she wanted to. Her limbs were wooden, her head heavy, her breathing labored. She hoped Kain didn't notice. "They know she's here!" he yelled. He held a device to her forearm. She braced herself for pain, but all it did was flash and beep until he chucked it away, presumably having disabled the tracker.

"I remembered you taller," she said, unconcerned. Her tongue was stiff, but she managed to sound natural. The last time she had faced Kain, she'd been afraid. Now she felt cool, wearing the knowledge that she would be his demise as a talisman. Even with her tracker disabled, if the Society hadn't been monitoring her location, it didn't matter. She never expected to go back. Hopefully it just meant Kain took her videtonin before it was too late.

"A sense of humor!" said Kain, raising an eyebrow. "I don't remember that from the last time we were together."

"I changed my clothes, too. What do you think?"

"Ah, yes. Society armor. How quaint. It'll certainly help you a great deal here, won't it?" He laughed and ran a hand over the stubble on her head.

Yara bit her tongue as his fingers crept toward her healing stitches. She wanted him to know that the frail girl he had once tortured and tormented into submission would be the one who ruined him. She just had to be careful and play her cards close to the chest, or it wouldn't work and it would have all been for nothing.

But she was running out of time.

They both were.

"Your Guardians care very much for you," said Thuja, leading Yara to a shelf on the far side of the cold-storage locker. "And your Catherine."

Guilt burned in Yara's stomach.

"It is natural that they do not want to lose you, Yara Rivers," said Thuja. "They do not understand the true nature of life in this universe. They will miss your consciousness."

Thuja opened one of the glass cases and pulled out a box of vials. They clinked happily in their hands.

"This is what you are looking for."

Yara stared down at the small vials.

So this was the Omega Project. The Society's most powerful weapon, their greatest shame, all distilled and stored in these glass containers. They looked relatively harmless. When Yara bent down to look more closely she saw that the liquids were unlike any she had ever seen. One of them was orange and moved like spitting lava, trapped within its glass prison. Another blue one swirled angrily like a miniature hurricane.

"They're all different," said Yara.

"Yes. Each one from a different nymph."

"Which one do I use?"

Thuja let their hand hover over the vials, vines growing from their fingers and wrist, curling around each one. "Water will drown. Fire will burn. Light will consume."

Yara didn't know what she wanted. What the best one to use on Kain would be. On the one hand, she wanted it to last. If she was infecting herself, she needed to have enough time to get caught. But once Kain was infected, it had to move quickly enough to beat his healing powers. "It needs to last," she said finally, deciding it was more important that she survive long enough to infect him. "It needs to take as long as possible."

All the vines retreated back into Thuja's hand, except for one, which lifted a small vial filled with a viscous brown liquid.

"Oak. The flora will take the longest."

"How long?"

"An hour," said Thuja. "But once you are infected, it will be hard to move. Your body will harden."

An hour. It wasn't much. But it would have to be enough.

"You are afraid," said Thuja, their dark eyes locked on Yara.

She shook her head. "Afraid it won't work."

"It will not be easy. And it will be painful. Both here," they placed a hand on Yara's chest, "and here." They placed the other on Yara's head.

Yara could feel the familiar grip of fear, but she clenched her teeth, her lips pursed. "I can do it." Her voice wavered and she was ashamed of how weak she felt. But she thought of Erik, of Aunt Catherine, Robin, and Carter. She thought of every person who had shown her kindness, of the other hyden, of poor dead Anna. "I can do this," she said again, this time her voice stronger.

"Take this, too," said Thuja. They pressed another vial into Yara's hands, this one hot. Looking down, Yara saw the spitting orange virus. The one that looked like lava. "Fire," said Thuja, though Yara could tell just from looking at it. "Fire gives you strength, but it does not last. It will burn. It will kill quickly. Whatever you choose, use only a little, or you will not have enough time. Even with flora."

"Thank you," said Yara.

Thuja nodded, and as they headed for the door, Yara stopped them. "Wait."

Thuja turned. "Yes, Yara Rivers?"

"Is there one… a virus, I mean, from the moringa tree?"

Yara couldn't be sure, but she thought she saw Thuja's beetle black eyes twinkle knowingly.

* * *

Yara could feel her heart struggle to pump her poisoned blood through her body as it thickened from the virus distilled from a nymph of the moringa tree.

Kain frowned suddenly. He held up a hand and the movement of the two identical blonde Shadow Men stopped as they awaited his orders. "What did you just say?"

"Nothing," Yara spat.

He cocked his head. A gesture she knew all too well.

He was reading her mind.

Foolish. How could she be so careless! She closed her eyes and, desperate to avoid any thoughts of the Omega Project, pictured the first thing she could think of: Erik.

"Stop that," said Kain, his voice much closer. She could feel his breath on her cheeks. She squeezed her eyes shut tighter.

Erik. Erik Erik Erik.

There was a prickle in the back of her mind as Kain probed her thoughts. It was impossible to hide. All she could see was Erik in their last moments together, how she had longed not to leave when he had asked her to stay, and his nutty smell - the same smell as the virus…

Oh no…

Yara froze. She opened her eyes and saw Kain's widen. He looked both livid and excited. "Do you know why I had to map out your brain, Yara Rivers?" He was so close that he barely spoke above a whisper. Her bottom lip was trembling and she bit it to stop. He had read her mind. She hadn't been able to hide her intentions. This would all have been for nothing. "You might wonder why I couldn't just tap into your brains once I know where your special hydan hormones are produced." He turned his head slightly and Yara saw fresh sutures around his ears. She thought of Luan and his bat-like ears, essential for his ability to echolocate, and felt a surge of revulsion toward Kain. Willing to mutilate himself in order to pilfer Luan's ability. "You see, every hydan is different. You all produce different hormones, and they all make your brains work differently.

"An incredible organ, the brain," he went on. He pressed his cheek against hers. He was hot and sweaty. His unshaven jaw scratched at her skin. She wanted to recoil from him, but she could barely move.

"You see," he continued, "I needed to see how each of you make your abilities work, otherwise I could never use them myself. I wouldn't know how. But now I know how, Yara Rivers. Which is why I am able to read every… single… thought… in your mind."

Don't think, don't think, don't think—

She looked around the room, desperate to focus on something other than what he was saying, but it was too late. She could see the tips of her fingers beginning to turn green…

"No!"

Kain had seen it, too. He gripped her hands and inspected her fingers. The color was creeping up her hand before his eyes. "What's this…" he said, more to himself than anyone in the room.

Unprompted, the memory of Thuja handing Yara the vial with the virus sprang into her mind. It caught Kain's attention.

No no no!

"What was that? What did it give you?"

"N- nothing! It was- it was from me. My videtonin. They want to do what you're doing. Take our abilities."

"That's impossible."

"They think it's the only way to fight you…"

Kain didn't speak and for a brief moment Yara thought she had convinced him, that there was still hope. But then, "You're lying."

"No," said Yara, breathing heavily. Her heart was slowing down, pumping sludge through her veins and working all the harder for it. "I'm not lying. Please." She was completely helpless. Immobilized by the goddamn virus. For all her confidence, Erik had been right. They had all been right. She should never have done this.

But she had looked. She had *seen* every possible thing she could do to fight him and they had all failed. Except for this. Except for this scenario, which she could not see the end of. And now she knew, it ended just the same as the rest. With Kain's victory. And she was going to die for nothing.

"It's not possible…" said Kain, and the change in his voice made Yara look into his eyes. It was the first time she had seen him look like that, and it took her a moment to recognize it for what it was: fear. "They wouldn't…"

He looked to the now useless tracker in her arm and let out a throat wrenching yell before gripping her throat and saying, through clenched teeth, "How many will come?"

"N-no one—" she managed, stars blocking her vision as the air was squeezed from her lungs. This was certainly unexpected. To think she had prepared to be killed by a virus and instead it would never get the chance. Kain would beat the virus to it.

"Stop lying!"

She was beginning to lose consciousness, spluttering for air, when something came out of nowhere and knocked Kain off his feet, sending him flying to the side. Yara coughed and gasped, her lungs filling gratefully with air. She blinked, taking deep, painful breaths, trying to clear the black spots from her vision to see what was happening. She couldn't tell if the disorientation she felt was due to the lack of oxygen or the virus.

Hands were on her, undoing her restraints.

"What—"

"It's OK, Yara, it's me!"

Erik's beautiful face swam in and out of focus in front of her. Was he really there? Or was she hallucinating in these, her final moments on Earth?

"Erik?"

"Come on. Remind me to kill you if we live through this." His words were muffled. Her head was full of foam.

He slung her arm around his shoulders and pulled her to her feet. The small room was a barrage of chaos. She could make neither heads nor tails of it all.

"How did..." she mumbled.

"Come on, we have to hurry."

Her body was so stiff that she couldn't bend her legs. She could not even feel her feet. "I can't..."

Carter and Robin were locked in battle with Kain. They hadn't even had time to put on their armor, dressed simply in their black uniforms, though at least equipped with gauntlets and solenoids. Kain's two blonde assistants were already dead on the floor. But Kain was no ordinary match. He was leaping around the Guardians with the supernatural skill of Emmanuelle - no shadow of his once useless leg - and moved as though he could anticipate every move before they made it. Which, of course, with the abilities of Bobby Diaz, he could.

"Yara, I need you to move. We don't have time, we gotta get out of here."

"I can't move, Erik," she said, tears falling down her cheeks. What had she done? She had ruined everything, and now they were all going to die because of her. "I thought it was going to work, it was supposed to work!"

"It's OK, it's not over, yet," said Erik.

The door they were headed for burst open and half a dozen Shadow

Men came pouring in. Erik was punched in the face, knocking Yara to the ground. He couldn't get back to her, pulled into a fight. From the ground, Yara could see both Carter and Robin forced to abandon their attack on Kain, defending themselves against the assailants. Kain, in turn, lunged toward Yara.

She tried to crawl away from him, but it took such effort to move and she was too slow. She felt him leap onto her, the breath knocked out of her. He roughly spun her around on her back and pinned her down with his legs, gripping her head as though trying to crush it. He looked positively crazed. His eyes were bugging, his mouth a crooked slash across his face, bearing his teeth like a rabid animal. She could feel his nails digging into her scalp, though it didn't hurt as much as it should have.

An enormous gash across his forehead had blood dripping into his eyes, staining them red. Yara watched as it healed itself, stitching together leaving nothing but smooth skin and a smear of red.

"You thought you could outsmart me," he snarled. "Little bitch! Now they'll all die because of *you!*"

Yara's mind was racing. She had no hope of fighting. He was stronger, enhanced with the abilities of six hyden, and she was quickly fading. Her hands were completely green, the same shade as the leaves she had plucked from Erik back in her quarters. The ones she had tucked into her pocket.

Her pocket…

She looked around and saw the same metal tray Kain had used to organize every injection he'd given her. It was close, almost close enough to reach. But Kain was pinning her down.

C'mon, Rivers, she thought to herself, her face scrunched with the effort to pull the tray toward her with her toe. She couldn't feel her feet at all anymore, so it was hard to know if she had managed to reach it.

Kain cocked his head and Yara realized too late that he had read her mind. He leapt up to push the tray away, but Yara was ready. In the split second it took for him to reach it she was able to yank it forward, slamming the metal edge into his face. He stumbled sideways, dazed, and the instruments on the tray flew in all directions.

It took every ounce of strength she had, pulling from a reserve deep inside her, to grab a nearby fallen syringe. Reaching into her pocket, she grazed the moringa leaves, but that was not what she was after. She closed her fingers around the glass filled with a burning liquid.

Had it not been for the stiffness the virus was causing, her hands would have been shaking too much, but she was able to jam the needle into the vial.

Kain, having recovered, lunged at her, sending the vial flying out of her hands where it crashed somewhere behind them with a sound like a roaring fireplace. But before he could pin down her arm, she jammed the needle still clutched in her hand into the nape of his neck and emptied it.

He screamed, the room suddenly quieted by his shrill cry of pain. He fell off of Yara, staggering backwards, gripping his neck. Yara was not the only one who was transfixed by the scene. All fighting had stopped to see what was happening.

Kain's skin was turning from red back to his normal ashy hue and then back to red, as though burning from a fever. He started to writhe. His legs buckled from under him. Yara couldn't tear her eyes away, horrified as his skin started to bubble and crack, then healing itself before burning all over again.

It wasn't long before the virus won out over Janya's stolen power, his skin blistering and smoke fuming from his mouth, eyes, nostrils.

At last, his screaming stopped, and Kain's scorched and blackened body fell in a heap, a few burnt fingers falling to the floor like ash from a cigarette.

The smell of burning flesh filled the air.

After a moment of stunned silence, the Shadow Men ran from the room. Whether they were fleeing or running for reinforcements, Yara did not know.

Her head fell to the ground. She was exhausted from having fought so hard against the virus, but it was over now.

Footsteps rushed over to her and Carter and Robin were at her side. She could barely make them out through the haze that had started to cloud her vision, tinging everything green.

"Did I do it?" Speaking was hard. Everything was impossibly heavy.

"You did it, kid," said Robin. She could not feel it, but she could see that he was holding her hand. Tears were pouring down his bloodied face, leaving tracks on his cheeks. She wanted to squeeze his hand, tell him to stop crying, but she could not move her fingers.

"I did it..." Her words were slurred. She was running out of time. "Erik?"

"He's here, Red. Don't worry," said Carter. Their glasses were smeared with blood and one of the lenses was broken.

"Erik..." she repeated. Every word took so much effort, she could only hope they understood.

Carter and Robin exchanged a look.

"I'll go get him," said Carter. They disappeared from view and Erik soon rushed over to her.

He brushed her face gently. "Hey," he said.

"I'm so sorry," she managed, her eyes burning with tears. She couldn't reach for him, couldn't see his face, but she could still smell him. Or maybe it was she who had the smell of roasted nuts, now her body was being fully consumed by the moringa virus.

"You have nothing to be sorry about," he said.

"I didn't even... get to say goodbye..."

"You can say goodbye now," he said.

Robin made a strangled sound and touched Yara's hand to his forehead, hiding his face.

"I love you," she said. Or at least she tried to, but the words got lost in her throat. She was petrifying. Her lungs could no longer expand, choking her. Her heart was slowing to a snail's pace, unable to pump whatever her blood had become.

She thought it would be more painful.

The world narrowed around her, the tunnel of her vision closing around Erik's face. It was the last thing she saw when everything went dark...

CHAPTER FIFTY-NINE

No Help

"You realize, Yara, that there's no way for us to cure you once the virus is inside you," said Carter.

"I wasn't expecting you to."

"This whole thing is incredibly foolish. We can't even guarantee it will work! You might be dead before Kain has a chance to be infected."

"It will work," said Yara. "I've seen it work."

Carter did not detect the lie in Yara's words.

No, she had not seen it work. She could never see past being infected. But Carter did not need to know that, because Yara could feel it in her gut. This was going to work.

"There has to be a better way to do this," said Carter again, rubbing their face.

"There isn't," said Yara. "And the longer we wait, the more powerful he might become. He might be planning to attack HQ as we speak, and he'll take us all back and we won't be able to escape again. We're not safe. Not while he's still alive."

"Maybe we can administer the virus to him without you needing to be infected. Set up a trap and just--" Carter mimed sticking Kain in the neck with a needle.

"You could try," said Yara. "I looked. I had vision after vision. I tested everything I could think of. But in everything I saw he killed me anyway, and if more people come, it just means more casualties. Using me as bait avoids an all out confrontation. It's the safest way. It's the only way. Nothing else worked. Works."

Carter shook their head for a long time, wiping their glasses against their *leg. Yara wanted to know what they were thinking, what options they were weighing. "I know," they said at last, putting their glasses back on.*

"I need you to do something for me, though," said Yara, and Carter lifted their head to meet her eyes. "I need you to tell the others. Annie and Robin and… Erik." She choked slightly on his name.

"They'll never forgive me if they know I agreed to this."

"I'm sorry."

"And what about the Society?"

"They'll never agree to it," said Yara.

"Look, Red," said Carter, their face solemn. "If you're serious about this, I mean really serious, you have to act fast."

"I know."

"No, I mean Black is planning to move the hyden to a more secure location. One that's difficult to get to. If we're moved, you won't be able to leave. Not without help."

Yara's mind was spinning. "When?"

"Days. Maybe less."

She had hoped she would have more time, but it was just as well. Less time meant less time to overthink, to second guess, to back out. "OK."

Carter sighed. "Look, I'll tell the others what you want me to say. And I'll wait as long as I can before informing Black. But… this goes way over my head. I can't… I can't help you."

Yara pursed her lips. She wanted to understand. She forced herself to nod, but before she could get up to leave, Carter laid a hand gently on her arm.

"But…"

Yara froze.

"There may be some information I can give you. Where to find what you'll need."

CHAPTER SIXTY

Waking

… but things were starting to come back into focus. Yara's breathing had returned to normal, and her heart seemed to be working fine. She blinked her eyes. Something wasn't right. The familiar chemical smell of Kain's laboratory was gone…

Yara wiggled her fingers, which felt stiff, but offered no resistance otherwise. And they were no longer green.

"Hello?" she called out cautiously, and immediately sound erupted all around her. Robin and Carter's faces came into view, haggard and exhausted. Robin's nose was bandaged, clearly broken, and one of Carter's amber eyes was swollen shut, a cut held closed with butterfly stitches running from their forehead to their cheek.

"Hey, kid! You're awake! How do you feel?"

"We were so worried, it's been almost an hour. Can you move your feet?"

"Wh— what's going on?" said Yara, completely flustered. "I'm supposed to be dead… Am I dead? Where's Erik? What's going on?"

Robin gave a dry sob and gripped his golden curls, his face bent toward the floor. Carter looked pale and wiped sweat from Yara's forehead.

"How do you feel?" they asked.

"Robin, what's wrong?" said Yara.

In answer, Robin took her hand and squeezed it hard, looking as though it was taking all of his energy to try to compose himself.

"Can you sit up?" said Carter.

With a little help, they managed to get Yara upright and moved into a chair. She was back at Headquarters. Back in the medical ward.

"Is someone going to tell me what's going on? I'm supposed to be dead. Aren't I? Am I?"

"We got you back to Headquarters before your heart stopped," said Carter. "Fortunately, when you first mentioned that you might be planning to go back to Kain with a deadly virus in your system, I told one of our Medics who started working on an antidote using Janya Varma's santocin."

"Her what?"

"The hormone she produces that allows her to—"

"—heal herself…" said Yara finishing their sentence, understanding washing over her.

Carter nodded.

"We would never have thought to use it. Ironically, it was Kain's work that enabled us to even find an antidote that *could* work."

"Where is Kain?" said Yara, tensing to get up again.

"He's gone," said Carter, putting their hand on Yara's shoulder, keeping her firmly in her chair. "You did it. You killed him."

Her stomach tensed at the words. The memory of Kain burning to ash came flooding back to her. She felt sick, a consequence she had not anticipated. After all, she hadn't expected to be alive to face the aftermath of her actions.

She had killed someone.

"I had to do it," she said in a small voice.

"No one is blaming you, Red. You did the right thing. He was a monster."

Even as Carter said it, Yara wasn't sure she believed them.

Robin pressed his finger between her eyebrows, trying to smooth her furrowed brow. "We didn't know ya had it in you, kid," he said in a weak voice. He tried laughing and nudged her in the arm, but she kept her eyes on the floor, and the smile faded from his face just as quickly as it had come.

"OK, so Kain is dead, you saved me with the santocin he took from Janya…" She was trying to make sense of things in her mind. "Where's Erik?"

Robin and Carter exchanged a tense glance before looking away, their heads bowed. Yara's stomach clenched and her hands started trembling.

"Carter, where's Erik?"

She could feel the words before they were spoken. She knew what they were about to say, as much as every part of her body was hoping against hope that she was wrong. That she had misread the looks on their faces.

"Erik is dead."

CHAPTER SIXTY-ONE

Gone

Erik is dead.

Just like that, the world had ended.

It couldn't be true... Hurt or injured, maybe. But not dead. They simply hadn't checked properly...

"But, he spoke to me." Yara's voice was distant. "Before I— he came over and he spoke to me and I talked to him—"

It was Robin who spoke this time as Carter looked away, ashamed. "We didn't know if you were going to make it, Yara. For all we knew, you were dying."

"So..." said Yara, comprehension and disgust dawning on her. She looked at Carter who looked as guilty as it was possible for them to look. "So you *pretended* to be Erik? You *lied* to me?"

"You were asking for him. We didn't know what to do."

Yara stumbled off the bed, her legs wobbling under her, and managed to stagger over to a trash can and heaved, but her stomach was empty and all that came out was bile. She was shaking, and she couldn't tell if it was anger or grief.

"He was there... in the room, wasn't he? His body?"

They didn't say anything, but she could feel them watching her.

"He was lying somewhere," she managed between sobs, "dead, and you put his face on and spoke to me like— I really thought he was— I didn't know."

She collapsed on the ground, and somehow Robin was there and had managed to catch her just as he always did. They sat together on the floor, crying for what felt like forever. Carter remained seated, afraid to go near her. The air was hot. Her skin burned from tears, her stomach hurt from sobbing, her knees were aching from kneeling on the tile floor, but none of it mattered.

Erik was gone.

CHAPTER SIXTY-TWO

Just the Beginning

The relief that should have accompanied the knowledge that Ramsey Kain was dead, that he had fallen, and that his Shadow Men had disappeared, was marred by the numbness that now accompanied Yara everywhere she went. She had been too young to appreciate the heaviness of the deaths of her parents. Besides them, she had never lost anyone. She had never been close enough to anyone before, except, of course, Aunt Catherine.

Yara had never spent much time thinking about death, or life after death, or the lack thereof. Even when faced with her own. But she was haunted by images of Erik's limp body. Horrible, distorted facsimiles drawn up by her own imagination.

The Society was not much for pomp and circumstance when one of their rank died in action. There was no funeral service, no viewing, no memorial. Whatever they had done with his body, she didn't know.

And without seeing it, she could not believe that he was really gone. Were they absolutely sure he was dead? Maybe his heart had still been beating, but too slowly and they just didn't listen long enough. And how could they really be sure that just because it wasn't beating meant he was gone? Maybe his brain could be preserved, his soul extracted, his heart jump-started. What if he was just stuck inside a lifeless body, calling for help, and they couldn't hear him? They should have tried harder! He deserved a second chance.

But life in the headquarters of the White Mask Society did not stop. People bustled around and asked her questions and called Robin and Carter away to meetings. Eventually, Yara and her Aunt Catherine were returned to their apartment. Aunt Catherine went back to work and Yara went back to school and half-heartedly started to look at colleges.

The apartment, once home, felt strange and cold, as though she were living in someone else's house. Her things did not feel like hers. Her clothes felt strange, and no longer fit like they used to. The pictures that papered the walls no longer felt like images of her life. She had changed during her time with the Society.

Now that she knew how to control her visions, her headaches had stopped. The nightmares of Kain never did. It wasn't uncommon for her to wake in the middle of the night, drenched in a cold sweat, still paralyzed, or else jostled into consciousness by the echo of a drill boring into her brain. Her hair was growing back in earnest, but she could still feel the smooth scar tissue at the base of her skull, knew what lay underneath.

Somehow, miraculously, she had gotten through the rest of her senior year of high school. She and Aunt Catherine had decided that Yara would benefit from a gap year before going off to college, which was a huge weight lifted from Yara's shoulders, knowing she wouldn't have to try to assimilate into a whole other world when she was still trying to figure out her new place in this one.

"Will I be able to visit you?" she asked Robin and Carter.

"We're still your Guardians," said Carter. "You're still our Ward. This isn't over."

"Isn't it, though?" said Yara. "Kain is dead."

Robin sighed and put his hand on Yara's shoulder with a wan smile. "I'm afraid it's not that easy, Yara."

While the city still looked - on the outside - like the same old city, she could not ignore everything she had learned. The Society was still there. Nymphs and shape shifters and maybe even other hyden walked among them. And Yara now felt more detached than ever from everyone around her. And though she had always been isolated from her peers, after having found companionship at the Society, she found herself longing for the company of the friends she had left behind, which was how she ended up spending most of her summer there. She used her self-defense training as an excuse to visit. She didn't know if it was strictly allowed, but Larry was always happy to see her, as were both Robin and Carter. Whether the news of her presence there ever reached Bora Black, she didn't know, and she didn't particularly care. Her Guardians didn't seem concerned.

Erik's vacancy had not yet been filled.

Bora Black stared at the document on her desk. Glover had dropped it off a few moments ago and had the good sense to leave her alone with this new information for the time being.

Every single White Mask had been interrogated. Black hadn't slept in weeks. The mood at the Society in the last few months had been tense as everyone knew they were being evaluated by the Tenebrae.

And now, finally, all the data had been analyzed, and here was the answer.

It was too unbelievable to be true. And yet...

The darkness that always surrounded Black was rippling off of her as her mind raced. She had to be sure this was true. She had to find a way to turn this to her own advantage. She set down the file of the White Mask who had betrayed them and began to concoct a plan.

One afternoon, on a sweltering weekday in July, Yara was having lunch with her Guardians at the commissary, still sweating from their morning training session. She was now not only comfortable using a gauntlet, but could control the solenoid with a degree of accuracy she was quite proud of, though training in the simulators always brought back painful memories of Erik. (She still had the branch she had plucked from his sleeping body, the only piece of him she could still hold onto. It had long ago dried up, but the vivid color remained. She saw his eyes every time she looked at it.)

Idly moving salad around her plate, she said, "I don't want to go home."

Robin raised an eyebrow. His nose had finally healed after having been broken by one of Kain's Shadow Men, but it was now permanently crooked, only adding to the roguish asymmetry of his smile. "Is that so?"

She shrugged. "I don't belong there now. I dunno. Isn't there a way I can just... stay here?"

"You have your aunt," he said. "And you can go to college. Build a life for yourself."

But Yara looked into Robin's eyes and she could see that he knew as well as she did that her place was with them.

"It wouldn't be easy, Red," said Carter.

"I know."

"You'd have to follow rules..."

"I know."

"I mean, *actually* follow them. Not only when you agree with them."

Yara bit her lip sheepishly.

Robin laughed. It was the first time she heard him laugh since Erik had died. "Black was expecting you would do this."

"Was she," said Yara, slightly bitter that the woman could anticipate her behavior. She didn't want to be predictable.

"The hours are long and hard. You won't have time for a personal life. You won't see much of your aunt. And that's only if you get the job."

"I figured."

"Training is grueling. No matter what field you join. Guardians or anything else."

"I can do it."

"Don't get too excited," said Carter. "Initiates are usually younger than you. Much younger. You may not even be accepted into the program."

"You would have to get through the evaluation and pass the assessments," said Robin.

"But there's a chance, though. Right?"

Her two Guardians exchanged an unreadable look.

"There's a chance," said Robin with a crooked smile.

"I can do it," Yara said again.

"We know you can," he said.

Yara's chest swelled. It took a moment before she recognized that it was joy - or something close to it. It was the first time she had felt anything other than numbness or grief since Erik had died. The first time she felt like there was something to look forward to. After all, the White Mask Society had been Erik's home. His everything. If there was any part of him left in the world, it was right here.

"What are you smiling at?" asked Carter.

She didn't know how to answer. Her mind was racing and her heart was beating hard. She looked at her Guardians, and felt stronger. Her place was here. With them. With the Deviants.

"Well, then I guess we better get started."

Epilogue

The Necromancer stepped carefully through the rubble of the laboratory. It was dark here, under the city, with nothing to see by save the one flashlight she had brought with her.

The White Mask Society had destroyed everything and taken all of her research. Or… they thought they had. Kain was nothing if not meticulous about his findings. With breakthroughs like theirs, he would have made copies and hidden them somewhere. She would find them.

The bodies of her Shadow Men were gone, too. As was Kain's. But it did not matter all that much. She did not want Kain's old body. To bring him back like that would not be sufficient. She just needed to find a glimmer of DNA and she could bring him back in a different way. If she deemed it necessary. He had, after all, been very useful.

It did not take long for the Necromancer to find Kain's hidden and protected store of information. The Society was stupid. Careless not to check for backups. Hidden in a corner of the lab, a hollow corner of cement had been easily broken open with a metal rod nearby. No doubt, Kain had accessed this remotely, more clean to open it with a computer than smashing it open. But she would not need to access it again.

One hard drive. The Necromancer laughed, despite everything, that all of their years of research could fit onto one hard drive.

Perfect.

It even fit in her pocket.

She tucked it away and started to head out of the room, but stopped suddenly. Something had caught her attention. She wasn't sure yet what it was. Something was tickling her consciousness, which, as a

Necromancer, was finely tuned to patterns of life and death. There was a murmur of something that was neither Kain nor Shadow Man. Something that excited her. She tilted her head, willing herself to find the source of this pattern that so intrigued her.

Left.

She turned her head and stared at the floor. It was barely there. Two drops, the color of rust, untouched by bleach or the destructive flame of a fire nymph. Two drops of blood which had been thrown from their host by a violent blow, all the way across the room. Had the Society been in a hurry, to do such a haphazard job of destroying the lab? Perhaps the Cleaners were losing their touch.

It did not matter. The Necromancer knelt by the drops. Dried, but still there, containing all the information she needed within each glorious molecule.

Footsteps behind her caused the Necromancer to stand up and face the approaching figure. She did not let her surprise show. The person before her was unfamiliar. The white half-mask of the Society was pinned on their collar, but they made no hostile movement toward the Necromancer. Their jaw was tight and their eyes narrowed.

"I'm here on Kain's orders."

The Necromancer smiled.

Keep reading for a look at the first few chapters of
The Guardians, the sequel to *The White Mask Society*.

Prologue

"You're absolutely certain that what you're telling me is correct?"

Bora Black stood with her back to her Second, darkness curling off her skin. There weren't many windows at the Headquarters of the White Mask Society, as most of the building was subterranean. But she had one of the few offices above ground, granting her a view overlooking the rundown corner of downtown Los Angeles where the building was located.

She saw none of it, however, her mind preoccupied.

Zak Glover responded in a voice too calm given the situation. "Yes. These are the results the investigation turned up."

"A diplomatic response," said Black. She considered his words for a moment. Considered her next actions.

There was a spy in the White Mask Society.

The ultimate betrayal.

A person in whom Black had bestowed so much trust had been responsible for the chaotic events of the last few months. An invasion of Headquarters; the kidnapping of six hyden, of one of her Guardians; the deaths of said Guardian and of one of the hyden...

"I'd like to hear your thoughts," said Black at last, turning to face her Second.

Glover was one of a few people who could stand their ground against her, somehow never intimidated by the unnatural stare of her obsidian eyes or the constant shadows that surrounded her. He straightened to his considerable height before answering. "I believe we could use this to our advantage."

"Explain."

"Let them stay. Find a pariah so they think we're off their trail. Give

299

them—"

"—give them false intel," said Black, finishing his thought.

He nodded.

Black considered him a moment. "Considering Kain is no longer alive, do you suspect they will continue to work against us?"

"Kain may be dead, but his mission lives on. If this spy really believes in the cause, it's likely they will find a way to resurrect the project."

"The Omega Project?"

Glover nodded again.

Black closed her eyes for a moment. She cursed herself for ever having approved of the Omega Project. Nothing good had come of it. "I want the situation monitored closely," said Black. "From now on, I want your first priority to be to keep a close watch on Xaili Williams."

Sweat dripped down Yara Rivers' forehead. She wiped it away impatiently, focusing instead on her crouched opponent. They circled each other slowly. Her muscles were aching with exhaustion and every part of her body was screaming at her to stop. But she could not stop. She shook her head trying to knock such thoughts from her mind. She was keenly aware of all the eyes watching her, not least of all those of the man in front of her.

His blonde curls, normally voluminous on his head, hung limp over his eyes, just as sweaty as Yara. He shook them out of his face, and, in that moment, Yara charged at him. He was fast, but she was faster. She managed to catch him at the exact moment he was off guard with a swift kick to the stomach, before tackling him and sending them both crashing to the floor. The onlookers cheered loudly. He quickly managed to regain control however, and used her own inertia to throw her off of him, leaping back to his feet as though nothing had happened. He laughed.

"This is pointless," said Yara, collapsing at last on the floor, her back throbbing from the impact against the ground.

"Are you OK?" said the man, hurrying over to her, the laugh fading from his face.

The cheering and jeering crowd flickered out of existence and the room around them evaporated, leaving nothing but the black glass walls and silver grid of the simulators, a virtual reality environment that enabled White Masks to train.

It was also fun to just play around in.

Yara blinked her eyes open to see Robin Green leaning over her, looking concerned.

"I'm fine," she said, grabbing his extended hand and letting him pull her up. She groaned in pain, clutching her backside. Blood was pounding in her face, making her feel both hot and cold at the same time. She was exhausted. "I don't know if I can do this, Robin."

"You can. When you're on form, you're better than any of us," he said, wiping the sweat from his face with the bottom of his shirt. Given how much experience he had, it was hard to remember that he was only a year older than Yara. She couldn't imagine anyone her age being as confident or self-assured as he was. "And you can't call me 'Robin' anymore, remember? From now on, it's 'R.'"

"You see what I mean?" said Yara exasperatedly. "I can't even remember that stupid rule. I'm really just not cut out for this."

Robin frowned at her. It had been nearly six months since Yara had decided she wanted to join the White Mask Society, an operation whose *raison d'être* was keeping a peaceful coexistence between humans and Deviants while ideally hiding it all from the humans as they did. "Deviant" was the name given to any humanoid beings who weren't quite... human. Yara was a Deviant. Specifically, she was a hydan, one of the last. Hyden were a rare race of people who had unique abilities. In Yara's case, she could see glimpses of the future.

Robin already occupied the job title at the Society that Yara was after: Guardian.

The training to become a Guardian at the White Mask Society was grueling and unforgiving. For the last six months, Yara had been up from dawn until well after midnight, spending all of her waking hours studying and training for the upcoming evaluation all Guardian initiates had to pass before being inducted. In that time, she had broken three bones, cracked a rib, dislocated her shoulder, and suffered one relatively serious concussion. Fortunately for her, the Medics at the White Mask Society were the best in the world. Their research on both humans and Deviants had enabled them to discover effective and fast-acting treatments. So no matter how badly Yara's leg was broken, she could be back to her usual schedule in no time at all.

She was happy not to have any down time, however, even though it meant getting back to training so soon after any injuries. The events of a year prior had taken their toll on Yara, and whenever she was alone or she closed her eyes, her mind would replay it all as though determined to drive her mad.

"You can do anything you put your mind to, kid," said Robin. He pressed his finger between her eyebrows, smoothing out her frown.

"Unclench, will ya? There's a reason you're here."

"Yeah, yeah, I know," said Yara impatiently. "I'm special, exceptions were made, blah blah blah."

Robin chuckled.

She'd heard it all too many times and was reminded of her special treatment whenever she was with the other Guardian trainees. Initiates applied young. Trained young. Yara had just turned 19, making her nearly three years older than the average Guardian initiate. She would have felt more awkward about it all if it weren't for the fact that, due to her small stature, she blended in well enough with all of the pubescent initiates.

"Black wouldn't have let you join the initiate program if she didn't think ya had it in you."

Yara rolled her eyes. "No pressure, right, *R*?" she said, putting an extra emphasis on the letter. "I think… I think this was just a mistake. You know, maybe I can still join the Society, but be like… a consultant or something. Maybe the resident oracle."

Robin ran a hand through his hair. "Look. Bottom line. Is this really what you want to do?"

Yara bit her lip. Not long ago, she had been sure that this was where she wanted to be. It was that certainty and a feeling of purpose she had never had before that kept her getting up with the sun and working as hard as she had been. Recently though, doubt had been creeping in. A crippling fear that she wasn't good enough. Would never be good enough.

But she wasn't about to tell Robin that.

Bora Black, the Head of the White Mask Society, had made an exception that had never been made in Society history when she let Yara become an initiate. Yara had joined training late in the game. Her Guardians had gone to bat for her, promising to train her themselves rather than take the attention of the other trainers away from the chosen initiates in the already ongoing class. Robin said he'd take full responsibility if she wasn't ready in time for the test she'd have to pass to get the assignment. He used the argument that she had started her training already, which was mostly true. She had practiced and trained with him and her other two Guardians in the height of the crisis last year, and she had been capable enough that she'd orchestrated the rescue of not only herself but six other prisoners. Not to mention, her parents' histories as Guardians themselves indicated she may have a natural born talent for the job.

"Maybe we should go grab some lunch," said Robin. "C said they would wait for us in the commissary."

C was Carter Knox. The second of Yara's three Guardians. They'd been assigned to Yara when she was under the threat of Ramsey Kain, a brilliant but evil man who had stolen Yara's and several other hyden's abilities. Carter was also a Deviant, though not a hydan like Yara. They were a shape shifter.

"Yeah, OK," said Yara. She and Robin left the sims, wiping the sweat from their faces as they walked.

"Hey, can I ask you something?" said Robin. He wasn't looking at her.

"What's up?" said Yara, scrubbing the towel along the back of her neck and trying to smell her armpits as discreetly as possible to make sure she didn't smell too bad to eat before showering.

Robin was silent for so long that Yara turned to look at him. He kept staring at the floor in front of them as they walked, evidently deep in thought.

"Y'know what," he said, screwing up his face and laughing. "Never mind."

Yara furrowed her brow, but smiled. "What?" she said, nudging him playfully with her elbow. "What was that?"

Robin waved his hand, brushing away the subject. "No, it was nothing."

"C'mon," said Yara, poking him with her pointer fingers and grinning, "you have to tell me!"

He gave a huge sigh and said, "I was gonna ask you if I could use your deodorant. I left mine in my quarters and I don't want to assault C with my pungent, manly, yet irresistible smell."

"Oh," said Yara. She may have had the supernatural gift of seeing the future, but she also had one not-so-supernatural gift: she could tell when people were lying. And Robin was lying now. She just didn't know why. She decided not to press the subject and said instead, "I didn't bring mine, either. Maybe my cucumber-melon scented lady sweat will cancel yours out and C won't notice."

"Let's just hope they don't shift into a bloodhound."

Robin and Yara made their way to the commissary, got a couple of sandwiches, and joined Carter, who was sitting by themself at a table reading something on a tablet.

"Hey, C," said Robin. "Is that the new edition of Guardians Monthly?"

"Does that exist?" said Yara, astonished.

Carter looked up, their glasses halfway down their nose, and shook their head, half a smile on their lips. "No, it doesn't."

Yara blushed, feeling stupid. She shoved Robin playfully. He nearly fell from his chair, off-balance from laughing, and recovered with a small "whoa!" before saying, "Right, sorry. So, what are you reading, C?"

Carter pushed their glasses up to the bridge of their nose and sighed. They looked tired. "New assignment from Black."

Just like that, boiling liquid filled Yara's stomach. She could feel heat rising in her face. She tried to stay cool, but feigning calm when she was anxious had never been her strong suit. She had known that this would happen. Dreaded it for the last six months. Carter and Robin couldn't possibly be her Guardians forever. The Society's purpose was not to give Yara friends; it was to help people. But a part of her had hoped that things would never change. That Carter and Robin would always be there. She had wanted Erik, her third and final Guardian, to always be there too, but…

Her thoughts trailed away and she stared down at her sandwich.

Thinking about Erik was painful.

"Red, you OK?" said Carter, noticing Yara's sudden change in demeanor. Despite Yara being an initiate, and the rules stating that she thereby was supposed to go by "Y," Carter had never gotten out of the habit of calling her "Red." It didn't bother Yara, though. She hated being called "Y." It always made her question herself, like people were always asking her, "Why? Why? Why?"

"Hmm?" she said, looking up. "Oh! Yeah. Fine." She took a large bite out of her sandwich and said, her mouth full, "So, you guys have a new assignment, huh? That's cool."

There was a little too much knowing in the look that Robin was giving her, but Yara ignored him.

"No," said Carter. "*We* don't have a new assignment. You do."

Yara blanched. "What? How is that possible? I'm not even officially a Guardian."

"Yet," said Robin.

Carter laughed. "You're a Guardian *short*. Black's finally found someone to replace— well, to fill in."

They had been on the verge of mentioning Erik. It had been hard for Carter and Robin, too, when Erik died. They had known him longer than she had, worked with him more closely, and while the whole point of avoiding using names among the Guardian division of the Society was to avoid becoming emotionally attached to someone in case they were lost in the line of duty, it was impossible not to. They had all loved Erik.

"Took her long enough," said Robin. "It's been a year."

"She trusted we could handle it, clearly," said Carter.

"Can we not handle it anymore?"

"You know the deal, R. Three Guardians is standard."

"So," said Yara, interrupting them, "you mean, you're still my Guardians?"

"I was actually thinking about requesting a change of assignment myself," said Robin with a heavy sigh. "You've just become too boring."

"Cut it out!" she said, looking from Robin to Carter. Hope filled her belly at the thought of Carter and Robin continuing to be her Guardians, but she was too nervous to trust it completely, and too embarrassed to ask for reassurance. Clearing her throat and trying to appear as casual as possible, she continued, "So, I'm gonna have a third Guardian again? What for? I mean, Kain's dead. It's not exactly like I still need protection."

"Why, you wanna get rid of us?" said Robin. He turned to Carter. "Can you believe this? She gets trained as a Guardian and all of a sudden, she's too good for us."

"You're still a hydan," said Carter, ignoring Robin. "There's not many of you left, and Black thinks it's a good idea to keep Guardians assigned to you, just in case. Obviously, it's not nearly as serious as it was before, but—"

"Cut to the chase, C. Who's the new guy?" said Robin, fitting the rest of his sandwich into his mouth and chewing the sizable chunk slowly, bits of lettuce sticking from between his lips.

"That would be me," said a voice from behind Yara. The three of them looked up to see a girl with a mischievous grin looking down at them.

"Red, R, this is Ash."

Ash With an A

Yara's first impression of Ash was that she was absolutely beautiful. Her second was just how young she looked. She was barely taller than Yara, which admittedly wasn't saying much, but Ash looked like she couldn't have been older than 18, maybe even younger. Her eyes were a shocking shade of yellow, much more striking than Carter's amber-hued shape shifter eyes. Ash's resembled the dying embers in a fire and flickered with the same quality of flame. Her long, black hair fell to her waist, streaked with red. Not the same red as Yara's hair, who was a natural ginger, but a bright red, made even more striking by the contrast of her dark skin.

"Hello," said Yara, suddenly painfully aware of her own short hair and rather plain face, still sweaty from training. She reached out to shake Ash's hand nonetheless. Ash didn't seem to notice and had already wrapped her arms around Yara in a quick but genuine hug. Ash's skin was hot against Yara's and smelled vaguely of smoke. Yara, who did not like being touched, froze until Ash pulled away.

"Hello, Yara Rivers," she said, beaming.

"A is a Vurwari. Fire nymph," said Carter to Yara as Ash hugged Robin, "in case you hadn't guessed." Yara barely heard them, watching as Robin grinned at Ash, introducing himself.

"What does that mean, exactly?" said Yara under her breath to Carter, hoping Ash wouldn't hear.

"It means I can do this," said Ash. Yara watched as, before her very eyes, a bright ball of crackling fire appeared in Ash's palm. She twiddled her fingers playfully and the fire, moving like a living thing, snaked its way between her fingers before licking her arm and flickering out of existence, leaving not even a trace of smoke.

"That was… I mean, that's…"

"But enough about me," said Ash, taking a seat next to Robin, her bright, fiery eyes fixed on Yara. "You're the Ward, here, right?" She laughed. A clear, infectious laugh. Yara gaped, feeling more and more self-conscious by the second. "A hydan! And you're thinking about joining the Society to boot?"

"Yup," said Robin, looking at Yara fondly. "She's training to be a Guardian. Initiation is tomorrow." He squeezed her hand, looking excited and proud. It made Yara's stomach feel queasy, and she pushed the rest of her sandwich away.

"Well, it was really nice to meet you, Ash, but I think I'm gonna go study before tomorrow."

"I'll come with you," said Robin, getting up to join her, but Yara shook her head.

"No, really. It's fine. I think I'll work better if I'm on my own tonight."

Robin sat back down, looking slightly crestfallen.

Yara walked out of the commissary, feeling bitter and jealous. They were feelings she wasn't altogether unfamiliar with, although she wasn't sure why she was feeling this way. The last time she had felt jealous was watching Robin interact with his ex-girlfriend, another Guardian named Nayla. But that had been a small twinge of jealousy, easily remedied by the fact that Robin spent almost all of his time with Yara. In any case, Yara had no claim over Robin. No right to feel jealous. After all, Yara had fallen in love with someone else. Someone who had loved her in kind.

Now with that someone gone, Robin had been filling a hole in her heart with his crooked face and easy laugh. She didn't want to share him with anyone else.

And Ash… she was so full of life. Ever since the events of last year, Yara had been too busy recovering, physically and emotionally, to have much joy. Yara didn't even know it was possible to have as much energy as Ash had already displayed in the last few minutes. Even more intimidating, she could control fire and probably do all sorts of other impressive nymph things.

Yara couldn't understand where these feelings were coming from. Why did it matter that Ash was more beautiful and more vibrant and probably more talented than Yara?

Because, said a little voice in Yara's head, *because what if Robin falls in love with her and not you?* Yara brushed the thought away, hating herself. Robin was his own person, and he had the right to love anyone he wanted. Nothing had ever happened between them. Yara wasn't even sure she wanted anything to happen. She still felt a painful ache in her heart every time she thought of Erik. She still loved him. And it wouldn't be fair to herself or to Robin if she started a relationship with him or anyone else. Besides, relationships were near impossible in the Society, as people kept reminding her.

There were just too many reasons it was a bad idea.

She found herself back in her quarters. She had meant to walk to the library, but her feet had subconsciously brought her here.

In the time she had lived at Headquarters, she had personalized her room by papering the walls with photographs, taken from her old room at her aunt's apartment. But now, in addition to the photos of her and Aunt Catherine that she had cut and pasted over picturesque calendar pages, she now had pictures of her new life.

There was only one with Erik. Guardians weren't much for taking selfies. She loved that picture the most of any in her whole room. It was the four of them in the training cubicles, back when her Guardians had first started teaching her self-defense. Yara was wearing a white workout uniform, and Carter, Robin, and Erik were in black. They looked exhausted but happy. Erik was glancing sideways at her. The Yara in the picture had not noticed he was looking at her, but the Yara staring at the four of them now could see very clearly where his green eyes had been pointed.

Robin and Ash stayed with Carter at the commissary, chatting and getting to know each other. Ash was vibrant, energetic, joyful. Her devil-may-care attitude would certainly be different from Erik, who had been a stickler for the rules. Up until the end, at least.

Carter didn't speak much as Robin and Ash talked. Carter didn't mind. They liked listening just as much as participating. It was a good way to get to know people. Robin mentioned his two brothers, but glossed over some of the uglier history with his family, while Ash told a graphic story about when her entire family got food poisoning. Robin was in stitches by the time Carter had to excuse themself to return to their duties.

They bid their two fellow Guardians goodbye and got up with their mind already on what awaited them tomorrow, when they ran into someone unexpected on their way out.

"Oh," said the man in polite surprise upon noticing Carter.

"Darwin," said Carter.

Darwin Jackson was just as lovely as Carter remembered. He had soft blonde hair, ears that stuck out, giving him a sort of elfish appearance, and the same almond-shaped eyes as his sister, Nayla, who was standing right next to him.

"N," said Carter, turning to her in kind.

Nayla, usually charming and quick to ease the tension, seemed at a loss for words. "I'll meet you inside," she said gently to her brother. She gave Carter a meaningful look and left the two alone.

Darwin was apparently just as caught off guard as Carter. But how could he not expect to see Carter here? The shape shifter, after all, worked at the Society. Darwin did not.

In an attempt to seem calm, Carter forced a smile, trying to appear as though they were pleasantly surprised to see Darwin after such a long time apart.

Their relationship had started on test day for the initiate class the year after Carter graduated. Family for the new initiates had come to see the new recruits take their tests, and there, amongst the cheering family members, had been Darwin, watching his sister become a Guardian. He was as beautiful then as he was now, and the way he looked at Carter was unlike anything they had ever experienced. His gentle eyes made Carter feel like there was no one else in the world except them.

Carter hadn't expected to receive any attention from a civilian, but Darwin had taken to them instantly. He hadn't had any misgivings about Carter's gender identity and, instead, was fascinated with the fact that they were a shape shifter. Expecting him to just be another human wanting to see magic tricks, Carter had been pleasantly surprised when Darwin, instead of asking Carter to demonstrate their ability, started questioning how the Society handled Deviant-human conflicts. Initially somewhat reserved, he turned out to be funny and smart once he became more comfortable amidst the chaos of Headquarters. He could have joined the Society as easily as his sister had, but he had another objective. He was studying law at the University of Southern California, and from the moment he told Carter that his greatest ambition was working for a non-profit law office that fought for animal rights, Carter's heart melted.

The beginning of their courtship had been slow with both of them so busy. But they still found stolen hours throughout the following months to get a cup of coffee, to take a walk, to huddle up together in

Darwin's apartment and hide from the world, laughing and talking until the sun came up.

In the year that Carter and Darwin were seeing each other, Nayla was busy with her own paramour, Robin, who had been in her initiate class. Nayla and Robin had fallen fast and hard for each other with none of the reserve that Carter and Darwin shared.

Then a year after that came Erik, who—in turn—fell for Yara.

Carter watched from the outside as their two fellow Guardians were swallowed up by their feelings, for better or for worse. And then Carter started to see in themself behavior reflected by Robin and Erik. Being in love made their jobs matter less. It was becoming too hard to be away from Darwin. Carter loved him and wanted to be with him. It had begun to make Carter resentful for having to work instead.

So Carter had ended the relationship with a breaking heart, hoping that perhaps one day when Darwin had an established job and Carter had graduated from the field they could find each other again.

Darwin had never forgiven them.

"Lunch with the sis?" Carter managed in an attempt at being nonchalant.

Darwin nodded, but couldn't seem to meet Carter's eyes. He had never been good at hiding his feelings. It was impossible not to read every single thought in his eyes. Carter had told him as much back when they were dating. Ever since they stopped seeing each other, Darwin made a concerted effort not to look Carter in the eye, as though determined to hide whatever he was feeling.

"I'm sorry I can't join you," continued Carter, not at all sorry. "I was just on my way out."

"Yeah," said Darwin, speaking for the first time. They were standing so far apart from each other that they were drawing some curious looks from a few passersby. Even though Carter couldn't see his eyes, they knew there was something else he wanted to say.

"How's school?" said Carter in an attempt to fill the silence. Once, it had been so easy to be around each other. Now, it was as though they had forgotten how to speak.

"Good," said Darwin. "Graduating in May."

"Congratulations," said Carter, genuine happiness expanding in their chest.

At the change in their voice, Darwin finally looked up, his innocent eyes locking onto theirs, causing a small jolt of electricity to surge through Carter's gut. "Thanks."

"You must be so excited. You finally get to pursue your dream."

Darwin's eyebrows creased, a small show of sadness. "I'm not sure we're really there. You know, at the place where we can have honest discussions about how we are."

Carter nodded sadly. "Right. Sorry."

"I didn't mean—"

"No, no. It's fine. I understand. I'll, uh…" Carter looked around and shoved their hands into their pockets. "It was good to see you. Take care of yourself."

Carter started to walk away, could feel Darwin's eyes on their back, but they did not turn around. Darwin belonged to another part of Carter's life.

One that no longer existed.

Night had fallen, but sleep did not come to Yara.

More so because she had nothing else to do, she had taken a long, hot shower, then turned the knobs all the way to cold and doused herself in the freezing water for a full minute before stepping into the fogged bathroom.

She stared at herself in the mirror, still dripping water. If someone had taken a picture of her now and showed it to her a year ago, she would not have believed it. She still had the same high forehead and the same pointed nose, but it was a different person staring at her in the mirror. It wasn't just that she now kept her bright red hair short rather than long, or that her face had lost the baby fat in her cheeks making her chin more pointed, but there was a gleam in her eyes that hadn't been there before. A kind of fierceness she could barely believe was in her own face. Her time in Kain's laboratory had hardened her, and if she was being honest with herself, a part of her that had broken on his table had yet to heal.

The loss of Erik still felt painfully fresh, even after a year. She hadn't expected the pain to still be this fresh after so much time. She had been so young when her parents had died that it had never felt like anything more than a distant dream, a missed opportunity, but while she had only known Erik a couple of months, she had loved him.

She felt a twinge in her heart.

She had loved him.

He'd entered her life when she was confused and vulnerable, and while she was only a year older now, looking back she seemed like a child. How could she have understood what she'd felt for him? What she felt for all of her Guardians?

Yet Erik had loved her back. He had made her feel like a normal teenager with a normal crush on a normal boy who also had a crush on her. It was like what high school should have been and never was for the awkward girl who didn't like to be touched. She could never have that normal-ness again. That naivety had died with Erik.

After drying off, Yara lay in bed for an hour before deciding she was still too nervous about initiation to sleep. A few times, she toyed with inducing a vision to see whether or not she passed, but it felt like cheating somehow. And what if she saw a future in which she failed? Would she even go through with taking the test at all? It was dizzying to think about, and the easy solution was simply not to know. Then she wouldn't have to think about paradoxes and fate.

She got out of bed, pulled a graying Society hoodie over one of her father's old t-shirts, soft and worn with age and sporting a logo for a music store in Burbank that now no longer existed, and headed silently out of her room. It was nearly midnight. The halls were empty. She followed her feet until she found herself at the Hall of Memoriam.

It was a small room tucked away in a far corner of Headquarters with walls of white marble. Unlike most aspects of the Society, technology had not infiltrated this room. It was lit by oil lamps, giving the room a warm, yellow glow that flickered on the smooth walls, casting the engravings in shadow and light. Every inch of the walls was carved with the names of those from the Los Angeles branch of the White Mask Society who died in the line of duty. It was weeks of visiting Erik's memorial before it occurred to her to look for her parents'. Aunt Catherine only told Yara when she was 17 the truth about Sierra and Theo Rivers. Yara had looked for their names, not really expecting to find them, but they were there.

SIERRA TANNER RIVERS

THEO RIVERS

Yara had asked for details about their deaths. Glover told her a story of heroics and noble sacrifice.

He'd been lying, but Yara never pressed for the truth. She didn't visit the names now. The lack of emotion she felt at her parents' memorial always made her feel guilty. So instead, she walked toward Erik's name without thinking.

"Hey," she whispered in the silence. Her fingers ran over the grooves of his name.

ERIK CARPENTER

No pomp, no circumstance. He had only been 18, had died to save her, and this was all there was to remember him. No dates, no empty words of comfort to mark him as "brother," "son," "beloved."

Sadness washed over her. She leaned against the cold wall and let herself slide to the floor, her eyes closed.

"I didn't expect to find anyone down here at this hour."

Yara's eyes snapped open with a small cry of surprise to see Carter standing in the doorway. There were deep circles under their amber eyes, which flickered with the light from the lamps.

"Hi," she said as Carter sat next to her on the floor. "What are you doing down here?"

"Same thing as you, probably," said Carter with a smile. Both of them leaned their heads against the marble and fell quiet.

It helped to have Carter there. They were calming, as though they could simply absorb her anxiety. The two of them sat like that for a while.

"Nervous about tomorrow?" they asked eventually.

"I guess so," said Yara. "Can I ask you something?"

"Of course," said Carter.

"What if… what if I'm not sure I want to be a Guardian?"

Carter was quiet for a few moments before turning to look at her. Yara turned her head to meet their eyes. "I would say you'd probably wanna be sure before becoming one."

"I don't want to upset Robin. He vouched for me."

"I'm sure R just wants you to be happy."

Yara bit her lip.

"What's on your mind, Red?"

"It's just… my parents were Guardians and you guys are Guardians, and you're the first friends I ever had, really. I think I just jumped into this because I thought it was expected of me. But if you're being honest with yourself, do I really seem like Guardian material?"

They pushed their glasses up the bridge of their nose. "It doesn't matter what I think. What matters is what you want."

Yara imagined herself dressed in Guardian gear, armor and all, battling unknown enemies, risking her life on someone else's orders. She had never been good at following orders. She was too stubborn, always questioning, and inevitably thought she knew better. Being a Guardian meant being a soldier who would put their faith in their commander and obey blindly, believing that what they were told to do was the right thing just because someone higher-ranking told them so.

Was that what she wanted? Was this what she was good at? After all the training, after all the broken bones and hours of grueling exercises... maybe it wasn't.

"It's normal to have doubts," said Carter after a moment. "Sometimes those doubts come from a real place. But sometimes they come from a fear of failure that's simply masquerading as doubt. It's easier to quit than it is to fail at something you care about."

"So what am I feeling, then? Is it real doubt? Or fear-doubt?"

"Bad news, Red. You're the only one who can know the answer to that."

"I was afraid of that."

"Either way, don't let R be a factor in whatever you decide."

"You really don't think it would make Robin mad?"

Carter chuckled. "It's pretty hard to make R mad."

"Yeah," said Yara. "I can't even imagine what that would look like."

"It isn't pretty."

"You've seen it?"

Carter smiled, their eyes out of focus as if they were recalling a memory. "Here and there. E used to get under his skin. The two of them could always rile each other up."

Yara laughed, and the laugh caught in her throat and came out more like a sob. "I just miss him so much," she said eventually, fighting the tears that burned in the corners of her eyes.

"Me too."

"I don't think I can do it, Carter," she said quietly.

Carter squeezed her arm but said nothing.

When they left the memorial for their beds, Carter bade Yara good night as they headed to their quarters and she made her way to hers. Initiation was in less than seven hours, which meant she had until then to figure out how to tell Robin and Bora Black that despite all their efforts in training her, all the exceptions they'd made in her favor, that she would not be taking the test after all.

She hoped Robin would forgive her.

Stifling a huge yawn, she pushed the door of her room open and screamed.

"Please don't scream!" said the man standing in her bedroom, holding his hands out, pleadingly. "I... I didn't know where else to go."

Yara's breath was shallow and rapid. She thought she might hyperventilate from the shock.

"Erik?"

Want to stay up to date with A.M. Colwell? Check out

her website:

ayliacolwell.com

Or follow her on social media!

 @AMColwellWrites

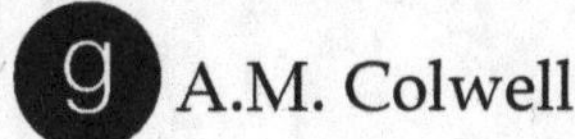 A.M. Colwell